Neil Bailey was born in Luton, England in 1961 and lives in Greenwich, London with his wife and daughter. After working over 30 years in the publishing industry for Time Inc, IPC Media, Northern & Shell and Mad magazine, Neil is now writing fiction full time. His first novel, *When She Was Bad*, was released in 2016 to five star reviews and much acclaim. The follow-up, *Bad For Good*, continued the adventures of Barclay and MacDonald.

Learn more about the author at
www.neilmbailey.blogspot.co.uk

Barclay & MacDonald

An Omnibus

Neil Bailey

COPYRIGHT

Cover design by Jenny Bailey
Cover photography by Tina Pugh

When She Was Bad

For Jen

There was a little girl,

Who had a little curl,

Right in the middle of her forehead.

When she was good,

She was very good indeed,

But when she was bad ...

Henry Wadsworth Longfellow 1807–1882

Later...

I had aimed at his shoulder but it was the side of his head that exploded. So much for shooting to wound rather than kill. Shit. Barclay would be furious.

So I ran. Ran like I'd never run before in my life. Drop the gun? Keep the gun? My fingers felt welded to its grip. I couldn't let go, the warmth of the metal strangely seductive.

Run.

Was she chasing me or seeing to what was left of her fallen lover? I wasn't waiting to find out, didn't even turn to see. I just ran. Arms pumping, cheeks puffing, breath already shortening. Run, girl, run.

I turned left, down the dark alleyway that led round the side of the abandoned warehouse. There were no lights, no paving and I stumbled on the uneven surface but I couldn't stop, I ran as fast as I could, my legs, sides, lungs all protesting at this sudden call to action.

There was wire fencing a few yards ahead. Could I take it in my stride like in the movies? From behind I could hear a shout for me to stop. At least she'd stopped screaming. I slipped the gun into my coat pocket and jumped at the fencing, surprising myself by getting a firm grip with both hands and hauling myself up like I was on an assault course.

'Stop, bitch!'

Well that's nice, I thought as I dropped over the other side, my ankle turning slightly on landing but just a tweak. I could understand she was upset, but there was no need to make it personal. I brushed myself down then started to run again, though every muscle was howling for me to slow down. Just too out of condition for this running lark. If it hadn't been for the adrenaline rush I'd have been finished already.

I could hear the blood hammering in my ears, felt my lungs close to bursting. Any further and I was sure I would collapse. I turned left around another building and then suddenly there was a pool of light ahead, a single streetlamp picking out the familiar Fiat parked at the roadside.

Had he heard the gun shot? Or was Barclay oblivious to the drama I'd suddenly ignited?

'Barclay!' I attempted to shout as I neared the car, so short of breath I thought I would die.

He saw me and wound the window down.

'All go to plan?' he asked.

'No it…no it fucking didn't.' I fell against the passenger side and wrenched the door open, clambering in.

'Where's the money?'

'What?' Barely able to speak.

'The money. Where's the money?'

'He's dead. I shot him. He's dead. Drive!'

'Fuck.'

He turned the key and the engine coughed into life. Slamming it into first and flooring the accelerator, we shot off, as fast as the little rust trap could manage.

Chapter 1

Before I found the man who would change my life, I found his bag.

It was a December Thursday and the morning commuters had long since shuffled from the platforms when I arrived to catch the train for yet another boring job for my pompous paymaster at Marshalls Design. 'Got a mission for you, Claire. Go pick up a package from Thompsons,' he had commanded, not even looking up from his laptop and critical game of Candy Crush, sending me, his always-obliging Intern, away with a careless wave of his hand. Git.

I didn't know what would be in the package – I didn't care, to be honest, I wasn't paid to think, just do – so off I went, entirely at his beck and call, picking up or dropping off, whatever he deemed was essential to keep the planet spinning and the gods happy.

The bag was a lonely black Prada rucksack, resting against the glass wall of the Waterloo sickly-sweet doughnut place. Did I mention it was a Prada rucksack? Not any old bag, not even an expensive rucksack but a *ridiculously* expensive one. It was certainly not something you would expect to see left and forgotten at Waterloo station on a cold winter's morning. I quickly glanced around. No obvious owner in sight. I couldn't believe my luck.

I should have reported it to a member of the police, but I was, for once, walking on the wild side that morning. Besides, terrorists don't buy Prada, surely – that just draws attention and they don't want attention. At least, not until things go bang.

I walked over to it and knelt down, admiring this neglected example of decadent luxury that had been so sadly abandoned by one careless owner. I'd never owned anything so glorious and instantly wanted one of my own.

It was such a very nice bag even though it was about to become second-hand – pristine condition, not leather but synthetic, Prada synthetic, probably even better than leather. It was in perfect nick, spotless, scuff-less, not a mark on it, and even the buckles looked freshly polished, the chrome sparkling in the unseasonal December sunshine. It looked so new I was surprised it didn't have a price tag still attached. I didn't know my luxury goods back then but I knew expensive when I saw it, felt it, smelt it (and it smelled divine). This was top of the line.

And I'd been thinking of getting myself a new bag.

So, a few more quick furtive glances left and right, just to be sure, and I took it, hoisting it over my shoulder and walking quickly, purposefully, for platform 8 and my waiting train.

It was heavier than I'd expected but not excessively so. I decided I'd throw the contents when I got to Reading. I had never stolen anything before in my life, but I was enjoying this adrenaline kick and the danger of my sudden impulse. A guard's whistle blew and I jumped, my anxiety getting the better of me. I skipped through the closing doors and the 11.07 lurched into life, departing platform 8 a few minutes' late but not that anyone really noticed or cared. I didn't realise it at the time but looking back that was the beginning. It wasn't just Waterloo station I was leaving, but also my tedious life of the 9-to-5, of Claire MacDonald being a good girl and doing as she was told. Blame a moment's unbidden impulse for me turning to the Dark Side.

I had the carriage pretty much to myself. There was a spotty kid in a dishevelled school uniform sitting a few rows down, ears plugged into her music, staring out the window at the factories and warehouses as the train pulled out and started to pick up speed. She should have been at school – I had no idea why she was on a train at this time of day. Maybe she was bunking off. I'd never had the courage to do that when I was that age. Good for her.

I hoisted the rucksack onto the small table. It was quite beautiful (as rucksacks go) but not so beautiful as to probably justify the ludicrous price its (former) owner had likely paid for it – a small shiny brand label the tasteful reminder of its quality and price tag. There was another even smaller label that just had a printed mobile number on it, presumably the owner's, useful if my guilty conscience finally got the better of me. There was no lock and the zip easily yielded to my impatient pressure.

The first thing I took out was a laptop. A gossamer thin, featherlite top of the range slice of Apple, designed in California, forged in China, a computer so elegant I wanted to stroke it and purr at its delicate sleek brushed aluminium finish. Beautiful.

Sadly I realised that this would be useless to me. It would be secured and encrypted with passwords, possibly even booby trapped to delete everything or explode if my clumsy fingerprints should glance over its state-of-the-art keyboard. The bag may not have been secured but I'd put money on the laptop being locked from prying eyes and fingers. Bugger. This would have to go back; just too good to throw away, too hot to sell, too password-protected for a simpleton like me to use. Besides, said my guilty conscience suddenly finding its voice; the laptop may have critical stuff on it for someone. I would need to call that mobile number and return it – I may just fifteen minutes earlier have become an opportunist thief, but the rucksack alone would need to be enough.

Putting the laptop to one side I dug a little deeper into the bag. There was a bright red cashmere scarf and a copy of *Catcher in the Rye*. A well-worn, well-thumbed vintage seventies edition that looked much loved as though it might be a much-travelled constant companion. I was starting to feel bad about digging through someone's most personal possessions. It was not a good feeling. I was invading a stranger's privacy. But still I dug deeper. It's what us Bad Girls do.

Rootling a little further I found a boxed Epipen, one of those hypodermic things for people with serious allergic reactions, anaphylactic shock and all that scary stuff.

No messing now. I really should get that at least back to the owner if it was for medical emergencies. My angelic conscience was no longer whispering and was getting the upper hand over my newfound criminal intent. The Epipen's box was unopened and although its Use By date had long since expired I needed to return it or I'd never sleep at nights ever again. Thief? Maybe. Killer? Definitely not.

The other contents were less interesting: a packet of travel tissues, Rennies, a broken Chunky KitKat, a packet of three ('ribbed for heightened pleasure'), a Tom Ford glasses case (empty), some keys (including an impressive looking one for an Aston Martin), leather gloves (presumably Prada too) and a handful of USB thumb drives, unlabelled.

There was something bulky in a compartment at the back of the bag that was zipped shut. Whatever it was would be what was making the bag feel heavy. I unzipped it and, before I realised what I was doing I placed a gun on the table.

'Fuck me!' I whispered to the almost empty carriage (fortunately the girl was still lost in the music). A gun. I'd never seen a real gun before, let alone touched one. Keeping an eye on the girl lost in her daydreams I picked it up and tried the grip for size. I was surprised just how heavy it was. I didn't know anything about weapons back then, but it looked the real deal, a serious handgun for serious crime. Unlike the bag it was old and dirty, slightly oily, and looked like it had been used a number of times.

(It was probably my imagination, but I'd swear it felt slightly warm, as if it had been recently used.)

Mild panic took hold. I couldn't put the stuff back into the rucksack fast enough. I scratched the laptop's pristine surface ramming it all back in (sorry, my beauty) but I didn't care. Any thought of keeping this deluxe treasure trove immediately left. I should leave the bag on the train, dump it, throw it away, run a mile.

I suddenly went cold. I'd have been caught on the CCTV with it, the cameras at the station and would be seen dumping it in a bin at the other end. They even had CCTV on the train ('We are watching you for your protection' proudly boasted the sign on the carriage wall). Hell, they may even have me on CCTV getting the gun out. I quickly looked around the carriage. I couldn't see any obvious cameras. I tried to convince myself that they wouldn't be looking that closely for my 'protection', would they?

I'd call the rucksack's owner. I got my ageing Nokia phone out but saw there was no signal. Damn. The call would just have to wait.

I decided my bad girl days were already over. Barely half an hour all told, off the straight and narrow. I was reverting to well-behaved type – this was not a world I was comfortable with (exciting though it promised to be). I would call the bag's owner as soon as I could get a signal and arrange to return the bag and its dubious contents at the very earliest opportunity. I needed shot of it. I needed a strong drink and the comfort of a re-assuring cuddle. I needed to get back home quickly to discuss this with clearheaded Mr Rational, my all-so-perfect Henry, boyfriend-in-residence. He'd know what to do – I was clueless and couldn't handle this kind of madness alone.

Sadly, when I got back home to my flat in Deptford that evening, I found another kind of madness.

'You're what?' I was incredulous

'I'm going to India for a year,' Henry said.

'No you're fucking not.'

'Yes I am, Claire. And please calm down.'

'Calm down? Calm down? I'm completely fucking calmed down.' (Looking back on it, I wasn't.)

'It's not as if I hadn't mentioned it…'

True. He had been talking about overseas voluntary work for ages and ages, but then he was all talk, wasn't he? No fear of action surely. For all the nights down the pub righting the world's wrongs, we all knew he was never going to skim the waves as an environmental warrior for Greenpeace saving whales from the evil Japanese, didn't we? Henry was 100% mouth but a big zilch in the trouser department. But now this? Desertion! I was not happy.

'A fucking year?' Every time I swore he winced.

'Twelve months, with a review possibly extending it a further twenty-four.'

'Three fucking years?!' Louder. I think Henry was starting to worry more about what the neighbours would say rather than what I was saying: I was not being quiet.

'Possibly yes.' Every time I moved towards him he started

to back away

'And what does that mean about us? What about me? What am I supposed to do whilst you're saving the third world?'

'I think we should see it as a break,' he said.

'Like Ross and Rachel? A 'we were on a break' kinda thing?'

He was mystified. I don't think he'd ever seen *Friends*. Not cool enough for his sensible sensibilities no doubt.

'A break. A time to consider things and where we're going in this relationship,' he said.

'I don't want to consider things – I thought we had a good thing going. But it's quite clear where you're going, at least. India! What the fuck for?'

'It's that voluntary placement we've been talking about.'

He may have been talking and talking and talking about it but as I say it had never been remotely real to me. Just talk. My brain knew I needed to take it down a notch or three but the message was getting lost before it got to my mouth. If anything his reasonableness was winding me up more and more.

'No break,' I declared.

'What? You're coming with me? That's great!' It was his turn to be surprised.

'No, we're finished.'

'Oh.'

'Done. Kaput. No more.'

'I thought you might think that.'

'But that didn't make you stop and think? Three fucking years?'

'As you always say, 'If a job is worth doing…''

'Don't use my clichés against me.'

'You're not being rational.'

'I know. Mark it down as Tough Love.'

'Oh. Okay.'

I didn't know what to think. What to say. Too angry. Too shocked. Too heartbroken? Possibly. It hadn't been great but it had been good and sometimes good was good enough. Already with the past tense…

'When are you leaving?' I asked.

'I have to be in Paris on Monday for Orientation.'

'Then you'd better get packing,' I spat.

'Can I leave my stuff here?'

'No you fucking can't. Put it into storage if you can't take it with you.'

'Will you help me? Nice bag by the way – is it new?'

'No I fucking won't and yes it fucking is.' I couldn't take any more of this. I stormed into the bedroom and slammed the door behind me.

I didn't want him to see any more tears.

Chapter 2

It took an hour or two but by the time I got around to calling the mobile number printed on the back of the rucksack I had calmed down to the point where I felt I could talk to a complete, possibly unstable stranger about his bag without the sobs getting in the way. There was an outside chance that I might even make some sense. So far, nothing else had made any sense whatsoever that day.

I guess I had always known deep down that things with Henry were never going to be permanent. Sometimes relationships stumble along more on hope than judgement, don't they? We weren't a perfect fit, we were simply too different on so many levels (I've never bought in to that 'opposites attract' nonsense). My absent family may have found his worthiness and charitable nature endearing, it was not something I empathised with. Besides, what did they know? They'd only met him the once so most of their judgement was based on hearsay rather than personal experience. Mum may have referred to him as 'a keeper' but for me, once the initial thrill of waking up with a grown man in my bed had lost its novelty (snoring can do that) it was never going to be the real thing. It had become strained and forced, and recently there had been more to complain about than compliment. Henry's permanent benevolence and righteousness was tiring and irritating. He was just too earnest, too *good* for me.

I tried to rationalise my shock, wrestling the rampaging emotions into some semblance of order. Him going was a good thing, an acceleration of the inevitable, an acceptance of the obvious. Let him piss off to India and help the genuinely needy, flee our First World trivial distractions to make a better hash of the Third. That was for him and most definitely not for me. I had no desire whatsoever to experience a life tougher than I was already living first hand. Life was too short. Comfort too important. Henry could tackle those charitable challenges very much on his own as far as I was concerned.

It didn't make me a bad person, didn't necessarily make

him a good one. At least I was about to demonstrate that I had the virtue of being shamelessly honest; that bag wasn't going anywhere without me making that call and returning it to its rightful owner. Having a gun in the flat was not something I could cope with, and I'd decided it all had to go, elegant luxury rucksack and all.

I made the call. It was brief and business-like. The man who answered the phone said his name was Barclay, and I agreed to meet him the next day at some pub nearby. He sounded calm, cold even, not a gun-toting nutter but not exactly gushing with gratitude either. I was a little put out that my virtuous, honest gesture was being taken completely for granted. Maybe he was one of those quiet psychos, the madness going on behind the eyes. I would soon find out.

He said he needed the laptop for some work he was doing. He didn't mention the gun. Neither did I. It didn't seem to be the right moment. I just wanted to be shot of the damned thing. 'Gun'. 'Shot of'. Hilarious.

My nerve started to fail me as I approached the pub. It was just a short bus hop from my flat in Deptford. It didn't look like a rough place, nestled in Greenwich's sophisticated Victorian residential streets rather than some dodgy factory wasteland. This would be safe, I thought. Safer, at least.

It was a small Shepherd Neame pub situated a short meandering walk from Greenwich High Road. 'Britain's oldest brewery' the sign boasted proudly and it looked welcoming enough, its livery recently painted in a bright red, gold and tasteful cream, a handful of unoccupied wooden tables and outdoor chairs neatly arranged on a front yard, a couple of empty pint glasses still sitting there from the previous night. Some underdressed builders opposite were noisily throwing bricks into an almost full skip, spoiling the back street tranquillity.

I was suddenly in two minds whether to call the police about the gun or not, especially given all that stuff on the news about some weekend street fights in Lewisham centre just down the road. 'A gun! I've found a gun!' I wanted to shout, but more out of childish excitement and bravado than out of any civic duty. I had been rational little Claire MacDonald for every second of my twenty-five years on this planet and it had done me no favours whatsoever in the 'exciting' game of life, but that was probably insufficient to justify me doing something as foolhardy as stealing a piece of luxury luggage then arranging to meet the guy who had lost said bag and its bloody not-so-safe contents.

I was not doing the right thing. I was not being sensible. Was this a new, post-Henry Claire? Was I being reckless? Did my actions seriously lack 'reck' (whatever that is)? The truth was that I was exhilarated by the bag and its contents, my humdrum life was about to have a much-needed jolt of possible thrills and surprises, I was going off-script and stepping out from my cosy comfort zone into the great unknown.

I walked up to the pub door then pulled away, indecisive, then turned to retreat and then turned back again, my courage ebbing and flo-ing. It did not go unnoticed – the builders opposite laughed at my impromptu okey cokey. Sod it. Grow a pair, Claire. In.

I pushed open a heavy door and entered what TripAdvisor would inform its American audience was 'a quaint traditional British pub', all polished wooden furnishings and tasteful William Morris print wallpaper, some faint jangling indie music creating a welcome warmth from the winter chills outside.

The lounge area was almost empty, just a student barmaid dressed all in black, an assortment of piercings adorning her ears and nose, and a lone guy leaning against the bar, nursing a half-empty pint of something or other.

Was that him? Barclay? My god, he was gorgeous. Very tall and well built, his shoulders and strong muscled arms were barely contained by his tight white designer tee shirt. He had pale blue eyes twinkling out from a fading summer tan, his hair shaved fashionably at the sides but topped off with an expensively cut oiled hipster wedge.

Down girl.

'Mr Barclay?' I asked, barely able to contain my excitement. I couldn't believe my luck.

'No, I'm Barclay,' said a voice behind me. I turned and saw another man had followed me into the pub.

His voice was deep and resonant, rich in timbre like that guy who played Snape; a 'voice for late night radio' you might say. But he was not beautiful himself (unlike that hunk at the bar) – his face had character rather than conventional beauty, strong cheekbones and curls of black hair falling in an unruly manner over small, intense dark eyes. He was tall, slender, immaculately dressed – his dark double-breasted overcoat looked ridiculously luxurious (much like his rucksack that I had over my shoulder), the suit underneath probably Italian, the white shirt something out of the pages of Esquire rather than off the racks at M&S. He wasn't bad looking, it was just that the other guy was so jaw-dropping that my standards had momentarily been elevated to new heights. There was an authority about him, a sense of privilege and certainty. I'd hesitate to define it as charisma, but there was definitely something about him. I just couldn't put my finger on it.

'And it is just Barclay,' he said, straight-faced.

I held out my hand which he shook lightly. 'I'm Claire. We spoke on the phone. Claire MacDonald.'

'And you have my bag, I see. Good. What are you drinking?'

'What?' I hadn't planned on staying a second more than was absolutely necessary. 'Oh, that would be nice, thank you. A Diet Coke please. Lemon, no ice. Thank you.' Even the newly morally questionable Claire was still impeccably polite. To be honest I was still rudely distracted by the other guy.

Behave, girl.

I didn't immediately warm to Barclay but he didn't strike me as a brutal terrorist or manic gang member; I had been right not to panic and call the police. Probably. Maybe he even was police, undercover? Or maybe he was secret service or a spy? MI5? MI6? MI7? Is there an MI7? There was certainly a whiff of Old School, expensive education, a twist of Cambridge perhaps. My Deptford Green education had not prepared me for this kind of company. I was moving up in the world.

He got the drinks while I found us a table with an excellent view of The World's Most Perfect Man; I needed that assurance that he was just a few steps away if I needed saving.

Barclay joined me, my crass Coke in one hand, his sophisticated whisky (a solitary ice cube) in the other.

'I suppose I should say 'thank you' for calling me about my bag,' he said, placing the two drinks on the table, removing his coat and carefully folding it before placing it on a spare chair. 'I was concerned when I realised it went missing. I believed it had been stolen.'

'I'm not surprised you were concerned…' My nerves had returned and my voice sounded strangely unfamiliar. I instantly felt guilty for having explored its contents. 'I had to open it to find the owner,' I murmured, almost inaudibly.

'My number was on the label on the outside.' There was a flicker of a smile. He seemed to be amused at my embarrassment.

'It was lucky you had written it on the tag.'

'It is what the tag is for. They print it on there when you order one. My bag is important to me.'

'Yes.' I was staring at my glass. 'It's a nice one.'

'If one is going to have a bag, it is important one has to have something decent. You cannot be seen to compromise on the important things in life.'

'No, of course not.' I kicked my own handbag further under my chair. It was from H&M, knocked down from 19.99 in the summer sale, just a small step up from a Lidl plastic bag. There was no point in drawing attention to it. If he had noticed it he hid it well.

'I expect that you are anticipating a small reward for ensuring my bag's safe return?'

What? I looked up. I hadn't expected that.

'I thought so,' he said. 'Unfortunately, I don't have any cash on me at the moment.'

He clinked my glass but still didn't smile. 'Cheers,' he said. 'Here's to acts of kindness.' I couldn't say if it was with sarcasm or not – he was impenetrable, a face and demeanour too complex to read.

'Cheers,' I said, excited by the prospect of a little windfall to cover the month's rent.

The Diet Coke was warm and I should have asked for ice, its cloying sweetness was sorely failing in the refreshment department.

'I assume that all of my stuff is as you found it?' he asked.

'Yes.' I decided against mentioning that elephant-in-the-room handgun. 'Nice laptop.'

'The Air? Yes, a little underpowered but it does the job. Light on storage but that is what the Cloud is for. The eight oh two eleven AC is essential.'

His laptop had air conditioning? I had no idea what he was talking about, but smiled and nodded. 'Absolutely,' I agreed.

'Like I say, there is no point in compromise.'

'None whatsoever.' My own computer was a seven-year-old laptop from Curry's, still running the old version of Windows I had used in Sixth Form, more 'in a state' than 'state of the art'. I was out of my depth. Why couldn't that guy at the bar have been Barclay? The conversation would have been easier and the view spectacular. Sadly, he was finishing his drink and making a move, my bodyguard-in-waiting had tired of waiting. Another lost opportunity. Story of my life.

'What do you do, Miss MacDonald?'

'Do?'

'Work. Are you a student at the Uni?' Oh my god, he was attempting small talk. This was going to be painful.

'No, I work at Marshalls Design. We do web stuff.'

He raised an eyebrow. 'You are in technology?'

'Barely. I'm an Intern. Minimum pay. Maximum tea making and post distribution. But my stapling skills are second to none,' I babbled. 'The greatest challenge is staying awake. Spreadsheets, y'know?' I rolled my eyes, all too aware how colourless and mundane my life was sounding.

'And you enjoy that?'

I laughed. 'What do you think? Finding your gun was the most exciting…' I froze. I'd spoken of the unspoken.

'It may not the wisest thing to mention that in public?' he said under his breath.

'Sorry,' I mumbled. It was hardly 'in public' – the barmaid had disappeared and we were alone, but he had a point.

'But you work in technology. That is interesting.'

I could have pointed out that my technical prowess was limited to turning a computer off and on again, but not necessarily in the right order. I decided not to go into details.

'I dabble,' I lied. 'It's the future, apparently.'

'Actually, it is very much the present I think you will find.'

'Are you in technology, Mr Barclay?'

'Barclay. Just Barclay. I…dabble'

I smiled. 'Dabble?'

'Yes, I am *in* technology, as you so succinctly put it.'

'I'm told it's where the opportunities are.'

'They most certainly are.'

We were treading water. If the conversation shrank any smaller it would disappear completely. 'You mentioned a reward?' I ventured.

'What? Oh, yes. That. Sure. But you've got me thinking.'

'I have?'

'Yes. Let me check a few things but I may have something more interesting to offer you than tea duties and stapling.'

'Really? I'm not that kind of girl.' My attempt at humour fell flat.

'Behave. Let me make a few enquiries this afternoon and I will get back to you.'

Interesting. He said he would call me before the weekend.

'Whenever,' I said, hoping to appear nonchalant.

'If it turns out there is something, are you around on Saturday to discuss some details?'

Saturday? I should have been helping holier-than-thee Henry get his stuff packed up for the Big Orange Storage or whatever the company is, I should have been pretending to share charity worker Henry's excitement and listening intently to his nervous planning of the un-plannable. I should have been doing my bit for His Great Benevolence's selfless adventure.

But I'd had enough of doing what I *should* have been doing. It was time to stretch my wings and fly into my own great unknown. I wanted to see what this Barclay character had on offer. It couldn't be less interesting than the life I was currently living, could it?

'Sure,' I said. 'I'm free Saturday or Sunday. Give me a call if there is anything.'

He rose, downed the last drops of his whisky (presumably an oak-aged malt, nothing second best for Barclay), collected his handsome overcoat, and gave me a curious little salute with his left hand.

'Until next time,' he said.

I smiled and saluted back. 'Until tomorrow?'

'Good girl,' and, as I bristled with being called 'girl', he left.

'What's going on?' I asked myself. One thing for certain, I was not going to accept compromises any more. No sir.

I finished my sickly warm Diet Coke and left.

Chapter 3

The bus ride home was my thinking time, my opportunity to weigh up the seismic shifts of the previous 24 hours. What did I actually know about this guy Barclay? Would I really put my future in the hands of a guy who I knew absolutely nothing about except he had a gun and an expensive taste in clothes and accessories? It was the most un-Claire thing imaginable.

The double decker was one of those ugly, bulbous scarlet monstrosities that the ugly, bulbous scarlet Mayor of the day had foisted on an unsuspecting London public. I had taken a seat upstairs and at the back. Normally I attracted the nutters on a bus like a powerful nutter magnet, but mercifully on that particular day they stayed away.

Maybe reckless Claire had scared them away?

So what did I know?

The obvious thing, and the biggest, was that I needed a serious change. My life, at twenty-five, was going nowhere at a pace that would have the guys at Guinness World Records taking an interest. My internship, contrary to the initial promise of high tech training and unlimited opportunities, had matured into endless tea brewing (my office nickname was 'Two Sugars Sweetie'), casual (but hurtful) sexism, and day long trips to Reading to drop off or pick up brown padded envelopes that always weighed a little more than you would have thought. Was I being used as a drug mule? Should I have been grateful they were at least using padded envelopes and not considering other, more personal hiding places? No, of course not. I didn't know exactly what was in them but you've never seen a company more straight laced and straight faced than BORING Marshalls Design. It may have boasted it did 'web design' but in the fast moving super highway of the Internet they weren't just in the slow lane, they were parked permanently on the hard shoulder. I had to move on, tell them to stuff their 50p more than the minimum pittance and call it a day. The days of stewing rather than brewing needed to come to an end. Stewed tea's loss would be my gain.

And what about Henry and my tattered, broken attempt at an adult relationship? Now that the shock had passed and the emotional tsunami had quietened to be less choppy waters, that was really a good thing, him going, not something to get angry about. I could only have feigned interest in his self-interest for so long. I'm not a charitable person I'm afraid. Like the men I'm attracted to, I'm too self-centred and self-absorbed to win any popularity contests. (Don't be shocked – I'm just being honest. More people should be. We're all in it for Number One, aren't we?)

Whisper it quietly, but I'm not even sure Henry is genuinely genuine. I mean is he really, truly, deeply, in it for anything more than improving his own social standing? 'Everyone loves Henry', 'he's so giving', 'always thinks of others, never considers himself', etc.

Bollocks. It's all about how others perceive him, not what he's doing as much as what he's *seen* to be doing. I give this India thing three months max. A couple of bouts of Delhi belly and some painful bloating and a Malaria scare or two and he'll be out of there. Once everyone's noticed and congratulated him, once the 'good old Henry' cheering has subsided and life returns to normal he'll quietly come back and pick his next Do Gooding exercise of self-importance. I guarantee it. Three months. Or sooner.

I had to get on with my life and forget him. It wasn't going to be difficult for me, but Mum would be upset (I would have to steel myself for the inevitable 'how's my lovely son-in-law?' questions before I let her down gently). My know-all of a little brother for once had been right – that guy was a loser. At least Dad would understand. Assuming he even noticed.

I had the opportunity of a clean slate on the relationships front then. Not that this Barclay would be a contender – simply not my type, too cold, aloof, distant. I sometimes play a game with my Mum where you have to sum up a person in three words. Three for Barclay; Cold. Aloof. Distant. No, I'd say 'Dangerous' would be a better fit than 'Distant'. At school I had always insisted that my three should be 'Amazing', 'Funny' and

'Pretty' but no one ever agreed and little kids could be so cruel. 'Dull', 'Boring' and 'Plain' were about as good as it got, and that was from Polly Dee, my best friend when I was growing up. (We used to call her 'Dolly Pee'. Like I said, kids can be cruel like that. I'm sure it made her cry when we weren't around.) I could be a little bitch at times. I wondered what Polly was doing now? One day I'd track her down on the web and see whatever happened to that little tightly-wound ball of premature neuroses.

But I digressed. This wasn't about the past; this was about my future. No more 'Dull', 'Boring', 'Plain'. What did I want in life? And how did I get there? Maybe this Barclay would open a few more doors, provide a bridge to a different life.

I bloody hoped so.

Home was not where the heart was. It was bloody uncomfortable. Charitable Henry ('Earnest. Worthy. Fake') was doing a fine impression of someone who was expecting the world to be at his feet, helping him pack all his immaterial material goods into a large stack of cardboard boxes he'd half-inched from out the back of the local Sainsbury's. That it had been raining hadn't helped – a number were damp and likely to burst if tested with any significant weight.

Henry would have liked that – even the elements conspiring against him. If he had believed in God he would have taken it as a sign, but he didn't (although he professed to be 'a christian with a small C') and so he muttered and cursed his way through the packing process.

'Need any help?' I reluctantly asked from the doorway. I don't think I've ever uttered three words so insincerely.

'No. I'm fine.'

Fine then.

I decided to take him at his word.

'Okay then. Want a cuppa?'

He huffed and puffed, heaving a pile of unread Hemingway paperbacks into an already over-filled cardboard box, previously the home of 48 Pampers. Somehow, it seemed appropriate seeing how full of shit he was. 'Two sugars,' he said.

'Yeah. I remember. I'm good like that.'

As I made the tea, dripping out the last drops from a carton of semi-skimmed, I wondered briefly if I should make the peace with him or let him, much like my tea, stew. On the one hand, I hated leaving things messy (although it was him doing the leaving). On the other, I didn't want to spend my weekend helping him pack and reminiscing about what a wonderful three months we'd had since he moved in (we hadn't but memories are often deceptive when warped by departures).

I decided to go for the middle ground. The tea was a start, even if it did look a little on the strong side.

'You're still going then?' I was asking the bleeding obvious.

'Yes. Of course.'

'Where in India, exactly?'

'Bengaluru.'

'I've never heard of it.'

'It's the real name of Bangalore. You've heard of that?'

'Southern India. Lots of people. Just below the malaria line. Most of the population working in Western call centres for the hard-of-paying.' I was good at geography at school and we'd done India and an hour or two on Bangalore as a project. Only it sounded like it wasn't called that any more.

'Eight and a half million people – more than Wales and Scotland combined. Most live in abject poverty. Horrible. And the divide gets worse every year.'

'I'm sure you'll make a tremendous difference.'

He grimaced at my cruel sarcasm and I almost felt ashamed. Almost. 'I'll do what I can, which is more than most.'

I let that hang in the air. No point in getting into an argument about the futility of his gesture (because that's all it was, a gesture).

'I will be gone on Sunday morning,' he said. 'Flight to Paris from City, a week's training and orientation, and then the direct Air France flight next weekend.'

'You've never been to India,' I said unthinking, as if he may not have realised.

'Nope. About time I lived it for myself.'

'Nothing going on in Africa caught your fancy then? Peckham poverty not good enough for you?'

He gave me a weary look.

'We're not a good couple, are we?' It was like the penny had finally dropped for him.

I sighed. 'No. This is good for both of us.'

'I think you're right.'

It was one of the very few times in the recent weeks we had agreed on something and we chinked our mugs of builders' tea in recognition of that. I wouldn't miss Henry, we had irritated each other from the very moment he'd moved in, after the limited 'thrill' had gone. We hadn't eaten the same food (he was Vegan, I liked my meat, the more processed the better), read the same books (my passion for tacky thrillers and real life crime out of place on his Guardian-recommended shelves), enjoyed the same classic films (how could he not fall in love with Butch and Sundance?) – we were Matthau and Lemmon, an Odd Couple best de-coupled.

Forget it being a break, this needed to be the real deal, a full break-up.

No half measures. No compromises. New Claire was taking over.

Chapter 4

Saturday had been my last night of sharing a bed with Henry but there had been no final throes of bedtime passion. We were both uncomfortable with him staying in the flat over our last weekend now that things were ending so he had made arrangements to stay with his bestest buddies Dominic and Sam for the Sunday; they had a van and were going to pop over to move out his worldly goods when I popped out to Tesco. Dom and Sam were a couple I'd miss them tremendously – they were originally Henry's friends and I knew whose side they would go to once we split. But it was time for the change.

The bed was cold that night, as it had been most nights in recent memory. We had never been a passionate couple, Henry was not a great or even competent lover, and that night we slept as we did normally – back to back, to minimise the impact of his window-rattling snoring. I was not going to miss that. The more I thought about it, the easier this separation was becoming.

Barclay hadn't contacted me though. Broken promises already. But then no one but Mum ever called me to be honest – Vodafone probably wondered why I even bothered with a phone. Poor, lonely Claire. I managed to fall asleep quickly and stave off the threatening melancholy. It had been a particularly arduous afternoon at Tesco after all.

I woke and rose early the next morning but Henry had already risen and was finishing the dregs of his packing. Good man. I hate goodbyes, especially potentially emotional ones. I was more upset when Dom and Sam arrived – I'd miss those guys hugely, we'd had some good times together, sometimes even with Henry, and we all knew that this was the end of the line for us as friends. There were tear clouds gathering and my voice broke as I helped them pack the last of the boxes into their old rusty van. Henry probably thought all the emotion was for him and he strode forward to hug me, but I was stiff in his arms to avoid any doubt.

And then so quickly they were gone, Henry was gone, and I

was alone to make my own mistakes in this world.

It was Monday and Barclay still hadn't called, despite my hopeful glances at my Nokia every hour, on the hour, all weekend.

It all felt like a massive anti-climax, and my life seemed to have forgotten the exciting promise of the previous Friday with Barclay.

Work. Marshalls. Same old same old.

But no. When I got to my desk it looked odd. As in 'where's all my stuff gone?' odd, a lone Post-It in the centre, curling to hide its message.

'Please see me in my office. Peter'. That was not good. This was signed 'Peter', my boss's more formal corporate ego, not the less clenched, more approachable everyday 'Pete' I normally worked for. As I approached his door I saw him look up from his laptop. He was dressed in his best Top Man grey wool suit, a white button down Oxford and subdued red silk tie. Management personified. Suddenly I felt leaden in my step and dry mouthed. This wasn't looking good.

'Ah. Claire. Do come in and please shut the door behind you.'

By the book. No 'how was your weekend?' though, so he wasn't following the HR script 100%, but definitely not good. I quietly closed the glass door (a sound barrier only – so much for privacy). I figured I could always slam it on my way out for extra impact.

'Feeling any better?' he smarmed. He did insincerity very, very well. It probably featured highly on his LinkedIn profile. At least he'd noted I had been off on Friday.

'Not really,' I croaked, a final play for sympathy.

'Now Claire, sorry to catch you as soon as you walked through the door but it's best to get these things sorted as soon as possible I always say.'

"'These things'?' I put on my best confused look, but I was pretty sure what was coming.

'As you know,' he continued, ignoring my attempt at a furrowed brow, 'things have been a little tough of late for us at Marshalls Design and we're going to have to make a few economies to be ready to kick off in the New Year from a sounder base, peel the onion on those costs and take a helicopter view of the operation. Some potential hot prospects for us to warm up for but we need to be fitter and a little flatter to gear ourselves up for the challenges ahead and…'

Uh oh. No doubt now where this was going.

'I'll save you the words,' I interrupted. 'You are going to tell me that my year as an Intern is coming to a close and you have reviewed the option of making my position permanent but at a time of commercial austerity and difficult trading in the web game and the threat of off-shore outfits outpacing and undercutting us, etcetera etcetera. Sorry to spoil your speech but I'm sure we both have better things to do with the day so just tell me how much I'm getting and I'll go.'

That hit him slap bang in the middle of his mono brow.

'Er well yes, exactly Claire. How very perceptive of you. Thank you for your understanding and your contribution to …'

'Marshalls Design. Yes, got that. How much?'

'We'll pay you up to the end of the month. Including the holidays of course.'

So generous.

'Perfect. That's my first round sorted out.' I held out my hand for a final shake from the most ineffective man-child it had ever been my misfortune to encounter. 'Good luck and all that. It's been a blast.'

It hadn't been, but if I'd learned one thing from Peter Marshall it was insincerity that could be vaguely convincing. I didn't slam the glass door on my way out – what was the point? – and I wasn't in the least bit surprised to see a younger, cheaper, prettier prospective Intern standing outside his office waiting for a few minutes of his valuable time.

'You're next,' I smiled, and left without another word.

Chapter 5

Barclay finally texted me that lunchtime. It was succinct and to the point:

Ashburnham Arms. The quiet table at the back. 2pm. B.

How did he know I would be free today? Did he just assume he could click his fingers and I would come a-running?

It was the same pub as before, so it would be safe neutral territory and I did have the afternoon to kill, the rest of the week now. Rest of my life even. At least I was going to meet a dangerous man in a non-dangerous place – that pub was the kind where you couldn't imagine people getting even slightly tipsy, let alone a fight breaking out. The landlord probably considered calling the police when someone went 'tut' under their breath just in case all hell broke loose. I got to Greenwich and the pub a little early. Barclay was already there, sitting at the table furthest from the front door as if hiding from an imaginary throng of fellow customers – the place again was completely empty, not even any bar staff although there was the sound of someone moving crates of empty bottles out in the rear garden.

'Good afternoon,' he said, not rising to greet me. He was wearing a wonderfully cut jacket – pale grey, with a black shirt underneath. I felt underdressed in my best discounted Gap combo of jeans and overwashed bulky wool jumper.

'Hello,' I said, taking the seat opposite him.

'Would you like a drink?'

'I would like a coffee if that's possible.'

'When Keiran gets back I'll ask him to do you an espresso – they do a decent Nespresso here, better than that High Street rubbish.'

I don't like espresso – far too strong for me. But that day was now all about new Claire, maybe even Nespresso Claire, rather than boring old Nescafe Claire, so I let it ride.

'With milk on the side please,' I asked.

'You mean cream, surely?'

Of course. Cream. No compromises with Barclay. He had a glass of something clear and fizz with a slice of lime and ice.

Possibly a G&T but I couldn't read the guy at all.

'So you have something for me? Are we talking a job?' I asked.

'Did you classify your work at Marshalls as 'a job'? That was paying below minimum wage, you know.'

'I thought it was little more, but close enough.' I was taken aback that he had somehow found out my salary and appeared to be aware that I was no longer working there, but then this guy seemed to know everything.

A barman (presumably this was Keiran) appeared and Barclay got his attention with a nod and held up two fingers, in the polite way. Keiran nodded and noisily began dissecting the coffee machine.

'I need an assistant, someone who can drive,' said Barclay.

'I…I don't have a car,' I said.

'I know. A car comes with the job. You have held a clean licence since you turned eighteen and that is all that is required. I have a new car coming for you.'

'You've already done that? What if I said 'no'?'

'You are not going to turn this down.'

'Apparently not.' The arrogance of the man. And how did he know about my driving licence and no car status?

I remembered the car keys I had seen in his rucksack. 'It must be expensive to insure an Aston Martin,' I said.

He raised his eyebrows. 'It is. But I don't drive that anymore. There were…complications. This work requires a more anonymous car.'

'That's good,' I said. 'I don't think I'd be comfortable driving something that costs more than I've earned in my entire life. I thought you said this work was going to be technical?'

'But you're not particularly technical, are you?'

'Not massively, no.' Rumbled.

'The work I do does involve mobile phones and computers, but it is the driving that is the pressing problem for me at the moment. I've been…' He hesitated, what was to follow was causing him some embarrassment. 'I've been banned for six months.'

I laughed. 'Banned?'

'Speeding. Parking. Driving while suspended, that kind of nonsense. Nothing major but it all totted up. I probably should have gone to the court thing about it but I had something else on that day. They weren't happy about me being a no-show so they hit me where it hurt. It has left me with a problem you can assist me with.'

Our coffees arrived, tiny half-filled white cups with a thimbleful of espresso in each. Even adding the cream made barely a mouthful.

'I just need to go to the loo,' I said. 'Need to make room for that.'

He nodded, but still no smile. Maybe he was shy and slow to warm up with beauties like myself. I left my handbag with him and made my way to the Ladies. When I returned, Barclay was rifling through my bag.

'What are you doing?' I asked.

'You went through my bag,' said Barclay. 'I'm going through yours.'

'Put that down!' But I wasn't quick enough and he had it open, the contents tipped onto the table.

'Calm down. Fair is fair. Now, what do we have here?'

He picked up my mobile phone. It was not going to impress Mr Barclay, that was for sure.

'Nokia? An early Nokia?' he sneered. 'I think my late grandmother had one of these. Do they still work in the 21st century?'

I made a desperate grab but he pulled it away, easily avoiding my lunge.

'It's all I need.'

'Really? Interesting.'

I felt like a sub-species. Was it too soon to call him cruel? After all, I'd only met him a few days before. 'At least you won't find a gun in there,' I snapped.

His eyebrows arched. 'No. Nothing so interesting. Oh my, what is this?' He held up my Kindle, pinched between thumb and forefinger. 'This really is the lowest of the low. A Fisher

Price toy. There's no excuse for such a device you know – I would rather have an Etch-a-Sketch to read on. You can have too much technology – paper will always be superior. And more secure.'

I dropped my head at his cheap put-down and he continued to rifle through my possessions. I was too shocked to stop him. He ignored my lipstick, mascara and blusher; when you carry a loaded handgun in your own bag, the everyday contents of a nobody like me must make boring fare.

And then he found them. He held them up to his nose and took a deep breath.

'Ah, disappointing. They're a fresh pair.'

'Bastard!' I lunged, but again he easily evaded me. He balled my flimsy spare knickers in his left fist.

'Care to explain?' he sneered.

'I'm going,' I said, rising to my feet. 'And I'm going to report that gun to the police.'

He laughed. 'Sit down. And what will you tell the police, about stealing my bag at the railway station and then rifling through its contents before bothering to contact me? Why didn't you hand it straight to the police?' Ah. He had me. 'And what on earth did you do with my wallet and cards? I swear they were in the bag when I lost it but you appear to have failed to return them.'

My mouth made the motions but nothing came out. The gall of the man. 'Your word against mine,' I said, deflated.

'Good luck with that – my father is a high court judge.' (He wasn't, I later discovered and his father despised him.)

'Oh.'

'And a lovely pink umbrella, a Hello Kitty purse – what are you, twelve? – and some chewing gum. Scintillating. Here, have it back.' He threw the bag across the table at me. 'But I'm keeping these.' He shoved my knickers into the pocket of his coat.

I hated this man. But I couldn't move, his gaze didn't waver and I found myself transfixed. I drank my coffee in a single gulp. It was delicious. I needed four more.

'Now then, after that little distraction, let's talk about payment for the driving work and the reward for the return of my bag.'

'You are assuming that I want anything to do with you,' I said, surprising myself; I'd seemingly 'grown a pair'.

'Of course you do. This is exciting for you.'

'And how do you know so much about me?' I asked.

'I know more about you than you know about you. The internet may be a dangerous playground but it is a fascinating one.'

'Such as?'

'Well, let me cover the basics first,' he appeared to be enjoying himself, enjoying my discomfort and all too aware of the hold he had on me. 'Name; Claire MacDonald. Age; 25, birthday September 13th. Born just down the road in Greenwich Hospital, sadly an institution no longer with us. Parents; Desmond and Deidre MacDonald, now resident with your brother Paul, in Edinburgh. You went to school at Deptford Green High School but never went to college or university after Sixth Form. You have eight GCSEs but did not excel at any single subject. You live in a rented flat at 13 Dutton Road in Deptford. Your rent is £750 a month, which is going to be a problem now that your Ex, Henry has run away to India. But you are undoubtedly better off without him as it will give you the opportunity to work for me. Your closest friends were originally Henry's so they will leave you, too. Sad.' He pulled a sad face. I was not amused. Going through my bag was a very bad thing but this man had seemingly gone one step further and worked his way through my entire life.

'You were paid weekly on Thursdays by Marshalls Design as an Intern (Temporary), but the work and pay are both desultory, insulting, so them making you redundant this morning was no bad thing,' he continued. 'You complained bitterly about the company and your work colleagues on Facebook to anyone who will listen, but you do nothing about it. And no one listens, no one reads what you post. Did you know that? No one.' That was cruel – I didn't need to hear that. 'Shall I go on?'

'There's more?'

'You are very public online. Like I say, I know more about you than you do yourself. Do you know how much is in your current account? Or, more to the point, how much you owe NatWest?'

My jaw went slack. I'd heard about this kind of privacy intrusion on Watchdog and the like, but that happened to old people, the hard of thinking, surely, not real people. Like me. Who was this guy?

'No. Let's not go there. I don't need to hear any more, thank you very much.'

'The reward then, and a little retainer for your services as my driver and assistant. Shall we say five thousand pounds?' He pulled a pen and cheque book from his jacket pocket.

Suddenly I needed a drink. A strong one. 'That…that would be welcome,' I stammered as he scrawled the necessary on what would be my first ever cheque from a bank called 'Coutts'. That would raise a few eyebrows at the bank when I paid it in. He slid it across the table and rose from the table.

'I suggest we celebrate with dinner at Dion by St Paul's this evening. I have booked a table for two at eight.' He held his hand out and I surprised myself by rising from my seat to shake it.

'8 o'clock,' it was all too fast. 'I'll meet you there.' I was operating on automatic, damn near speechless as he left. I went to the bar. 'A gin and tonic please. Double. Light on the tonic.'

'Sure. Are you going to settle up Barclay's tab, too?' the barman asked.

You bastard, Barclay…

Chapter 6

I surprised myself and managed to arrive early, a whole half hour to wait for his majesty before I told him where to go. Or not. But that business with the spare knickers I keep in my bag had really riled me and I was favouring the easy option.

The restaurant he had selected for our 'celebration' was possibly the best I had ever been to. Situated right on the door step of St. Paul's, it had the kind of floodlit views of Wren's cathedral that would impress all but the most travel weary tourist. The place was crowded with noisy, opinionated City types in their dark pinstripe uniforms and pressed white shirts, the only women either staff or demure arm candy. Not the company I usually kept, of course (I have higher standards) but excellent for people watching nevertheless. I played Mum's old 'Three Words' game and found that I was applying the same three words to everyone there: Wealthy. Opinionated. Loud. Junior managers were lording it over their silent subservient worker bees, deep privileged tones were occasionally rising above the hubbub and spouting macho nonsense to the masses, inevitably punctuated with an overdramatic laugh.

I ordered myself a Diet Coke and pretended to read something on my mobile. It looked even more out of place than I did in this land of shiny smartphones and tablets.

So this man, this Barclay, what to make of him? The facts at hand: he had left an expensive bag (very expensive: I looked it up online and they go for around a grand and the laptop was worth even more) that I had picked up and, admittedly a few dark thoughts later, I had returned to him, intact, as any good, law-abiding citizen would. He had then undertaken a detailed, possibly illegal, certainly exhaustive online investigation without permission on yours truly and by all appearances he had harvested what felt like every online detail about me, including stuff that I probably don't even know about myself. School reports? Credit history? Medical records? My so-called friends bitching about me on Twitter behind my back? (Is that called 'twitchering'?) Had I been hacked? Had he hacked my bank, my email, my doctor? Did it matter? What could I do about it?

So many questions. And what did I know about him? Only what I found in that bag. I didn't even know his full name – was 'Barclay' his first or surname? Was it his real name? What was his line of work? Why did he require a gun? All I had to go on was his mobile number and a cheque, which had his bank account details and that was about it – the account name was simply 'Q. H. Barclay'. 'Q'? That sounded more like a name from a James Bond movie than real life. I couldn't even think of a male name that started with Q.

And why me? Was it my honesty in returning the bag, or my dishonesty in taking it that appealed to him? And who pays a stranger five grand for returning a bag? Was he buying my silence over the gun? Was I now an accessory after the event (or whatever they call it)? What was happening? Maybe I should get up and leave while I still had the opportunity. And yet…Barclay arrived a few minutes after eight, dressed in almost exactly the same costume as the City clowns (minus the pinstripe – not Barclay's style) but carried it off with pure panache. You could criticise him for many things (and I was assembling a pretty long list myself already) but you had to admit the guy had style. The head of the restaurant knew him, they exchanged pleasantries in French, and we were moved to a different table right at the back, away from the main crowds. Cosy. So much for my thoughts of possibly making a rapid exit.

'This is not a date.'

'It is not a date. We have been very clear on that,' said Barclay.

'It's just a getting-to-know-each-other meal.'

'Exactly.'

'We are not celebrating, more clarifying.'

'If you say so.'

As you can tell, the conversation was uncomfortable at first. We discussed the menu and its expensive dishes which seemed individually to cost more than my weekly shop. We ordered, me keeping an eye on the prices just in case. Barclay however seemed to be pushing the boat out. Surely he couldn't leave me to pick up the bill again?

Suddenly, without warning, he said; 'Sorry.'

'What?'

'That foolishness with your bag. That was stupid and childish of me. Not a good way to start things. Sorry.'

Disarmed, I said 'S'okay' under my breath.

'Forgive me?'

'Maybe.'

The starters arrived almost too quickly: the curse of ordering from the set menu.

'Tell me more about this work then. Where's your office? What are the hours? What will I be doing? I haven't said 'yes' yet, you know.'

'I've got a little mundane, boring stuff, and some not-so-mundane-stuff that's not strictly, exactly one hundred per cent…' He paused and looked around – there was no one listening. '… that requires that you display a degree of moral flexibility.'

I knew it! I smiled. He smiled. 'How illegal?' I asked.

'Justifiably illegal,' he answered cryptically. 'You have my word that no one gets hurt. I will always have your back. You will sleep soundly at nights, I can assure you of that, and I'll take any heat if things get too...' He let that one drift, probably realising that he was saying too much.

''If things get too…' what, exactly?'

'Claire, you've got to ask yourself what exactly do you want from life,' he said. 'Do you really think the best that life in this wonderful town can offer you is a nine-to-five existence as an underpaid, overworked junior for some anonymous bunch of losers too stupid to hack it at Google or Facebook?'

I picked at the rocket in my diminutive avocado salad with my fork. I didn't know what I wanted, but he was right – I was starting to know what I *didn't* want. I didn't want to work in an office for anonymous people who didn't appreciate me, didn't talk to me, didn't even see me the majority of the time.

'You work with me, Claire,' he emphasised the 'with', 'and you'll never be bored again. I guarantee it.'

I had no answer to that. I was bored with my life. Twenty-five and already dreading the morning alarm, the sardine squash of the commute, the monotony of the blinking cursor on my screen, the pile of meaningless paperwork I had to complete and file for no one to read, the trip to Starbucks for everyone's latte but mine. Only another forty plus years of this to go – it will just fly by – and then I can curl up in front of my one bar heater with a mug of Horlicks waiting for the minute of conversation with that nice young man from Meals on Wheels. Bliss.

Barclay was smiling at me, knowing he had me. I tried not to smile back, but it was almost painful not to.

'And a car?' I asked.

'One appropriate to the work we will do.'

My mind started racing. Obviously something classy if I was to chauffeur him around for his meetings and engagements. This guy wouldn't be cutting corners with his wheels, that was for sure. A Jag? Beemer? Bentley? This could get very interesting.

'Do I get a chauffeur's cap?' the child in me asked.

He chuckled and shook his head.

'And my salary? I'm looking for thirty k,' I suggested.

'Then in that case I think you will be looking at a Job Seeker's allowance as I can't cover that,' he responded.

'And you're looking at Uber or an Oyster Card.'

'Touche. Twenty.'

'I'm sorry?' I cupped my hand to my ear, suddenly hard of hearing. Hilarious, I know. 'Twenty-five k.'

'Twenty-two. Done.'

'Twenty-five.' But it was too meek: he knew I was beaten.

'Twenty-two. And a cut of any extras we make together.'

I had no idea what that would amount to but I found myself grinning. I couldn't help myself.

The deal was done and there we were. Barclay and MacDonald. Partners in something or other.

Once we'd eaten and opened the second bottle of red:

'An excellent wine list here,' Barclay boasted. 'Makes up for the so-so food.' I wasn't complaining: those were undoubtedly the best salmon and crab fishcakes I'd ever eaten (on account of them being the only fishcakes I'd ever had not made by Birdseye. I thought it best not to mention it.)

'So tell me more about this Barclay guy,' I don't think I was slurring but maybe ordering a second bottle hadn't been a great move.

'What do you want to know?'

'Full name for a start. Is Barclay a first or second name?'

'It can be either.'

'Yes, but with you?'

'It is my surname.' He hadn't answered the original question but I let it pass. 'Born in 1986, to Mr & Mrs Barclay of Berkshire residence.'

'Do you see mum and dad much?'

'Only at Christmas. Torture.'

'Brothers and sisters? Cousins'

A small shake of the head

'Significant other?'

'No.'

'Ever?'

'No.' He shifted uncomfortably in his chair and took another sip from his glass. For the first time in our short acquaintance I felt like I had him on the ropes.

'Friends?'

'When I need them. I don't need them often. They are more like acquaintances, colleagues even. You?' He had switched the focus – had I hit a nerve?

'You know all about me.'

'Only what I found online. Surely that is not everything?'

'It seemed pretty extensive from what you said the other day.'

'That is not Claire MacDonald, the person. That is Claire MacDonald the online persona. I assume the two are very different – I would certainly hope so. And before you say anything I did no more than any employer would do when assessing a prospective job applicant. Surely you don't really think all that stuff people post on Facebook is private do you?'

I hadn't really considered it. I knew there were privacy settings, much like there was also all kinds of legal stuff, Terms & Conditions and other pages and pages of legalese that you were supposed to read before clicking 'accept', but who had time to look at that? No one I knew, that was for certain.

'I guess not,' I said.

'So Horrible Henry has gone?'

'He's not that Horrible, but yes. He and all his worldly have moved out and are scattered globally. His body is now in Paris, his mind already suffering in India, his boxes of books and other shit are deposited in some anonymous damp, rat-infested warehouse out Woolwich way. Good riddance.'

'You do not mean that so callously, surely?'

'I do. We weren't a good fit. He wants to help the world, stop global warming, feed the hungry, free the oppressed, clothe the naked, house the homeless…'

'Busy man.'

'Ha! If he spent less time talking about it to his mates and their girlfriends and more time actually doing something that would be a start.' I was sounding bitter, but the truth was I genuinely didn't care at all. He was gone. End of.

'So little Claire is all alone now in the big, dark city?'

'Hardly. I've got loads of friends.' It sounded like a boast.

"Good for you.' He didn't sound convinced. Neither did I.

'But most are away at the moment.'

'Not good for you.'

'That's the great thing about Facebook and…' I paused, remembered that he'd been so dismissive of my Facebooking; apparently no one reads my stuff. No one cares. I was posting to the un-listening. That hurt. 'I find it difficult to make new friends, like I'm being disloyal to absent friends,' I said.

'I do not have that problem.'

'You make friends easily?'

'No, I meant I have no loyalty issues. I am not very loyal to anyone.'

'But you'll be loyal to me?'

'If you work with me? Yes. Of course. But loyalty has to be

earned.'

'You'd make a rubbish dog.'

'Don't mention dogs,' he scowled, uncomfortable for some reason.

'You don't like dogs?' He shook his head but I couldn't say I was that surprised. This man's idea of a best friend was probably an Italian sports car or an expensive vintage cellar. Or a Prada rucksack.

Before I could stop myself I said, 'I get lonely sometimes, especially the evenings when Henry's out saving the world.' Uh oh. The alcohol was doing my talking for me. It just slipped out. Damn that second bottle.

'Who doesn't?' Was he being sympathetic or sarcastic? I couldn't tell.

'You don't strike me as the lonely type.'

'Everyone is lonely. It's just that some of us find it difficult to admit to it. Money doesn't always buy happiness. I would like to think I'm a loner but sometimes…'

And he left it there, hanging, unclarified. In time I would get used to it, but it was surprising that evening. Later I realised that with Barclay it was all front, all bravado. But deep down, further down where he didn't let you dig, there was a lonely, unhappy little boy. Spoiled rotten, unprincipled, sad even. The bugger just wouldn't admit to it. One minute it felt like he was opening up, only to slam that door shut with the next breath. Infuriating.

The restaurant had emptied out almost completely by the time we had finished our food so I figured I was on safe ground to mention the unmentionable.

'Can I ask you something?' I ventured.

'Sure.'

'The gun.'

'Ah.'

'What's it for?'

'I don't have it on me if you're worried.'

'I appreciate that,' the wine made it sound more like 'happreshiate'. 'But what's it for when you do have it?'

'Encouragement. Deterrent. The usual.' His voice drifted

away as if that wasn't the whole story.

'Will I need one?'

He laughed. 'No.'

'So you've never shot anyone?'

'No.'

"No, you have' or 'No, you haven't'?' I pressed.

He sighed. 'It was in my bag because I had to meet this guy who was being difficult over some money he owed me.'

My eyes widened. 'You threatened someone with that gun? Shot him?'

'No. Of course not. What kind of man do you think I am? Even I would not do that just for money,' said Barclay.

'Good,' I said.

'But I may have killed his dog.'

'You shot a dog?'

As Barclay was getting quieter I was getting louder. The restaurant was now empty except a few staff well out of earshot. Just as well.

'Keep it down. No one can claim to be perfect. Not even your Ex. Look at you – you stole a bag,' he replied.

'No I didn't. I picked up a bag that some idiot had lost. I gave it back.'

'Eventually. I didn't shoot a dog. I shot *at* a dog. And I missed. Deliberately. The dog had a heart attack. It was not my fault.'

'You believe that you are completely blameless for its death?'

'Pretty much.'

'And you did this because this guy wouldn't pay you?'

'He owed me money.'

'So you shot his dog.'

'*At* his dog.'

'For money?'

'Why else would I do it? I like dogs.'

'You have a funny way of showing it.'

'Look, he owed me money. A lot of money. Fifty grand. That is a lot of money. And he was refusing to pay, so I needed to shake him up a bit and remind him of his obligation.'

'Bang. Dead dog.'

'Actually it was bang bang bang, woof, topple, dead dog. I am not very good with guns.'

'Evidently. But effective nonetheless.'

'So it would appear. Look, Claire, I do hope this will not come between us…'

'There is no 'us'. I'm not sure I want to work for you anymore.' But my eyes were smiling

'But we have a deal. 22k.'

'I thought we'd agreed on twenty five? So if I now say 'no' you'll shoot me? Sorry, I meant 'shoot *at* me'?'

He smiled. Damn it, I found myself smiling, too.

'It's going to be fun,' said Barclay.

'No guns,' I said.

'No promises,' he replied, and ordered another bottle.

Chapter 7

He had probably answered all of my questions. I had possibly asked all of my questions. Sadly, the large quantity of quality wine consumed meant that I could remember nothing with any certainty, so I was none the wiser. The following morning all I had to show for the evening with Barclay was a Saharan mouth and the dull, unrelenting pounding in my forehead. Oh, and a business card that had just BARCLAY printed on it. On the reverse he had scrawled his mobile number, a Docklands address (presumably an office?) and a time: 11am.

It was 10am when I read it. Despite my head screaming that I was in no fit state to rise I forced myself out of bed and dressed with the clumsy, lethargic motions and lack of care of the truly hungover. I decided to skip the shower and make up and my breakfast consisted of a mouthful of Colgate foam.

So much for making a good impression on my first day.

Mercifully the sky outside was dull and grey – I don't think I could have coped with any brightness that morning. There was a dampness in the air that wasn't quite drizzle that softened the hard lines of the buildings as I made my way to the local Docklands Light Railway station. At least the commute would be easy – Barclay's office looked like it was about half an hour away. Plenty of time to sober up and start feeling human again for my first day in my new life.

But it wasn't an office. The building was a sharp-cornered modern glass and steel tower of an apartment block, built for a sparkling future that still hadn't quite arrived despite the promises of the developer's brochure. My doubts returned and I still wasn't quite sure I was doing the right thing. I was going to his flat? Even newly liberated Claire wasn't wholly comfortable with that particular step into the unknown. But it was too late to walk away, and I was pretty confident I could take this Barclay character in a fight. Even so, my hand reached into my bag for the calming assurance of my attack alarm key ring, though going on previous experience it was as likely to deafen me as much as any attacker.

And then suddenly there was my prospective 'attacker', holding open the building door for me, beckoning me inside. And … smiling? Was that a smile?

'Good morning. You look…tired,' he managed, about as polite as I could have expected in the circumstances. In stark contrast Barclay looked like he had spent the last few hours with his personal barber and tailor – if I said he looked 'immaculate' I'd have been understating it. Even his teeth looked newly polished.

'I work from home,' he explained. 'But you won't need to come here very often. Everything will be on the laptop I've got for you and the car's being delivered this afternoon.' We had walked to a bank of lifts and entered the one he had presumably just descended in. He pressed the button marked 'Penthouse' and we started our ascent.

The giddy girl in me I had tried so hard to contain was easily impressed and quite excited. I was going up in the world, both literally and figuratively.

'Make yourself comfortable over there at the desk. I'll get some coffee on – you look like you need it.'

Barclay disappeared behind what was presumably a kitchen door and I was left alone to take in the eye-watering views of Docklands and the almost-as-stunning apartment. I tried not to look too awestruck, but it was bloody difficult.

So this was how the other half live.

It was a large monochrome high tech flat, the furnishing was sparse: a designer recliner here, a matching sofa there, a state of the art work desk and chair all chrome and glass and leather sparkling under the halogen lights set deep in the ceiling.

So was this Barclay's home? Wow.

Barclay's deluxe lifestyle trappings weren't limited to the contents of his rucksack. The polished steel of three TV-sized computer screens jostled for dominance with laptops, iThingies, keyboards and mice on a smoked glass desk that was more like a futuristic work bench than a table.

The entire far wall of the room was obscured by three of the largest televisions I had ever seen, effectively they *were* the wall. Boys and their toys, huh? All the gear and no idea.

But curiously the room was stylish but without style, a show home lifted from the pages of *Wallpaper* magazine or *Esquire*. There were no ornaments or plants whatsoever, cables had been tucked away out of sight and it all felt artificial and false, the result of either chronic OCD or someone desperate to impress. It was very much a personality-free zone. Polished but seemingly unloved, there were no feminine graces. This was a cold room, almost antiseptic in its detachment from a personal touch. The only softness in the entire room was from a single grey fake fur rug that leaked out from under the work bench, concealing the cables presumably for all that technology piled up on top.

All I could learn about Barclay from this room was from what wasn't there rather than what was. There were no pictures on the walls, no family photos, no newspapers or magazines or CDs or DVDs or books or paperwork or even post.

The more I looked the less I found. Few cupboards, one set of (locked) filing cabinets, not even a coat rack. Presumably everything was crammed into the bedroom, which I had no intention whatsoever of visiting.

How long did it take a man to make coffee? I needed a drink and felt like I could pee like a grizzly coming out of hibernation. There were three doors leading out from the main room. Barclay had gone through the one on the right to make coffee, so presumably that was the kitchen. The one on the left, which would presumably share the stunning views of the main room, was likely a bedroom so I guessed the one in the middle, slightly ajar, would be the loo.

I pushed it open and clicked on the light and entered. The bathroom was five-star hotel spotless, a shining example of just how sparkly chrome fittings and white tiles can be. Mr Muscle would be so proud. My eyes did not appreciate the additional jolt of polished surfaces and tungsten brilliance. I did my business and helped myself to a glass of water. It really was like a hotel – the glass was in a little plastic bag.

When I went back into the lounge Barclay was sitting at the table, two tiny clear glass cups of espresso proudly sitting before him. Oh, for a cup of instant.

'Sorry it took so long. Kitchen's a bit … untidy,' he apologised.

'Nice place,' I said.

He nodded but said nothing. Instead he pushed one of the laptops towards me as I sat in the other chair at the table.

'This is for you,' he said, lifting the lid of what looked like the Apple laptop that had been in his bag. I spotted the scratch I'd made on its perfect skin while on the train and my cheeks reddened.

But it was like being reunited with a lost love. I'd swear there were tears in my eyes.

'Thank you.'

'Unfortunately the work I need you to do on it today is far more mundane. I need help completing my Self-Assessment tax return and … actually, I don't need help as much as I need you to do the whole thing. I've got to go and sort out your car at the dealer, so let me just get the receipts and stuff and I can leave you with it while I get the car.'

I'd noticed the Audi dealership on the train over. Or maybe it was that Jaguar place opposite? I wouldn't mind filling in his boring old tax return while waiting for the keys. Besides, a man's tax filing can reveal all kinds of things about an individual, surely?

He went into his bedroom and emerged with a small box file and his coat.

'Okay if I leave you here? I'll be a few hours.'

'Sure,' I said.

'Ciao,' he said, pulling on his coat and whipping a Paul Smith silk scarf around his neck.

'Ciao'? Had he really said that? How totes Eighties…

Barclay's tax return was a massive disappointment. Sorting through a nominal handful of receipts and bank statements yielded precious little information about the man and, much like his apartment, it was what was missing that spoke more about the man than what was there. It wasn't going to take a massive amount of work to complete it, but at least there were a couple of surprises that made it more interesting to do than my old job's paperwork.

Surprise number one: his full name was Quentin Horatio Barclay. Quentin? So that was the 'Q' on the cheque. Mystery solved. Hardly a name to be ashamed of these days – old Tarantino had done the world's Quentins a massive favour, even if it would never quite be cool. I'd been thinking more along the lines of 'Quincy' or 'Quigly' or even 'Qatermass'. Quentin was disappointingly conventional, and I couldn't see his problem with it.

(But I guess 'Barclay' fed his ego better, of course.)

Surprise number two was that his taxable income for the entire year was eighteen grand. Eighteen! And his sole employer during that period appeared to be a local coffee shop where he worked as a barista. Seriously? The coffee he'd made me that morning was okay but nothing out of this world – Barclay was a barista?

I sorted through the receipts he'd left me and poured over the bank statements. It was not what I'd expected, a man living pretty much on the breadline, a current account dipping into overdraft most weeks, topped up with tiny dribbles from the coffee place that barely paid off the previous week's deficit. He'd even asked me to put his home address as the same as the coffee shop rather than this high tech palace.

I looked around the flat. How could he afford all this? And the clothes he adorned himself in? And an Aston Martin (or whatever he'd sorted for me)? Something wasn't adding up.

I could only guess that his declaration to Her Majesty's Revenue puppets was at best a sleight of hand to keep them from his real lifestyle and earnings. I'd only been working for him a few hours and I was already guilty of filing a false tax declaration and fraud.

Oh Barclay, you're leading me astray.

I finished the online form and checked and re-checked my work. All in order. I pressed send and clicked 'yes' a zillion times and then it was on its way. Crime number one neatly wrapped up and delivered on day one. Imagine how productive I'd have been with a clear head?

The hangover had subsided a little and I'd calmed its temper with a succession of glasses of tap water from the bathroom. But having finished the main job at hand I needed something more, some food perhaps. He'd warned the kitchen was a mess but how bad could it be?

Bad. As I opened the kitchen door I almost retched. In contrast to the designer perfection elsewhere the kitchenette was a devastated disaster zone, stacked high with unwashed plates and cutlery and what looked and smelled like a week's worth of discarded takeaways. I instinctively held my breath: abandoned food was everywhere. The nauseating stench of several half-eaten stale curries competed with the sickly aroma of rancid sweet and sour chicken. A token pedal bin was overflowing – it hadn't been emptied in weeks.

Desperate for a drink I opened the fridge. Empty, except for an unopened, out-of-place bottle of Dom Perignon Champagne. It looked like it had belonged in someone else's home. (From what I'd already learned of Barclay, it probably had.)

I needed a drink but the coffee machine looked too complicated. Maybe he was a barista after all? Nothing around that looked remotely as practical as a kettle. I settled for another glass of tap water in the last clean glass, then ran from the kitchen before the combination of last night's excess and the cloying smells of Barclay's culinary depravity proved too much. I needed to get out and draw in a lungful or seven of fresh air. I grabbed my coat and bag. I'd leave the door on the latch – I'd only be gone a few minutes, I just needed to clear my head and, most importantly, my nasal passages.

'Oh. Hello,' he said.

For some reason I hadn't expected to meet anyone in the corridor outside the flat but I guess stranger things have happened, even to me. (Barclay, for one.)

The guy looked confused and a little lost. 'Is Barclay in?' he asked.

'Er, no. No one home I'm afraid. Were you after him? I was just leaving.'

'No. Yes. Are you… are you his girlfriend?'

I laughed. 'God no. Just a …' (friend? employee?) 'I'm Claire,' I said, holding out my hand in a ridiculously formal manner.

He was confused but amused by my business-like gesture and shook my hand nevertheless. 'Tom. Thomas,' he said.

"Tom Thomas'?' I grinned. 'Really? Did your parents think that would be funny or something?'

He laughed too. 'No. I'm Tom, but I'm trying to be 'Thomas' now and it's not quite working. Tom Pedakowski.' That explained the slight American accent I was picking up.

'I prefer Tom I think. Don't be a 'Tommy' though. It would make you sound about five years' old.'

'Tom it is. I'm thinking of cutting the surname back to something more British – it sounds too foreign and I end up spelling it out on the phone all the time. I've been test driving 'Thomas Peters'. Can't get used to it myself. I keep forgetting then correcting myself.'

'I like your glasses,' I said out of nowhere.

'They're Tom Ford's,' he said.

'Doesn't he miss them?' I cracked. 'It's amazing the prescription works for you.' Hysterical, I know.

He smiled again, revealing near perfect teeth, a credit to the great American dentist profession. I like good teeth. He had a nice smile. He was a little lacking on the height front (around my height) but he wasn't unattractive. Blondish hair, a little unruly, light stubble, probably late thirties, casually dressed but smartly so. On the old Claire-phwoar-meter (now back in use in the post-Henry world) he was an 'Interesting' but not in the 'Drop Dead G.' category. Close, but not quite.

Whatever. Maybe it was the dim light in the hallway or the relief of being away from the horror of that kitchen and back in the real world, but I suddenly felt myself relaxing, the day brightening up. I was in no rush to go and my head was feeling surprisingly clear.

'Why are you after Barclay, Tom Thomas?'

'I quite like that. I might go for that.'

'You're welcome. It's of no use to me.'

'I need to sort something out with him. We occasionally do business together but it's all gone a bit messy and I just wanted to straighten it out before it went to far.' He paused. I think he was considering how much to tell me. 'We had a bit of a disagreement.'

'You run the coffee shop?' I said, all innocent.

'No, not a coffee shop.' His bemused look was a firm indication he didn't have a clue what I was talking about. I moved on.

'A disagreement? He's quite a disagreeable sort. I don't know him that well but I can see how he rubs people up the wrong way.'

Tom nodded. 'He sure can. I think there's something faulty with his wiring, sometimes he seems to be oblivious to the way he makes people feel. Like that medical condition.'

'Asperger's? I don't know it's that extreme but I haven't known him that long. He doesn't seem to care what you think.'

'It's not an endearing quality,' said Tom.

'So shall I tell him you called by? I've just been tidying up some paperwork for him.' I thought it best to make it absolutely, 100% clear that there was nothing going on between me and Mr Barclay. 'He should be back shortly. He went to see a man about a car.'

'Another Aston Martin? Man, I loved that DB7, that was just beautiful.'

I grinned uncontrollably. Soon it would be mine.

'Shall I..?'

'Yes please. Actually, no. Don't bother. I'll catch him at some point. It wasn't important, just me wanting to tie up some loose ends and not leave things unspoken.' He pushed the button for the lift and the doors opened – it hadn't gone anywhere since his arrival. 'Going down?' he asked. I nodded and joined him.

The lift descended uninterrupted. We stood in silence, uncertain where to look. Instantly strangers again. As we neared the ground floor, he said:

'I was just wondering…'

'Yes?'

'I was wondering if you'd like to have a drink with me sometime?'

I didn't know what to say – it had been a while since someone had asked me out, and this guy was a complete stranger. I didn't know anything about him or…

'Sure.' The word surprised me but it had definitely come from lips. 'That would be nice. I don't live around here though – I'm over the river. Deptford.'

He hummed the theme from Neighbours. 'I'm in Lee. Maybe before Christmas? I've got this trip home I'm heading out on next week.'

'Home? America?'

'San Francisco.'

'Very nice. Yes, before Christmas suits me.' This was all going too fast for comfort but I wasn't resisting; it was just one of those days when things span out of my control. We exchanged mobile numbers and I held my hand out for another overly-polite shake. 'Nice to meet you, Tom Thomas.'

'Nice to meet you, Claire.'

He walked off towards a parked BMW and blipped the blippy thing as he approached it and it blipped back in recognition. I waved then took in a few deep breaths of the damp air I'd been so eager to consume just a few short minutes earlier.

'Well,' I said to myself, 'That really was quite pleasant.' A date? So soon after Henry? Things were looking up. Tom Thomas – it was growing on me, even if it wasn't his real name.

Two new men in a week. And it was still only Tuesday. A girl could get a reputation with that kind of hit rate.

Chapter 8

The car was not exactly what I had been expecting.

'It's a classic,' said Barclay, sensing my disappointment.

'Is it?' I was definitely not convinced. 'A classic what, exactly?'

'They don't make them like this anymore. Actually they probably still do, down in South America or somewhere. A classic never goes out of fashion.'

'Assuming it ever was in fashion in the first place. What exactly is it?'

'It's an early nineties Fiat Uno. Car of the year in its day. The first supermini. A racing hot hatch. 55 metric horsepower.' The words were English but he was talking a different language.

'I thought it would be ... nicer.'

'This is as nice as you'll find a Fiat Uno these days. They're pretty rare. This is a great example of Italian style and engineering.'

It was like dealing with a second-hand car salesman, only this car looked distinctly fourth or fifth hand. Barclay was gamely trying to sell it to me but it was a pretty herculean task to convince me to even step closer, let alone step inside.

To describe it as 'boxy' would be unkind to boxes. For one thing, boxes look more solid and even a soaking wet box would appear more secure. It was square and angular in a way they just don't make cars these days, you could almost cut yourself on the sharp corners that had only been slightly softened in the interest of aerodynamics. It was as if it had been designed with just a ruler. At least the wheels were round, and, presumably, the now-missing hubcaps had been too. The wing mirror (there was only one, on the driver's side) looked like it had been glued on, a plastic afterthought added to scrape through an MOT.

It occurred to me that it may have been maintained as a failed school metalwork project, there was definitely some DIY welding on one of the rear doors and some of the rust had been painted over, possibly with household emulsion.

Colour? Well it had several in truth, even the rust came in

several fetching shades. It was possible that in a past life it had been red and quite dashing in its youthful eighties' heyday, but now it was several dull, faded pinks, darker on the driver's side for some curious reason like an old Royal Mail post van parked under a blazing hot sun for a decade or two in exactly the same place.

I circled it to see if it had a better side, maybe the light was playing tricks.

Nope.

I reached to open the driver's door but pulled away sharply, as if my touch would confirm the new ownership.

'Don't be timid now,' said the used car salesman who also happened to be my new boss. 'It won't bite.'

I gritted my teeth and clasped the handle. With a sharp tug it was open, and a stale odour of mildew knocked me back on my heels. Involuntarily I tried to swat it away as if it were a cloud of midges.

Barclay laughed, but it wasn't an infectious laugh. I felt like crying.

'I thought…I thought it would be something special,' I whined.

'It is special Claire. A white one of these killed Princess Di!'

I had no idea what he was talking about. I made a pantomime dusting motion at the driver's seat then engineered my butt into the vehicle.

Actually, it wasn't too bad. No, I'd got further than that, it was quite comfortable, firm in support and the dashboard was clean and functional. It would have been out of place in an Aston Martin, but then so would I.

'And you want me to chauffeur you around in this thing?' It didn't make sense.

'Sure. A bit of retro chic never hurt anyone. Besides, it will be dark, no one will see us.'

'Dark?'

'Yes. Didn't I mention that?'

'No.' What else hadn't he mentioned? 'What exactly is this driving job, Barclay?'

'Nothing to be alarmed about. I just have some business deals I'm doing in the next few weeks and need a driver to help me…'

'Get away? Flee the scene? Do a runner? Are these dodgy deals you're doing in the small hours, Barclay?'

He gaped at me in surprise, hurt even. 'Dodgy is a strong word. At worst I'd suggest they're 'below the line'.'

'But I'm a getaway driver?'

He looked suddenly tense, concerned, unsure where I was taking this. 'I guess so, yes,' he said, doubt crossing his face for the first time. 'I've got it all planned, it's very straightforward and…'

'Cool!'

I was grinning, I couldn't help myself. 'When do we start?' I asked.

His relief was visible, his shoulders relaxed and the old Barclay arrogance immediately returned. 'I need picking up at three tomorrow morning. It's not far. You'll be tucked back safely in bed by five and you can take the rest of the day off.'

Generous. I turned the Uno's ignition and unexpectedly it bit first time, a little coarse, throaty even, but it hadn't misfired and it sounded surprisingly assured. I gingerly pressed down on the accelerator and the engine responded, making an almost manly growl. The cold hard plastic of the steering wheel felt good in my hands and suddenly this didn't seem at all bad. I'd never had my own car before and I had to start somewhere. Okay, so Barclay probably had been paid to take it off some crook's hands at a scrap heap, but it worked and felt curiously cosy once I was inside. Snug even.

'Take it for a spin,' he said, closing the door and patting the roof.

With a little too much effort I managed to get it into first and lifted the clutch. A jerk, a jump, and I was moving, a little nervously (I hadn't driven at all for a few months) but my confidence grew as I took it through the gears. I could get used to this, I thought. My initial disappointment was, much like Barclay, disappearing fast in my rear view mirror.

Claire MacDonald. Getaway driver. You heard it first here, folks.

I was in the Fiat Uno parked on the edge of an abandoned DIY store car park at just passed four in the morning on a freezing Tuesday in December. Ignoring Barclays' instruction I had left the engine running to keep the heating ticking over – he couldn't expect me to freeze, surely? I was bored out of my mind.

And maybe, just maybe, a wee bit scared.

'Ten minutes. Tops,' he'd promised. That had been twenty minutes earlier and to be honest I'd never expected it to be "ten minutes, tops", he didn't strike me as a punctual person. But now though I was unsure that this little 'below the line' caper of his was actually going to plan. He had disappeared around the corner of this shuttered not-so-super superstore to do the pick-up and there had been no sign of him since.

Maybe I should have turned the car off, but I was still nervous that it would restart easily on my command – 'reliable' wasn't one of the three words that sprang to mind when considering the Uno. The heating was hardly worth it, more noise than heat and Barclay could have been out there screaming for me for all I knew and I wouldn't have heard it. I know what I should have done. I should have turned it off and wound down the window and listened for him, that was what a professional getaway driver would do.

Mind you, a professional getaway driver would probably have demanded a better set of wheels than that little ageing Italian runaround, that I was actually quite taken with. He had told me that the most important thing in this line of work was that we had a car that nobody would look twice at. Well, with the Uno they might have, but the first look would have been shock and the second more like pity.

Despite my new confidence behind the wheel I was secretly hoping that I wouldn't have to 'burn rubber' and get involved in a high speed chase. The badge on the back proudly boasted that it was an Uno 55 –was that its top speed? It seemed nippy enough, shifting up through the tricky gears, but it did start noisily vibrating, almost straining when I got to thirty and I'd been reluctant to push it passed fifty in case bits started shaking off. That car may have been able to park on a postage stamp but I feared it would be a serious stretch of its abilities to reach 60mph. Going downhill. With a strong headwind behind it.

I turned off the engine. Instantly it was as cold inside as outside, but, I reassured myself, at least it wasn't raining.

Splat on the windscreen. Splat splat splat. Typical.

The high flying criminal life could be trying at times.

Where was he? Where was Barclay, the man who was supposed to be saving me from a life of office-tied tedium and evenings of DVD box sets and lonely bottles of Merlot for one?

I waited. And waited. And waited. 'Come on, Barclay, where the hell are you?' I muttered to myself. At least those first drops of rain didn't live up to their promise. I checked my watch and it was almost half an hour passed drop time.

Something had gone wrong. Something must have gone wrong. I lowered the driver's window, the cold air rushing in, instantly releasing the last vestiges of warmth.

Just the noise of faraway traffic. I heard a dog bark off in the distance and I noticed again the slight mildewy dog smell of the ageing fabric on the car's rear seat. Maybe the heaters had brought out the worst of it. It must have been a previous owner's pooch: Barclay never struck me as a pet person. At least he hadn't taken a gun with him – 'no animals were harmed in the making of this getaway'. Or did he have the gun? Why did I trust that man?

I was being stupid. That bark was from the wrong direction. There was no dog there to get in the way. Calm down. I had the easy job, sitting in a car, waiting. Well worth it for a few quid. And Barclay knew what he was doing, right? He said that he'd done this kind of deal without a hitch dozens of times before.

But had he? I only had his word for it of course. I was starting to have my doubts. I was tapping the steering wheel like I was waiting for my driving test result. Couldn't panic. No need to panic. It was just Barclay making sure everything was in order and…

And then suddenly he was there in the rear mirror, jogging gently, a large holdall in hand, something resembling a grin on his face.

I reached over and unlocked the far door. He climbed in, the bag down between his feet and rubbed his hands together.

'Why so cold in here?' he asked.

'You told me to turn the engine off to avoid attracting attention!'

'Are you mad? It's below freezing out there.' Incorrigible. 'Let's get moving.'

Suddenly nervous I turned the key and the over-confident engine coughed and revved into life. Go! First gear into second, third gear just minutes away now folks. I felt that the world record for fastest getaway was safely ours.

'All good?' I asked, gripping the wheel like Lewis Hamilton but driving more like Lady Hamilton.

'Yes. He was a little late. Sorry about that. He couldn't wait to give me the bag. Almost threw it at me. Then ran away. A dream pick-up.'

'And that bag's full of cash?'

'I haven't counted it but it looks and feels good. He looked like a nice guy.'

'Really?'

'No, not really. Didn't get a good look at him, and he didn't even glance at me, so we can … hey! Slow down!'

We were barely doing thirty, but already the Fiat's minuscule engine was straining.

'Don't need a speed camera ticket, do we?' he half joked.

He had a point. I had one thing to do and I was closer to panic than I had ever been in my life. It's a cliché but I could feel a pounding in my chest. Literally. I had never known a thrill like that before. This was the adrenaline-fuelled life I was destined for. Bonnie and Clyde! Barclay and MacDonald!

Fucking hell – I was a getaway driver! Woo hoo!

(At 29mph in a built-up area on a deserted street.)

He was rifling through the holdall, counting out the bundles. "Yes, all here. Easiest money you'll ever make."

But I was barely listening. The blood was rushing in my ears, my heart was racing, pulse throbbing in my wrists and I had a grin as wide as a psychotic clown's. We had done it and now we were heading out of town and on to whatever was next in my new life of crime. Our new life of crime. It would be dark for several more hours on that crisp, cold night, but already my day was brightening faster than the December sky.

I floored the accelerator. The Uno protested but was up for it. Barclay was gripping the holdall's handle. We were both smiling as a light fog enveloped us and we made our first getaway.

'Well,' said Barclay. 'That was something pretty special.'

My heart was still racing and I could hear the blood in my ears throbbing. "Yes." I was still out of breath.

'Exhilarating even.'

I nodded. 'Sure was.'

I clenched and unclenched my hands several times to try to calm myself down.

'I'm sorry if that was all a wee bit too fast for you,' I said.

'Isn't that supposed to be my line?'

We both laughed. I may have blushed a little; it was difficult to tell as I was still feeling quite flushed. Oh my god, we did it. We really did it.

'In my defence it was my first time,' I said.

'Could have fooled me. I felt like I was in safe, experienced hands.'

'Thanks.' It was an unexpected compliment. 'Felt a bit fumbly at first.'

'Didn't notice. You're a natural. This is going to work.'

I nodded, still catching my breath.

'And you sound like you enjoyed it?'

I hadn't expected to, I thought I'd be too nervous and would cock it up and let him down, let us both down.

'I was a teensy weensy bit nervous,' I confessed.

'Teensy weensy? Aren't they the Teletubbies?'

I hadn't expected Barclay to do funny. I also didn't expect him to know about the Teletubbies. This man could surprise for Britain.

Then he laid another one on me; 'I still get a bit nervy, too. I think the adrenaline is all part of this, part of the thrill. I'd like to think I'm ice cold and calm and James Bond-like, but that would all get quite boring after a while. It's that edge that makes it, losing a little bit of self-control every now and then.'

My eyes widened. 'So you're not as cold and heartless as you first appear? Not as manipulative as I thought?'

'Manipulative, yes. But I'm no Daniel Craig.'

'Your eyes are too dark.'

'And I don't have those ears.'

'Nor the hair?'

He snorted in derision.

'Nor the body?'

'Nor the body. Although I'm probably taller.'

He did remind me of someone famous though, but I couldn't for the life of me remember who. Certainly not Daniel Craig. Maybe someone off the telly?

He turned to me and fixed me with those dark, impenetrable eyes. 'What you're really saying is that I'm not as shallow as you thought?'

'That's another way of putting it.'

He paused. Whether for effect or humour or genuine reflection I couldn't tell. Despite what had just happened, we were still two strangers. I was beginning to wonder if we always would be.

He sat straighter. 'No. I am pretty shallow. I might surprise every now and again but I'd say that what you see is pretty much what you get with me. No great hidden depths here to explore.'

He was drawing the Barclay blinds down. Show's over for tonight, folks. As if to emphasise the point he said 'Time to call it a night.'

It was actually nearer morning, but the streetlights would burn through the mist for a while yet.

We sat in silence. I was smiling, still enjoying the moment. He turned to the window and gazed into the distance, shutting me out from his thoughts.

Chapter 9

'So how old are you?' I asked Tom Thomas.

'Thirty-three.' A pause, a correction to cover his embarrassment. 'No, thirty-seven. Sorry, don't know why I said that. I'm thirty-seven. Bizarre.'

I picked up my glass of the overpriced Rioja and took a quiet sip to fill the yawning seconds. Shit, I thought, he sounds mad. The man doesn't even know his own age. This was a bad idea. Like the thing with Barclay, I was jumping in to this far too fast. The last few days had just been too …no. This was fine. He was just nervous, like me first date jitters, and we both needed to relax.

He smiled. 'Look. I'm thirty-seven. Honest.' He played the sympathy card. 'I'm a little jumpy. It's been a while since I've done this kind of thing.'

'Me too,' I said, smiling. It was only the smallest of white lies.

'It's a reflex answer I seem to have developed. Can't explain it. It's a bit like when you're a kid and someone asks you what your favourite colour is. I always said 'blue'. But I don't have a favourite colour – who does? – but I didn't want to sound odd or different, so I said I had a favourite colour and it was blue. I liked some blue things, – sky, the Pacific at the beach – but not everything blue. That would be odd, if you liked things simply because of their colour. I'm talking too much. Shut up, Tom.'

'Thomas,' I corrected him.

He smiled.

'Is the Pacific really that blue?' I asked. 'I've never seen it. Never been to America in fact.'

'It was in my childhood at least. Probably more grey than blue though these days, with a delicate sheen of spilled oil to add to its twenty-first century charms.'

'I was asked to name my favourite colour last week,' I said.

'Really? How old are you exactly, Miss MacDonald?'

I laughed. 'Thirty-three! No, I'm twenty-five.'

'So who asked for your favourite colour? Isn't that kind of

question normally left behind in a kindergarten?'

'Maybe. It was some internet thing on my laptop. One of those security questions things that you always forget as soon as you type in an answer. I put 'blue'. I was buying some shoes. Boots, actually.'

'Good for you. We have something in common at least, albeit a lie.'

We both laughed and clinked our glasses in a silent toast. It was going to be all right after all.

The waiter arrived and took our order. He poured an unnecessary top-up into our glasses before disappearing into the kitchen.

'The pedant in me says that he's overfilled that,' I said. "What I know about wine can be written on the side of a fag packet but I know that red needs to breathe in the glass. More importantly, if you overfill, you can't do that pretentious swirly thing that makes you look like you know your stuff. Like you were doing.'

'I like the way it rides up the side of the glass. A little bit dangerous on a first date given that I have a propensity to spill it.

Wine talk. Small talk. This had doomed date written all over it.

'Is this a date?' I asked.

'Technically and mathematically yes. Socially...maybe. Let's play First Date Questions,' he suggested.

'Okay,' I was cautious. 'Fire away. But keep it clean.'

'Of course. Right, where were you born?'

'Greenwich. The London original, not the village in New York. America's probably got hundreds of Greenwichs.'

'A few I know of, no doubt dozens I don't. I was born in San Diego, but my folk now live further north, outskirts of San Fran.'

'Mine live in Edinburgh. The family abandoned me when my grandmother died and left us a huge house in the cheap part of the city. I've got to go back up there next week for Christmas.' I pulled a face, suggesting it was the last thing on earth I wanted to do.

'You have my sympathy. Okay, let's move to easier ones. What's your favourite film?'

'Easy. *The Notebook.*'

The look on his face told me that Tom had never heard of it.

'Oh, that one with whatsisname?' bluffed Tom.

'Ryan Gosling,' I tried to help.

'Yes, him. I preferred him in that other one, *Green Lantern.*'

'That's Ryan Reynolds.'

'Burt's brother? I'm not very good with my Ryans.'

'There aren't a lot of Ryans to get confused by.'

'I still struggle with my Ryans.'

'He was in *Deadpool*, too.' Another blank. 'So what's your favourite movie?'

'*Green Lantern.*'

'Isn't that supposed to be shit?' I'd never seen it.

He laughed.

'It is shit. I paid good money to see it and it was a disastrous date, probably the last one I'll own up to, and I'm still trying to convince myself it wasn't a waste. I tend to fall asleep in superhero movies – an understandable habit but not exactly endearing on dates. Let's never go to a superhero movie.'

'Deal.' We were both relaxing, the wine was helping.

Maybe a cinema date next?

More questions followed. Favourite book? I said mine was *Gone Girl* (I'd made it through the first fifty pages before shelving it); he was a Stephen King fan. Favourite music? I admitted to my soft spot for Adele but spared him my impression. He predictably cited the Beatles. Uh oh – my Beatles-bore warning bell started to ring but it was a false alarm, and we quickly moved on, like he could see my eyes glazing over. Quite different from the odd conversations I'd been having with Barclay where I could never be sure if the man was actually listening to a word I said.

We politely small talked our way until the food finally arrived and we made the appropriate noises of delight. Once the waiter had left I said: 'That looks good. Mine is somewhat spectacular though.'

'Agreed. I don't think I've ever tried soufflé – it looks like an omelette on steroids. Makes my sole look…' he lifted the fish with his fork. ' … a little flat.'

Ho ho. Tom didn't do pretentious by the sound of things, such a contrast to Barclay, such a welcome change.

(Get out of my head, Barclay.)

The soufflé was delicious. I found Tom's company charming. We ate in silence, the odd murmur of contentment as we relaxed into the evening.

The waiter cleared away the dessert plates and brought our coffee. Proper coffee in a mug, none of that espresso nonsense that lasted seconds. Tom suddenly looked serious, which was a shame after such a nice meal.

'Barclay,' he said.

'Barclay?' I asked. 'There's nothing to it, honest, just a work thing.'

'Of course, but he's dangerous. How much do you know?'

'I only started on Monday. I know he's … interesting, fun even.'

'He's not fun, he's dangerous. You need to get yourself out of that thing.'

Two 'dangerouses' in quick succession. Tom looked stern. There was an awkward silence.

'I can handle myself,' I assured him. 'I'm thirty-three, remember?'

He smiled but his eyes had turned cold. 'I'm not joking, Claire. You need to get out of whatever's going on with him. It'll end in tears. Or worse.'

'I'll be fine.'

He didn't look convinced.

'Please don't get hurt, Claire.'

'I'll be fine,' I smiled, patting his hand. 'Shall we go?'

Outside it was a little chilly, a cool wind had picked up while we had been eating and I only had a light jacket, fooled into it by a late burst of winter sunshine at the end of the afternoon.

'Would you like my coat?' he asked

'I'm fine.' It was my word of the evening, a poor, insincere word that rarely gives anyone the assurance it promises.

'Let's get us a ride home,' he said, waving down a black cab that had freakishly materialised south of the river. Where was home, I wondered. Mine or his?

I was not an 'easy' first date but I'd have been happy if we had gone in either direction. Henry was barely gone forty-eight hours and this dirty trollop Claire was already considering taking another man between the sheets.

And I didn't care.

'So how do you rate our evening overall?' he asked.

'Oh, definitely an eight.'

He started to pull me closer then stopped, squeezed my hand and kissed me quickly on the lips.

'That was … nice,' I managed, our noses still gently touching.

He kissed me again, a little longer this time but still chaste, affection rather than passion.

I squeezed his hand. 'Maybe a nine?'

'It gets a ten in my book.'

'Does it need a nightcap to elevate it to a ten?' I asked.

Before Tom could answer the cabbie interrupted: 'Where are we going then?'

Good question, sir, an excellent question. I had no idea.

Chapter 10

The morning text from Barclay was succinct and to the point:

Pick me up at 3pm. B.

No 'please' or 'if you'd be so kind'. Really, the manners of some people make you despair. At least it was a 'pm' this time – much as I had enjoyed my first driving job, that early hours-of-darkness start had not been appreciated and a similar early rise the night after the night before was not what the hangover doctor ordered.

The late afternoon time suggested that it wouldn't be another getaway featuring a bag stuffed with used twenties taken or stolen (but certainly not voluntarily donated) from god knows where. Which was a little disappointing but presumably a tad more legal.

Ho hum, how innocent was I?

As I dressed after a much-needed shower my mobile rang. It was Mum, checking that I was still heading 'home' to Edinburgh at the weekend for her family Christmas. I loved my Ma more than anyone on Earth but boy she could chat for Britain. This proved to be yet another one of those conversations where I managed to contribute one word (usually 'uh-huh') for every thousand or so of hers. She was a great talker, possibly the greatest, but not so big at the listening thing. Worryingly, Mum seemed to be getting worse and sometimes she even had to stop herself after a few minutes (that felt like hours), unable to remember who exactly she was talking at. She was harmless enough and probably a wee bit lonely and it was, after all, her phone bill she was running up. Resigned to losing the rest of the morning I tucked my phone under my chin and tidied the flat as she droned on and on about my errant brother Paul, her best friend Sharon, my dad's job security, and that nice boy down the road at number ten. I think she was referring to the Prime Minister. I thought of pointing out that he was neither nice nor living down the road, but it was all one-way traffic and I wasn't going to take the risk of lighting the political debate touch paper.

After an hour I'd had enough. With no little skill I somehow managed to engineer the one-way conversation to a close and was able to make my escape. Parents, huh? Can't live with 'em but you can never really move out of their lives either. I couldn't waste the entire day. I had work to do.

The sudden noise had stopped several passers-by on the street in their tracks. I could understand their sudden distress.

'That's unusual,' said Barclay, emerging from his apartment building and climbing into the Uno's passenger seat.

'A little surprising, I agree,' I said. 'I haven't used it before. Must be the Italian heritage.'

The Uno's horn had proven to be deafening yet surprisingly melodic, shattering the office hours' calm of the street where I was collecting Barclay. There was no modest toot or peep from my little runaround, oh no; some previous owner had added a powerful two-tone klaxon under the rust-encrusted bonnet of my Eighties' marvel and the car was now very loud and extremely proud. I wouldn't be using the horn again in a hurry –the last thing we wanted was to draw attention to ourselves as we went about our business.

Or, I should say, Barclay's business. I was just the driver, and his reluctance to give me any useful details about the nature of said business was rapidly becoming irritating.

'I need to go to Eynsford in Kent,' he said, sharing the bare minimum with his woman-servant. 'Something I need to check on. I'm a little concerned.' He was wearing some snazzy designer sunglasses so I couldn't read his eyes. Barclay, concerned? Really?

'Okay,' I said, hoping to learn more. But he wasn't forthcoming and I was out of luck. I crunched the Uno into first gear and we pootled south to the Garden of England, the bright, low winter sunshine pleasantly warming in my steadfast Italian chariot.

It had been a beautiful day but the sun was setting fast and I figured it would be almost dark by the time we got there. As we joined the queueing traffic departing London early for the evening, I asked;

'Barclay. Your tax form. Was that all in order?'

'Yes. Nice job.'

'But it said you worked in a coffee shop.'

'Yes.'

'And that you earned eighteen thousand last year. Just eighteen thousand?'

'Yes.'

'And that it was your only employment?'

'A little white lie.'

'As is the eighteen grand?'

'You're a fast learner.'

'I take it that anything else is pretty much 'cash in hand'?'

'It's difficult to define it any other way.'

'Isn't that illegal?'

He yawned. 'You didn't seem to mind when I gave you that cheque the other day.'

'I didn't say I minded, I asked if it was illegal.'

'I'm not a lawyer,' he said. 'They can't tax what they can't see.'

'But it's a crime.'

'A very small one. Best they focus on the Amazons and Googles and the big boys. Why bother the baristas?'

'What if everyone did it?'

'But they don't.'

'But they could?'

'But they don't.'

'I could do it.'

'But you don't. Or, I should say, didn't.'

He had me. I decided to let it rest. I had a feeling that tax evasion was the least of Barclay's crimes.

To describe Eynsford as 'picturesque' is an understatement, on a par with 'that Taj Mahal, it's okay for an old building'. Take a right just before the turning for Brands Hatch and follow the road down the slight dip and round to the left. You can't miss it: a short high street lined with colourfully quaint higgledy-piggledy terraced cottages and shops from some bygone era, packed shoulder to shoulder in a disorderly fashion as if in denial of modern planning laws. It was like we had turned a corner and travelled back a century. 'This is lovely,' I thought to myself as I dropped to a pedestrian ten miles an hour to take in the view. Barclay didn't say a word. He hadn't spoken since I had questioned his tax legality. He may have fallen asleep.

A Volvo honked in annoyance as I squeezed passed it. Barclay's eyes snapped open, startled.

'Nice kip?' I asked.

He frowned and for a moment didn't look himself.

'Bloody Volvo drivers. Something on your mind?'

'I am … concerned, as I said. This man I want to check on has just gone silent and that's not like him. He has not been responding to my emails, texts, calls, he's posted nothing on social media, I rang and he hasn't been seen at his office for over a week. Nothing.'

'Is he a friend?'

'Hardly. He's the guy with the dog I mentioned.'

'The dog you shot?'

He had woken grumpy and wasn't amused. 'At. I shot at.'

'Yeah, right.'

'He still owes me the money.'

'What for?'

There may have been tumbleweed rolling in the deafening silence.

'Eynsford's pretty' I said, keen to change the subject.

'His house isn't. It's one of those ugly monstrosities up there on the right, just before the station.'

The cute little lost-in-time high street petered out after a few hundred yards and was replaced by a small but perfectly-inappropriate housing estate, a shocking modern day eyesore after the tranquil rustic idyll we'd just passed.

'Urgh,' I said, unable to conceal my disgust.

'Not so pretty, see?'

I nodded in agreement.

Barclay pointed at a small detached red brick house at

the far end of a cul-de-sac, away from the main street. Its driveway was dominated by an enormous, ostentatious white BMW 4x4 that dwarfed its surroundings and made the house behind appear undersized by comparison. It was a testosterone-enhanced brute of a car, bought to impress and intimidate the simple minded.

Tutting under my breath I parked my Toy Town car in front of it, blocking the drive in case it decided to steamroller its way out.

'I'll be ten minutes, tops,' said Barclay, exiting and striding up to the front door of the house. He rang the bell.

Nothing. He tried again, this time following it with a firm percussive knock, then hammering on the door with the side of his clenched fist. Still nothing. He peeked through the letter box, then peered through the downstairs window, the room behind unlit despite the darkness.

He turned to me and shrugged. I shrugged back. He walked up to my side of the car and I unwound the window.

'No one in by the look of things, and the post is pretty stacked up in there. I'm going to see if I can get in around the back. You stay here and keep watch.'

'What do you mean 'see if I can get in'? You're going to break in?'

'Sure. Think of me as a bailiff, collecting what's mine.'

'And I'm your look out?'

'Someone has to be.'

'What if someone shows up?'

'Then you honk that macho horn of yours. I should be able to hear it in there.'

'And wake up the whole of sleepy Kent? You're joking, aren't you?'

'Okay. Maybe not. Come and get me if you see anyone heading directly for the house.'

'And then what will we do?'

He nodded at the Uno.

'Another getaway?' I asked.

'If we are walking calmly so as to avoid suspicion I'm sure

we'll get away comfortably. Stop being so negative.'

"Walking calmly? Are you serious? But…'

He turned his back on me and disappeared down the side of the house.

Brilliant. More hanging around waiting for Barclay. The opportunities just kept on coming.

Moments later there was the distant sound of a grown man foolishly trying to shoulder his way through a locked door. Thud. Grunt. 'Fuck'. That hadn't worked. A slight pause for him to gather his composure then the sound of a small window being broken, only slightly softened by what I assumed was Barclay's coat. Another pause, then he appeared at the front window and waved before drawing the curtains closed. I looked nervously around the street – no one, not even a solitary dog walker. And the ridiculous BMW tank was proving a blessing in disguise, concealing much of the front of the house from any prying eyes.

Long seconds stretched into long minutes, the sky grew darker and the street lights blinked into dim, early life. I stared at the dashboard clock and drummed a nervous, erratic rhythm on the steering wheel. Come on Barclay, get a move on.

Barclay had worked his way upstairs, pulling the curtains across before turning on the lights. I was getting cold with the window open but needed to keep an ear as well as an eye open.

In the rear view mirror I saw a silver car, one of those Japanese save the planet things, pull up at the far end of the road, its silent electric engine catching me unaware despite having my window open. I turned around too quickly and ricked my neck. Ouch. Fortunately, it was a good fifty yards or so from where I was parked so I saw no reason to panic Barclay. A couple of uniformed school kids jumped out the back, and a woman clambered from the front seat, struggling with armfuls of school bags as she juggled with her keys. She stumbled to the front door and let the excited kids into the house before slamming the door shut on the outside world. As an afterthought, the car's lights flashed orange as she locked it from inside the house.

I turned back to see Barclay peeking through the curtains – he'd seen the Prius, too – then he pulled back and I guess resumed his search.

What was he doing in there?

What was he looking for?

What was I doing outside?

As if to answer me another car, a bigger one this time, sort of sales exec Mondeo-y I guess, turned into the cul-de-sac and drew up about twenty yards away, pulling into the drive of a house just three along from where Barclay was fucking about. Too close. Its headlights dimmed slowly but nobody got out. I could see the driver just sitting there. I gave it a few minutes but still no movement, nothing.

Not good. I needed to warn Barclay.

I unbelted and attempted to look composed as I left my car. No bleeping locks with my bleeping relic from the last bleeping century. A few cautious glances left and right before I stole down the side where Barclay had disappeared. There'd still been no movement in the newly arrived car.

It was even darker around the back of the house but I could just make out that the back door was ajar, a small glass pane by the handle had been smashed by Barclay.

My mouth went dried and I swallowed hard as I entered, adding breaking and entering to my growing charge sheet alongside tax fraud and aiding and abetting. I was willing to bet that the Uno's MOT was probably dodgy, too. Not a bad list for a few days' work.

'Barclay?' I whispered as loudly as I could, pointless I know but it seemed wrong to shout. 'Barclay?' A little louder.

There was a scrambling noise from upstairs and the banging of wardrobe doors. I made my way through the dark kitchen, tripping over a dog's water bowl by the door. That was sad. Barclay had killed that dog.

On tip toe I hurried through the shadowy sitting room, too nervous to have a nose around. There was a light from the top of the stairs and the sound of Barclay hunting for whatever he'd come for.

'Barclay!' Still whispering, but very, very loud whispering.

'Claire? I'm in the main bedroom.'

'There's another car pulled up but no one's got out yet.'

'I know. I saw. Odd.'

'Barclay, what's that smell?'

I pushed open the bedroom door and screamed.

The wardrobe was half open and there was a naked man hanging from a belt pulled tight around his neck. He looked like he'd been there for several days. He smelled like he'd been there far longer.

'Shhh!' said Barclay, calm as you like.

I couldn't say anything, just shoved my fist in my mouth and stared at the naked body. It was heavy set and ugly and the folds of flesh had a pale, waxy texture. If I hadn't known better, I'd say it was still sweating, like old cheddar left in the sun. It also seemed to be entirely shaven, not a hair on it. It's strange the things you notice when in shock. But the smell, the smell was unlike anything I'd ever experienced before.

'Yes, I was a little taken aback I must say. Try to control yourself, Claire.'

My voice spluttered back into life. 'Taken aback? That's a dead fucking body!' I couldn't blink, couldn't breathe.

'Like I said, odd.'

'Odd? ODD?' I grabbed his coat and pulled him towards the door. 'I'll tell you what's so fucking odd – us still being here is bloody odd. Let's go!'

'But I haven't found what I came for.'

'I don't care. We need to go. Now.'

He resisted at first but my persistence got the better of him and he reluctantly followed me down the stairs, I lost my footing under his weight and almost fell.

A body! What the fuck was that all about? I tugged him down after me and, with no small effort, dragged him through the house and out into the back garden. He stumbled over a watering can as we made our clumsy exit.

So much for 'walking calmly so as to avoid suspicion'.

Thc new car had gone. We were alone again.

'What...what was that all about, Barclay?'

'It was his thing, his sexual peccadillo. I didn't expect him to go all Kung Fu on me but he liked the old erotic asphyxiation thing and it was only a matter of time. Poor guy. Anyway, it's not like he's going anywhere soon. I'm going back in,' he said, pulling away from me, and disappeared once more into the gathering late afternoon gloom.

'Fuck,' I muttered. No way was I following him. That was his funeral. And what did he mean 'go all Kung Fu on me'? It felt like were were speaking different languages at times. I got back into the car and angrily crossed my arms. I like to wallow in a good sulk, although I was not sure what I was actually sulking about. Why hang yourself in a wardrobe? And completely shaven from skull to toe? That's just plain weird. Well, weird to you and me, but Barclay seemed to be taking it all in his stride, like it was all in a day's work for him.

Barclay emerged after another ten minutes. He waved a carrier bag at me then trotted over to get into the car.

'About time, too,' I harrumphed. 'Did you find what you were after?'

'Not exactly, no. Some cash in the house but probably only a few hundred quid. I did pick up some cans of Coke from the fridge and some crisps in case you were peckish.'

'No thanks,' I murmured. I didn't think I'd ever feel like eating again. Certainly not cheese.

I started the car and we pulled away, re-joining the main street and the traffic heading north. After a few minutes I asked;

'Seriously, what … what was that all about?'

'Looks like he just pushed it too far. Been gone a few days, much like the milk in his fridge. I thought he might make a run for it but...'

'He must have really loved that dog.'

Barclay nodded.

'So he hung himself?'

Barclay turned to look at me, shaking his head.

'Can't pretend to understand that. I knew he was into all kinds of kinky stuff but that's not something I know anything about or can easily explain. Different strokes and all that. Wasn't there a rock star in the nineties who went the same way?

Most peculiar. It was quite cold, you know, to touch I mean. The body.'

I shuddered. 'You touched it?'

'Couldn't resist. Back of my hand though, so no prints.'

I was shaking my head. I just couldn't process this.

'What did he do, that guy?'

'He is … was… a Financial Advisor, believe it or not,' Barclay said. 'Very quiet, as corrupt as sin but so clever and cautious with it.'

'And how did he owe you money?'

'A long story. Maybe later,' he said, and turning away from me stared out the window at the dark street as the car gently shook, straining to make the sixty I was demanding of it. I needed to get out of Kent pronto.

'Should we tell the police?' I asked.

'Tell them what? That we found a body hanging in a wardrobe when attempting to rob a house?'

I really should have given that 'thinking' thing a go before asking those kind of questions.

'Maybe not,' I mumbled.

We drove back to London in silence, neither of us absolutely certain what the fuck we had just witnessed.

Chapter 11

Tom was distracted. The cherry tomato was doing its third lap of his salad plate, looping around the inner rim propelled by his fork. He hadn't looked up for five minutes.

'You're not listening, are you?' I said.

'What? No, of course I am,' he lied. 'Something about going to Edinburgh for Christmas?' It was a shot in the dark and we both knew it.

'That was ten minutes ago! I was telling you about my family. Mum, Dad, brother Paul.'

'Right.'

'What's up?' I kicked him playfully under the table.

'I've got work stuff I'd hoped to sort out before flying home, and it has kind of gotten more complex, rather than sorted.'

Didn't I know that feeling!

'Bummer,' I said. I liked talking American to my new American friend. He looked up and smiled.

'It happens. I don't like taking work home over the holidays but I'll have to make some calls I guess, and that's not easy from the West Coast.'

We had decided to have a quick lunch before he jetted off to the US and I got on my train to Edinburgh; him for 'The Holidays', as they call them over there; me for good old fashioned Christmas.

It was a nice little bistro cum patisserie Tom had suggested, on a side street just off Great Marlborough Street and its non-stop traffic. Later that evening I would be heading to St Pancras, he'd already be on a United flight to California. I know which trip I would have preferred to have been doing.

I was deliberately not mentioning Barclay and our Eynsford escapade to Tom but it was never far from my thoughts that lunchtime. After Tom's warnings about Barclay it was a strictly taboo topic of conversation as far as I was concerned, so I decided to play it safe and keep things civil and a little dull.

'What is it you do again?' He'd said something about being a consultant but we hadn't gone into details.

'I told you. I'm a consultant. In law enforcement.'

My fork dropped and bounced noisily off the bistro table onto the floor. Several other diners turned to see me open mouthed and possibly going into shock.

'Really?' said my smallest voice.

Tom laughed, and it was a genuine laugh. 'Yes, really. I didn't expect you to react quite like that – let's get you another fork.' He signalled to our waiter and a replacement was quickly brought over.

'Got something to hide, Ms MacDonald?' he laughed. I laughed too, suddenly nervous, playing the innocent fool.

'When you said 'consultant' I just assumed it was finance or IT or strategy or something like that. Do the police use consultants?'

'Everyone uses consultants, it's the grease that oils the wheels of industry these days, the costs you can hide under the bottom line of the spreadsheets as 'Other Expenses'. With this government's budget cuts the police need them more than ever. Besides, I'm a specialist, an authority even.'

'What in?' I was almost too afraid to ask but my voice still sounded composed, mercifully.

'Cybercrime. Computer fraud. Hacking. I've been working here for a few years now. It's a growing industry, which is good for me but pretty shit for everyone else.'

Did that explain how he knew Barclay, I wondered? Barclay who 'dabbles' in technology? I wasn't going to ask and ruin our lunch date, but that would make some kind of sense.

'How's your work going?' he asked.

'S'okay, I guess. Done some paperwork. Got a company car. Been running a few errands.' For some reason I neglected to mention the tax fraud, speedy getaway driving from God knows what and…oh yes, how did I forget? Finding a decomposing body of a sex pervert in the bedroom of a house we'd broken into.

'Good. Steering clear of Barclay now, I trust?'

I looked down at my plate as I nodded. As lies go it wouldn't have convinced me, but Tom seemed to buy it.

'Hours not too demanding?' he asked. I started to wonder how much he knew.

'The odd early start, but the new boss is quite flexible with the time in lieu thing.'

'Good stuff,' he said, finally piercing his tiny tomato and popping it into his mouth. 'Why does your family live in Scotland? You don't sound Scottish.'

Thank god. No more work talk.

'I'm not. Obviously. They moved up there five or six years ago. I grew up with them in Deptford and we had a little two up, two down for me to charge around in, but then Mum had a few hospital things, the usual stuff, and they decided to slow life down and get out of the city and move up to a quieter life.'

'Edinburgh's quieter?'

'Everywhere is quieter. Edinburgh's cheaper. Or at least it was then, not so much these days. I never fancied it so I stayed here, first planned to go to art college or university but that never really happened.'

'Lucky for me.'

'Lucky for me too, I think,' I said, smiling as I polished off the last of my cheese toasty and salad.

'And your Mum – she's all well now?'

'She has good days and … less good days, but generally is okay. If it got bad Dad would give up work but he hasn't mentioned that at all so I guess it's all fine. They need the money from his job really – I've a younger brother, Paul, who arrived unplanned and keeps the expenses running high.'

'How young?'

'Twelve.'

'Almost a teenager.'

'Already a pain in the arse. Sorry, I meant 'pain in the ASS'.'

Tom laughed. 'I have two sisters in the States and haven't seen either since Thanksgiving last year. They'll be there this weekend, with their Ivy League husbands and pictures of their palatial houses, boring us with talk of their perfect lives of suburban prosperity. All money and equity talk, can't wait.'

'You're not going to get any sympathy out of me. Christmas

in San Francisco sounds brilliant to me.'

'It's okay. Just about bearable. My folks are good fun. You'll like them.'

He was thinking of me meeting his parents? Wow. Second date and that was the way his mind was working? That man was fast.

'Maybe one day,' I said.

'Let's hope so.' He looked at his watch. 'What time's your train?'

'Oh, it's not until this evening. I'm getting the sleeper up there. I've not even packed yet.'

'I'm going to have to make a move,' he said, signalling for the bill by signing the air with his forefinger.

'It's a shame we're going to be apart for a week,' I said, a little bubble of emotion getting caught in my throat.

He grinned and took my hand across the table. 'Time for a quickie?'

'Out the back by the toilets?' I joked.

'No. In the kitchen. Let's give the staff something to talk about. Sure beats tipping them.'

'You romantic, you.'

It wasn't even amusing but we both laughed hysterically as if it was the funniest thing either of us had ever heard. Oh, to be young and … in love? Too early. Oh, to be young and hysterical? Maybe. That would do for now.

The bill arrived and he tapped his contactless card to pay.

'That's so cool,' I said.

'The wonders of technology. Pretty easy to hack though – you have to be careful in crowds with it.'

'You're the expert.'

He winked. 'I've seen things you people wouldn't believe.'

I clapped my hands together in delight. '*Blade Runner*! I just knew you'd know a decent movie or two.'

'I've even downloaded *The Notebook* for my flight.'

He remembered. He was so sweet.

'We can compare notes,' I said.

'Count on it.'

Outside the bistro it had just started to rain and umbrellas were being raised as lunchtime crowds were quickly making their way back to the office.

'So see you in a week,' he said.

'Enjoy *The Notebook*.'

He pulled me close and we kissed a long, sad goodbye kiss. It was delicious. I can still taste it.

'I will see you later then,' I said, clutching at the moment.

'Enjoy Scotland,' he said quietly. I nodded and reluctantly turned and left him in the rain with his suitcase on wheels. I only turned to wave three times. Four, maybe. I was still grinning when I headed down the steps at the tube station.

Chapter 12

Thank the lord Christmas only comes once a year. I love my family, I really do, but like all relationships that affection can rise and fall with the tide of conversations and circumstance. The annual pilgrimage from St Pancras to Edinburgh was getting harder every time, a solitary reminder on my calendar of the life that left me behind.

Ah, 'twas the season of family embarrassment and tedium, the hallowed time of me recalling every tiny detail of the previous twelve months for my over-enthusiastic mum, barely-there dad and whatever uncles and aunts were dropping by for the free scotch and G&Ts and bowls of leftover-from-last-year nuts. In the past it had been difficult to drag out anything of any note from my boringly monotonous life to fill the painful, prolonged silences, the airless gaps in the chit chat when conversation just died on everyone's lips and you could hear the mice scurrying around under the floorboards. But that year it promised to be even worse, I wanted to tell them everything, boast even – but I could say nothing. Torture.

I had been dreading the conversations with Mum in particular. I didn't sleep much on the train journey up as I played out over and over what she would say, what I would say, how I would keep 'mum' about Barclay and Tom (funny girl; ho, ho and a seasonal ho for luck).

So much had happened in the last week, so much that I would normally turn to Mum to for advice and comfort, but I couldn't face the prospect of tipping her out of her cosy, comfortable world of tickity-boo Claire. Dad had been suggesting for some time that Mum's forgetfulness and the one-sided conversations were symptoms of a bigger problem, possibly even an early onset of dementia, but none of us were brave enough to take it any further, and Ma was so terrified of doctors and tests that it was never openly discussed, least of all with her.

I did consider telling her about Tom, but it was still too early, too unsure. Knowing Mum, she would instantly be working on finalising the wedding gift list and the reception seating arrangements before I even got to pronouncing Tom's real surname. 'Claire Thomas' I could fantasise over and possibly live with but 'Claire Pedakowski' was a non-starter. A nice, orderly life for nicely ordered Claire is all Mum wanted for me, and no loving daughter should ever go out of her way to dampen that hope.

Before I knew it I was sitting there at the kitchen table with Mum updating me on Paul and that he was twelve now of course and it was his last Christmas before he became a teenager and how we won't see him for days on end and he will be lost in his Xbox world and… on and on she went, fretting about kids these days and how dangerous it is out there (if only she knew) and how she was worried that he will be led astray by those video games and that horrible Internet and he won't turn out nice like me…

I couldn't tell her. Not a word.

'And can you please make an effort this year, Claire, to be nice to him?'

'Me?'

'Yes you, dear. None of that backchat and sarcasm. Do it for me, dear.'

'Of course,' I kind of promised. It would not be easy and I was sure he would not reciprocate. Little bastard.

It had been different with Mum when we talked on the phone, where I could hide behind a silence or quickly move things away from talk of the 'new job' with a random digression. But once I was in the kitchen with her, once she had me in her truth-seeking steely gaze over our 'catch-up coffee', all milk and too many sugars, once there was nowhere to run or hide and nothing to distract, I was convinced I was going to slip up and she would know immediately something had changed, that this new boss certainly wasn't like the old boss and that there was something different going on with her sweet little Claire bear.

I could hardly tell her about my new employment as a small hours of the morning getaway driver, the afternoons of tax evasion and burglary, could I? How would that have gone down on Christmas Day as we prodded the over-cooked sprouts and unpleasant sage and onion and the driest turkey that no amount of her watery gravy could moisten? That would have been a real choker. And that was assuming that every one's heart would keep ticking merrily along after the shock of learning that their eldest, dearest offspring had now opted for a life of crime with some posh wide-boy ne'er-do-well.

'How's Henry? Mum asked.

I stared at my mug as if hoping that it could answer the question for me. Stick or twist?

'He's okay. I guess.'

'What do you mean, 'you guess'?' She could still be as sharp as a paper cut when she wanted to be.

'He's gone to India for a few months. It's for work.' Translation: He's left me and run to India for a few years to ease his moral conscience and make a futile gesture he can bore his friends with when he finally deems to return to our lives.

'Oh, that's a long way. I hope he writes regularly.'

'He texts when he can get a signal. It's different out there.' I hadn't heard a peep out of him. I doubted it was a signal problem but I didn't feel like discussing it – Mum had such a wonderful, if somewhat naïve, view of relationships and didn't like the idea of things not following her preferred "and they all lived happily ever after" script.

Besides, I just couldn't mention the other guys now on the scene, the heart stealer with his bewitching schoolboy charm and the intriguing boss, all devil-may-care attitude, conversational eyebrows and steepled fingers.

'I like Henry.' She wasn't making this any easier. 'He's a keeper.' Thanks, Mum. Somehow I was expecting that one.

'Yes.' It was easier to keep up the pretence; I saw no point in causing her world to come crashing down with reality on Christmas Eve, that would just be cruel. Almost Barclay-esque.

'And how is that new job working out?'

'It's okay. Not as boring. I've been doing some of the work in the evenings and the pay's a lot better so I'll see how it goes in the new year. I haven't decided yet completely if it's for me.'

'Oh. You should talk to your father about that. You shouldn't give a job up on a whim.'

'I will,' I assured her.

There had been some culinary disaster in the kitchen ('it's okay – your mother is fixing it') and we found ourselves sitting at the table in a state of muted apprehension, awaiting our overdue dinner as Mum wrestled with whatever tragedy had struck with such unfortunate timing. The comforting aromas of roast turkey, sage and onion from the kitchen appeared to be slightly tainted by a faint odour of charcoal.

Paul, Dad and me: an unholy trinity at any time of year, but somehow in this season-to-be-jolly a particularly mismatched trio, not a wise man amongst us.

Dad wasn't good at small talk. He didn't excel at big talk either. Silence, apart from the odd grunt or clang from the kitchen. Dad's unease was proving infectious; the thunder clouds gathering behind the kitchen door adding to the tension.

'So,' Dad began, then paused as if the sound of his own voice breaking the silence had surprised even him.

'So?' I asked. 'A needle pulling thread?' They didn't get it – Mum was the only film fan and she was locked away performing unspeakable acts with a cumbersome dead bird.

'So your mother tells me you've started another job. I take it it's better than the last one?

Yes, I'm a getaway driver cum apprentice burglar for an egocentric, self-centred misogynist who does god knows what, who is obviously breaking the law in a thousand ways ... oh, and he randomly kills dogs.

'S'alright,' I actually said. 'A bit of paper pushing, spreadsheet stuff, a bit of evening work, gets me out and about and pays the bills. Irregular hours. Moving money around, that kinda thing.'

'Booooooring,' yawned Paul. 'Boring boring boring. What's the point of living in London if all you do is stare at screens and shit like that all day?' Little twat – what does he know about real life? What would he make of his big sister living a life that makes his world of Grand Theft Auto look pedestrian? I was old enough to know better, but…

'It's not dull,' I said through clenched teeth. 'It's actually very interesting. And I'm not office-bound any more – I'm out on the road for much of the time, meeting new people, even changing their lives in some ways.'

'Gripping.' His sarcasm was galling and I found myself rising from my chair, my balled fists tightening. Every time he did it. Every time I fell for it.

Dad attempted to calm things, aware that a catastrophe was pending in the kitchen. 'Hey, Paul, no need for that. I'm sure Claire is a better judge of how interesting her new job is than you are.'

I sat down. Two against one. My kind of odds.

Bravely, Dad attempted a digression. 'And how's your man Henry? He's a keeper.'

'He's in India. Doing some work there.'

'What a loser,' said Paul.

Get back up to your bedroom, child. Don't rise to it, Claire. Keep a lid on it.

'He's a good man,' said Dad.

'He's a twat,' said Paul. It was the happiest I'd seen my evil brother in years. 'India. What a sucker. Fucking A!'

Dad and I both stared aghast. Swearing was strictly taboo in this house and this was a first from Paul. He was growing up too fast.

'Fucking shit bastard bird!' came Mum's cry from the kitchen.

We all burst into laughter, the paralysing tension finally released.

The meal was overcooked and we all knew it, but still the compliments flew Mum's way ('great spuds, love'; 'I love these purééd sprouts, Mum') and she batted them away with false modesty as she helped herself to another slice of bread sauce.

Most families drink their way through the Christmas pain but the MacDonalds are not a boozy congregation regardless of the occasion; the lone bottle of M&S sparkling white was still only half empty by the time we all slouched in front of the TV for whatever feasts Auntie had scheduled for her license-paying devotees to sleep through in their stupor.

Mum didn't last five minutes, and soon her full-on snoring was competing with the telly for our attention. Sadly, the remote could only temper one of the competing sonic forces. Dad made a motion with his head – he wanted a quiet word with me by the look of things. Either that or he was developing a frightening tic.

We quietly left Mum to her unquiet slumbers and Paul considering his own escape options and returned to the kitchen, where every encrusted pan and plate and bowl my family owned was stacked high and unloved in and around the sink, the baked on, burnt on food demanding our immediate attention. It didn't get it.

'It's about your mother,' he said, and my heart grew heavy.

'How bad?'

'Nothing big, but I thought you should know that she's struggling again, getting forgetful and angry with herself.' This wasn't easy for him to articulate nor for me to hear. The great unspoken was being spoken of.

'Will she see a doctor this time do you think?'

'I've tried to raise it but she's not listening,' he said, his eyes suddenly looked bloodshot and tired, as if he'd been crying for hours. I put my arms around him and hugged him tight, an action sadly all too unfamiliar to both of us. He relaxed into my embrace and we stood in silence, both afraid of the words that remained unsaid.

'What can I do? Do you want me to see if she'll talk to Claire Bear?' I whispered.

'No, I don't think she'll listen. I'm going to talk to Sharon next door and see if she can help Mum see some sense. If it works, it might be easier to go private than get her down the doctors – she's always thinking she's going to run into someone she knows down there and word will get around.'

'That won't be cheap.'

'Any chance that you could help in …' He couldn't finish

the sentence.

'Of course,' I said, pulling him tighter. 'Not a problem, Dad. I'll do a cheque when I get back to town.'

Chapter 13

I was struggling. Chivalry was truly dead. Despite the hurrying crowds there was absolutely no one at St. Pancras to help the poor maiden with her mum-packed, bulging suitcase and collection of overstuffed plastic bags off the train. Could no one see how overloaded I was, how much distress I was in? Worse, I now had to bustle my way down the stairs onto the packed tube platforms and wrestle my way onto the packed holiday carriages. I suddenly had renewed sympathy for the bag ladies of this world.

Just when I thought it couldn't get any worse my Nokia rang and I jumped in surprise, dropping a Top Shop bag and spilling its contents under my fellow traveller's trampling feet. Shit shit shit.

'Claire?' I don't know why he asked, it was not as if there was anyone else likely to answer my mobile.

'Hello, Barclay.'

'I need your services again. Tonight, pick me up from the usual place. 3am.'

None of that nonsense chat. No 'How was your Christmas, Claire?' 'Very nice thank you, Quentin Horatio, and how was yours?' palaver. And it was only December 27th, so no extended holiday for me this year. No rest for the wicked, they say.

'Same car? Please tell me you got a new car for Christmas.' I was only half-joking – the Fiat may have had its own, curious charms but was in all honesty an accident waiting to happen, even doing twenty on a quiet side street.

He sighed. 'I have already explained this, Claire.' The tone, the tone – it was if he were talking to a five-year-old. 'It is important that your car is anonymous. We simply cannot have something that stands out. It has to look like it belongs to the streets of South London, not newly escaped from some Porsche showroom or something hot-wired for an early morning joy ride.'

'I suppose so.'

'Tonight then. Same time. Same car. And we will be going

to the same car park. Be ready on time if not a little early.'

'Okay. Got it. See you later. And Barclay?'

But the line went dead. No fear of a long, drawn out goodbye with Barclay.

When I got home I was knackered. It's funny how sitting on a train motionless for hours on end can do that to you. I could have gone straight to bed but needed to keep going for a few more hours, so I spent my time clearing out the last physical remains of Henry from the flat – he said he'd taken everything but I'd found some neglected underwear at the bottom of the laundry basket, a lone shoe under the bed and he hadn't even bothered with his CDs. His loss was to be Oxfam's gain, although I thought the chances of them taking soiled underwear were pretty slim. Even charity only goes so far. After that I thought I would try to get a few hours' kip before the late night/early morning start with Barclay, but I half expected that the adrenaline would kick in and I'd struggle to get even twenty of the prescribed forty winks.

I woke at three am. I had, for the first time in a long time, slept like a babe. It was a good job I'd set the alarm on my Nokia or I would have fucked it up completely. Six hours, a solid six hours. Brilliant. I was ready for anything.

I trotted to the bathroom and splashed my face with a shock of ice cold water to clear the last remnants of sleepy Claire, brushed my teeth and hair, then dressed in my blackest outfit. Black jeans, black shirt, that tight knit navy polo neck jumper from Gap, even my undies were black. Getaway drivers can never be too careful when doing night work.

I picked Barclay up from outside his building in the Uno. He was right – it was as anonymous a car as you could possibly imagine. Not one of those funky little new Fiats with the bright colours and the cheeky styling. Not quite. For me this was the car that took the word 'super' out of supermini and firmly trashed it. A car so anonymous even its mother wouldn't recognise it. Maybe I should have considered cleaning it – I felt dirty just looking at it, and touching its failing paintwork made me want to scrub my hands with a Brillo.

It was another particularly cold night and even inside the car I could see our breath forming as we spoke.

'Good morning.'

'Hiya,' I said. 'Hop in.' I'd kept the engine running, still not sure if turning the motor off was going to prove to be a final, fatal act. I'm sure the Italians make some excellent engines, objects of breath-taking engineering beauty and stylish mechanical efficiency. This was not one of them.

'Shouldn't take long tonight. This is normally pretty straightforward.'

'Good.' I still wasn't ready to ask what exactly was going on with these 'jobs' involving picking up large amounts of anonymous cash at four in the morning in desolate car parks on the edge of town. Chances were that it may have been a wee bit dodgy. Who was I kidding? I knew from the off that it was, without question, highly illegal and probably morally suspect, too. But it was one hell of a thrill and the shy, grateful coward in me figured that the less I knew the easier everything would be, so I didn't ask any questions and just did as I was told. I was being paid to 'do', not 'think'.

We pootled through the Blackwall Tunnel and around the quiet night-time streets of South London, the last dregs of late night humanity shuffling out from desperate looking all night takeaway dives. Even through the Fiat's windows I could hear the distant howls of police sirens competing for trade with those of emergency ambulances. It was not pretty. This area didn't do 'pretty' at this hour. Or any hour, come to that.

True to form, we drove in silence. I wanted, desperately wanted, to ask about the hanging body, but just couldn't find the courage to raise it again, so to speak.

The car park was deserted. The wayward anarchist in me parked badly over two bays at an uncomfortable angle.

'Right,' said Barclay. 'I will be ten minutes. Tops.'

'You said that last time. I reckon you'll be twenty at least.'

'Not tonight. Too cold to hang around out there.'

'Too cold to hang around in here, too.' There was no way I was not going to have the almost-heating running tonight – it was close to freezing outside and there were wisps of a light mist gathering, already threatening to blur the orange of the distant street lights. I should have worn gloves. Maybe I could buy some of those ridiculous leather driving gloves with this week's money? Mind you, woolly mittens may have been more useful that night.

He was gone just five minutes. He suddenly appeared, sprinting around the corner, a jumping sports bag strapped across his back. Panic? Barclay? Maybe this time. I'd never seen him run before and it was not exactly poetry in motion, flailing arms and uncoordinated legs. Tall men can't run. Official.

I threw the passenger door open for him. He hurled the bag in the back and jumped in.

'Drive!' he barked, eyes wide and staring.

I stamped on the clutch and fumbled the gear stick into first. We lurched off, jumping almost into a stall, then I dragged it into second and third in one of my more impressive gear changes. I didn't stop to check the exit, just shot out onto the A2, heading west.

'Fuck fuck FUCK,' said Barclay.

Into fourth, the Uno's engine surprisingly coping with the urgent call to action. Thirty. Forty. Fifty. No other traffic. The lights at the foot of the hill were mercifully green as we shot across the junction. Barclay still hadn't put his seat belt on. Deptford sped by. New Cross and its one-way congestion nightmare loomed. I slammed on the brakes, dropped into third, much to the disgust of the engine, and threw the Fiat down the sharp left at Goldsmith's and we shot up a quiet residential street. I started to slow – there were no lights in the rear view mirror and I guessed that whatever had shocked Barclay was gone.

'Why are you fucking slowing down?'

'What?'

'He's on a bike – he'll easily fucking catch up!' Suddenly there was a single headlight growing in my mirrors and the sound of an accelerating motorbike. But despite Barclay's sudden panic I was thinking calmly – surely he wouldn't know Barclay was in this particular car?

Almost nonchalantly I slowed further, indicated left and parked on a yellow line next to an overfilled skip. I killed the lights as the speeding motorbike roared passed us and raced up over the hill.

Sometimes I surprised even myself.

Barclay was breathless but I was calmness personified. I wanted to nonchalantly light myself a cigarette and look like I'd done it a hundred times before. If only I smoked. I hadn't smoked since that coughing fit behind the school garage with Dolly Pee. For just a moment, I needed a cigarette to look as cool and collected as I felt.

'That…' he panted, 'That was…good.'

I smiled. 'That's what I do.'

'Yes. Excellent.' His breath and composure were slowly returning. He took a minute, taking deep, meditative breaths. That had not been a Barclay I had seen before. Panicked, even fearful. I found it quite unsettling.

'What exactly happened?' I asked.

'It wasn't a set-up but not to plan. He had second thoughts and wouldn't let go of the bag. Idiot. We wrestled with this,' he motioned to the bag, 'and it all got a bit ugly. Bastard.' I noticed Barclay's trousers were torn and there was blood, as if he'd fallen clumsily. 'I whacked him with the bag. I ran for the car and saw he was going towards a parked motorbike I just hadn't seen. Lucky you were ready.'

I gave him a knowing smile. 'Nothing lucky about it. You're in safe hands, Mr Barclay.'

For once, he didn't correct me.

We sat in silence as I drove us back to his building, but I was far from uncomfortable. Who was the Muppet now, eh Barclay? He should have spotted the bike. He shouldn't have panicked. Thank god for Claire MacDonald, her serenity in the face of adversity.

Smug? Me? Too bloody right.

I pulled up outside the building. It was 4.30am, not a soul around. Barclay had been counting the bundles of notes in the sports bag. He dropped a handful in my lap.

'Here. Half tonight. You deserve it.'

I couldn't speak – there must have been over a thousand quid there, even some of those oversized fifties you hear about but never get from the cashpoint.

'Thanks,' I managed to say.

'And don't read anything in to this, but I need to ask a favour of you.'

'Sure.'

'What are you doing over New Year?'

Was this really Barclay sitting next to me, or some defective clone who'd come out in his place? Was he asking me out on a date?!

'It's not a date,' he clarified hurriedly. 'Not a real one. I need a … companion when I go and visit my parents for their New Year's Day lunch, it eases some of the pressure, you know, and I was hoping, if you didn't already have plans, if you would join me? No funny business, it's only the lunch so no 'whoops, we need to share a bed' nonsense, no obligations…'

I was taken aback but the adrenaline was still pumping. 'It'll cost you,' I chanced.

'I…er…I thought it might. But I've just paid you and…'

'…a new set of wheels.'

'What?'

'Barclay, if we are doing this seriously we need a more reliable car. This is great, I love it, we're really attached and everything, but it's a sick, sick motor and it will let us down when we really need it. I thought it may have died on us tonight but we got by, but it will cough its last any moment and, it may well be anonymous, but we have to be driving something better.'

He was silent.

'We cannot outpace a motorbike in a thirty-year-old Fiat Uno,' I campaigned. 'Let alone a police car. It doesn't have to be a Porsche or anything flash, but it does need to be sound and reliable and trustworthy. Keep it as anonymous as you like, but we can't rely on this rust bucket for another getaway.'

I'd made my point, set my price. He nodded in reluctant

agreement. 'Okay,' he said. 'Let me see what I can sort out. But you're good for New Year's?'

For some reason, that seemed to be so important to him. 'Yes, I'm good to be your beard for the day,' I said.

'It is not like that. When you meet my family you will understand.'

I was sure I would, but nothing was going to take anything away from my triumph that night. He got out of the Uno.

'I'll be in touch,' he said with a wave.

I grinned and waved back without thinking.

I was too high to sleep. Instead, I did what every right-minded criminal would do with their ill-gotten gains: I sat at a table and counted out the cash. I had never had so much.

I made myself either the last coffee of the night or the first of the morning. It was mix of notes; fivers, some tenners, just a few twenties, so counting it was more of a chore, albeit a pleasurable one. There was a little smile on my face when I'd counted out the first hundred, an even bigger one when I got to three, a quiet 'fucking hell' when I reached six and a hysterical laugh when I got to nine.

I had never held so much cash, let alone owned it. Counting it was an obsession and my coffee had cooled. I put the mug into the microwave to warm it back up. In all there was £980. I guess we had been short-changed by twenty quid? I didn't really care. Just twenty-four hours earlier twenty pounds had been a lot of money. Suddenly it was small change. I couldn't have been happier.

I started to consider the commitment I'd made Barclay. Was I really going to play the part of 'faux-girlfriend' for this man just to meet the family that spawned him? It seemed like a small price to pay, especially as I'd managed to add in the promise of a better car into the deal. I would do it. Besides, I might even enjoy myself.

Chapter 14

Barclay had said that the traffic might be bad, so he wanted to make an early start. I said I'd be ready 'whenever'. He suggested 10am to miss any drivers who were still pissed from the night before, which made sense. I said 'whatever'. He suggested I make 'an effort' to look nice for his parents. I said 'fuck off'.

As you can see, we were developing our witty rapport.

At ten to ten I was ready. I hadn't made a spectacular 'effort' but my recent investments in the shops around New Bond Street had certainly paid dividends, and the dark skirt complemented the white silk shirt and linen-mix cardigan. Hark at me – H&M girl makes good. I'd had my hair styled too, after one quip from brother Paul too many. I went to somewhere really expensive on Oxford Street and instantly felt like I had walked into a different reality. Funny people, hairdressers, not like us humans at all. All that conspiratorial giggling and looking distracted and far too much interest in my holiday plans for my liking. Nice haircut though – I don't think I'd ever felt so fab. I was sure it wouldn't survive me washing it with my all-in-one Superdrug shampoo then blasting the style out of it with my bargain basement drier.

Maybe I had made an effort, but it was very much for my benefit rather than Barclay's.

I couldn't believe we would be rolling up at the Barclays' family estate in the rusty old Uno, but there had been no word from His Lordship about the new car he had promised. I pulled the Fiat up outside his building, parking behind some boy racer's pride and joy that was hiding under a protective tarpaulin cover. Bastard. Some guys have all the luck.

I woke the neighbours with a honk of my too-proud, too-loud Italian horn and, moments later, Barclay appeared at the door. He was grinning. It was unnerving.

'Good morning' he said, a spring in his step as he strode over to the concealed car in front of me. He grasped the tarpaulin in his right hand and pulled it majestically away like the flamboyant conjuror he evidently imagined himself to be.

'Ta-daaa!' he beamed.

Oh. My. God.

I had stopped breathing. Was I dreaming?

I couldn't stay in the Uno a second longer. For me? This was for me? There were tears in my eyes as I clumsily clambered out of my humble shit heap of a car.

It was a 1962 Volkswagen Karmann Ghia. Of course I didn't know that at the time, I only knew that it was undoubtedly the most beautiful car I had ever seen. Every curve, every line was handsome, perfect, and it shimmered with an almost feminine glamour. It was a vision in sea blue and cream steel, its polished surfaces lustrous in the sunshine.

'Oh, Barclay,' I whispered as I timidly reached out and stroked its aquamarine contours for the first time. It was, possibly, the most erotically-charged moment of my life. I staggered back a step. Bloody hell. I'd wanted new wheels and the man appeared to have listened.

'Just for today,' said Barclay, but even that disappointment couldn't kill my new ardour. 'Are you ready?' he asked.

'I…I certainly am.'

He threw me the keys and I opened the door, only to notice that the steering wheel was on the other side.

He laughed. 'Left-hand drive only, I'm afraid.'

I frowned. 'I can see that.' My self-esteem took a stumble but at least no one else had seen me standing on the wrong side like an idiot. No one except Barclay. He'd enjoyed my seconds of embarrassment but I just didn't care – let him have his pathetic humiliation. Today was my day. Our day. Me and Karmann's day.

I dropped slowly down into the cream vinyl driving seat, lower and softer than I was used to. The interior was, if anything, even more basic inside than that of the Uno, but what was sparse and stark in the Fiat was charming and delightfully considered in the VW. The dashboard was shockingly bare, just three unpretentious dials for guidance. A fragile knitting needle of a gear stick poked proudly erect from the bare floor, accompanied by a cold steel handbrake rising from an ageing, wrinkled fake leather skin. It was all that was needed – anything more would have looked crude and ostentatious.

I had met a new world of sixties glamour and was smitten. Damn you, twenty-first century and your technology-driven complexity.

Barclay opened the passenger door and joined me, clearly delighted with my reaction. I inserted the key and, at the second time of asking, the VW announced itself with a bark and a splutter.

'Oh my.'

'Good Christmas?' he asked.

I couldn't answer at first – that world seemed a million miles away and I was tightly gripping the hard plastic of the outsized steering wheel, scared I'd wake from the wonderful dream, still lost in my rapture.

'What? Christmas? Oh yes, we had a good Christmas, thanks. You?'

'Later. Shall we go?'

I shuffled my feet on the pedals, pressed hard on the clutch and wrestled the gear stick into first. The engine gave a throaty splutter as I gently revved the accelerator and we jumped away from the curb. At last, at the tender age of twenty-five, I had fallen in love. I loved that car from the moment we met.

Barclay said something but I didn't hear it. I was driving with a fierce concentration as I negotiated the quiet Bank Holiday streets. God, I hoped Barclay's parents lived a thousand million miles away and it would take us forever to reach them.

We sailed through the West London streets towards the M25 and the countryside freedom beyond. Sitting so low in a sports car was not something I was familiar nor 100% comfortable with, the other traffic felt overbearing and monstrously large, passing buses and vans seemed to thunder overhead as the engine maintained a steady forty. For once I was a cautious driver, the car feeling delicate on the road amongst the twenty-first century beasts surrounding it.

We were still travelling in silence. Barclay's casual

conversations were painful at the best of times, and I was still savouring the car. But he was bored, so:

'And things were all good up in Glasgow?'

'Edinburgh. Things were fine. Things were normal. Mum asked after Henry. I didn't tell her we were finished, just said he was in India for a bit.'

'Have you heard anymore from him?'

'There were a couple of missed calls on my mobile but no texts. Are we going far?'

'Gloucester, so a couple of hours. Just outside Stroud. Traffic's not too bad by the look of things.' Bliss. Even though the engine felt like it would hit its limit at fifty I was happy to take my time. Can cars saunter? If so, we were sauntering.

A few more minutes passed, then he said:

'There's something I didn't tell you about my family.'

Uh oh. That didn't sound good.

'I have a sister, Dawn. She can be a little … odd.'

'Is that 'odd' like as in 'Barclay odd', or is she in a different league of odd?'

'You think I'm odd?' He looked quite pleased with my description.

'I think you're one of a kind. Are you saying your sister means that there are actually 'Barclays' blessing us with their presence?'

'We are … not similar.'

'Why didn't you mention her when I asked you about the family before?'

'I forgot her.'

'You forgot? You forgot you had a sister?'

'Sometimes I forget I have a mother and father, too. It's not that unusual. Everybody does it.'

'No they don't.'

'If they were more honest, they would admit to it.'

I really didn't know what to say to that. I guess there was maybe a small element of truth to it, after all, families are funny things and who hasn't wished at some point that they would all just go away? And if there's a list going I would like to volunteer my brother for it right now. But has anyone else ever really *forgotten* they have a family member? What a bizarre thing to say.

It wasn't worth an argument, but I was more intrigued than ever to meet his father, mother and, new addition folks, sister Dawn at stately Barclay manor.

I had pictured the Barclay family home as some kind of minor royalty palace. Maybe it had a pool? Huge expansive gardens that were prime for fracking? Nothing could have been further from the truth. As we left the A roads behind and I coaxed the VW around winding country roads I slowed at the turnings for each isolated, wind-swept mansion, only for Barclay to wave me on, 'not yet, not that one,' he muttered. His earlier chirpiness had quietened as we neared our destination, and when he finally said 'here', pointing to my left, my astonishment no doubt added to his embarrassment.

It was no five star hotel. It would barely have rated two. It was a modestly-sized and somewhat shabby pre-war detached house, three or four bedrooms at most, desperately in need of some TLC and a slathering of paint to protect it from the elements that had clearly taken their toll. I doubted if it had ever been impressive and, stranded in the middle of an overgrown, unkempt garden littered with long-abandoned childhood swings nestling in the weeds and wildflowers it looked sad and unloved, almost derelict.

This was 'stately Barclay manor'? Bugger me.

'What's that then?' asked Barclay's father. He waved a glass of seasonal sherry at the snowy drive out the front of the house where our decorous German classic was parked. He didn't seem to be surprised that we had arrived in a car oozing style and class. Maybe the Aston Martin keys I'd found in Barclay's rucksack had been genuine after all.

'A 62 Karmann Ghia,' said Barclay. 'Not many around these days, but worth the hunt. A bit tight now I'm a couple.' His arm had somehow worked its way around my waist and he gave me an 'affectionate' squeeze. Not happening, mister. I pulled away, but surreptitiously so as not to cause a scene. 'But I may be looking to trade it in soon. I may go for something more modern – the new Aston's due in the spring.'

'Boys and their toys,' tutted Barclay's mother, shuffling into the room with yet another bowl of dry roast peanuts. 'Nut?'

I noticed that Barclay almost instinctively put a little distance between himself and the bowl of nuts, and I suddenly remembered the adrenaline Epipen I'd found in his bag a few weeks back and wondered if he actually had a nut allergy. And his mother didn't know about it? How strange. Were they that distant?

Nothing was going to surprise me though about this family – 'odd' was the word Barclay had used to describe his sister (who I still had not met) and it was very much a family trait. The Barclays' house had several large rooms that could have been referred to as the lounge. They even had a room that only seemed to be referred to as 'The Other Room', as if it were inferior or secondary for some reason. Needless to say it seemed perfectly adequate and normal to me.

The room we had settled in was decorated with a peculiar nostalgic mix of Seventies and Eighties furniture, presumably salvaged from the various Barclay family homes over the decades; a sagging leather sofa, a wicker throne that wouldn't have looked out of place in a corny porn video; a low mahogany coffee table whose sole purpose was to support a collection of unread coffee table books; one of those oversized American recliners parked in front of a television that must have been many decades old. And what a TV – only junk shops stock ones like that these days. It was in an enormous dark wood cabinet with shutter doors pinned back, revealing the antique marvel within; a telly as deep as it was high, with what by anyone's standards was a small screen, curved slightly with rounded corners. Underneath was an ancient VHS video recorder with large clunky buttons for playing, rewinding and FF-ing. Like something from the ark. As was the small library of video tapes in their cases; *The Far Pavilions*, *Brideshead Revisited*, *Jewel in the Crown*. Programmes from before my time but I'm sure my Mum knew them. Mrs Barclay ('call me Jean, dear. After all, you're almost family already!' she had said) and Mum would get on well – they shared a common place in the home (the kitchen) and in time (the eighties). They'd never meet of course – we were playing a game, Barclay and I, and doing it quite convincingly. We certainly had Mrs B. convinced, but that hadn't proven particularly difficult.

Mrs B had curious tastes that wouldn't have been out of place on an edition of *Antiques Roadshow*. There were the ornaments; a collection of cutesy-pie Hummel figurines sitting uneasily with his father's ancient darts trophies on flimsy ancient stained pine shelving. The little ceramic children were in classic Heidi-esque lederhosen and chequered dresses, Swiss oddities that somehow looked dated and timeless simultaneously. They were possibly worth an absolute fortune, or had cost one but were now sadly worthless. I made a silent resolution to myself to look them up on the web when I got home. (I never did.)

There was snow on the ground outside and temperatures were around zero, but there was no excuse for the thermostat being turned up quite that high. Even stripped of my coat, scarf and woolly hat I was still baking.

'And you're sure you don't want a sherry?' his father asked me.

'No thanks, not really my drink,' I said. 'A glass of cold water would be nice though?' Mr Barclay nodded and waved his hand at Mrs B, who disappeared at his command to fetch one from the kitchen.

'And you?'

'No thank you,' said Barclay. 'You know I'm not a sherry drinker. Do you have any of that Chablis we had last year?'

'Of course I do, but I'm saving that for a special occasion,' his father said.

Right on cue his mother returned from the kitchen.

'And Quentin's only visit of the year isn't special enough?' she asked. Barclay visibly flinched at the mention of his hated given name.'No,' answered his father.

'Oh.' Head bowed, she shuffled back to the kitchen to fuss over some other unwanted side table snacks. It seemed to be norm, her husband belittling the poor woman and putting her firmly in her place. He didn't show any sympathy for her and her oppressed life as unappreciated cook, cleaner and housebound servant. I felt for her. No one deserved such scorn.

'How is London life?' Barclay's father asked him.

'As exciting as always. I've got a new opportunity, just needs some seed capital and…'

'If you can afford to replace that bloody car, I'm sure you don't need to ask for anything from me.'

I didn't have a clue what Barclay was talking about, but he couldn't have it both ways; pretend he was loaded (the car, the clothes, me on his arm in all my new finery) and then ask for a loan.

Muppet.

'Would you at least like to hear about it?' Barclay chanced.

'No.'

That killed the discussion stone dead, a welcome chill suddenly dampening any illusion of joy at this tired, tiring family reunion. With impeccable timing, Mrs Barclay reappeared.

'Nuts?'

The late New Year's Day lunch had proven almost unbearable. As the enmity between Barclay and his father developed further they descended into a succession of prolonged uncomfortable silences, only broken by Mrs Barclay's imploring for us to 'eat up – there's plenty more'.

Barclay's 'forgotten' sister Dawn had proven to be a no-show. No mention was made of her and every time a car passed outside I looked at the window in curious hope, but there was no relief from our unspeaking quartet.

I wasn't sure Christmas Day leftovers were still good to eat a whole week later, and I was even less sure that they'd been anything special when they'd been fresh. For someone who appeared to spend an inordinate amount of time in the kitchen Mrs B didn't appear to be particularly gifted in the culinary skills department. At least the wine was good – excellent in fact. A girl could get used to this taste of luxury at least.

I needed to get out of there, even it was just for ten minutes. It was suffocating and I think my credibility as Barclay's 'girlfriend' was hanging on by a rapidly unravelling thread; Barclay was neglecting to play his part and I was buggered if I was going to make up for his shortcomings on that front. If the subterfuge was going to last the visit I needed a break.

'I need some air,' I said. 'Okay if I pop out the back?'

Only Mrs B showed any concern – Barclay was gazing at an old movie playing silently on the dining room's telly.

'Of course dear,' she said. 'The back door's open.'

'Thanks. That was delicious, Mrs Barclay.'

'Jean.'

'Jean.'

Like I say, suffocating.

Outside it was mercifully clear and crisp, refreshingly cold. The stars were already blinking in the darkening sky, a sight so unfamiliar to us light-spoiled city mice. If I'd been a smoker this would have been an excusable break, but I'd probably only have a few minutes to gather my thoughts and gird my loins for more of the same. How I longed for the solitude of my beloved Karmann.

'Hello.'

I jumped. I hadn't noticed anyone else out here when I'd stepped out but I could now see the amber glow of a cigarette tip and smelt its faint aroma on the light breeze.

'Hello?'

A girl, no more than sixteen, stepped into the light from the kitchen window. She wore a heavy winter Parka and was wrapped against the elements, hugging herself to keep warm. She was tall, probably taller than her brother, and slightly ungainly. Her hair was blue black and cut with a strikingly harsh fringe just above the pierced eyebrows. Her nose had a septum piercing, her ears resembled curtain poles, adorned with rings almost too many too count. She was thin, punky, gothic in her style and clothing. Probably tattoo-ed all over.

Even in the dim light I could see that her eyes were

breathtakingly blue. She was confidently beautiful, quite exceptional.

'You must be Claire?'

'Yes. And are you…Dawn?'

She smiled.

'Bad in there, is it?' she asked.

'Horrendous. I had to get out. I couldn't breathe.'

'I've been out here for hours. Told Mum I was going round some friends but I wasn't. I just hate it in there. Christmas really is the worst time of year.'

'I can only imagine.'

'I wanted to see Barclay but I've lost my nerve. He doesn't visit often.'

'I can see why.'

'Him and the old man. It's horrible. I'm sorry you had to experience it. Must put you off him.'

Before I realised what I was saying I said, 'Oh, we're not a couple…'

Ah. My boo-boo. It just slipped out. Sorry Barclay.

'I didn't think so. Barclay can't do relationships. Not even friends.' She drew hard on her cigarette. 'It's good of you to come with him. I think he's a lonely soul, but I didn't tell you that. You seem too nice for him, but my parents won't notice that. Too subtle for them.'

That was nice to hear but we'd only known each other for a minute or so. 'Oh, you don't know me. I'm actually quite bad and Barclay makes me do bad things.'

She laughed. 'Yeah, I'd imagine he does if it's work. So you work for him?'

'Yes. I'm his driver.'

'I didn't know he had a driver. I wasn't even sure he had a car. That VW is a rental, isn't it? Just for the day to impress the old folk?'

Of course. Bloody hell, Barclay.

'He's done it before,' she continued. 'Asked some poor schmuck to be his girlfriend for these visits, to act as a parental distraction. Drives up in a flash car to impress. A few hours of empty, uncomfortable silences and then he disappears again for another year or two.'

Somehow I felt smaller, almost insignificant. 'I would imagine so,' I muttered, looking at my shoes and the patterns the heels had made in the light snow on the grass.

'Don't feel bad. He uses people. Always has. Always will. It's never personal. He gets it from Father.'

I was starting to feel the cold but I was warming to Dawn. She was the normal one in the family. Maybe that's what Barclay meant by 'odd', as in 'odd one out'.

'Are you still at school?' I asked.

'I'm older than I look. I'm at art college on my Foundation. Just home for the holidays.'

'Where's college?' I asked.

'Camberwell in London.'

I was stunned.

'I live in Deptford – we're almost neighbours.'

'I thought we might be. Barclay lives in Docklands somewhere but never makes the effort.'

'Do you live in Camberwell?'

'I wish. Too expensive though. I live in Peckham, a few miles down the road. A smelly bedsit above a smelly shop.'

Suddenly I had an idea. Unlike me I know, but I was already so far out of my comfort zone I couldn't stop myself. This was New Claire. Living dangerously. I was probably doomed to failure so what the hell?

'I don't suppose you're looking for somewhere to live?'

She looked at me quizzically, a smile playing on her lips.

I was speaking without thinking. Slow down Claire, before you say something you'll regret.

'I've got a spare room in the flat and my ex has just moved out. I need help with the rent and I'm looking for a flat mate and…'

Her face lit up. 'That would be brilliant! How much?'

Henry used to reluctantly contribute £750 a month.

'Five hundred?' I suggested.

'Wow that would be great!' Over-excited she hugged me like

a long lost sister. I barely knew her and I had invited her to live with me.

'I'm getting too cold now,' I said. 'I need to go in. Let's talk about it later.'

'I'll join you,' she said. 'It'll be a distraction for them. Let's not mention the flat just yet though …we don't want it to become a discussion.'

'Agreed.'

I put my hand out and she shook it, laughing. (What is it with me and the hand shaking thing? Am I a closet business woman?) She stubbed out her fag on the paving – she had amassed quite a collection underfoot I noticed. She really had been standing out there all that time.

'No smoking in the flat,' I said.

'You're going to be as good for me as Barclay is bad for you,' she joked as I opened the kitchen door and we both stepped into our shared private hell.

'You what?' Barclay was genuinely surprised. Stunned even.

'I asked your sister to move in with me,' I said, calmly smoothing my coat as I climbed into the passenger seat. He swung my door closed, threw a cursory wave over his shoulder at his family (he needn't have bothered – they'd already gone back inside) and strode round to the driver's side. Once we were out of sight we would swap – the illusion was everything.

And Barclay was not happy.

'But you hardly know the girl!'

'I know her enough. Probably know as much about her as I know about you.'

'But I don't live with you!'

'Then I will get to know her better than I know you. I like her. She's nice. No wonder you find her odd.'

'I find you bloody odd,' he muttered, turning the key, stalling, then igniting the engine of the temporary Barclaymobile.

'And this is a hire car, isn't it?'

'Yes of course it bloody is.'

'And it's back to work in the Fiat when we get back I take it?'

'Of course.'

'You promised…' But he wasn't listening, preferring instead to pretend to be concentrating on his driving rather than talking to me.

'Fine,' I said, crossing my arms in another huff. 'So I did this for nothing?'

'You got a free lunch.'

'It *was* a free lunch…it was week-old leftovers.'

'And you got to meet my family, including your new flat mate.'

'And what a bizarre bunch they are, too. No wonder you're so fucked up.'

He glanced over at me, brow slightly furrowed. Hurt? Probably not.

He drove for a mile before he pulled up and we swapped seats, all legal now. The VW had turned ice cold from being left alone and unloved for most of the afternoon and it was taking forever to warm up. A hush descended again, uncomfortable but I wasn't going to break it. Damn him, I was going to savour my last moments with the car. I didn't care that my plans with Dawn had clearly rattled him – he didn't own me.

He didn't own anyone. He didn't even own the car I was driving.

About a mile along the M25 the Karmann coughed and spluttered its last and died an undignified death on the hard shoulder. It took a garage four hours to reach us; by then, my brief passionate affair was truly over and I longed for my Uno.

True love can be such a bitch.

Chapter 15

Dawn was looking for a corkscrew to open the second bottle she'd 'borrowed' from her father's cellar. The first had been the familiar screw cap and had been possibly the most delicious thing I'd ever tasted in my life. It had barely lasted thirty minutes. I couldn't recall if I'd ever used a corkscrew before – it's a generation thing now, I guess – so I didn't hold out a lot of hope for her finding one in the 'all the other stuff' drawer in the kitchen amongst the rubber bands, probably-dead batteries, wooden spoons and that curiously sadistic-looking thing for lifting the spaghetti.

I was wrong. 'Success!' she beamed, triumphantly holding a near-antique penknife-like object aloft. 'A sommelier knife!' These Barclays, they all spoke an entirely different language.

'A semolina what?' I asked, completely bemused.

'A sommelier knife. It's got a blade to cut the foil and a lever if you're feeling a bit feeble and even a bottle opener. One of the great inventions. It's an old one but will do the job I'm sure.' She sat back down with me on my sofa and went about attacking the top of bottle number two.

'This one's from some fancy place in Italy I think – a Barolo. Father's favourite and rather special. He'll be furious it's gone. We really should let it breathe first.' I nodded wisely in bemused agreement. 'Have you got a decanter at all?'

'I didn't know I had a corkscrew.'

'No worries, we'll let it breathe in the glass, but we can decant the next one now if you've got a clean Pyrex lying around.

That I did have, and collected it from the cupboard where it had been gathering dust since Henry's departure. She uncorked a third bottle (three? Was she expecting guests or something?) and splashed the contents into the litre sized measuring jug.

Back to bottle number two. 'Cheers!' she said, raising her glass.

'Cheers.' Was Barclay junior going to add to the life of depravity her errant brother had introduced me to by turning me into an alcoholic? I could think of worse paths of destruction to stagger and stumble down, especially if all the booze was this exquisite. I would never look at my Jacobs' Creek with quite the same lust again.

She had arrived shortly after five like Taz the Tasmanian Devil from Cartoon Network, a whirlwind of frantic activity and volley after volley of incessant chatter. Whereas Barclay himself would frequently withdraw into silence mid-sentence, his sister didn't appear to even draw breath and was non-stop energy. She arrived pulling a large bright pink suitcase on wheels and a battered wine carrier thing with half a dozen chinking bottles ('I can always ask them to send more if we need it,' she had half-threatened, half-promised). She certainly wasn't going to over-clutter the flat, which was a relief, but from the evidence of the first few hours she was still going to be more of a handful than I had been anticipating.

She was the antithesis of Barclay; in fact you could have called her the anti-Barclay. Her laughter was infectious and long, Barclay's was controlled and brief – a sharp bark at best. Where he was reserved and cold, she was warm and open. She thought aloud whereas he preferred silent contemplation. Did they really share common parentage? The immediate evidence suggested otherwise.

'And what exactly does 'driving Barclay' entail?' she asked, picking up our conversation from a few days previous.

'That's a good question. I'm not really sure, it's only been a couple of weeks. He's banned at the moment.' Her eyes widened. 'I just do the quick sprints around town in the Fiat Uno.'

She laughed and spluttered in her glass. 'A Fiat Uno? Whatever happened to the DB7 he had last year? The Aston Martin?'

'He's got some keys but I've only ever seen the Fiat Uno and Karmann. Endearing little rust trap. He's promised me something better but I'm not holding my breath. The Uno's not reliable for what we're doing…'

'Which is?'

'Tearing away from car parks in the middle of the night with a bag of cash.'

She almost dropped her glass. 'Seriously?'

'Yep.' We were both grinning like mad things.

'You're a fucking getaway driver?'

'I fucking am!'

'That is so cool!'

'I know.'

'And where does he get the bags of money from?'

'I have absolutely no idea.'

'That's even cooler! Don't know, don't care! I love it!'

'It's the new reckless me. Cheers!'

We chinked glasses again, instant BFFs.

'Can I come on one of these getaways?' She was hugely excited. I couldn't imagine Barclay welcoming a passenger – the Uno struggled enough carrying the two of us.

'Maybe. If he gets a bigger car. It would be a squeeze in the back of the Uno. We do seem to do this pretty early in the morning though.'

'How early's early?'

'Three, four.'

'Bummer. Okay. Maybe not.'

'Late riser?'

'Kinda. Certainly not that early. I don't think I've ever seen three in the morning, at least, not as a starting time. Looks all blurry as a finishing time though.'

I nodded in agreement and we started sharing stories of wild nights on the town we'd enjoyed. Mine were part-drunken recollection, part-fabrication. My wild social life had pretty much ground to a halt since taking the Intern position and attaching the ball and chain of Henry. Dawn's were epic – long, rambling tales of partying into the small hours followed by quest-like journeys home that even Frodo Baggins would have baulked at. She had certainly packed a lot of living into her eighteen years – heaven knew what she'd get up to when she was old enough to drink legally.

We talked long into that first night together. She was due back at college the next day, first day of a new term and she had said she planned to get in bright and early and bushy tailed. All three of those were looking a trifle ambitious by the time we hit the Pyrex of red, bottle number three.

'Tell me about Barclay,' I slurred.

'What do you want to know?'

'Oh, everything. Tell me everything.'

'Everything I know. Sure. But I don't know everything. I can't tell you where he's getting that money from for a start.'

'Whatever,' I said, waving my glass too casually and spilling a little of the red stuff. Didn't care. Beyond caring. Does red wine stain? Surely this stuff was too good to stain.

'Older than me by a good ten years or so. Wasn't around when I was tiny – they packed him off to some posh public boarding school. He got weirder every time he was back for holiday – even little me could see that. Never wanted to play, showed no interest in my best friend Tinky Winky…'

'Your best friend was called Tinky Winky?'

She laughed and playfully hit my knee. 'My best friend was a guinea pig – I was a lonely kid. Don't look so shocked. You've met the family. So that had been a big deal for me and my idiot brother disappeared into his bedroom at every opportunity rather than entertain his only sister. Then he just vanished from our lives completely. Mum said he'd gone to University to do something with computers. She didn't know what. Father didn't either. Neither seemed to really care and he kinda disappeared from our lives for a while, never mentioned, never seen. By the time I was at high school myself I'd pretty much forgotten all about him. I didn't get the posh expensive school they'd wasted their money on for him – they weren't going to be bitten by that one twice, and besides, money was suddenly a little harder to come by. Once father became 'Sir Desmond' and Mum was a Lady they instantly seemed to become less wealthy.'

'I didn't know your dad was royalty!'

'It's not royalty, just a knighthood.'

'What was it for?'

'I never asked. We never talked about it. All a bit embarrassing really.'

‘So Barclay’s as much of a mystery to you as he is to me?’

‘Pretty much,’ she said. ‘We’re not close and both prefer it that way.’

‘Fair enough.’

We chinked glasses again. It didn’t look like I was going to learn that much more just yet, which was just as well as she could have shared the secret of life that night but the vast quantity of quality alcohol would have ensured it still remained a secret for all eternity the following morning.

Chapter 16

Barclay and I were sitting in the Uno (yes, it was back) in a half-empty car park, but this time it was late on the Monday afternoon, with the supermarket winding down but still with a few people milling around, last minute shopping for dinner or emptying their recycling into the overflowing bins and so straight onto the floor (so much for saving the environment). Barclay had told me we were waiting for someone who was going to help him on the next pick up, due later that week. Tom Thomas's warning was playing on an endless loop in the back of my head – he was coming back from San Francisco that night and I was desperate to see him.

'I know you think it's best that I don't know what goes on, deniability is the best defence and all that, but could you at least give me a clue?' I asked.

'I would rather not. Deniability and all that. I can tell you what it is not, if that helps.'

'It would be a start I suppose, something to chew over while I'm sitting in the eight by eight holding cell waiting for the judge.'

I was only half joking. I hadn't developed a guilty conscience or anything as extreme as that, but, as Dawn had pointed out earlier that morning, trust was not something Barclay had actually done anything to earn from me. I guessed it was illegal – otherwise he'd get the money through a bank transfer or cheque or something, so it must have been dodgy to require that the payment was untraceable and off-the-record.

'It is nothing to do with drugs, if that is keeping you awake at nights.'

Well, that was a relief. Didn't fancy getting tied up in anything like that.

'It does not involve violence. Not by design, anyway. Sometimes a threat of violence is required…'

'Like the dead dog?'

'That was most unfortunate, and more to do with the animal's existing health condition than any action on my part.'

I didn't buy that but let it rest.

'It is not theft, burglary or anyone being robbed of their life savings. The money comes from people who can easily afford to give it without their lives being wrecked as a result. It is not fraud, counterfeit goods or that kind of activity. It does not harm people.'

I was checking a list off in my head. He'd got the obvious ones I'd thought of earlier and I was starting to run out of guesses.

'It's not murder is it?

'I said it does not involve violence by design, so obviously not.'

'Kidnapping?' I asked.

'And where am I keeping the kidnap victims?' He was enjoying this game of riddles.

'But it is illegal?'

'In most countries, well, yes. Actually, it is probably illegal in every country, but not punishable by the death penalty anywhere as far as I … ah, here he comes.'

I struggled to turn in the tight confines of my seat belt, only to see an absolute hulk of a man approaching the car. He was as wide as he was tall (and he was at least a six footer), the result of too many hours pumping iron and gobbling handfuls of steroids, a veritable goliath of muscle and brawn. His arms and chest were so horribly overdeveloped they didn't seem to fit together properly, his broad head meeting his broad shoulders with no obvious neck in-between. Despite the plummeting temperature, he had no coat, only a short-sleeved black tee shirt that was struggling to contain the distended, stacked muscles upon muscles beneath. He walked with a heavy, wide gait, almost a waddle, his formidable thighs uncomfortably rubbing as he moved towards us and I shrank down as low as I could manage. He was possibly even larger than the Uno.

This was a colleague of Barclay's?

I was simultaneously revolted, terrified and fascinated. I didn't know the human body could become that…that enormous.

He raised his hand to Barclay in greeting. There was no smile, no words. Barclay exited the car, holding his right hand out in welcome. I wouldn't have done it – that was not a handshake anyone who valued their fingers would attempt – but the man mountain gently encompassed Barclay's bony fingers in his own and they shook.

It (I wouldn't say 'he' – this was not a person in the conventional sense) grunted.

'Good of you to come,' said Barclay. 'Let me introduce you to our driver. Claire?'

I am not ashamed to admit that I was cowering, making myself as tiny as I possibly could in my seat. Barclay indicated I should leave the safe confines of the car and meet this shaven Kong. I pulled my bag up onto my lap and half hid behind it for protection, a little shake of the head to demonstrate my reluctance to join them.

'I'm fine here.' It was barely audible even to me.

'Claire? We have not got all day for God's sake.'

I swallowed hard and whispered a godless prayer. I unclenched my body and made a hesitant exit from the car, ensuring I kept the door open and vehicle between us. Not that it would have offered much protection if the guy made a hostile move.

'Claire, this is Thug Number Two.'

'What?'

'He prefers people not to know his real name. Thug Number Two – this is Claire,' said Barclay.

'What?' I was stunned. 'So it's okay for him to know my name but I can't know his?'

'Be realistic, Claire. It is only being sensible. It is not like you are on every European security service's Most Wanted list, is it?'

Not yet, I thought.

'What's he wanted for?' I couldn't address Thug Number Two directly, couldn't look at him in case – the horror! – he looked back. I felt if I could avoid the eye contact he'd not see me.

'Nothing with sufficient evidence to prosecute with any

certainty that I'm aware of.'

'Well that's reassuring.' My voice sounded tiny.

'Thug Number Two will be joining us in our work this week. I wanted you to meet him and to see if he can get into the back of the Uno.'

He was joking, wasn't he? It was more likely he could swallow the Uno whole himself.

'I don't think so,' my quietest voice suggested. 'The rear axle can only take so much…weight.' I took a step backwards in case that offended it in anyway.

'Yes, I can see that now. Silly me. Number Two – it looks like we will need a bigger car after all. Do you agree?'

The mighty beast's head nodded slightly. Still no words. No smile. No relief from the relentless menace I felt just being a few yards away from it.

'Okay then. I will see what I can do.' Barclay turned to me. 'It looks like you'll get your wish after all Claire – we're going upmarket with the vehicle.'

I forced a smile. 'Thanks.'

Thug Number Two, or 'TNT as I preferred to think of him as – it seemed appropriate – turned and started lumbering slowly away. My relief was audible. Barclay smiled.

'Goodbye monsieur. We will pick you up on Tuesday, 2am. Please try to be on time.' The creature waved without looking back at us.

We climbed back into the Uno. I was shaking and tried, unsuccessfully, to conceal it.

'Yes, he can do that,' said Barclay. 'Quite magnificent though, isn't he?'

'Chatty chap,' I ventured.

'He is not one for small talk, I agree.'

'Is there a Thug Number One?'

'We don't talk about Thug Number One.'

'Oh.' Leave it, Claire.

I started the car and we set off.

'I felt after the last little episode that we needed a little… muscle…to help oil the wheels of commerce, to bump up the protection.'

'It looks like you've gone for more than a little.'

'True. I think he's been working out since I last saw him. I honestly thought he would be able to squeeze in the back of this…thing.' I was having trouble shifting into fourth gear, the clutch action was not the smoothest or quietest.

'So he will just be along for the ride?'

'Pretty much.'

We entered the streets of Camberwell and turned onto Peckham Road. I wasn't particularly comfortable with the thought of meeting TNT again but I wasn't in a position to raise an objection. At least he would be on our side.

'That's Dawn's college over there,' I said, pointing out the Art College, an awful windowless concrete monstrosity that had been built in the most appalling Sixties manner. It was unspeakably ugly, even by Peckham standards.

'Charming,' said Barclay. He couldn't have been less interested. We hadn't talked about Dawn and I didn't even know if he knew she was now it town and my new flatmate. He'd made his disapproval of the arrangement perfectly clear on the drive back from his parents and it wasn't a topic I was going to raise again, especially as I was still coming down from the fight-or-flight endorphin rush of meeting TNT.

We drove on in silence, our earlier game of 'guess the crime' forgotten. I was starting to realise that this was getting serious and there was no turning back. It was exciting. It was terrifying. Would I mention my encounters with Tom Thomas and his words of caution?

I didn't think so. It was not the kind of thing easily explained, especially as I didn't have a clue what was actually going on.

Chapter 17

'What…the fuck…is that?'

It was a reasonable question, given the sight before me. It was early, 1.30am, on a particularly parky Tuesday morning and I'd not even attempted a few hours of sleep but I felt I was in a nightmare. My eyes were sharp and alert though thanks to late night Nescafe but still I couldn't quite believe what I was seeing.

Barclay had left the driver's door open and stood by it, beckoning me forward like an over eager car salesman once more.

'Your chariot awaits.'

'Fuck off.' I wasn't joking. It was quite simply the ugliest car I had ever seen in my life.

Barclay looked hurt, but fired me what he clearly thought was his winning smile.

'It is a Fiat Multipla,' he beamed. 'A design classic from the nineties. Stylish but practical. Winner of Top Gear awards many times over if I recall correctly.'

'It…it looks like a duck!'

'What?' He took a step back as if he hadn't really been looking properly before. 'A duck?'

'Like Daffy Duck's head. In the Looney Tunes cartoons.'

He shook his head. He wasn't seeing a resemblance.

'I do not understand you. You wanted, nay, you demanded a new car, and here it is, big enough for Thug Number Two and certainly a better runner than the Uno. There is no pleasing some people.'

'Sorry to sound ungrateful but it looks like a little car parked on top of a slightly bigger one. Whatever happened to us having an anonymous, inconspicuous motor? There'll be no mistaking this on Crimewatch.'

'I hear your very small point, but needs must. It is wide enough for Number Two and that's the main thing.'

'Can the rear axle take his weight?' I was genuinely sceptical that this was a step up from the Uno, which was proving to be my dream car compared with the alternatives Barclay was sourcing.

'Of course. Do I look like an idiot?'

Best not to answer that one – if he was seated in the driving seat of the Multipla, my answer would definitely be a resounding 'yes'.

'Get a move on,' he said, walking around to the passenger side. 'We don't want to keep the man mountain waiting.'

He had a point – TNT was not a man to be left waiting by the roadside – he would be an obstruction to passing traffic for a start. I climbed into the car and was surprised to find it was even more like something from another planet on the inside, three seats across in the front like a builder's van.

'Ooh, roomy,' I said before I could stop myself.

'See? I know what I'm doing,' he smiled. But I wasn't convinced.

The dashboard was a very nineties idea of what a 21st century car would look like: not a straight line in sight and everything swelling against convention as if to prove a point that cars don't need to be practical … or attractive. Everything was curved and bulged at jaunty angles, more Fisher Price than Fiat, a child's delight. Even lit under the dim glow of the interior light it was breath-taking in its misshapen, warped ugliness.

'It's…what…how…' I just couldn't find the words.

'The gear stick is there,' said Barclay, helpfully pointing to a short, swollen knob that jutted out from the sea of plastic in a vaguely pornographic manner.

'I'm not sure I'm going to be one hundred per cent comfortable touching that,' I complained. Barclay laughed.

'Oh do get a grip, Claire,' smiling at his own joke.

I sighed and reluctantly turned the key. The engine caught first time but it shared the same rattling voice of the Uno, more grumble than purr, sounding like it needed a damn good cough to clear its throat.

I did a double-take before grasping the stubby gear stick and shifting it into first, a surprisingly smooth action after the faltering jerk of the Uno's.

Barclay belted up.

'Number Two lives over by the Dome. We'd better get a move on. I'm seeing the money at two thirty.'

'You're the boss,' I muttered. As if there had ever been any doubt.

After ten minutes' driving through the sleeping streets of Greenwich I was a little more appreciative of the new car. A little.

It still looked like it had been panel bashed by a particularly over-sized Ugly Stick wielded by a drunken blind man in a debauched Pinata ceremony. To its credit though it was surprisingly comfortable, like sitting in an elevated armchair, and it made me feel like I had a better view of the world around me, almost like riding at the front on the top deck of a bus. And Barclay was right – it was a better drive than the Uno, comparatively smooth although it tugged a bit to the left and the width made it difficult to judge the Blackwall Tunnel.

Barclay directed me through the maze of roundabouts and lights that surrounded Greenwich's own Yuppy backyard, the Blair legacy that is the Millennium Dome and its ugly collection of unaffordable housing and apartment blocks, the Greenwich Peninsula. If this was modern living you could keep it – my home in Deptford was looking cosier with every turn of the wheel.

After a couple of mis-directions from Barclay we saw TNT ahead, waiting under a flickering streetlight. He hadn't lost any of his phenomenal bulk and could have easily been mistaken in silhouette for a small gathering rather than just a lone individual.

'There he is,' said Barclay, unnecessarily. I flipped the wipers by mistake before flashing the headlights at our companion. It was as friendly as I was willing to get with Mr Intimidation. He waved. No smile though. Not his style.

TNT opened a rear door and climbed in. It may have been my imagination but I swear the car reared like a bucking bronco, front wheels rising with the dramatic shift of weight. And something cracked – I'm sure something cracked in the

Multipla as it accommodated his immensity. He filled all three rear seats and was touching both sides of the interior.

Timidly, I moved into first gear, half expecting the car to surrender and die, but somehow it took the extra weight in its inelegant stride and we eased off without a hitch, none more surprised than me.

Barclay had said that this was to be a drop-off rather than a pick-up. Why that meant bringing TNT I wasn't quite sure, but the more questions I had the fewer I raised. I really was happier in my ignorance.

The drop was a few miles further south, yet another anonymous, dimly-lit car park Barclay had selected from a seemingly endless list of dodgy rendezvous destinations he had. I was too frightened to speak as I got to grips with the bizarre car's steering and uniquely personal eccentricities. TNT's mouth-breathing was loud and unsettling and I put the radio on to try to drown it out. After a burst of Thin Lizzy's 'The Boys Are Back In Town' I thought better of it. A shame we hadn't brought any cassettes with us to ease my tension. Not only could I hear TNT's breathing, I could smell it, taste it, like a foul dashboard air freshener it filled my every pore.

'Here. This is it,' directed Barclay, much to my relief. Another car park, abandoned, its pot-holed surface, wet from the earlier rain, littered from the overflowing bins that had been stuffed by the daytime January sales bargain hunters.

I engineered our Noddy car over a couple of parking bays and turned the engine off.

'Ready, Number Two?' asked Barclay. The response was a guttural grunt. The rear door opened and I felt the suspension bounce in relief as he exited.

'We will be ten minutes, tops,' said Barclay. 'Should be less drama this time with Number Two here.'

They disappeared around the corner of a darkened warehouse with a sports bag, presumably full of cash, and I was alone. I turned the car's electrics on to keep the car warm and decided to try the radio again. The subtle melody of Dusty Springfield's 'Look of Love' wrapped me in its sexy embrace and I instantly wanted to see Tom again. Never mind, just a few hours and we'd be together again. I love that record, and it put a smile on my lips, even in my nervous excitement of waiting for Dastardly and Muttley to return from another escapade.

I didn't have to wait long. As the fading strings signalled the end of Bacharach and David's song the familiar figure of Barclay jogged back into view, another rucksack slung over his shoulder. TNT followed, walking rather than running, despite Barclay's protestations to 'hurry along'.

'All good?' I asked as they re-entered the car and I started the engine.

'Yes. He was surprisingly agreeable. No need to shoot off this time. In fact…' Barclay paused, thinking through an idea by the look of things. 'Actually, let's hang around for a few minutes. I'd like to follow him.'

'Follow him? But we're not exactly inconspicuous in this thing are we? Surely he's bound to notice this balloon car crawling up behind him with the world's largest man sitting in the back?'

'Oh, Number Two can hunker down, can you not, sir?'

TNT grunted in agreement but I couldn't see it myself. Just wasn't going to work. Oh well. Who was I to argue?

We sat in uncomfortable silence for a few minutes then Barclay did a condescending little wave of his hand and I pushed the phallus into first.

We inched out of the car park and I turned in the direction where they'd disappeared just a few minutes earlier. Up ahead, scurrying under the bright streetlights of the high street, was a small figure, furtively glancing from side to side as he scampered from the rendezvous.

'I take it that's the guy?' I asked.

'Yes. That's him. Stop here and let's see where he goes.'

I pulled up on a double yellow. Our target was heading straight passed the closed shops and looked like he was heading to the all-night supermarket on the corner. Despite the bright lights of the High Street I couldn't make him out much. He had skinny jeans and a hoodie up over his head, topped with an inflated puffer jacket. At that hour he looked like just the kind of guy the police would want to call upon when rounding up the usual suspects. And to think I was worried about us looking conspicuous…

'Jumpy,' noted Barclay. 'That's good. He's been a pain in the arse recently. Very good. Go passed him and we can take a final look. Number Two: make yourself small.'

It was never going to happen, but TNT gave it his best shot and tucked his head down into his Olympian shoulders. Fail. I still couldn't see out the rear view mirror.

I moved the car forward and we picked up a little speed in second. As we neared him he threw his hood back and, as we passed, I glanced and got a quick look at the nervy, agitated guy Barclay and his massif had just been doing something dirty with.

The air left my chest. I recognised him. What the hell?

It was Tom Thomas.

Chapter 18

Was it him? Had I really been falling not-so-slowly but definitely-surely for a man Barclay was exchanging bags of cash with? Had my exciting new world of Crazy started taking the dubious blue pills to elevate its status to Even Crazier Totally Fucking Nuts World?

Driving back to the flat (having deposited the incredible hulk and infuriating sulk off at their respective homes) I replayed that quick glimpse of the guy over and over and over again. Tom Thomas? Seriously, that nice, witty Tom Thomas? But he had been so nice, so easy, so natural, that little twinkle in his eyes, the smile, the teeth – Jesus, I found myself grinning just thinking about him. He'd warned me off Barclay but I'd ignored him, pushed the thought away, figured I could cope with any supposed danger. He said I should make sure I didn't get hurt. How much did he know? More than me, no doubt, but that wouldn't be difficult. Why had he been hanging outside Barclay's flat when we first met? What had he said – that he and Barclay used to be business partners? And then there was the investigation thing? I was tired and couldn't think straight, and I'd kept schtum about Tom with Barclay, just in case. Barclay doesn't share so why should I?

When I got home and had parked the Multipla in a space where I prayed the neighbours wouldn't see it, the temptation to wake Dawn and tell her what had just happened was almost irresistible, but resist I did and lay on my bed covers, fully dressed, eyes wide.

Suddenly that evening's date with Tom wasn't looking like such a good idea. I needed time to think, to talk to Barclay. Had it *really* been him? It was a split second glance, a blink-and-miss moment. It could have been just a similarity – all men in hoodies look the same don't they?

I was all over the place and not thinking straight, straying dangerously into implausible explanations and my exhausted mind was racing with doubt after doubt. I really needed to get some sleep and maybe it would all be right in the morning.

Hell, it was morning already, wasn't it?

Was it him? Nice Tom? Tom Thomas, the Green Lantern fan?

What if it was?

'Please don't get hurt, Claire.'

(It was the 'please' that stuck in my heart.)

Over and over I played it, replayed it, asking questions, answering questions but lacking conviction, asking them again, answering them again, round and round and round. I must have fallen asleep eventually, but it was a fretful, almost painful slumber. So much for Barclay's promise that I'd sleep well at nights.

My phone woke me with a start. Fumbling in the darkness I stared at it as if for the very first time. Shit. It was five past ten already. Fucky shit. It was Tom Thomas calling.

You know the guy; 'Please don't get hurt, Claire' Tom. That's the one.

Do it, Claire, just talk to him. This was the time for to-the-point, no bullshit Serious Claire, and Serious Claire was going to have a serious conversation she didn't really want to have.

'Hiya,' he said. 'I'm back. Are you still on for tonight?'

'Depends,' said Serious Claire. 'I need you to be straight with me.'

I could hear a deep breath at the other end.

'Straight?'

'Yes. It's about Barclay.'

'Ah.'

'Yes, "ah" indeed.'

'You've talked to him?'

'Not about what you said, no. But I can't get your 'Please don't get hurt, Claire' and 'he's dangerous, Claire' out of my head and it's fucking me up, keeping me awake. It's seriously … fucking me up, Tom.' He could hear I was close to tears.

'Sorry.'

'Dangerous how? Hurt how?'

'I'm just warning you. All I can tell you is that…' he paused, hesitant, as if he was about to talk before thinking. 'Look, Claire, this isn't easy, I shouldn't tell you anything, shouldn't have mentioned it.'

'Tough. Too late. You did.' Serious Claire was a serious bitch.

'He ... Barclay … he's involved in the investigation I'm working on, he's heavily involved, and it's highly confidential. I wish I'd not mentioned it.

'But you did.'

'Yes, I did. Not my finest hour. But I don't want to see you hurt.'

'Hurt how?'

'I can't tell you. It's not nice.'

My heart felt leaden. 'Drugs?'

'God no. At least I don't think so.'

'So not drugs. Does it involve animals? Dogs?'

'What? Dogs? Why dogs? What makes you think…'

'Okay, so forget the dogs thing. So if you're involved it's a hacking webby internet thing.'

'That's part of it but I'm not the best person to talk to about this…'

'So who is?'

'Barclay. You need to find out from him what he's up to, get it from him. Leave me out of it. Make your own decisions.'

'You want me to be an informer?' I shouted.

'God no. But I want you to be informed, to know what you've gotten yourself into.'

'But you won't tell me?'

'I can't tell you. And please don't mention to Barclay that you know me. That would get me into trouble with my superiors if it got out.'

'Does he know you? Have you met?'

'He doesn't know as much as he thinks he does. Talk to him. I'm not important.'

'But I'm asking you.'

'But I can't…'

'So if you can't, you shouldn't have said anything. He's my

boss. He pays my wages. I need the money for Mum. And he clothes and feeds my imaginary children, cares for my fictional ailing grandmother in her fictional convalescence home, he … I need him, Tom!'

'Sorry but…'

'Don't 'sorry but' me, Tom, I need more than 'sorry but' and a vague warning.'

'It's unpleasant,' he whispered. 'Blackmail.'

'What?'

'He's blackmailing people. Dangerous people.'

'Blackmail? Over what?' I was faltering.

'Like I said, I can't share the details. It's not good.'

Blackmail? Suddenly it all made some kind of sense, it explained the untraceable bundles of second hand cash, the nervous pick-ups, the need for a fast getaway in case of … what? Police? Vigilantes or…

'I'm not fucking about, Claire, he's playing a dangerous game. People are unhappy. It won't end pretty.'

'Well, maybe people shouldn't have done whatever people did to make them so blackmailable.'

'Sure, there's maybe some truth in that, but it doesn't make what your Barclay is doing acceptable or right.'

'Very much depends. And he's not 'my Barclay'.'

'But you are 'his Claire'.'

'Only for work.'

'That's as may be, but it's still something you should end now. He's an extortionist, Claire. And if you're an accomplice, that's a custodial sentence if you're caught. When you're caught. And that's assuming it's us that catches him and not one of his targets or victims or whatever he calls them. These people aren't happy and I don't know how far they'll go to sort this and Barclay out. It never ends well for someone like Barclay and he'll drag you down with him. Steer clear, Claire.'

Easier said than done. (And not that easily said, come to that.)

My moral high ground was starting to crumble beneath my feet. Tom was caring, looking out for me with kindness and concern and I was arguing with him like the heartless, amoral monster I appeared to have become. I needed to calm down, think this through. I needed time.

My silence wasn't welcome.

'Let's talk about it later,' he suggested. 'We still on?'

'I guess so' I said, almost under my breath. Lost for something to say I said, 'Mum's not well.' It came out of nowhere, a play for sympathy to signal the departure of Serious Claire.

'Oh Claire, I'm sorry.'

'Dad says she's showing all the signs again, forgetting things that happened just hours before, not making sense. There've been a few falls…' I was close to tears again – suddenly saying it aloud brought the latent emotion to the surface that caught in my throat and took me by surprise.

'Oh Claire…'

'So I need the money… I need Barclay.'

'No you don't, Claire. You're better than that. Better than him.'

'Maybe I'm not,' I said, and hung up the phone.

Blackmail? So bloody obvious really. I suppose it could be worse.

I'd have been more worried if it was drugs or something that was hurting people or robbing the poor, but as crime goes blackmail isn't all that bad. For a start, it can only happen if the blackmail-ee has done something really bad and naughty that they're ashamed of to be blackmailed over. If anything, it's almost like a middle man operation, Barclay finds someone getting away with whatever and makes a few quid that they'd rather pay him than pay a judge or do the time behind bars.

Barclay, judge and jury, though. That logic had more than a hint of vigilantism about it? But it's a crime based on shame, I tried to convince myself, so if they have nothing to be ashamed of, there's no crime.

I wasn't assuring anyone, least of all myself. I needed to find out more. I needed to talk to Barclay.

'Claire? Pick me up at noon. I have an …'

'No.'

'... appointment with an associate who...I'm sorry, what did you say?'

'I said 'no', Barclay.'

'What do you mean, 'no'?'

'I mean 'no, I will not pick you up at midday or ever again come to that unless you tell me what the fuck your game is.'

He paused. 'I take it you didn't sleep well?'

'I slept fine thanks. Stop playing games with me Barclay, I need to know what you do, what we're doing. And don't give me any that 'best you don't ask any questions' shit.'

'Ah.'

'Does Thug Number Two know?'

'He doesn't ask questions.'

'He doesn't say anything, so that hardly counts.'

'True. Okay, Claire, so let me try this again. Pick me up at noon and I will answer your questions.'

'That's more like it.'

'And what do you think it is I do?'

'I think it's blackmail.'

He paused for a second that felt like a minute, and then said 'smart girl,' and the phone went dead.

'So I'm right, it's blackmail, is it?' I saw no point beating around the bush as he climbed into the ridiculously inflated Fiat.

'What's blackmail?' he said, combing his hair with his fingers. 'Nice to see you, by the way.'

'Blackmail. You blackmail guys for vast quantities of cash.'

'So?'

'So...why didn't you tell me?'

'The less you know the safer for you.' He was smiling. 'Are you going to try blackmailing me over the fact that I am a blackmailer? Ooh, the irony.'

I remembered how he gathered all those details about me from the web when we first met and realised that he had resources beyond the ken of luddites like myself.

'What do you blackmail them about?' I asked.

‘Pretty much whatever they have to offer,’ he said.

‘Such as?’

‘Financial improprieties. Affairs. Non-mainstream sexual preferences. Illegitimate offspring. You would be amazed how easy it is to find once your control someone’s computer or phone.’

‘And that’s what you do? Hack them?’

‘Pretty much. Ever heard of phishing?’

Even I knew what that was. ‘People opening a dodgy link in an email?’

‘Exactly. Or a tweet or text or anything else. People are stupid, you know. No matter how many stories they hear or how many times they are told, they still do it without a thought. They deserve everything they get.’

‘And you don’t draw a line?’

‘No two are alike, each target is different. Unique. And so are the principles I apply. I do have a moral code, but it’s …’ he hunted for the word, ‘flexible.’

‘So the guy last time for example,’ I ventured, meaning Tom Thomas. ‘What had he done?’

‘That one was slightly confused...’

I was desperate to know more but didn’t want to alert him to my interest in Tom so I let it lie.

‘One I’m currently working on is quite different though,’ said Barclay. ‘A young married schoolteacher having an affair with a 15-year-old boy. I will not be needing the services of Thug Number Two for that one: she should be fairly compliant.’

‘She’s a ‘she’?’ I was surprised. To date the targets had all been men.

‘Yes. Newly married but still carrying on with him. Husband a City millionaire, her career would be on the line. She’s already agreed ten k for me to keep that one from her husband and school.’

‘And what guarantee does she have that you will do that?’

‘Why wouldn’t I?’

‘So she just has to trust you, a blackmailing stranger?’

‘Basically, yes. But what you may find surprising is they

actually do trust me, and, unless I find them a particularly irksome individual, I am good for that promise of it being a one-off demand. Maybe they find some odd comfort in knowing that their secret is out there, albeit just with me, and it acts as some kind of release for them. I don't know.'

'So you never go back? Unless you need more money I suppose.'

'Why take the risk? They just want me out of their lives and I'm not greedy by nature, everything's small scale, below the police radar. Occasionally, if I get a sense that they may try to resist, I have to involve additional assistance.'

'Such as your rather over-developed thug of a friend?' I asked.

'Yes, he is quite the charmer, isn't he? Depends on the target. I'm not the most intimidating chap, hence I sometimes have to call for Number Two.

'And what if they don't pay up?'

'Like I say, sometimes I have to call Number Two. But he's all bark and no bite – I don't think I've ever seen him actually hit anybody. He's not the violent type.'

It all sounded too easy. Too innocent. Surely there was something in this that didn't make sense otherwise everyone would be at it.

But I couldn't think of it. It looked like he had thought it all through, had all the bases covered. It may not be legal but as these kind of things go, it seemed pretty fool proof.

'Why me? Why did you rope me into this?'

'Pure chance. I would have left it with the bag but when I looked into your details there was something about you that suggested you would be interested in something a little more exciting, perhaps more dangerous than some duller than dishwater office job.'

He was right there. 'And you didn't leave the bag to entrap me?'

Barclay smiled. 'No, like I say, it was pure good fortune on my part. I did not deliberately entrap you, Claire. That would have been naughty. I met you. I liked you. I saw opportunities. I sensed a wildness that I could use.'

I smiled. My closeted Bohemian side liked the idea of being regarded as 'wild'.

'Besides,' he continued. 'Even I would not leave such an expensive and dangerous item just lying around for any Thomas, Richard or Harold to pick up, would I?'

I guessed not. Barclay was, for once, being surprisingly honest and open.

'So who's this associate you're off to meet?' I asked.

'Change of plan. I'll skip that. Look, seeing as you're getting cold feet, why don't I show you first hand the kind of individual I'm talking about?'

It was all getting too real, but he was so convincing, so involving, so goddamned logical, I was in deep and thrilled by the danger, the illegality of it all and Barclay's curious take on moral justice.

Tom was wrong. He should go after the real criminals. This was different. Personal. Besides, it was simply too late for me to step off the Barclay merry-go-round.

Chapter 19

'That's the guy?' I pointed at a short, overweight City-type, smart in his pinstripe suit, pale blue shirt and woven tie. He didn't give an immediate impression of being a likely blackmail victim, but then who did? Even from a distance he didn't look like the kind of guy I'd trust with my money.

'Don't point,' said Barclay. 'It is rude, you know. Did your parents not teach you that? Besides, it may give us away.'

We were sitting outside a Costa in a quieter part of Docklands, away from the upmarket shopping arcade and its lunchtime heaving throngs of already-exhausted office workers. It was mild for January but not mild enough to be comfortably seated outdoors. I was wearing too light a jacket for the time of year that needed an additional layer or two underneath it to stop my teeth chattering.

Barclay had surprised me by lighting a cigarette but had not been smoking it, just letting it rest between his fingers.

'I didn't know you smoked.' I said.

'I don't. But why else would we be sitting outside when there are plenty of empty seats inside?'

'Clever.'

'Thank you.'

'And that's him?'

'Yes. Queues for his sandwich every day at that little Italian place. Every lunchtime the same routine, even the same lunch – chicken escalope and salad in a ciabatta roll. You would have thought he would be a few sizes bigger as a result but he's quite trim, considering.'

'Predictable chap. So what do you know about him? What's he done bad?'

Barclay stirred a sugar into his macchiato. 'His name is Anthony Bartholomew. He's fifty-nine years' old and is a senior director at one of the major trading houses around here. Which particular one is irrelevant to what we are doing, but they're a household name even if he isn't. He would be though, if what I have on him ever became public knowledge.'

'Dirty is he?'

'Unbelievable. He's been creaming off the top, bottom and sides of almost every business relationship he's had for years. No single big take, just a plethora of just-below-visibility dips into the swill. When all added together it runs to millions, tens of millions even. He is one of those I have absolutely no remorse for; he already earns more than he could ever possibly spend in a single lifetime, several in fact, and yet he still has the greed to take more and thinks nothing of the consequences of his actions. He has no scruples over what he dabbles in as long as it lines his pockets. He's traded arms with terrorists, committed financial fraud on a global scale, many of his clients, friends even, have gone to the wall because of his actions, yet there's no regret or remorse on his part. He's very clever, he would be the last any of them would suspect but I got him.'

'How did you find him?'

Barclay hesitated before replying. 'I was put onto him by someone I know. Initially we were looking at someone else but that one turned out to be of no use. Then we saw that Bartholomew was involved in a few of his larger transactions, acting as an 'advisor'. I hacked into his personal laptop and looked a little closer. He's so clever yet so dumb – his password was just 'password1'.'

I laughed, making a mental note to change my laptop's password when I got home, from something that was awfully similar to something that wasn't. Barclay continued:

'And I saw that this advisor role consultancy was off his company's books, very much off-the-record pieces of work. It wasn't the day rate that he was charging that alerted me – that was pretty modest in the banking game – but the travel and expenses he was passing through. Tens of thousands without receipts or an audit trail. So I dug a little deeper and found that it was the tip of the proverbial iceberg. Expenses fraud that would make even an MP blush. By my estimate he draws over three million a year through this additional income.'

'Wow.'

'Oh, that's pretty small in the circles Bartholomew mixes

in – you wouldn't believe the bonuses they get just for turning up to an office three or four days a week.' Barclay pushed over his phone to me which displayed a small spreadsheet with some very large numbers on it. 'That's his additional income for last year. He won't be paying tax on it as it's undeclared, its privacy secured by his friendship with clients. He harvests broadly – think of paying a builder cash in hand, we all do it if asked, small amounts, where's the harm? – but if you add it all up it soon takes on a different dimension. That's thousands by the way.'

Oh. My. God. The numbers were dizzying. I sipped my flat white: suddenly Costa coffee didn't seem quite the extravagance I'd previously regarded it as. The money involved was astronomical. I think it was fair to say that I was not feeling any sympathy for this guy.

'And how easy was it to get him?'

'He was easy. He does everything on his laptop and smartphone but never updates the software on it – it's wide open, easy pickings. Spends a fortune on cars but has the cheapest, most vulnerable technology you can imagine. I just phished him, and once he clicked the link I was in and I had everything I needed. He's a dangerous thief, ruins lives. Deserves to be stung.'

'How much for?'

'He's in a different league from the business I usually do. I normally keep it small, a few thousand here, a few there, below the authorities' radar and nothing that's going to bankrupt anyone. No point in being greedy. 100k. Small change to him, but he'll be nervous about the drop. When we … I made the demand he offered to do a bank transfer – a bloody bank transfer! Does he think I'm stupid? Always cash and always in person.'

'There's no danger of him getting someone else to do the drop, someone we should be scared of?'

'I doubt that very much, he's not going to involve anyone else. We'll have Number Two along just as a precaution. I do undertake a full and extensive background check on targets before I put in the first call – I've never been wrong in the past. Nearest to that was the guy with the dog. I should have seen that he takes the bloody mutt everywhere, can't leave it on its own or it would tear up his furniture. I won't make that mistake again.'

Bartholomew had reached the front of the shuffling queue and had collected his sandwich. He didn't look any different from the dozens of other suited gents quietly milling around the small parade of lunchtime eateries amongst the towering glass edifices of Docklands. Who would have thought, eh?

'So what time tonight?'

'Pick me up at 1am, I'll have Number Two already, and we're not going far from home ground.'

'Good,' I said. 'I'd still like to get more involved if you need me.'

He smiled. 'I'd appreciate that. I think we're a good team, Claire, and I'm glad you are a little more comfortable with what we do. I was cautious about involving another person but this feels good and you're right, I should have told you earlier.'

I smiled back. Now that he'd been open and I knew what was going on in detail I was more at ease and happy. He was a bright man, had thought of every angle, every nuance, every possibility. It seemed so simple.

I couldn't imagine anything going wrong.

As I put my key in the door I heard laughter from within, then two familiar voices loudly entwined. Dawn and …

'Henry?' I gasped.

'Hi there!'

My Ex was sitting there at the kitchen table, a mug of tea, that wretched old mug of his, I noted, steaming in his hands.

'You're back?'

'Yep.'

'Already?'

'Yep.'

'That was…quick,' I observed needlessly.

'Turned out I'm too sensitive a soul for the first-hand experience,' he was beaming, like it had all been a big joke.

'And now I'm back.'

'So I see.' I pulled out the spare chair from around the table and sat with a bump.

'Tea?' asked Dawn. 'The kettle's just boiled.'

'Yes. Thanks.' It was taking a few seconds to get my head around this. I thought I'd seen the last of him.

'Yes, I was explaining to Dawn who I was and where I've been,' he didn't appear to be capable of stopping the grin and nodded to the younger Barclay who looked demurely to her lap – was it my imagination or was there something between these two? Surely not.

'You never told me much about Henry,' said Dawn.

'I didn't see the need to be honest. I thought he was confined to history,' I said.

'As if,' said Henry. 'You can't keep a good man down.'

'Or a boring one, apparently.' I wasn't buying that 'all friends again' crap.

'It's nice to see you too, Claire. You look well. Dawn was telling me that you've got a new job.'

'I've got new work, I wouldn't call it a job. You couldn't cut it in India then?'

He shrugged. 'Not my thing. I'm more useful here I think.'

'Couldn't stomach the poverty and distress up close? Too painful for you?'

Looking down he shook his head. 'It's difficult. More difficult than I thought I'd find it. I've seen things…'

'You were only there a few weeks.'

'It felt like forever.'

'I'm sure it did. What did you expect?'

'Look, it's easy to sit here and criticise from wintry Deptford but…'

'I don't want to hear it, Henry. I'm not interested.'

'I am,' said Dawn. I wasn't mistaken. She was looking at him with something somewhere between fascination and adoration. What had happened between them this morning? Had I misjudged her? Him? Was this a 'love at first sight' thing going on? In my kitchen? Ridiculous.

He smiled at her – he always lapped up any female attention going and certainly wasn't getting it from me. It was more cloying than touching.

'Nice of you to drop by,' I bit.

'I thought you might be happy to see me. But sadly it appears I was wrong. I'd forgotten to take my favourite mug.' He held it aloft for my benefit.

'You're lucky I didn't bin it.'

'I recall it was you who bought it.'

Not exactly. It was something I'd stolen from the office from the IT guy. 'Have you tried turning it off and on again?' it asked on one side. 'Have you tried fucking off?' it answered on the other.

'Yeah,' I sighed.

He took a final, noisy slurp and rose to leave.

'So I'll pick you up tonight at seven? he asked Dawn.

What?

'Great. See you then,' she said.

Huh?

'Nice to see you again, Claire. I hope the new work goes well.'

I shook my head as if it would get him out of my hair sooner. 'Bye!' I managed.

He was gone. Dawn was grinning. I raised my eyebrows.

'Wow. He's nice,' she swooned. I was beginning to feel nauseous.

'Maybe at first. Seriously? Him? Henry? Where did that come from?' I was shaking my head. 'I should have warned you, should have said something.'

'He turned up whilst you were out. Had a key but still knocked first. Very polite. Quite a gentleman.'

'Him? You'll learn.'

She laughed. 'Well you can't blame me for trying, surely?'

'I don't know why I'm so surprised that I'm surprised. The Barclays are constantly surprising me.'

'It's a family thing, it's what we do. Anyway, Henry's taking me out for a drink tonight.'

'I gathered. Take a good book with you. I give it an hour before you tire of his preaching. Don't bother to set the box to record that film tonight – you'll be home before nine.'

Dawn laughed. 'We'll see,' she said. 'Don't wait up.'

But I knew better.

Chapter 20

I had been wrong. When I pulled away in the Multipla from my building at 1am the next morning there was still no sign of Dawn coming home. I found it oddly unsettling that she seemed genuinely happy with the man I had so easily brushed out of my life just a few weeks earlier. Had I misjudged him or was she not quite the girl I'd thought she was? Maybe she was just too young to know better? Perhaps I should introduce her to TNT. He might be even more her type.

It's not as if my own love life was anything to boast about. My evening reunion with Tom proved a frosty, short lived encounter. Our earlier phone call had clearly unsettled him as much as it had me, and after ordering a couple of bottles of Peroni he was fishing for an excuse to leave early.

'Do you mind if we skip dinner? I've got a lot of work to catch up on. The investigation has been busy and ...'

'Let's not talk about him,' I said.

'Did you talk to him?'

'Let's not talk about him or me.'

'Oh. Okay then.' He couldn't look me in the eye. I couldn't look at him, either. The whole evening had been a mistake, and I'd committed to picking up Barclay and TNT for the Bartholomew job in a few hours.

'I'm not feeling too good,' I lied. 'Can we call it an early night?'

'Sure. Sorry you're not so good.'

God, what a painful mistake the evening had proven. It was supposed to have been a joyous, passionate reunion, but Barclay had come between us and it felt more like a wake for our relationship. The conversation stuttered, stumbled and died, and we left and went our separate ways without even touching once. Broken? It sure felt broken, fragile at best.

But there was little time to dwell on it – time for work. I had to go and collect my colleagues and we were going to get that dirty embezzling fat bastard and extract a ridiculous amount of loose cash from his greedy porky paws.

When I got to Barclay's TNT was already there. At least from a distance I think it was him – it may have been an abandoned overfilled skip.

'Hiya,' I said as Barclay wrestled with the seat belt. 'How are you doing, Number Two?'

Not even a grunt back. I wasn't going to take it personally. He didn't bother with a seatbelt – it's not like he would have bounced around the interior in an accident, jammed in as he was.

I pushed the gear stick into first and we moved off. The traffic was light almost to the point of non-existent and Barclay directed me west into the labyrinth of dual carriageways and roundabouts that form the East India Dock area, brightly lit by the orange streetlights but bereft of any signs of life. So this is what London will look like after the zombie apocalypse.

I was having trouble with the car's gearbox – shifting down to second seemed to be stiffer, jerking and loudly protesting its discomfort when I slowed for corners.

'Wasn't like that the other night,' I said. 'Can't seem to make it any smoother. The clutch feels like it's hardly working.'

'That's not good,' muttered Barclay. He seemed pre-occupied, nervous even.

Nothing from TNT. In the mirror I could see him gazing transfixed at the bright signs atop the Docklands banks and business towers, like a child with the Oxford Street Christmas lights. I half expected him to coo 'Oooh, pretty' but it wasn't happening. At least, it wasn't happening outside his head.

Pity.

'Next left, then a right, then a left,' directed Barclay. 'Right, then left and a sharp left, right and right at the roundabout.'

'Aren't we going to end up back where we started?' I asked, only half joking. This wasn't looking like a straightforward exit route and it was making me nervous. What's more, as we moved from the main thoroughfares into the side streets the lights were further apart and it was getting harder to tell the turnings from the warehouse entrances. I had no idea where we were or how we'd get out in a hurry. It was not feeling good. My stomach was suddenly prickling with nerves.

'Almost there,' said Barclay.

'Did he pick this place or you?' I asked.

'I did, although I have to admit it was easier to navigate on Google Maps than it is in real life at this late hour. Just to the right up here.' He pointed to an entrance to a parking area with a broken barrier. 'Dimly lit' didn't do it justice – there were no streetlights and it was unnaturally dark, countryside blackness in the heart of the new City. The concrete surface was badly pot holed and the Multipla's suspension tackled them with the grace and finesse of a stampeding blind elephant.

'Steady there,' said Barclay.

'Sorry,' I apologised.

I pulled up and dowsed the lights. Not a sign of life. I could just see the dock waters through two dark warehouses, high tide by the look of things, the wind whipping up small, tame crested peaks.

'Okay, Number Two. We're going to wait for him over there under that light.' It was about fifty yards away and was pretty much the only light in the immediate area, hanging off a broken wooden sign that had promised 'Fresh Fruit and Vegetables' in better times.

TNT eased out of the three rear seats, the Multipla's suspension bouncing in joyful relief as his feet hit terra firma.

'Ten minutes. Tops,' said Barclay. It was becoming his catchphrase. It had yet to prove an accurate estimate.

They walked over together to the distant glow, their silhouettes vaguely resembling a diminutive zookeeper taking a giant silverback gorilla for a walk. They reached the spot and Barclay waved. I waved back, involuntarily, forgetting he couldn't see me with the car's lights off.

It was quiet, deadly quiet. We'd driven far enough away from civilisation that there wasn't even any distant traffic to disturb the peace. I wound down my window (electric – the Multipla was an improvement on some of the Uno's more dated 'features') and a cold wind reminded me of the season.

Brrrr. Back up it went. Whatever I was about to witness could play out as a silent movie.

This was actually going to be the first time I'd actually seen a pick-up – I'd always been stuck 'round the corner' or 'out the back'. The dream team were quite a distance away and Barclay must have figured it wouldn't be a risk for the car to be in plain sight as it was too dark and distant to make out our getaway car, even one as distinctive as the Multipla.

Lights suddenly appeared around a corner and a second car, a hatchback appeared. It was being driven cautiously, nervously and the driver had just the sidelights on as he approached Barclay and TNT. Barclay raised his gloved hand and waved. All seemed to be going to plan.

Suddenly the car roared and accelerated directly at them, tyres screeching, the headlights blazing on full beam, blinding them with their dazzling brilliance. Instantly the hatchback was on them. Barclay threw himself towards the warehouse with startling agility but TNT was clumsier, slower, too slow, and the speeding car caught him side on. He span, pirouetting with surprising grace as the car swerved, then corrected itself and accelerated away, killing its lights and back into the darkness.

Shit. Fuck shitty fuck.

I needed to stay calm. I turned the ignition, put the lights on and drove rapidly over to Barclay and his fallen comrade.

This wasn't in the script. Someone had torn up Barclay's perfect plan.

Both of them were still lying on the hard, uneven concrete. Barclay was attempting to pick himself up, dazed and hurt, but it looked like he would live.

TNT was motionless, almost as tall horizontal as he had been vertical. His eyes fluttered briefly before closing. There was a dark puddle appeared to be growing under his head. His short legs were lying at odd angles. Not 'funny' odd though, 'badly broken' odd.

'Fuck,' I said, clambering out of the car.

'Fuck,' said Barclay.

That seemed to pretty much sum things up.

I'm no doctor, but I knew who was in more trouble there. I knelt by TNT and could see he needed help, serious help, nothing my fundamental First Responder skills could handle. Even unconscious he was an awesome sight up close, still surprisingly intimidating for one possibly no longer with us.

Barclay stood at my shoulder.

'Fuck,' he said. 'He looks pretty fucked. Let's try and move him.'

I gave Barclay my most withering look. 'Are you serious? Move him? Us? What's he weigh, thirty, thirty-five stone? Move him?'

'Yeah, maybe. Sorry. Not thinking straight. He doesn't look good.'

'No he fucking doesn't. That's blood, isn't it?' In the near darkness the puddle under his head was black and sticky looking, and it was definitely expanding. 'Probably best we don't move him, actually.'

'Yes. Good point. Fuck.' Barclay pulled his phone out. 'I'll call an … shit, no signal. Fuck.'

I got my phone out and found one bar. Sometimes I loved my Nokia more than words could say. I pressed the Emergency fast dial button.

'Hello? Ambulance. Emergency. Hit and run incident,' I sounded remarkably calm, considering. 'Sorry, what?' I looked at Barclay. 'Where exactly are we?'

He gave me the address of the nearest building which I passed on to the operator. 'Ten minutes. Okay. Yes, of course.' I hung up. 'They want us to stay with him.'

'We can't,' said Barclay.

'What? We can't leave him here!'

'How do we explain what we were doing here?'

'We have five minutes to think of a bloody good lie. You can do that Barclay, surely?'

'What good do we do by staying? He's down. Man down. We can't do anything for him. Best leave it to the professionals.'

'What if they miss him, don't find him?

'Even flat out he's unmissable. They'll find him. Get the

torch or warning thing out the back of the car.'

Without thinking I followed his instruction and went to the Multipla's rear door. In there was a plastic traffic red triangle for use in accidents on motorways and, now, for alerting police after a hit and run on a pick-up. I brought it over to our fallen comrade.

'They won't be able to miss seeing that,' said Barclay. He seemed to be calming whereas I was feeling panic rising. 'We can leave him.'

'I'm...I'm not comfortable with that.'

'Okay. You stay. He's your boyfriend and you got lost walking back from a club. That's easier to explain than if there's three of us.'

'My boyfriend?'

'It'll work. Trust me.'

'But I don't even know his real name!'

'He's just picked you up at the club. You're an easy pull.'

'What?'

'Say anything. It'll work. Trust me.'

'I'm not doing this.'

'Then we go. Your choice.'

My panic levels were rising into the red zone. I looked at TNT. Still no movement. My mind was racing, couldn't think straight.

'Okay. I'll stay. You go,' I said.

'Good girl.'

'Okay. Okay. I'll be okay,' I muttered to myself, not convinced.

Barclay quickly climbed into the Multipla. 'You call me as soon as you can.'

'Yes. Sure.' My voice had shrunk like my confidence. 'I'm doing the right thing, the good thing.' Barclay climbed into the Uno and drove off. Illegally, but that was the least of our concerns right then.

I knelt again by Number Two, bravely brushing his cheek with the back of my fingers. He was still breathing but it was shallow and almost imperceptible.

'Stay still, Number Two,' I whispered. 'Help is on its way. You'll be okay, it's just a little knock. It's all going to be okay.'

But I wasn't convinced, and when the tears came I was crying both for him and me.

Chapter 21

Well, that sure went to hell in a hurry. I wanted out.

I tried calling Barclay when the ambulance had arrived, just minutes after he'd departed the scene. No luck. I was probably too generous in assuming that he was still out of signal. Bastard.

The ambulance crew were fast but there were only two of them and they immediately called for further assistance once they'd assessed the situation. Moving the unmovable was a challenge beyond the two strapping young chaps, I was told. TNT was all muscle, heavy muscle. They'd need a small army to move him.

They asked me to step away and leave them to it, which I willingly did. I thought of mentioning my First Responder course but decided against it – there was nothing I could help with.

The police arrived ten minutes later and I stuck to Barclay's hastily concocted story. I was shaking, partly due to the cold, more likely in shock and the adrenaline. The police and crew were gentle with me, caring even.

'Which club did you say you were at?' asked the policewoman who had introduced herself as Joan.

'I don't know. It's over there somewhere.' I waved vaguely in the direction Barclay had indicated. 'We were lost. I'm not sure.'

'And you don't know his name?'

'He said…' think girl, quick. 'Derek.' Ridiculous. TNT was no more a 'Derek' than I was.

'No surname?'

'I don't recall. Sorry. I'm not thinking straight. I had a few Breezers and it's all muddled.'

'Understandable, Miss. I'll slow down. And you didn't see the car?'

'It was very fast and the headlights were really bright. I don't even know what type it was. I'm not very good with cars. Small. Smaller than…Derek.'

She scrawled something on her notepad, angling it to try to

catch enough light from the police car's headlights to write by.

'Is he going to be okay?' I asked.

'Probably too early to say. He's breathing and they've staunched the bleeding from his head. They're trying to figure out how to move him.'

There were now five figures clad in luminous yellow safety coats gathered around TNT discussing the logistics of lifting him.

'I'm not judging you, but he…he is a big fella.' Policewoman Joan was stating the bleeding obvious. She'd made me a cup of instant coffee, primed with about a dozen sugars. It tasted good. Anything would have.

'I like them big,' I lied. 'He makes me feel… safe.' Which was less of a lie. But not safe enough, apparently. Joan nodded.

She took a few more of my details and said I could go. 'Can I have a lift?' I asked.

'Is there no one you can call?'

'I'll try. But it's late. What if he's not answering?'

'Try him first. We'll be here a while and you probably need to get safely home. Bit nippy, isn't it.'

More in hope than in expectation I made one last attempt and called Barclay. He finally answered, but only after it rang for all eternity.

Barclay pulled the Multipla up a good fifty yards from the Police and Ambulance, who had now called for even more reinforcements to try to move 'Derek'. I strode angrily over to the banned driver. He vacated the driver's seat for me. Big of him.

'I take it you don't want to get too close in case they remember you're banned from the wheel?' I bit.

'That's the least of our problems. What did they say? Is he okay?'

'Like you care.' He looked shamefaced and offered no response. I put the car into gear and we pulled away.

'I can't believe you were prepared to leave him there,' I eventually said, almost too angry to speak.

'He knows the risks of this work.' It was lame and indefensible and we both knew it.

'If that had been me, would you have left me?'

'It wasn't you.'

'But if it had been me, would you?'

'Probably not.'

"Probably'? That's not very reassuring.'

'It's better than 'possibly'.' He attempted a smile.

'This isn't a joke, Barclay. I'm serious. If that had been me knocked down, would you have stayed?'

He hesitated before answering. 'Yes. You're different.'

'In what way?'

'You're my responsibility. I got you into this. It's new for you and that's down to me.'

'What if I want out? I didn't sign up for this.'

He didn't respond and we sat in awkward silence as I drove us cautiously back to Barclay's place, his only words a quiet navigation of 'left heres' and 'next rights'.

'What is his real name? The police asked and I said Derek. I'm betting he's not a Derek.'

'No, not a Derek. He's an Hugues.' Barclay pronounced it 'Oog'. 'He's French, you know? I can't pronounce his surname but he'll have fake ID on him for the hospital.'

French? I'd never heard TNT say anything but he didn't look particularly foreign. Mind you, he looked unlike anyone, any*thing* I had ever seen before.

'You think he'll be okay?' I asked.

'What did they say?'

'They said it was difficult to tell and he'd been hit pretty hard. Any one smaller may have been killed instantly.'

'Then he's lucky. I'm lucky – could easily have been me. He pushed me away at the last moment.'

I had been mistaken – it was TNT's reflex reaction that had saved Barclay, not his. Lucky, lucky Barclay. What had he done to make Number Two so loyal?

'Wow.' Under my breath. 'And you would have left him?'

He didn't hear that, or least pretended not to have. 'Wow

indeed. I owe him,' he sighed.

'Let's just pray he's around to know that,' I said.

'Amen.'

The flat was silent when Barclay dropped me off. There was no sign of Dawn or Henry. Good – I don't think I could have coped with the sounds of a noisy first date fumbling from her room.

I stripped and had a shower. I felt dirty and suddenly I was trembling. The shock and emotion quickly returned, bubbled over and I crumpled to my knees, shaking uncontrollably.

Chapter 22

'He's okay,' said Barclay.

'Thank god for that,' I sighed in relief. 'How okay?'

'Well, he's alive but a little bit broken.' Barclay seemed a little broken himself. His usual overpowering self-confidence had seemingly deserted him and I was surprised to still find him shaken by the previous night's events.

'How broken?' I asked, sipping my morning brew. We were always the only customers in Barclay's Docklands café and I was starting to wonder how it kept in business. There was certainly no fear of being overheard there, and the tea was certainly a step up from the sludgy coffee. I still didn't think I'd risk it with the food though.

'Cracked skull, four broken ribs, possibly five, left shoulder and arm, possibly multiple fractures in the left leg but they cannot say for sure until some of the swelling calms down. They said they weren't sure what was swelling and what wasn't.'

'Ouch.'

'Very ouch. It will be a while before they let him out. Hopefully he can get sufficiently well before Interpol catches up with him. That ID he carries won't deceive them for long – the physical description is pretty unmistakable.'

Interpol? I didn't know if that was a joke or not. Neither of us were in a joking mood.

'Were you serious? he asked. 'About wanting out?'

'I was. But I'm not so sure now. It was a heat of the moment thing.'

'I need you with Number Two gone.'

'He's out of action for a while?' I asked.

'He will want to lay low once released, go back to France I expect. He has in the past proved to be a fast healer but I have never seen him taken out like that before before. Months, possibly worse.'

'But they expect him to make a full recovery?' I sounded desperate, desperate for good news, better news at least.

'As far as they can tell. Like I said, they don't know the full extent of his injuries yet.'

'What happened exactly? I couldn't see much from the car – it was too dark and all happened so fast.'

'Someone decided it was a better option to take us out. I told him this was too big, too risky.'

'Told who?'

Barclay didn't answer. There was someone else involved?

'It wasn't Bartholomew driving,' Barclay said. 'Someone else, someone brought in to do the dirty work. Maybe Number Two spooked him. Too big, this was too much.'

I nodded in agreement – TNT had spooked me even when he was lying there unconscious and bleeding.

'Has this happened before? Someone tried to shut you up rather than pay up?'

'No.' Barclay couldn't look at me directly. 'This one was bigger than what I'm normally doing. I told him...'

'Told who? I thought this was just us?'

But he dismissed my questions with a wave.

I tried to lighten the mood; 'I wonder how the other guy is, the hatchback?'

Barclay smiled. 'I'd imagine our friend left quite a dent.'

'I'd be surprised if it was still in one piece.' It hadn't been an entirely one-sided content.

'And how are you?' Barclay suddenly asked. It seemed a genuine question and he made a movement to touch my hand but then withdrew it hastily.

'I'm doing okay.' He wasn't convinced. 'No, really. Bit shaken last night but slept like a log and I'm fine now. All okay.'

'You're a tough one, Claire.'

'I'm going to need to be if there are many more nights like that one.'

'There won't be.'

'Is there anyone else you know who can cover for Number Two until he's mended?' I asked.

'There's no one like Thug Number Two,' he said, stating the obvious.

'Is there a Thug Number Three for emergencies?'

'No.'

'And Number One isn't available?'

'I told you, we don't talk about Thug Number One.' Time to change the record, Claire.

'Dawn went out with Henry last night.' I needed to lighten the mood, get things back to what had been counting as 'normal'.

He raised his eyebrow. 'Henry? Your Ex? He's back from India already?'

'Yes. The wayward worthy one turned up on my doorstep yesterday morning and swept your sister off her size fives. Went off on a date last night when we were out there and hasn't come home yet.'

'The tart,' spat Barclay, without much humour.

'Hey, steady on. That's my new best friend forever you're talking about.'

'And my sister. Well I never. No changing some people.'

'I had no idea she was so … easy, so easily impressed. And still not home yet.'

'Probably eloped. If they come back, charge them both rent and double it.'

'She can handle herself for sure, and Henry is hardly public enemy number one. At worst, he'll bore her to death or worthy her into submission.'

He managed a pained smile.

The conversation slipped away, having pretty much exhausted itself. We still needed recovery time and to reflect on what had happened. Then something bizarre struck me; it appeared that we'd somehow mutated into a conventional couple, comfortable in our shared silences. When did that happen? When had I lost that compelling need to fill every pause and gap in a conversation? It was unnerving to say the least.

'We should go,' suggested Barclay. 'I've got someone to update on last night's episode.'

'Who?'

He shook his head. 'Too big,' he muttered.

Thanks for sharing, Barclay. But I guessed the less I knew, the easier it would be to walk away if I needed to.

By the car he touched my sleeve, a token, uncomfortable attempt at comforting me.

'See you later,' I said, finding it suddenly difficult to look directly into his eyes.

Something may have been happening. I was not sure it was to my liking, not sure it wasn't. I was losing control of my life in so many ways I should have been terrified.

But, somehow, despite everything, I just couldn't let go.

When I returned home I was exhausted, the stress and emotion of the last twelve hours were finally catching up with me and knocking me for six.

And Dawn was back. Finally. Sans Henry, but giddy and giggly like a love-smitten schoolgirl.

'What a night!'

I looked at my watch – it was three in the afternoon. I felt like an over-anxious mother, grateful for her arrival but angry that it had taken so long.

I wasn't sharing her good humour. 'Glad for you. Can we talk about it some other time?'

'What a morning!'

'I'm serious, Dawn. I'm not in the mood.'

'H'okay.' She danced off to the bathroom.

Kids, huh?

Was I angry at her, still confused over Barclay or was it delayed repercussions from the hit and run? Or was there a latent jealous over Henry rising? No, surely not. He was history to me and I'd looked under all the rocks and there was nothing there, not a scrap of emotional residue or longing for the guy. I had wanted a clean break and this one had enjoyed the full power pressure hose treatment. Nothing there. Nothing whatsoever. All gone. Nada.

Honest.

(I was almost convinced.)

*

'Barclay. It's Claire. I've been thinking.' There was no response from him. 'Barclay? You there?'

'Of course. Please share.'

It sounded like I'd called him in the middle of something – I could hear other voices in the background, street noises too.

'Is it a bad time? Can you talk?'

'I can listen.'

'What are you doing?'

'Selling the Fiat.'

'The Uno? Great!'

'No. The Multipla. I'm trading it back for the Uno.'

'What? You're joking?'

I knew he wasn't. Bloody hell. If this carried on I was going to buy my own bloody getaway car.

'You were thinking?'

'What? Oh, yes. Protection – we need a different type of protection now we're without Thug Number … without Hugues.'

'Please don't tell me you are joining a gym… we don't have the time and you won't have the dedication.'

'What do you mean I won't have…anyway, no, I'm not suggesting a gym. Remember how we first met?'

'Yes. My bag.'

'Exactly. And in the bag, the gun. Do you still have it? Can we get another one? Can you teach me how to use one?'

'No.'

'No to what? No you don't have it, no you can't get another, or no you can't teach me?'

'No, I can't teach you. You may recall I'm not very good with guns.'

'So we'll both learn.'

'Claire…are you sure you want to go down this path?'

'Never been surer.'

He sighed. He sounded disappointed, his apprentice was growing up too fast. I was toughening up. We needed to toughen up. He didn't like it? Tough.

'I can't teach you,' he sighed. 'But I know a man who can

teach both of us. One slight concern though…'

'What?'

'He's a little… You may find him quite unbearable.'

It didn't matter to me. I had been proving myself a dab hand in dealing with unusual and difficult men.

Chapter 23

His name was Owen Ward but he said that I could call him 'Wardy'. Apparently that's what everyone did, or that's what he told me. He was around Barclay's age, late twenties, early thirties, not as tall and a little stockier, like he worked out a little but not to the point of obsession. He had dull brown hair with a floppy fringe that was last fashionable in the previous century. It was immediately obvious that he quite fancied himself and thought that women were similarly minded. God's generous gift he was not, but sadly no one had actually told him that to his face.

Or, more likely, he just hadn't been listening.

Barclay had said on the way over to Ward's workshop that they had met at University and had been friends ever since, when it proved mutually beneficial to be so. Ward had stumbled along from one job to another since dropping out of the academic rat race, taking cash in hand whenever it was offered and never staying with anything long enough for it to be classifiable as a career.

After a string of failed business ventures, including one that had burned through his entire, not-inconsiderable family inheritance in a single week of breathtaking commercial incompetence, Ward had hit hard times and was taking whatever was on offer. Currently, he was providing MOT certificates for cars that would fail at legitimate garages, a much needed service in some circles, hence the workshop. I wondered if the Uno had been a recent 'patient' requiring his attention – that would have made so much sense.

Whisper it quietly, but Owen Ward was also building himself quite a reputation in south east London as a guy who could get you what you needed and teach you how to use it, no questions asked, cash not credit if you would be so kind. More importantly, Barclay assured me, he was discreet to the point of appearing disinterested.

Unless you were female.

Which, of course, I am. I thanked Barclay for the warning.

It was after sunset when we got there, a cold, damp and dark late January evening like every other January evening. The workshop was squeezed into a crumbling Southwark railway arch under one of the main rail tracks running from the garden of England into the capital. Either business was particularly bad or Ward had already moved out any cars currently under his dubious inspection. The place had been arranged into a makeshift small firing range with some paper targets pinned onto some loose plaster board on the rear wall some twenty or so feet from where Ward was standing.

'Well, hello there,' he said, smiling and striding towards me, openly leering. He walked passed Barclay, seemingly oblivious to his friend's offered hand of greeting. Ward's attention was already focused.

'Uh, hello,' I said.

'Hi Wardy,' said Barclay, unaccustomed as he was to being completely bypassed. I suspected that the snub was 100% deliberate on Ward's part.

'So you're Claire?'

'Apparently so. Hello, Mr Ward.'

'Wardy.'

'Got it.'

'And you need to learn how to hold and fire my weapon?' He made it sound filthy, pornographic and he hadn't wasted any time getting into a practised routine of less-than-subtle innuendos, that was for sure.

'Both me and Barclay, yes.'

'Well, I'm less interested in Barclay's grip,' he winked. It was like sparring with Graham Norton, but without the laughs. 'He's a lost cause,' said Ward with a smile and slight shake of the head. 'But you I can definitely work with.' I smiled back through clenched teeth. 'Ever worked with guns before?'

'No.'

'Lots to learn then.' He deliberately brushed passed me, too close for comfort. I tried to ensure this didn't become difficult.

'Barclay – are you having a lesson, too?' I asked.

'A refresher may prove useful.'

'Oh, you're staying with us? Pity. From what I recall, you're unteachable,' said Ward.

Barclay looked pained. 'I will accept I can be a challenging student, but nothing a good teacher can't deal with.'

'Touché, brother.' Their banter was neither comfortable nor genuine, and felt as though it was being forced for my benefit. So kind.

Ward went to a drawer and adopted a more professional demeanour. Presumably he assumed I would be back for more personal attention from him later, maybe after Barclay had left.

Sucker. Not a chance in hell.

'I've got Claire the same handgun as you, Barclay.' He put on the dirty worktop a gun identical to the one I had found in Barclay's rucksack.

'It's an a SCCY CPX 9mm, the best-selling handgun in the States, and the Yanks know a fine piece of weaponry when they see one. Every home should have one. Take out those pesky raccoons and immigrants without a second thought.' He formed a childish finger gun with his right hand, actioned as if to fire it like a pre-school cowboy and blew on his 'smoking' forefinger.

Sure, that would impress even me.

'May I hold it?' I asked.

He went wide eyed and smiled, 'With Barclay here?' then feigned disappointment: 'Oh, you mean the gun.'

I rolled my eyes. Barclay was already looking at his phone.

'Hold on, before you touch let me run you through the basics. Gun law I call it. Wardy's Laws. Four golden rules. Barclay! Do pay attention 007.' Barclay couldn't have looked less interested.

'Rule one; always treat the firearm as if it were loaded. Never, ever, even if you are 100% sure it is 100% empty, treat it as if it isn't. Respect the weapon.

Duh.

'Rule two: never fart around with a weapon. Always point it in a safe direction and where it can do no one or nothing no harm. It ain't a toy and accidents easily happen. Think safe.'

I was wondering if he'd mistaken us for a pair of six-year-olds. Barclay was already checking his phone again. I was counting bricks in the ceiling.

Ignoring our wandering attention, Ward continued: 'Rule three. Keep your finger outside the trigger guard until you have made a conscious decision that you are going to shoot. That's why there's a trigger guard. Don't be tempted to rest your itchy forefinger on the trigger.'

Barclay yawned but I resisted the temptation.

'And finally, always look not just at your target but what's beyond it if possible. You don't want to hit a passer-by or shatter a window if you can avoid it, do you? All that nasty paperwork and police time can kill an evening's fun.'

I stifled another yawn and nodded. I could have learned this in five minutes from Google. 100%.

'Got that? Good. Now we can start shooting those bad guys.'

('But aren't we the bad guys?' I asked myself.)

Barclay sighed and took his own pistol from his rucksack, ignoring rules one, two and three immediately by waving it around before pointing it directly at Ward with his finger on the trigger. Ward frowned. 'Barclay…' he said in the weary voice of a teacher who had better things to do with his time.

'Whoops. How careless of me. I really should pay more attention, shouldn't I, Mr Ward? You have me, sir. 100%.'

Ward smiled the tiredest of smiles. Barclay really was the most trying of pupils.

Ward may have been even more condescending than Barclay, but he was thorough, which was welcome if draining. He instructed us how to hold the guns and why a two-handed grip was not just essential for the beginner but also even for an experienced gun hand. It was exactly how you see them do it on the telly, one hand on the gun, the other to steady, the pose familiar from a thousand cop shows. My gun was new, slightly oily, cold and so heavy to my hands. My pose was pure Hollywood, legs slightly apart and arms out rigid. Too rigid for Ward, and I tensed as he moved behind me and made tiny, unnecessary adjustments to my posture just for the thrill of the contact. Creep. 'Relax,' he breathed in my ear. 'Not so tense.' I did the opposite.

But the feel of a real, honest-to-goodness loaded gun in my hands was, I can't pretend otherwise, exhilarating.

'Relax,' he whispered again.

It was a clumsy, unsuccessful seduction, and dangerous for him to persevere with it when I had my hands full of lethal metal.

'Barclay! Stop fucking around!' he barked suddenly, making me jump. Barclay pointed a finger at his chest and pulled his best 'who, me?' look. I'd missed what he'd been doing but I would have put money on it contravening those four rules of gun law again.

Ward turned his attention back to his star pupil. 'Are you ready to fire your first load?' he asked.

It was making me feel nauseous. 'Yep.'

'Right. Aim at that target there and take your time.' I closed my left eye, bit my tongue in concentration and took aim. 'Don't jerk it, take the slack out of the trigger then squeeze, increasing the pressure until …'

Fuck me, that was loud. Echoing around the arched walls of the workshop it deafened us all and had both of them covering their ears but too late to save them. Barclay was shouting something at me but I was momentarily deaf. For seconds I thought I would live forever in a world of silence but slowly my ears adjusted and started to make sense of the world again, sounds edging in around the high pitched whine that would stay with me for the rest of the evening. The recoil and shock from the gun hadn't been as bad as I had expected, but the loud explosion of that first shot was painful.

A greater shock though was when we inspected the target. Wellwadayaknow? Bullseye! Slap bang in the middle of the target, which sadly looked larger close up, deflating my immediate sense of achievement. Ten out of ten. Ward looked genuinely impressed and tried to give me a celebratory hug which I stepped quickly away from.

'Complete fluke,' laughed Barclay.

'Do better,' I challenged.

Ward produced three oversized ear protector muff things

from a cupboard. 'I should have got these out earlier.'

That was true. Barclay lifted his gun and took the pose, we covered our ears and he fired, not just once but four times in rapid succession.

The bullseye was untouched. The entire target was untouched. He had missed an A3 sheet of white paper from ten feet. Four times. Unbelievable.

'You've been practising, Barclay,' joked Ward. 'Last time you had trouble hitting the wall!'

I laughed and Barclay fired me his most withering glare. Ouch. How come he never missed with that?

'I'm tired, tired and bored,' Barclay offered as an excuse that no one was buying.

Even with the ear protectors my head was still ringing, my hearing dipping in and out as if there were child playing with the room's volume control.

But I didn't care. It was thrilling and I wanted to do it again. And again. And again. The purest of pleasure, firing a gun, was the biggest kick I could think of, better than sex, hotter than Chris Hemsworth, better and hotter than sex with Chris Hemsworth, this was intense yet intimate and just pure fucking amazing. More. I needed more.

And so we continued into the night. Me, an apparent natural even when we lowered the lights to better simulate the darkness we were accustomed to in our work. Bullseye after bullseye I hit, shredding the centres of the paper targets and hammering the wall behind like a drill.

Who would have thunk it?

And Barclay? Best we don't discuss his shooting prowess, as he was a sensitive soul despite all his front and bullshit and even he should have his pride respected.

But let me just say, he was absolutely fucking shit.

'That was unexpected,' said Barclay.

We were driving back from Owen Ward's after our evening of shooting the shit out of a workshop wall.

'You thought you would be good at it?' I asked, incredulous.

'I had to make you look good,' he lied, purely for his own benefit. He knew that I knew and I felt a warm glow inside at that fact.

We were back in the Uno, negotiating the potholes and puddles of an unadopted backstreet in the small hours. Street lighting was at a premium around here and the local council didn't think it was a worthwhile expense. I was enjoying the driving and manoeuvred the Italian antique with skilled dexterity that was not going to do my campaign to get a better set of wheels any good. I decided there and then that with the next pay day I would buy us a new car. I had seen a rather nifty looking black Alfa Romeo going for £5k on a car lot the day before and would make my move at daylight. That would surprise him. Fiat begone!

'Your shooting was exceptional,' said Barclay, a rare compliment indeed.

'You really thought so?' I mocked.

'Yes, Claire, I really thought so. And you know so. So let's stop pretending. I think by your sixth round we all figured it wasn't a fluke.'

'Maybe I've finally discovered my true vocation in life.' I was only half-joking. It had felt surprisingly… natural. I'd never been good at anything before. This was genuinely a first.

'Our gain is the British Shooting team's loss.'

I loved it.

'Claire,' said Barclay, snapping me from my daydream of Olympic Gold glory. It was never going to be an easy conversation when he used my name. There was something quite parental about that. 'Claire, are you absolutely sure you are comfortable with this?'

'What do you mean?'

'With us … and guns.'

'I'm not that comfortable with you and a gun, that's for sure,' I joked.

'I'm serious, Claire. This is not a path I expected us to go down.'

'But after Thug Number Two?'

'That was a one-off. I'm sure of it. It was careless and I didn't see it coming. I should have thought it through. We shouldn't have gone for someone like that, shouldn't have asked for so much but he... We will be more careful in future and shouldn't need the guns. Keep it small, like that school teacher I told you about.'

I wasn't convinced. 'We're playing a dangerous game here, Barclay, and it's only as a deterrent. If it hadn't been this one it could have been the next or the one after that. You know that. I know that. We've been naive thinking we could just walk away with the bag of cash every time and there was no risk.'

'A one-off.'

'It's not a one-off though, is it? That time without me when you shot the dog…'

'In the general direction of the dog,' he corrected me.

'Having seen you shoot, I think you aimed at the dog and missed from a yard away. Whatever. You carried a gun before and we can do that again. If you're uncomfortable with that I'll carry the gun and do the bloody pickups and drop offs and what not.'

'I'm not that comfortable with us being armed.'

'Well I'm not at all comfortable with us being unarmed. Especially as we're going to be without TNT for a few months.'

'TNT?'

'Thug Number Two. I think of him as TNT.'

'That's good. Hadn't occurred to me.' Barclay smiled, possibly for the first time in hours.

'So how about you trust me with this and I carry the gun then?'

'Like I say, I'm not happy about that.'

'Neither am I particularly, but I will feel safer.'

'We'll see,' he said. 'There may be other options.'

I seriously doubted it. We drove on but there were no more words, I wasn't going to change my mind, come what may.

The following morning I found a tired-looking Dawn sitting alone at the kitchen table.

'No Henry today?' I asked, making myself a quick coffee from the just boiled kettle.

'No. He didn't stay last night. He said something about feeding the homeless but…'

'But you weren't really listening?'

She sighed and smiled a defeated smile. 'You got it. Boy, how does he do it? Get him on a worthy subject and you can feel your will to live ebbing away with each word!'

I laughed. 'That is so true.'

'I know, I mean he is a good man, a kind man, a caring man but bloody hell, it can all be too much, can't it?'

'You've not even had a week of it,' I said.

'I'm not sure I can last that long. Surely it gets easier?'

I shrugged. They were doomed. End of story. Sad but inevitable, sorry to be the bearer of bad news. Pick yourself up and get yourself a gun. You won't believe the buzz, Dawn.

But that was a conversation maybe for another day. Instead I said: 'Barclay's in a funny mood these days.'

'How so?'

'We had a little accident the other evening and his muscle man got hurt. Barclay's taking it badly.'

'Losing his nerve?'

'It looks like it. I'm coming over as the tough one now.'

'And this guy's okay?'

'Should be, but its broken bones and they will take a while.'

'Oh.'

I was talking about TNT but my every thought was about the gun sitting tucked in my parka pocket upstairs. I was having trouble containing it, bursting to tell. I couldn't resist.

'I've got a gun!' I blurted.

'What? No way! Oh wow.' I couldn't tell if she was excited or scared. Probably a little of both.

'Have you shot anyone with it?' she asked.

'No. Don't be stupid – it's just for protection. But I had lessons last night and get this – I'm really, really good with it. I mean, Olympic medal good!'

She grinned, pleased that I was pleased.

'That's so cool.'

'Isn't it? I had no idea. Top marks. And get this – your brother can't hit a target from ten paces! Five paces even!'

We both laughed.

'Doesn't surprise me. That must have been so funny to see,' Dawn said. 'You should have filmed it – that's why God invented YouTube, you know. I love it when he's embarrassed. Hilarious.'

'It was bloody fantastic,' I said. 'The better I got, the worse he was. Not just laughably bad, hysterically bad. And he couldn't see the funny side of it at all, got more and more sullen. We were killing ourselves!'

'We? Who were you with?'

'An old friend of Barclay's, he was the instructor. Owen Ward.'

Even in through the laughter I could see Dawn shudder at his name.

'Oooh, that creep. I don't like him. Tried to feel me up once. Nasty piece of work. Avoid.'

'I think we agree on that one.' I sipped my coffee. Too cold. 'I'm going to make another – want one?'

'Sure. Thanks.'

And with two mugs of Nestlé's finest, we sat and talked the morning away, setting the world to rights and Best Friends Forever.

My Nokia burst into life just as I was preparing lunch, an unappetising sandwich using ancient dry bread, even older shiny ham and cheese that was putting up a losing battle against the gathering mould.

I saw that it was 'Home' calling. What did Mum want? She only normally called at weekends, we had our routine, Sunday mornings at eleven. Odd.

'Hello?'

'Claire? It's Dad.' I don't think he'd ever called me before. My blood turned cold. He sounded serious.

'Hi Dad. What's up?' I was trying to sound flippant but this felt ominous.

'It's your mother, Claire. She's…she's been taken ill.'

I sat down on the kitchen stool with a bump.

'How ill?' a little voice asked.

'She's had a stroke. She's in hospital.'

Ohmigodohmigodohmigod. I couldn't think, couldn't speak. All noise disappeared from the room except his voice.

'Claire?'

'When?' I murmured, as if knowing details would make a blind bit of difference.

'Yesterday evening. It was very sudden. We've been in A&E all night. She's still there.' He was talking dispassionately, a newsreader on the telly talking about a humanitarian disaster thousands of miles away.

'One minute she was peeling potatoes. The next she was on the floor. Staring. She was just staring.' His recall of the details was un-Dadlike and alarming, as if he'd been taking notes for a memoir.

'I'm coming up,' I said without thinking.

'There's no point Claire. She's being looked after and is comfortable. The doctors sent us away. Paul's at school. I'll go back once I've had a few hours' sleep. Sharon from next door will go with me.'

Sharon may have been Mum's best friend, possibly her only friend outside of family, but Mum needed me.

'I'm still coming.'

'No you're not. She's okay. Not fine, but okay. I know it's hard to hear but there's nothing any of us can do and we just have to give her time to recover.' He was trying to sound as if he had this all under control and was an alpha male assuming his rightful position as head of the clan, but Dad was no alpha male, barely a beta bloke.

'I'm coming.' I was determined.

He sighed, resigned to my resolution and perhaps the recognition that I was heading north not just for Mum but for him, too. And me. This was, of course, mainly about me.

Chapter 24

Google suggested that the journey from London to Edinburgh would take four and three quarter hours. Trainline disagreed and promised four hours twenty minutes. I booked on Trainline, but they both lied.

The journey took an eternity.

Dad's call had hurled me back down to Earth with an unfeeling, vicious bump. A crashing descent, from the thrill and highs of the shooting lesson to the harsh reality of ageing parents and fragile health. I felt empty, shaky, it was impossible to think straight, I just couldn't relax.

Dad was right: there was nothing else I could do, but I had to do something. Morbidly, I tried to recall my last words to Mum, something about the Attenborough show that had been on last week. So meaningless. So trivial. Was that it? Her last words? It sounded like she'd had a stroke. Would she be able to talk? Walk? Feed herself? Would I ever hear her voice again?

My mouth was dry no matter how much of the bottle of Volvic I drank. I stared, bleary-eyed, at the bleak, grey landscapes flashing by. Did the train normally take this long? Surely we were at least halfway there by now?

I checked the time on my phone. Barely an hour gone, not even a quarter of the journey completed. Dad said he'd pick me up from the station but I declined and said I'd get a cab.

I didn't want to put him out. He'd never find anywhere to park, anyway. I just didn't want him to drive.

I had no idea what to expect when I arrived and saw her. Strokes and heart attacks were what happened to other people, not us MacDonalds.

Fuck fuck fuck.

My thoughts blurred with the speeding scenery out the window. I just couldn't focus on anything for more than a second or two.

The rest of the journey dragged by at a snail's pace and I sat numb and dumb, motionless, emotional, still too stunned to move. By the time we pulled in to Waverley I was exhausted.

*

Well, she looked fine. Happy and rested even. She smiled at me from her hospital bed and my heart sang and danced with joy.

But she didn't speak. Just smiled. For that moment, that would be enough. She had a loving smile and I felt as warm and special as I ever had in my life. It was all going to be okay.

The nurse, far too young for such responsibility, was talking but I was catching one word in three.

'Minor. A few weeks. Too early to tell.' Words, just words. Meaningless words.

I took Mum's hand, ignoring the tube and savage needle that had punctured her precious, pale skin, and smiled back.

My eyes were brimming, cold tears running unchecked down my face.

'I'm here, Mum. Claire's here.'

She smiled. Just smiled. Her eyes moist but the recognition all there.

Like I said, that was enough.

Dad drove me back to our house, their home.

'She's not spoken since she fell,' he said, suddenly looking like a broken man. 'She looks okay but they don't know what's going on inside there.' He tapped his head with his free hand.

'Oh.' There was nothing that I could add.

'The doctor said her eyes are sharp and she's recognising us, but she's very sleepy and keeps drifting in and out. You were lucky; Sharon sat with her for hours and Mum just slept through it.

'Is that normal?' I asked.

'I don't know. Probably.'

I nodded. Life for Mum was going to be a series of 'probablies' and 'possiblies' from now on, nothing certain, nothing definite.

'She may have to stay in care for a while they said, depending how things go.' His voice was struggling to contain the emotions and dark thoughts that were best left unspoken.

'She'll be fine, Dad,' I touched his hand and he smiled.

‘God I hope so,’ he whispered, then he too went silent.

Home was cold. Literally and figuratively. Paul had locked himself away in his room and wasn’t interacting with Planet Earth. That was a relief.

I made us our millionth cup of tea and broke open a pack of Digestives for comfort. Mine and his.

‘She’ll be fine,’ I said for the thousandth time.

‘I know,’ he replied for the thousandth.

We weren’t fooling anyone: we knew nothing.

Dad took his mug in both hands and looked on the verge of tears. I’d never seen my father cry before. Not out of sadness. Not out of fear.

‘Claire. If she needs … rehabilitation, professional assistance, would you be able to help me with some money?’

I nodded. ‘Of course,’ I managed, almost a whisper. He was still in shock, struggling to make sense of it all.

‘Thanks.’

We stared at our mugs, too numb to talk further.

Dad had been right. There was little I could there, nothing I could help with. Sharon was ‘popping in’ and sorting out the cooking and cleaning, Mum’s fall giving her suddenly something to fill her empty hours next door, her husband having walked away several months earlier. Mum had always said she was too good for him.

Mum had always said…

‘Dad, I can stay for as long as you need me.’

He straightened on the kitchen chair, pulling his shoulders back momentarily before they slouched again.

‘Thanks love, but I’m fine. We’ll be fine. She’ll be fine. Stay the night but I think you should get back down to The Smoke and that new job of yours tomorrow. All okay with that?’

He always referred to London as ‘The Smoke’; I’ve no idea why. Personally, I found the Scottish city air, especially around Murrayfield where they lived, far dirtier.

‘It’s going fine thanks. Busy. Learning new skills, new stuff.’ Just don’t ask exactly what I’m doing, Dad – we didn’t need a heart attack to the add to the stroke.

'And the money's good?'

'Better, and I can spare some so please don't worry about it. I know it isn't easy but I've got plenty. I want to help.'

'I hope so,' he said. 'I think we'll need to look at moving your mother into a private home. The hospital says she'll be okay to come home in a few days but it will be a long time and I'll need help. Professional help. Sharon's been brilliant but your Mum needs more than that and I think they need the bed back. Bloody cuts.'

'Sure Dad. Whatever it takes.'

'Thank you Claire Bear, you're a godsend.'

'How much exactly will it take?' asked Claire Bear.

'It's expensive.'

I knew it would be. 'How much, Dad, and I can transfer some today?'

He took a sharp intake of breath. 'Ten thousand for a few months' care.'

Christ. My silence spoke volumes I guess, and he quickly followed with: 'Too much?'

'No, that's fine.'

'You sure? I hate to ask but…'

'Don't worry about it Dad. I'll sort it out when I get home.'

'I will do, Claire. And thanks. That's tremendous. One less thing for us to worry about.'

'No worries,' I said, but he could tell that I was lying.

Our conversation stumbled and stuttered on through several more cups of tea and the whole packet of biscuits. What to talk about? We didn't want to talk about Mum or the money and I certainly didn't want to open up about Barclay or Tom Thomas and we had nothing else – any family reminiscences would have been tinged with the uncertainty about the future. After an hour I realised that this is why Dad wanted me not to come – this was almost as hard for him as the stroke that had taken Mum away from him, the realisation that he didn't know me at all and I hardly knew him.

My visit was proving a sad and empty gesture, salving only

my guilt and comforting no one.

The following morning I sat at the breakfast table, the dry toast in my mouth tumbling like laundry, unswallowable. This was doing no one any good.

I headed home, boarding the 9.30 from Waverley Station and back to Barclay.

Chapter 25

It was cold and dark outside, but the atmosphere in the Uno was even colder and darker. I had brought my gun with me and Barclay was not a happy bunny, no sir.

'I thought I told you not to bring that,' he said.

'Not in so many words. You made it clear that you weren't comfortable or happy, but there wasn't a definitive 'no'. Besides, you're not my keeper.'

'I am your employer, your boss.'

'I prefer to think of it as you're the brains of our gang, I'm the more practical one.'

He considered that for a few seconds – I don't think he'd thought of it like that before.

'I do not think you should be armed. It's asking for trouble.'

'And I would be happier with TNT with us. But you can't have everything.'

He said nothing.

We were parked around the back of some abandoned warehouses in the East India docks, the demolition notices suggesting that this was the next target for the insatiable developers' non-stop glass and steel roadshow. We were half an hour early, and Barclay had asked me to park a distance away from the pick-up in case I got ideas with the gun.

As if. Even I would have trouble hitting anything from that distance in the dark.

So we had plenty of time to fill the air with a continuation of the stuttering disagreement about my sudden lust for weaponry.

'It's only the teacher this time. You don't need a gun.' He was sounding like a broken record.

'Ward said I should get comfortable with having it on me at all times.'

'What does he know?'

'He knows enough to be the expert you brought in to teach us,' I snapped.

'But this woman is twenty-five years' old and it's only ten grand. Lunch money to her. She's as timid as they come. She is not going to pose a physical threat whatsoever.'

'If she's in a car she's as dangerous as the guy who hit Number Two.'

'She won't be.'

'Or if she's armed, we should be armed too.'

'Great, the American gun lobby argument. There's the arms race in a nutshell. They may have one so we have to have one.'

Silence. He may have had a point but I wasn't biting.

'I think the guy last time was spooked by Number Two. We won't have that problem again,' Barclay said.

'You're not scary on your own. I'm not exactly terrifying either.'

'You scare me at times, Claire. Not who you are, but what you are becoming.'

So dramatic. I attempted to laugh that off. 'You think I'm out of control? Am I not the monster you were hoping to create, Dr Frankenstein?' I mocked.

He almost smiled. Almost. 'I think your independence and appetite for danger are heading a little out of my comfort zone.'

'Not necessarily a bad thing. Beats complacency hands down.'

'Possibly.'

'Definitely.'

'Probably,' he conceded.

I looked at my watch. Almost time. Just as well, the car was getting colder despite the pathetic efforts of the Fiat's blowers.

'I tell you what, I'll prove you can rely on me to stay calm. I'll do this one.'

'What?'

'Let me do this pick up. Like you say, what's the harm? She's a young teacher at a posh private school for Christ's sake, where's the risk in that? It's ten grand or her career and reputation and marriage and easy life down the pan. She's the easiest pick up we've done and I won't exactly terrify her with my size 10 mega frame, will I?'

He raised an eyebrow. He wasn't convinced.

'It will be fine. I will be fine. Ten minutes, tops.' I winked as

I released the seat belt and opened my door. He shook his head, but knew he was beaten.

'I'll move the car over under that light so you can see it easily when you get back.'

'Keep the engine running,' I said.

'Of course.' He waved and I turned to go, making my way around a high wire fence to the agreed rendezvous point at an old, disused garage just off the main road. Behind me I heard Barclay rev up the Uno's engine and I turned and saw him move it under the street lamp.

I felt pretty pumped up. It felt good. And, more to the point…

I still had my gun in my pocket if I needed it. My TNT-sized worries were a thing of the past.

The pick-up point was around the corner from where Barclay had manoeuvred the car. Fifty yards away stood a desolate, deserted petrol station, a long dormant sign had shouted the Texaco brand in more prosperous times. Now it stood as a sad reminder of how the much-vaunted redevelopment of East London in 2012 had stalled and failed to live up to even its modest promise of regeneration for the area. A streetlight flickered and died, then relit itself only to die again. It just couldn't be bothered and I could understand that; as inspiring landscapes to illuminate, this one left a ridiculous amount to be desired.

Barclay sure could pick 'em.

There was no sign of the teacher. No sign of life at all at first, and then, as if to deliberately prove me wrong, a fox ran up to one of the long-dead pumps. At least, I hoped it was a fox – the rats out this way can grow pretty big I'd been told. I shivered involuntarily. Not a fan of rats. I have a thing about their worm-like tails. Urgggh.

I waited five minutes, hands pressed deep into my coat pockets, seeking warmth but just finding some old crumbs and sweet wrappers. And my gun. My breath formed pale clouds in the cold and I amused myself for what must have been seconds seeing if I could form smoke rings with my mouth.

Don't bother trying it. You can't. It doesn't work. Not for the first time I wondered if I should take up smoking for nights like these.

Suddenly the fox scurried away – something had spooked it. Coming from the opposite direction was a huddled figure, glancing from side to side.

The teacher?

But as she neared I realised that there wasn't just one person but two, the taller's arm wrapped tightly around the shoulder of the smaller. Shit. There was a bag held in the taller person's left hand. Presumably the money. Definitely the teacher, but who was she with?

For the first time that morning I had doubts and I found my hand crawling unbidden to my coat's inner pocket, finding and rubbing the gun's grip for comfort, possibly assurance even.

Not to plan. What would Barclay do? Fuck it up probably, going on his recent efforts. Never mind. I strode purposefully towards them and they didn't back away.

It was the teacher.

I was about twenty feet away from them and could now see a blonde woman, dressed in a thick, dark expensive looking coat with a taller young man, much younger than her that was for sure. Her schoolboy lover? He certainly didn't look like a sixty-year-old City millionaire, that was for sure.

Interesting. I coughed to clear my throat and spoke, my voice startlingly me with its nerveless assurance that broke the night's silence:

'Samantha Fielding?'

She nodded but moved behind the boy for protection. In the darkness he looked mature for his fifteen years, already six foot tall but slender as only teenage boys can be, a bulky puffy jacket giving the impression of a greater bulk but it was his spindly legs in slim fit jeans hanging below that gave away the true slightness of his frame. He looked vaguely absurd, all Uniqlo bulk and teenage un-muscled gangly limbs, the torso of a dark Michelin man balanced precariously on a couple of spindly sticks.

I could take him. Easy. Was this really the best protection she could find? She should mix in lower social circles.

'You were supposed to come alone. That was the arrangement,' I said, short and sharp in my disapproval. Although the words came from my mouth I couldn't believe that was me talking. I was so authoritative. I was just so in command. There was no quivering of nerves in my clear, succinct delivery.

Claire my girl, you're a natural.

Samantha shrank further behind the puffer jacket's protection.

'Sorry.' So quiet I barely heard her.

'We have the money,' said the boyfriend.

'So you did understand the instructions,' I said. 'You just chose to be selective about which ones you followed.'

'You can't expect Samantha to come here alone. No woman would feel safe in a place like this.'

I don't know – I didn't feel particularly threatened myself. I was actually enjoying how this was turning out, truth be told.

'Bring the bag here, please.' I said, then silently cursed myself for the sudden politeness of the 'please' – and I had been doing so well with my tough girl impression. Damn. Concentrate.

He edged forward, the quaking teacher moving with him, still hiding behind his back as if she thought it concealed her from my steely judgement.

'How much?' I asked.

'Ten thousand in tens, as you demanded,' he said.

'Doesn't she talk?' I asked, nodding at the figure cowering behind him.

'We decided that I'd be better at the talking.'

'But you're not supposed to be here, are you?'

'No, but I am. Here's the money.' He dropped the bag on the floor, but it was still too far away for me to reach it. I took a step forward and he put a foot on the bag.

'I thought we should talk first though?'

I straightened. 'Talk? You are not really in a position to make demands, are you? Neither of you. You've seen what we have on you two. Think of the consequences for Samantha if we shared that. There is nothing to talk about. You've been playing naughty, illegal games and these are the naughty, illegal consequences.'

'If you take this, how do we know that you won't call again and ask for more?'

'You don't. But we won't. You already live with the guilt of what you have done. At best you have my word that this is it, a one-off transaction. You won't hear from us again.'

He shook his head. 'I'm sorry, but that's not very reassuring. All we know about you is that you're blackmailers who hacked Sam's phone. That doesn't make you super trustworthy in my book.'

'Then like I said, you don't know. And chances are you will continue to jump with every phone ring or rattle of the letterbox, fearing the worst. But you already do that. Paying us … me … is the only way you have to stop this.'

'Or I could stop you…'

Suddenly he reached into his inside pocket and before I could register his movement he had a gun in his hand. Smaller than mine, it could have been a fake or a starter pistol – I just couldn't tell. But it was a gun nevertheless. Pointed straight at me.

Fuck.

I froze. The teacher shrank away from him. 'Anthony, you said you wouldn't…'

Instinctively I put my hands up. 'Hold on there,' it was almost a whisper, my bravado just about holding on. 'Don't do anything hasty here.' I needed to step this down a notch. I had to think quickly. In a flash of inspiration, I surpassed myself. 'This is all being filmed by my colleague.'

That got him. Confused, he looked quickly around the open dark spaces behind me, searching for the fictional cameraman I'd just invented. Nothing. Nowt. Well, what exactly did he expect? He'd already said I was untrustworthy.

When his nervous gaze returned to me I had my own gun in my hands, pointing straight at him. A classic Tarantino Mexican stand-off.

His pistol was wavering but I held mine firmly in both hands, my left supporting the rock steady right. Legs slightly apart. The perfect firing posture feeling suddenly so natural.

My finger was tellingly already on the trigger. Unlike him I knew exactly what I was doing. I had been trained by a professional. One whole lesson. I was ready. Steady Eddie ready.

'Hold on there,' he managed, echoing my sentiment of just a few seconds earlier. 'We can talk…'

But he fired, more pop than bang, a clumsy mess of a shot, whistling off into the night's darkness, all bark and no bite.

I didn't make the same mistake. I shot straight and true.

Chapter 26

I had aimed at his shoulder but it was the side of his head that exploded. So much for shooting to wound rather than kill. Shit. What would Barclay say? All those assurances I'd given him and I fuck it up at the first hurdle.

So I ran. Ran like I'd never run before in my life. Drop the gun? Keep the gun? My fingers felt welded to its grip. I couldn't let go, the warmth of the metal strangely seductive. I loved that gun. We were inseparable.

Run.

Was she chasing me or seeing to what was left of her fallen lover? I wasn't waiting to find out, didn't even turn to see. I just ran. Arms pumping, cheeks puffing, breath already shortening. Run, girl, run.

I turned left, down the dark alleyway that led round the side of the abandoned warehouse. There were no lights, no paving and I stumbled on the uneven surface but I couldn't stop, I ran as fast as I could, my legs, sides, lungs all protesting at this sudden call to action.

There was the wire fencing a few yards ahead. Could I take it in my stride? From behind I could hear her shout for me to stop. At least she'd stopped screaming. I slipped the gun back into my coat pocket and took the shorter route, jumping at the fencing, surprising myself by getting a firm grip with both hands and hauling myself up like I was on an assault course.

'Stop, bitch!'

'Well that's nice,' I thought as I dropped over the other side, my ankle turning slightly on landing but just a tweak. I could understand she was upset, but there was no need to make it personal. I brushed myself down then started to run again, though every muscle was howling for me to slow down. I was just too out of condition for this running lark. If it hadn't been for the adrenaline surge I'd have been finished already.

I could hear the blood hammering in my ears, felt my lungs close to bursting. Any further and I was sure I would collapse. I turned left around another building and then suddenly there was a pool of light ahead, a single streetlamp picking out the familiar Fiat parked at the roadside.

Had he heard my gun shot? Or was Barclay oblivious to the drama I'd suddenly ignited?

'Barclay!' I attempted to shout as I neared the car, so short of breath I thought I would die.

He saw me and wound the window down.

'All go to plan?' he asked.

'No it…no it fucking didn't.' I fell against the passenger side and wrenched the door open, clambering in.

'Where's the money?'

'What?' Barely able to speak.

'The money. Where's the money?'

'He's dead. I shot him. He's dead. Drive!'

'Fuck.'

He turned the key and the engine coughed into life. Slamming it into first and flooring the accelerator, we shot off, as fast as my beloved Fiat Uno could manage.

'Fuck. Fuck. Fuck.' He was scolding himself, not me, and he muttered curses under his breath like a repentant litany.

There was nothing I could say. What had I done? WHAT HAD I FUCKING DONE?

I think I could safely assume that I was not popular. Barclay's near silence was more menacing and abusive than any emotional volley of derogatory vilification he could have thrown at me. I shrank into the passenger seat, cowering in my shock, cowardice and shame.

He drove surprisingly slowly, but snatched at the gear changes and was late to signal when turning. The roads were surprisingly busy and I was for once grateful for the anonymity of the Uno. His ire was all too apparent. I was furious with myself but I didn't think he'd be sympathetic.

It was all Claire's fault. Muppet.

Before we reached the main road he stopped the car and we swapped seats. There'd been a shooting. The police would be everywhere. No point in taking any stupid risks with him driving us.

Any more stupid risks, I should say.

I turned the Uno's headlights back on and we pulled away, just another couple in a clapped-out car on the streets of South London.

'You said 'he'?' he asked, glaring at me.

'It was not my fault!' I pleaded, knowing that was at best only half true. 'The teacher had come with her boyfriend and he did all the talking. He drew a gun on me and said he was going to silence me.'

'Really?'

'It was all so quick. He may have said 'stop' rather than 'silence', I'm not sure.'

'But he had a gun?

'A pistol. Honest, Barclay, honest.' I touched his sleeve to reassure him but he flinched it away. I still could not make eye contact.

'I heard two shots. The first was more a pop,' he said.

'That was him. Not me, him. It was a small gun.'

'So you shot him?'

'I aimed for his shoulder, Barclay, I didn't try to kill him, just wound.'

'His leg would have been an easier target.'

I didn't think so – I recalled the spindly legs – but decided to keep that to myself. It was not a time for flippancy.

'Maybe,' I mumbled.

'And you killed him stone dead?'

It was all so quick. Was I certain? 'There was a burst of blood and stuff.'

He groaned. 'Shit. Not quite the crack shot you thought you were then?'

'No.'

Suddenly I started shaking uncontrollably as I tried to blink away the tears.

Barclay said nothing. He knew there was no need, that the impact of what I had just done had finally hit me. I shuddered in dry sobs for minutes, uncontrollable, inconsolable. There was nothing he could add.

Chapter 27

I couldn't sleep. I lay wide-eyed on top of my covers, fully dressed, waiting for the police to break down the door, surge in, guns drawn, and drag me away.

But there was nothing.

Every muscle tensed with every dog bark and car passing in the street. My mind just wouldn't rest. I tried in vain to sleep. Toss, turn, toss, turn, flip the pillow, toss, turn.

I'd killed a man. No, not even that. I'd killed a schoolboy.

I put the bedside radio on and listened to the local station's all-night phone-in marathon, straining my ears and holding my breath with every news bulletin.

Nothing.

(Not yet, anyway.)

I replayed those final moments of the boy's life over and over again in my mind, the pop of his pistol diminishing in my mind's echoes, the explosion of my gun amplifying.

In my head I shouted, 'drop the pistol or I will shoot' before I fired. I screamed, 'please put down the fucking gun', but to no avail.

I still shot. He still fell.

I tried to slow the harrowing images down to zoom in to assess the impact of my fateful bullet. But there was only the burst of blood and bone, his collapse, the screams of the teacher.

The teacher. No doubt to be referred to in police reports as 'the witness'.

I sat bolt upright. She would be a witness. She had seen me. She could select me from a line-up. She would point the finger that locked me away for life.

My heart was galloping in my chest, my skin suddenly cold and clammy as the penny dropped. I tried to calm the panic, telling myself that the hoodie and bulk of my scarf had hidden my face sufficiently, but I was convincing no one, least of all me.

But it had been so dark out there, I couldn't see them clearly, surely they couldn't see me? Identify me?

I wasn't buying it.

I was, in a word, fucked.

The 6am news was the first to mention the shooting:

'Reports are coming in of an overnight shooting, believed to be gang-related, in South-East London. Police were called around 2am and a fifteen-year-old youth has been taken to hospital with gunshot wounds. Lewisham hospital described his condition as serious but not life threatening. A number of witnesses are helping police with their enquiries.

'In football, Chelsea lost again…'

I sat upright, suddenly alert. The relief washed over me instantly. He was alive. 'Thank fuck!' I cried out.

He was alive! Every word was precious to me.

What did a 'serious condition' mean? Can't be as bad as 'critical', surely? That was good, wasn't it?

Why did they say it was 'gang-related'? There had been the recent spate of shootings across South London at weekends, maybe they thought this was another?

Why the plural, 'Gunshot wounds'? I had only shot once. For a second I started to wonder if this was a report on a different incident, another fifteen-year-old felled in his prime but I quickly dismissed the idea. This was South East London, not LA. No, I guess they wouldn't know how many times he'd been shot until they cleaned the mess up and got the forensic teams in. I could tell them, but there was no way I was going to help in their investigation on this one.

And what was this all about 'a number of witnesses'? Even Barclay hadn't seen what had happened.

My relief at the schoolboy's survival proved momentary as doubt took hold – what had happened? Had we been truly alone? Had there been another car out there in the darkness? Or maybe some over-attentive fly in the ointment passer-by had heard the guns? That would make some sense, although the boyfriend's pistol had made an almost comical pop, no louder than a Christmas cracker, whereas my gun had detonated with a deafening roar, shaking windows and glass for miles around.

My claim to have fired second was not going to stand up in court.

I spent the next hour waiting for further updates but the morning news was all about plunging stock markets in the Far East and tributes to an actor who had died over the weekend, much to the surprise of most of the world who had thought he'd died decades ago.

The 7am bulletin added nothing. I decided to get up and get over to Barclay's as soon as I could. No point whatsoever in hanging around. I knew far more than the BBC and probably the police, and I wasn't going to share with anyone except Barclay.

I was still fully dressed and didn't bother changing. I needed to move quickly, get over to his place and discuss this.

Dawn was in the hallway.

''Morning. What's going on, fake sister?' she asked innocently.

'I need to see Barclay. Now,' I said, pushing passed her.

'Woah. Hold on there, cowboy. What's up? Why all the noise and naughty words?'

'I…I…I fucking shot someone, Dawn.'

Open-mouthed, she staggered back. 'What?'

'It all went wrong, too fast. He shot, I shot. I shot a boy.'

'You? Shot? A? Boy?' Repeating each word, hammering home my pain.

'Yes. Yes. YES. I'm going to see Barclay.'

'I'm coming with you. Give me five minutes.'

I tried to explain it to Dawn as we set off for Barclay's, but I was making little sense. She couldn't take it in. Shock was the order of the day. We took the train – the Uno suddenly looked even more risky an option than usual.

'So you were shot?'

'Shot at. But not hit.'

'Did it hurt?'

'I wasn't hit. I told you.'

'But you shot and hit him?'

'Yes. In the head. On the head. The side of his head. Maybe his shoulder. He's not dead. It's only serious. It's not critical.'

'There's a difference?'

'I think so. I hope so. Serious isn't critical.'

'Or fatal?'

'You're not helping, Dawn,' I snapped.

'Sorry. Well, that's good then,' she said.

'It's not good. I don't think I'd call it good.' I was talking too fast.

'It could be worse.'

'I'm not sure how. I'm a wanted woman, Dawn. And not in a good way.'

'Let's see what Barclay thinks.'

I think I already knew what Barclay thought.

When we arrived I felt immediately that something was seriously wrong. Correction, something *else* was seriously wrong. Dawn and I stepped out of the lift into the tasteful luxury of the 12th floor hallway. There were just two penthouse apartments, two doors, and one was ajar: Barclay's. Dawn was distracted by the minimalist elegance of the corridor, the art deco wall lights and spectacular Docklands views through the windows, but I feared the worst and muttered 'no, no, no' under my breath as I approached his apartment and knocked tentatively on the open door.

'Hello? Barclay?' No response. I pushed it wider. 'Hello?'

The last time I had been here it had been a stunning, impeccably decorated pristine Man Cave of technology, a dazzling show home designed to take your breath away.

But now…

My hand rose involuntarily to my mouth.

'Shit.'

'Wow,' said Dawn. 'Way to go, bro.'

'Barclay!' I called again, louder. 'Barclay!'

The three shattered over-sized TVs hung from the walls by their cables. There was broken glass everywhere; the beautiful smoked surface of Barclay's desk had been destroyed by what looked like crushing hammer blows, the computer monitors suffering similar devastation. No sign of the laptops or computers, but keyboards had been stamped on and cables ripped from their cubby holes were everywhere. The filing cabinets had been forced open and hundreds of pieces of paper were scattered around the room. The leather of the sofa had been slashed with a knife and ripped open, the filling disgorged over the floor. Adding to the disarray someone had kindly thrown old, discarded takeaway food from the kitchen at the room's white walls, adding a pernicious odour to the brutality of the wreckage in the room.

What had happened here? I strode around the room, too stunned to take it all in.

'Barclay?' There was a slight tremor in my voice. I don't know why I was still calling as it was pretty obvious that he wasn't there. Dawn ran into the kitchen where I had previously been so appalled by the filth and squalor. She ran straight out again, a look of disgust on her face. It wasn't just me then.

Had Barclay run riot in his anger? Unlikely. Very unlikely. Someone else had done this…this…

I ripped open his bedroom door, the overturned bed was littered with his expensive shirts, coats and suits ripped from their hangers in some frantic wardrobe search, overturned drawers and their contents strewn around the room, the full-length mirror smashed into a million pieces. There was a smear of blood on the wall. I touched it. Still wet. Barclay's? His attacker's?

Or had he now abandoned me? Damn you, Barclay, we were a team, weren't we? I needed you as much as you needed me.

Suddenly Dawn cried out. I raced out of the bedroom and almost sent her flying as she fled from the bathroom. She turned back and pointed at the sink, staring, wide-eyed, hand over her mouth.

There, by the toothbrush and glass, were four adult fingernails. Not clippings, but whole, bloody fingernails. Male. Manicured. And a blood-soaked pair of heavy duty household pliers.

I screamed, too.

We both ran for the door, then stumbled into the lift and out of the building and back outside as fast as we could.

That had been horrible. Unthinkably horrible.

We just had to run.

We clambered up the stairs at the DLR station and threw ourselves through the closing doors of a departing train, breathless and scared. Scared shitless.

Oh Barclay.

Chapter 28

We had only been gone an hour but that had been sufficient time for some arsehole to break in and ransack my place, too. The busted front door was dangling from a single hinge, precariously suspended from the brute force that had torn it open.

Worse, that nosey cantankerous bitch from the flat above was sitting on her stairs judging us.

'What was that all that noise?' she demanded.

'What do you think?' I spat, pushing the door open. 'We organised a wild party before we went out.'

She slammed her door at my sarcasm.

Since Henry's departure the place had never been the tidiest, but our uninvited visitor had elevated it to a new level of chaos. In truth, I had actually seen it messier, but this intrusion into my sanctuary had me reeling.

Dawn ran to her room but quickly returned.

'Fingernails?'

'No. God, no. Just all my stuff everywhere. Like they were looking for something. Nothing missing. A couple of bottles of wine smashed but that's the worst of it. The front room doesn't look that different from how we left it.'

She had a point. It wasn't that bad, more tossed than trashed, as if whoever did it had cared a little more than they had at Barclay's where they'd gone for maximum impact. In fact, if it hadn't been for the broken door and Mrs Nosey-bastard I possibly wouldn't have noticed immediately anything untoward had happened.

But that didn't make it good.

'My laptop's gone, the one Barclay gave me,' I said, spotting the empty space on the dining table where I'd left it earlier, the charger still there like a parentless child.

'Anything else?'

'Nothing I can… shit…' I ran into my bedroom, and, ignoring its upturned drawers and my clothes scattered on the bed and floor, reached up to the top of my wardrobe.

It had gone.

'SHIT!' I shouted.

'What?'

'My gun. They've taken the gun.'

The gun with my fingerprints all over it.

'Got any vodka?' asked Dawn.

I shook my head. Henry had left behind some pretty chamomile tea bags at the back of the cupboard. The packet promised that a 'delicious cup of calming tea would ease away the day's tensions and stresses'. Fat chance, but I was willing to try anything. The packet lied about it being delicious: we each took one sip from our mugs, pulled our best grapefruit faces and poured it down the sink in synchronised disgust.

'Coffee?' I suggested.

'That'll do.' She smiled, but it was forced. It was starting to sink in.

'I'll need to get that door fixed,' I said, attempting everyday conversation as I spooned the coffee into our two mugs and boiled the kettle again.

'Do you think it was the same people who turned over Barclay's?' Dawn asked. We were avoiding talking about her brother's disappearance and the grisly nails. It was just too shocking for us to process I guess.

'Could be. Doesn't seem as violent here though. Not much broken – the telly's fine, the bin's been rifled through but at least they didn't hurl the shit inside all around the place.'

'You've no idea who?'

'Not really.'

'And Barclay?'

I put her coffee down in front of her with a little more force than I'd intended, slopping some over the table.

'I think someone's taken him.'

'What do we do now?'

'I don't…I don't have a clue.'

'We can't call the police, not with the gun and everything.'

'No, no,' panic was rising in me again. 'Definitely no police.'

But I had to call the police. Kind of. I had to call the only person I could think of who knew Barclay, who might be able to help. I called Tom Thomas. He said he'd be right over. My hero. My knight in shining … y'know. Help was on its way. Sanity would return and it couldn't come soon enough.

As we waited an eternity for Tom I broke open a packet of Digestives and I tried to explain the shooting to Dawn. In the cold light of day, after what we'd just found at Barclay's and in our own place, it was starting to feel all too real and less dreamlike.

'It was all quick, really really fast,' I said. 'We'd been expecting just this teacher who'd been having an affair, a classic Barclay set up, seemed fool-proof, low or no risk, the simplest of jobs. After the hit and run we were both a little jumpy and we'd been arguing about the gun but I took it anyway. He wasn't happy but if I hadn't made a move we would have been sitting in that bloody poxy car all night quarrelling.'

'And she wasn't alone?'

'No, she had her underage teenage boyfriend with her, fresh out of nappies and all adolescent macho posturing in pimples, trying to impress her.'

'He's not impressing anyone right now,' she said.

I sighed. 'He wasn't exactly wowing the ladies last night either. He had the money but he had a gun, too. I don't think he had intended to kill me or anything, just wave it around a bit to try and scare me. But he was shaking so much when he drew it I thought it would go off whatever his intentions so when he threatened me I drew mine. He shot first. He definitely shot first.'

'So you shot in self-defence?'

'Pretty much. He missed, I hit. I'd been aiming at his shoulder but think I caught the side of his head. There was blood and skin in a puffy cloud but it was all so fast and I hope it wasn't as bad as it looked. It was dark so I couldn't see clearly. You want to know the funny thing? It felt faster than normal speed, like it was all playing on fast forward rather than the slow motion you see on telly.'

'Maybe you should go and see him in hospital, check he's okay?'

'Should I do that before or after I hand myself in to the police?'

Dawn shrugged. I'd thought overnight of both visiting him and the police and neither had made it onto my To Do list for the day.

'What happened then?'

'I panicked. I don't feel so bad about that now – it was a perfect time to panic. I just ran away. All too fast. I just had to get away from there. No point trying to be cool about it, just needed to escape.'

'And Barclay?'

'He wasn't exactly delighted. I don't think he'll be renewing his membership to my Fan Club.'

'He's probably got other things on his mind now.'

'Yep. Tom should be here in a minute – he only lives in Lee. There's something you should know about him.'

'Is it important?'

'He's a copper.'

The look on her face was priceless and I found myself smiling for the first time in what felt like forever.

'Seriously?'

'Well, not a policeman in the strictest sense, he's a consultant. And he's been investigating Barclay.'

I think she had stopped breathing. I started laughing.

'No way.'

'Yes way.'

'Oh, this just got stupidly interesting. At least he may have an idea who's behind this break-in shit and the nails and everything.'

'And where Barclay's gone?' I added.

'That too. Wow. You're a dark horse, dating the guy investigating you! His name's Tom Thomas?'

'Not his real name, that's my joke name for him. His real name's one of those American Polish names, Pedzinski or something like that.' I helped myself to my fourth Digestive.

I needed sugar and then more sugar and bugger the waistline. 'When we last spoke I was a bit short with him.'

'Amazing. Play with fire, girl.'

There was a knock on the barely-vertical door and a familiar face poked around the frame.

'You know that door's not very secure and ... Jeezus. What happened here?'

Nice to see you too, Tom.

'We had a visitor,' I said.

'So I see.'

'And this is Dawn, Barclay's sister and my roomie.'

'Hi Dawn.'

She smiled a stupid, tight-lipped smile, suddenly shy.

He took a chair at the table. 'So it was a bit garbled on the phone but you reckon Barclay's been abducted?' He helped himself to a biscuit – supplies were running dangerously low.

'Looks like it. His flat's been smashed up and there's his stuff everywhere but no sign of him,' I said.

'Bad?' he asked.

'Party of the Century bad.'

'And no trace of him at all?'

'Well, that's not strictly true,' said Dawn. 'There was a sign of him. Four in fact.'

I hadn't been sure how much to share with Tom but there was little point in hiding anything now: 'There were four fingernails, covered in blood, in the bathroom.'

'And some bloody pliers,' added Dawn, helpfully.

It didn't seem to faze Tom. 'I told you he played dangerous games, Claire.'

'Yeah, I know, but...'

'No buts Claire. I wasn't fucking about.'

I stared into my empty mug, unable to look into his eyes.

'Have you got any idea where he may be?' Dawn asked.

'I'll have to go back and check the files again, see if there are any clues there.'

'Those...those files,' I asked nervously. 'Do they mention me at all?'

'What do you think?' he asked, his gaze steely and unblinking.

'Yes?' I suggested, barely audible. He didn't answer and just left it there, cruelly, letting me have my moment of stomach-clamping fear. Then, quietly, he said:

'No. There is no mention of you in the files. There should be, but I couldn't do it.'

I wanted to hug him and kiss him and throw him on my bed and break it with my best 'thankyouthankyouthankyou' sex, but it wasn't the time or the place and I don't think Dawn would have enjoyed the floor show. The weakest of smiles crossed his lips.

'Let me check those files back at the office and see what I can find. We may have to try a few places but I guess you guys have nothing else to do today?'

We both nodded and thanked him.

My hero. My knight in shining…et cetera, et cetera.

Chapter 29

It wasn't until late afternoon before we heard from Tom again. The sun, what little of it we'd seen that week, was long gone and a light, irritating drizzle was confusing indecisive umbrella owners in the streets. My Nokia lit shockingly with its oh-so-last-decade ringtone.

'I think I've an idea where we may find him,' said Tom. 'I'm on my way over. I'll be about thirty minutes – rush hour and all that.'

'Okay. Will you need anything to eat?'

'I can pick up some Indian on the way over if you like.'

My stomach grumbled its agreement before I could answer.

'Indian?' I asked Dawn. She nodded furiously.

'Great,' I said to Tom. 'But don't get too much.'

'There's no such thing as too much Indian,' he joked. 'Besides, could be a long night. Best we fuel up.'

He brought too much. If I'd eaten another mouthful I would have gone all Mr Creosote over our newly re-tidied flat. Temptingly, that last poppadum was calling to me.

Man it was good. I was starting to feel human for the first time in an age.

'Where do you think he is again?' I asked.

'It's this Bartholomew guy I mentioned. He's a City financier, but that's just a cover for all kinds of illegal stuff.'

I wasn't letting on that I'd not only seen the guy but had also been with Barclay when our first attempt to pick up the money had gone so spectacularly tits-up, with poor old TNT paying the price – if Tom's investigation hadn't gleaned that, I was buggered if I was going to offer up the info.

'How illegal?' asked Dawn.

'Front page illegal. Headline News illegal. If exposed this guy would be international news, it's that big 'n' bad. We have our own investigations into some of his enterprising adventures but he has friends in very high places and we've nothing concrete to prosecute with. Barclay decided he would take a more vigilante approach I guess, cut out the middle man and just pump the guy for as much as he can.'

'How did he find out about Bartholomew?' Dawn asked.

'His usual methods, I'd suspect. He'd have hacked a laptop or Wi-Fi network or mobile. He's good with that kind of thing. There aren't many software flaws or bugs that Barclay can't exploit. That's how I first got involved. His activities have been known about for years in both good circles and bad, but it's always been anonymous – believe it or not he doesn't have the rampant 'look at ME!' ego that more often than not exposes the bad boys in the hacking community. He's not been after corporate dollars or making political statements, he's so low key, almost out of sight he's so low, never greedy and so … so good it's impressive. Very impressive.' He shook his head and smiled. 'So impressive.'

'But Bartholomew?' she asked.

'Bartholomew's different from Barclay's usual targets. Far bigger scale, a different league from the small fry our friend normally goes for. This guy's massively wealthy, and smart too. He knows people who know how to deal with irritations like Barclay. That's what I don't get – why go for someone who's just going to be trouble? Claire – you must have seen this?'

I was playing dumb and looked down, embarrassed. 'I just do paperwork and driving and stuff,' I muttered modestly to my lap. Dawn shot me daggers but, fortunately, Tom missed them.

'Maybe it's not Barclay,' suggested Dawn. 'If it's not his normal type, why has he gone for him? He mentioned someone else was involved with this one.'

Tom looked surprised. 'I … don't know about that. Normally Barclay goes for people with dirty sex secrets they'd rather weren't made public or smaller financial foul play, never too big, never too greedy with his demands, just little and often. He goes after normal people, every day types, people too scared to call for help, terrified that he'll expose them. The dirty little secrets, the affairs, the wicked lies that probably nobody cares about but are distorted and swollen in their own minds. He seems quite honourable, honour amongst thieves and all that. No doubt he considers himself a bit of a Robin Hood character.'

I had to smile at that; it was so close to the truth.

'And you think with Bartholomew he's bitten off more than he can chew?'

'What do you think? Looks like he has mastication issues to me.'

'If you're so sure Barclay is doing this, why haven't you picked him up before? It sounds like you have all the evidence you need,' asked Dawn.

'But I don't have enough for it to stand up in court. The victims won't come forward, too much to lose if word got out, so they never complain, they don't trust the good guys as much as the bad ones. That's where he's so darned clever – he's modest enough in his ambition to keep it low on the list of our priorities, especially with all the other stuff going on around here.'

He polished off the last, lonely poppadum I'd had my eye on.

'And it's very technical how Barclay does his stuff. The British couldn't get their heads around how his hacking works and, frankly, much of it is beyond me, too. He hacks iPhones. No one hacks iPhones. Even the US Government and the FBI haven't been able to do that. Even Apple can't do that. It's a shame he can't see beyond the easy cash. He's really every bit as good as he thinks he is, and that's saying something. I was hoping that the Bartholomew thing would blow it all wide open for us, two birds with one stone and all that, Barclay and Bartholomew. But it looks like Bartholomew decided that he's had enough of Quentin and has done something about it. Speaking of which,' he looked at his watch, 'we should make a move before it gets too late. If Barclay's where I think he is, it won't be pleasant overnight.'

'Assuming he's still with us,' I added, mournfully.

'Yes, assuming that he's still with us.'

And there was a look of sadness in Tom's eyes, and I realised that Tom, too, had fallen a little under the spell of the man known only as Barclay.

Tom hadn't brought his car – he did like his Oyster Card that man – so we all crammed into the Uno: me and Tom in the front, Dawn squeezed into the back. Tom said that Bartholomew had an old warehouse down in Kent, a few miles outside Rochester. It had been part of one of his businesses that had failed in the nineties but he kept the building for reasons the police just couldn't understand. Several raids on it, looking for dodgy imports or stolen goods had yielded nothing but embarrassed looks on the faces of those raiding. Eventually they'd left it well alone and it had sat there, unloved, seemingly unused for years.

But Tom said that he'd put a 'calling all cars, be on the lookout for…' request out on Bartholomew's car and it had been reported going south on the A2 heading just an hour ago, so that looked like as fair a bet as any. And we had nothing else to go on. Things were desperate. We were desperate.

Typical. There'd been some unspeakable accident on the A2 and we were stuck in the long tail back, stationary for what felt like hours in the long snake of impatient commuters' cars desperate for home and supper. Conversation had pretty much run dry, the radio had given up the ghost and all three of us were starting to regret having a large curry so quickly and then confining ourselves together in a small, metal box. The horror. The smell. All four windows were open but you could still almost taste the after effects.

Just when I'd thought things couldn't get any worse.

We edged forward inches at a time, the only notable movement being the flashing blue of the emergency vehicles, tantalisingly just a few hundred yards ahead.

Tom was starting to doze off, gently snoring in what was normally really irritating but strangely, in these most bizarre of circumstances, was quite endearing.

Very odd.

I looked at Dawn in the rear view mirror. She was smiling. I smiled too. Then we both jumped out of our skins as my phone burst into song.

It was Barclay.

I pressed the buttons so fast I almost cut him off.

'Where the fuck are you?'

'Hello … Claire.' It didn't sound like him. He sounded distant, detached, uncertain, almost unworldly. And breathless, as if calling had been agony.

'We've been to your flat. It's been wrecked! What happened? Are you okay?'

'I'll … live.' It wasn't the most convincing answer; he was faint and sounded like he was in pain. A lot of pain. His breathing was audible and laboured, distressing to hear between the few words.

'There were fingernails, Barclay, bloody ones. And pliers! Fucking pliers!'

'Yes.'

"Yes'?'

'Yes, the nails are … were mine. They'll grow back … I hope.'

'Who did this Barclay?'

Dawn was desperate to hear and sat close behind me, trying to force her ear next to the phone.

'That … that associate I mentioned. He's not happy about the Bartholomew thing…'

'The one we fucked up?' I paused. 'The *first* one we fucked up? He's not worried about the teacher fuck up?'

'He doesn't know anything about the … teacher thing. That was mine, on my own, not him, not big enough for him. No, he's the …' he was struggling for breath, 'genius behind the Bartholomew thing.'

'And he's not happy?'

'He wasn't happy, no. It got quite…nasty.'

'We saw.'

"We'?'

'I told Dawn and she went with me. We've been burgled, too.'

There was silence, then he asked gently: 'Are you okay?'

'Shaken but fine. They took the laptop. And the gun.'

'Oh. With your..?'

'Fingerprints. Yes.'

'Oh.'

'What do they want, Barclay?'

'He wants the money from Bartholomew. He wants a quarter of a million from him. I told him it was too much but he says it has to be the full amount. He was quite ... unrelenting on that. He wanted me ... us ... to collect it tonight. I said no and ...'

I couldn't speak.

'Claire. I can't do this. I didn't bargain on this. You need to get away. Dawn too. You need to run Claire. You and Dawn, you both need to run.'

'Run? Where?'

'Anywhere. You can't stay there.'

'But we're not there. I'm with Dawn now in the Uno. We're coming to get you.'

'To the flat?' he asked. 'I'm not there.'

'We're on our way to Bartholomew's warehouse in Kent.'

'Why? I'm not doing that pick up now. I told him I'd quit. Why are you going there?'

I shook my head. It didn't make sense. 'Barclay, what the fuck's going on,' I asked. Then suddenly it hit me. 'Barclay?'

'Yes?'

'This associate? His name's not Tom...Tom...' Damn it. I still couldn't remember his second name.

'I don't know anyone called 'TomTom'.'

'No. Tom...Thomas...'

'Pedakowski,' said Barclay. 'His name's Thomas Pedakowski.' And the line went suddenly dead.

My blood turned to ice. Pedakowski. Tom Pedakowski. That was it. That was him. And then I felt the cold metal of a gun press against my neck.

'Eyes on the road. Keep driving Claire,' he said calmly. 'The traffic's moving.'

I couldn't swallow. Could barely breathe. Dawn screamed.

Chapter 30

'That was him then,' said Tom.

'Yes,' I whispered. 'That was him.'

'And what did Barclay say?' he asked.

'He said it was … you. All of this was down to you, Bartholomew, the break-ins, the pliers … business. All you. All Tom Thomas.'

'Well, he would say that, wouldn't he?'

'You holding a gun on me isn't exactly persuading me otherwise, Tom.' My voice quivered.

'Good point. But needs must.'

'Are we turning back?' asked Dawn, her voice small and trembling too.

Tom twisted around sharply to face her, but the gun stayed pointed at me.

'No,' he snapped. 'We're going to the pick up.'

'But we are going to find Barclay?' she said, a question more than a statement.

'No. Barclay's gone.'

'Gone?'

He turned back and stared at the dark road ahead, saying nothing.

'We were never going to look for Barclay, were we?' I said.

'No.'

'This is the Bartholomew pick up, isn't it? You have no idea where Barclay is.'

No answer.

Dawn started crying, childish but understandable. I felt like joining her, but one of us had to stay strong and I was probably our best shot. We were on our own. Tom Thomas, you bastard bastard bastard.

In my head I was screaming but in the car we were silent. The traffic had started to spread out after the accident and we were making fair time towards Rochester, but the minutes felt like hours, there was so much to say but so little said.

Why so far this time? Everything with Barclay had been on our doorstep, but for this one it looked like we were heading a distance out of town. I guess the previous fuck up with Bartholomew had pushed both sides close to the edge.

I glanced at Tom, still pointing the gun at me.

'I thought you were one of the good guys, Tom.'

'And you were one of the bad?'

'I wouldn't go that far. Barclay says I'm an 'accessory' at worst.'

'I doubt a judge would see it like that. Some accessories are essential. Shoes and belts are pretty fundamental.' I was beginning to regret the ridiculous clothing analogy – it wasn't helpful.

'I'm not a bad person,' I muttered.

'Everyone has bad in them.'

'But I only got involved in this because Barclay got suspended from driving.'

'We all know that driving while suspended would prove to be the least of Barclay's crimes.'

'Can't we stop and let Dawn go at least? She's completely innocent in all this.'

'Stop? Where?' He had a point – we were in the middle of nowhere, crossing the Rochester bridge. 'No. She stays. She knows too much.'

'I don't know anything,' she managed to say between the sobs.

'No.' Hard. Final. He wasn't open to negotiation.

'We're doing this pick up, then? The one Barclay backed out on because he thought it was too dangerous, too big?'

'Barclay's biggest problem,' said Tom, 'is that he lacks courage and ambition. Sure, he lusts for the trappings, the designer clothes and snazzy apartment and fast cars, but he isn't prepared to take the risks to get them. He's brilliant technically but wants always to keep it small and manageable. I brought him ... opportunities beyond his limited vision.'

'Barclay doesn't let people get close to him,' I said.

'With me he had no choice. When they asked me to pick

up the Barclay investigation I saw he was onto something, his scams so simple yet effective. He just needed some guidance to make some serious money though, he needed encouragement, a brain, a partner.'

'And in return you'd keep the police at arm's length, slow things down, send investigations down dead ends when they got too close?'

'It's not difficult when the troops have been cut to the core by your government. Easy to turn a blind eye when there are so few eyes actually open. Besides, they have all that shit kicking off across South London to keep the boys in blue occupied but I've deflected them when I've needed to. We have a window of opportunity and we're using it. Barclay was perfectly happy with the arrangement. Until Bartholomew.'

'Barclay says it's too big.'

He shrugged. 'Typical. It's ambitious, I'll give him that, but Bartholomew can afford it. Barclay got spooked when his man got hit by that car, but I don't think that was planned or pre-mediated, just blind panic. That muscle Barclay took along was fucking intimidating – have you seen that guy? – and Bartholomew's guy panicked. I would have done the same thing. He won't be doing that again.'

'You sure?'

'You're hardly in the same scary monster league.'

'Me?'

'Sure, you're doing this one.'

'No way,' I said, shaking my head. He poked the gun at me then turned to the back seat and pointed it at Dawn.

'You really think this is the time to start arguing with me?' He wouldn't, surely? Dawn was wide-eyed, staring in disbelief at the gun pointing directly at her.

'Not her, Tom, not Dawn.'

'Pow!' said Tom, laughing. What is it with Americans and waving guns about? Didn't Mom and Pop tell them that was not the way modern societies worked? I tried to get him facing front again.

'Why this one, Tom? Why won't you let Bartholomew go?

Barclay said…'

'Barclay's gone.'

'So why me? Why take the risk? I'll fuck it up, you know I will. Why aren't you doing it yourself? You know the guy surely in setting this up.'

'Only by text messages and email. We're hardly dating. I've too much to lose. You have nothing to lose – you're already an accessory, remember? Besides, I'm one of the good guys, huh?' He smiled but it was cold enough to freeze hell over.

'You have a funny way of showing it.'

'Besides, you'll have some good old fashioned British male chauvinism to keep you safe. Bartholomew may be a complete asshole but he's a polite British asshole and he'll be less likely to do anything stupid when he meets you.'

'And afterwards?'

He said nothing and the silence returned to haunt us, the unsaid even more uncomfortable than the spoken.

'The turning's just up here. Next left,' said Tom. I flipped the indicator and changed down to second, the clutch fighting back and the gearbox rattling in protest. That Uno would be the death of us, I thought, silently cursing Barclay's insistence we kept it. Cursing Barclay, not for the first time but possibly the last.

At the junction roundabout Tom directed me left, then right, then left again. A mile down the road was a small cluster of derelict buildings, former factories and warehouses that had been abandoned after a fire had ripped through one and left its roof a jumble of dark timbers jutting up into the moonlit sky. The others, forlorn, forgotten, stood silent in the darkness as if mourning their fallen comrade. There was no Bartholomew warehouse, so no kidnapped Barclay for us to rescue. It was just yet another desolate, dilapidated location for another desolate, dilapidated pick up, this one by disconsolate, dejected me.

The earlier drizzle had cleared and there was a full moon, the sky clear of cloud for once, possibly the first time that entire winter. Barclay had preferred the dark for our work, but after the recent disasters I was quite grateful that we would have at least a little light this time around.

'Here,' said Tom, pointing to the burned out building. Nothing else was said as I pulled up on the concrete road by one of the buildings. There were no other cars. We appeared to be early.

'When you're out there, Claire, no heroics, no fucking around.'

'No fucking around,' I confirmed in a whisper.

He ran through what was involved, how I should identify myself to Bartholomew (not that there was going to be anyone else around to get confused with) and to simply collect the money and return to the car, walking calmly, not running. There was a password I had to give: 'Rosebud'. Someone knew their film classics at least.

It all seemed so simple. It was so simple. So why was I trembling? What did Tom have in mind for later?

'He should be in here in a few minutes,' Tom said, checking his watch for the hundredth time since we'd parked. I turned the engine off – it was getting warm in the car with the three of us – but Tom suggested I leave the lights on.

'He needs to know we're here, waiting,' he said. 'Otherwise he could renege on the deal. It will unnerve him that it's you doing the pick up.' Not as much as it was unnerving me, I was sure.

I noticed that one of the Uno's headlights was dimmer than the other. That car really was a pile of rusty shit. I longed for the relative comfort of the Noddy Multipla Barclay had sold – anything was better than the Uno. I'd fallen out of love with it again.

Another car turned off the road ahead of us and drove cautiously towards the rendezvous. A monstrous Range Rover. A Sherman tank of a car for those who have the money but lack the class. It looked like it hailed from a different species from our humble wheels. Anything would, truth be told.

The Range Rover stopped thirty yards away. The overweight bulk of Bartholomew emerged, wrapped against the January cold in a large overcoat that almost touched the floor. Fat little man. Big coat. Another of us bad guys. Where were the good guys, the men in white? Did nobody think to invite them along?

Bartholomew waved at the Uno, but there was nothing cheery or welcoming in the greeting.

'Ready Claire?' asked Tom, but I had already forced the door open and was on my way, striding purposefully despite the leaden nervous weight in my legs and stomach.

'Good girl,' I heard him say behind me. Dawn let out a small cry and I heard a smack as he cuffed her. Bastard. What had I seen in that guy? Was I just part of his games with Barclay, just another means to an end? I felt sick, used, abused, and foolish. Don't forget foolish, Claire.

Bartholomew put his clenched fists on his waist, elbows cantilevered outwards like an oversized sports cup.

'Who the fuck are you?' he snarled.

Nice.

'I'm Claire,' I said, and then instantly regretted using my real name. Think sharp, girl. 'Dorothy Claire.' Dorothy? Dotty for short? What was I thinking?

'Well, Dorothy, this sure ain't Kansas. You workin' with those wankers?' His accent was East End barrow boy made good, all the clothes in Jermyn Street couldn't hide the origins of that cruder, coarse accent.

I wasn't going to waste time with small talk. 'Rosebud,' I said.

Bartholomew nodded, stood a second longer then went to the back of his car and opened the boot. With a grunt and a groan and more effort than he was familiar with, he pulled out a limp body, bound and trussed and bruised and...Barclay.

He let him fall to the floor. Barclay barely moved.

'This is yours, I believe,' and he spat at the figure at his feet.

Bartholomew turned his back on me and climbed back into his car. He wound down the window.

'No money. Not now, not ever. We will never talk again.' A man who was used to making statements rather than asking questions. 'Oh, and I don't like loose ends.'

Loose ends? What did that mean?

The window slid smoothly up and his posh beast of a car gave an upmarket, luxury growl and it rumbled off over the potholed concrete.

I ran to Barclay, too heavy to carry but I managed to lift him into a seating position. His eyes were closed and his breathing shallow, rasping, bubbly. His face had been battered and broken, his nose shattered, bloody. It had been brutal and unforgiving. Oh, Barclay.

As the Range Rover disappeared from view I yelled out to the Uno for help.

Suddenly a gunshot rang out and my left leg was on fire. I screamed and my free hand grabbed at my thigh as I fell, dropping Barclay and sprawling onto the cold, hard concrete.

I heard Tom yell 'No!' into the darkness. The pain in my leg was blinding, unbearable, I was blacking out. I saw Tom jump out of the Uno and start towards me

Another shot, catching Tom in the shoulder and turning him round. Another. Tom's head exploded before his body could hit the ground.

Another. This one smacked into Barclay's prostrate body. It shuddered with the impact, then was still again. So still. Too still.

Fuck.

I struggled to heave myself up, the pain exploding and stealing my breath. I had to move. Had to get out of range. I could feel hot blood pulsing out, soaking my jeans as I dragged my throbbing useless leg behind me as I hauled myself toward the Uno. Pain. The pain. I'd never known pain like it.

I left Barclay. Fuck Tom. Fuck Barclay. Fuck this.

Dawn was screaming as I clambered into the driving seat.

'Shut it, Dawn,' I snapped and, much to my surprise, she did. Instantly.

I turned the Uno's key in the ignition. Nothing. The engine ignored my frantic action. I tried again. Nothing. Zilch. Nada. No. NO!

‘Why won’t she start?’ asked Dawn. ‘Why won’t she fucking start?’

I just shook my head.

‘Shit,’ I said.

Another shot rang out and a bullet bounced off the Uno’s bonnet, shattering the windscreen.

Shit indeed.

Chapter 31

Another shot, another bullet fired from god knows where, ricocheting god knew where off the bonnet.

'Is that…that Barclay?' Dawn pointed at her fallen brother.

'Yes. Bartholomew had him … I don't know why I … I'm not sure he's still alive … he's been shot. He's not moved since I dropped him.'

There was nothing I could say. We both just stared in horror at the two bodies lying motionless.

More bullets from the dark, slamming into the fragile metal around us, peppering it with their deadly intent.

'Well, Butch, what are we going to do now?' Dawn asked as we cowered low in our seats, desperately trying to hide from the unseen sniper. She'd replaced screaming with sarcasm. It wasn't appreciated. We'd watched my favourite movies together but this was neither the time nor place to start with the quoting memorable lines thing.

'Not so sure, Sundance,' I replied. I valued her trying to lighten the tension but we were both in shock and it was no time for levity. Besides, Newman and Redford didn't make it out alive in that movie. Was our very own freeze frame moment just seconds away?

Another shot. I'd stopped flinching – they were becoming the norm.

Instinctively I checked my mobile. No signal. And, even more alarming, the text on the screen jauntily informed me that I'd run out of credit and should buy some more. Dawn checked hers.

'No signal,' she said. 'Not a great surprise given where we are.'

'I've no credit, either,' I said.

'I can't believe you're on Pay As You Go.'

'I can't believe we're hiding from a gunman in the middle of nowhere and we're discussing mobile phone plans. I think I'd like my last words to be a little more profound than 'and how many texts do you get with that?'.'

Dawn laughed. It was false and strained, a familiar sound in an unfamiliar place, an odd little chuckle that seemed to neither rise nor fall. Within seconds we were both chortling away like maniacs. Hysterical. Hysteria. Shock and tension and fear make you do the funniest things. Suddenly Dawn stopped.

'Have you got the gun?' she asked.

I stared at her in disbelief. 'Barclay said no more guns!'

'He, whoever he is out there, doesn't seem to know that.'

'No shit Sherlock.'

'So you don't have the gun?'

'I don't, but Tom had one, didn't he?' She nodded.

Tom, or at least what was left of him, was lying a few yards from the car. The gun was still in his right hand.

'I can't go get it, Dawn, my leg's...'

'I'll get it,' said Dawn. Before I could argue she'd opened the door and had sprinted toward my fallen lover. Two shots in rapid succession rang out and bullets bounced off the concrete, missing her by inches. She wrestled the gun from his lifeless grip and ran back. No more gunfire.

Good girl. Thank fuck she was with me.

'Give it here, Dawn.'

She didn't, instead she pulled out the clip and checked its contents. 'Doesn't feel full.'

'You'd know a full one?'

She shrugged and handed the gun to me.

'Thanks,' I said. 'And why are we whispering?'

'I don't know. It's not like anyone's listening.'

'True.' I stared out into the dark but could see no sign of the gunman. Gunmen? There could be two of them. I had a handful of bullets and an unfamiliar handgun to hit someone out there we couldn't even see.

'He moved!' Dawn shouted suddenly.

'What?'

'Barclay. He just moved. Look – he's lifted his hand!'

I strained my eyes but saw nothing.

'Are you sure?'

'I think so.'

'I'll take the gun and see if I can get to him.'

'I'm not 100%.'

'We can't leave him out there.'

'Aren't we better staying here?' Before I could answer another bullet whistled off the bonnet. We were too easy a target in the car.

It was only about twenty feet I had to cover. I could fire the gun until it ran dry, one last despairing effort. Dawn was horrified:

'You can't just run out there he'll nail you in seconds.'

'We can't stay here. You make your way into this building here – if you stay low he won't hit you.'

She wasn't convinced. Neither was I.

'I don't like the odds on that, either.'

'They're the only odds on offer.'

Yet another bullet flew into the Uno's peppered body.

'If you get out through this side he may not see you.'

It was as near a plan as we had. I quickly unbuckled and slunk out onto the cold road surface, the unfamiliar gun heavy in my hand. My leg shrieked as I hit the ground. Dawn, her tall frame making it more difficult, did likewise. Bullets bounced off the concrete around us like deadly hailstones, a few feet from the car. A few feet from us.

'What if he hits the petrol tank?' she asked.

'I wouldn't worry about it. I forgot to fill up earlier, there's hardly any in the tank as it is.'

More gunfire, but this time I saw the flash that went with it. About forty yards away, behind one of the outlying buildings.

'Over there!' Dawn pointed in the general direction and I nodded.

'Right. Here goes.' I held up the gun in my best Bond-like pose, both hands on the grip. 'Good luck.'

Instinctively she pulled me towards her and gave me a hug.

'Stop that. Go!'

She nodded.

She turned and ran. I painfully lumbered my way towards Barclay, suddenly he seemed so far away.

I heard a shot and fired towards it. The gun barked and jumped in my hand, shooting blind into the pitch black. I heard another shot, and saw a flash with the next. I fired and fired and fired for all I was worth, then slipped on something wet and collapsed on the ground. One more from the dark. So close. I writhed on the floor, clutching my leg in agony. Suddenly there was the sound of a motorcycle starting up, moving off. I looked towards Dawn; she'd been hit and was holding her shoulder. I turned and saw a fleeing bike emerge from the moonlit shadow of one of the buildings and sped off. A lone rider. Our lone gunman.

Just a few more yards.

My leg cried in protest as I collapsed onto Barclay.

My God, he was breathing. Just. But they were fast, deep breaths and there was a gurgling sound that I will remember to my dying day. His eyes were puffed closed and and a ridiculous amount of blood had soaked through his shirt and beloved Prada coat.

I couldn't move. 'Barclay? Barclay!' I yelled.

And then it all went black.

Chapter 32

The policewoman was the nicest person I had ever met. Ever. Even nicer than policewoman Joan.

She'd wrapped my shivering shoulders in a warm blanket and handed me the sweetest cup of black coffee I had ever tasted.

'You're shaking, you poor thing,' she said, brushing my hair from my eyes.

'It wasn't a great evening,' I half-joked, surprised at my calmness given the circumstances. I was probably going into shock. I could feel dark clouds gathering in the back of my mind. It was only a matter of seconds before I'd be a heaving mess of sobs, tears and shakes.

'At least you two are okay,' she said. 'Those chaps weren't so lucky.'

Another policewoman was talking to Dawn, a silver foil blanket draped around her shivering shoulders. Tom Pedakowski had definitely breathed his last, the top of his head now a macabre bloody jigsaw the sight of which made one of the ambulance crew retch. Dawn had been hit in the shoulder and had, like me, been bleeding profusely. They were trying to bandage her up before whisking her off to hospital. Tom they were still leaning over, crowded around making calm conversation as if there was still a chance to save his life if they could just put all the pieces back together, a modern day Humpty Dumpty.

No way, Jose.

And Barclay?

I looked at the policewoman.

'The guy with the curly hair? Is he…?'

'I've no idea, Miss. You say he was breathing when you got to him?'

I nodded. After coming to I had managed to stumble away from the scene and had somehow, miraculously, managed to get a single bar of signal, just enough to call the emergency services.

An ambulance man pulled away from the group around

Barclay and came towards me, the headlights from the vehicles lighting up the scene but turning him into a silhouette as he approached.

'Are you related to the young man?' he asked.

I shook my head. 'He is…was…my boss,' I managed.

'He still is,' he said, 'but you may want to consider a change of profession if this is a typical bit of overtime for you. He's lost a lot of blood but he'll live. It looks worse than it is. He's taken a few bullets but only in the limbs and shoulder. The girl's going to be okay, too. The other chap though is dead I'm afraid.'

It would have been more of a shock if Tom had been still with us.

'So Barclay's going to be okay?'

'Barclay? That's an odd name. Bit of a character is he?'

'You could say that,' I said, and found myself smiling despite the circumstances.

'He'll probably live,' said the medic.

'Of course,' I said. 'He doesn't do death.'

'And the other one, the deceased?' he asked.

I shook my head. 'He is…was…a man I … knew vaguely,' I said quietly.

'He has a police ID on him.'

'Yes. He told me he worked with the police. One of the good guys. He was a consultant. I only met him a couple of times. Not even dates, really. Well, maybe one. Or two. I … he wasn't the guy I thought he was and he didn't … sorry, I'm not making a lot of sense.'

He nodded. 'Understandable,' he sighed.

My head was throbbing, spinning, and I just wanted to lie down again.

'Careful, you've lost a fair bit of blood.' A tourniquet on my leg was doing its job but I'd lost all sensation in my foot. I felt myself going under again.

It hadn't been a good evening.

And then the shock hit me like a tsunami and I lost all strength, dropping my mug and collapsing, sobbing uncontrollably before finally, mercifully, I closed my eyes and it all went away.

Chapter 33

'Black. Filter, not that Americano rubbish. And two sugars.'

The new young Intern sighs and scribbles my order on her Post-It pad. She's already bored with the day. And it is only 9.30. I know that feeling. Boy, do I know that feeling.

'And get one for yourself,' I say, giving her a tenner. 'And we can share one of those blueberry muffin things. Make sure you get a low fat one though.'

She smiles, surprised at being treated like a member of the human race after all. I'm not going to treat her the way they'd treated me when I was an Intern here, that's for sure. I've learned a lot in the last few months, all of it highly suspect and most simply out and out illegal, but that is no excuse for not being a nicer person when the opportunity arises. Maybe I can be a good girl after all. Maybe, though I doubt it, the angelic lifestyle will win me over and my bad days are behind me.

Like I say though, I doubt it.

I am back working at Marshall's. They had called a few weeks after I was released from hospital. I had still needed crutches but they needed the bed back and I was 'good to go'. My leg still hurts a lot and the throbbing pulses its way through the painkillers with remarkable ease, but I had to get back onto life's treadmill I suppose. Marshall's had a big contract land in their lap ('how big?' I'd asked, 'historically big,' he'd replied) and they needed to staff up really fast and, they said, naturally they'd thought of me.

Sure…

Of course, I was stealing stationery almost from the moment I walked back through their doors. This particular old dog isn't one for that new tricks fandango. Besides, it is good to be back amongst all the bored, scowling faces and those oh-so-critical spreadsheets and emails – it reminds me that it is only going to be a matter of time before I need to escape again. I can only take so much excitement.

And what of Barclay?

Ah yes, Barclay.

He is still in hospital, but is sufficiently recovered to have been charged with a whole list of offences dating back years, even back to his time at University with Wardy. They tell me the charge list is extensive and comprehensive, but, somehow, I suspect it's nowhere near complete. He appears to the casual eye to be a broken man, a battered, bruised stammering wreck, incoherent when answering their questions, almost to the point where they think he may have suffered permanent brain damage.

But I know better. It took a while, weeks rather than days, but that sly wink he gave me when the police weren't looking calmed my concern and warmed my heart. He's playing the long game but it's a game he'll win, I have no doubt of that.

Just how much of the stuff that was recorded in Tom's files will stick I have no idea. I do know that there was no mention of me or my part in Barclay's crimes, nor any of Bartholomew, so for that I guess I should be grateful to Pedakowski. From the polite police questioning I've had so far I'd guess that they actually know so little they'll never be able to piece together what happened that night outside Rochester, or any of it, come to that. Tom covered his tracks and Barclay's pretty much too. Peas in a pod, blood brothers, brothers in arms - pick your own cliché.

Of course, Tom was as corrupt and malleable as you could ever find and if they'd had the resources he would have been under far closer supervision and observation, but then you can't blame austerity and budget cuts for everything, can you? Besides, he wasn't really one of them, one of their own. He was an American, a foreigner, and, his worst crime most likely, a highly-paid consultant. He was an outsider from every angle. They got exactly what they ordered.

But Tom's gone now, and there's no one mourning his demise. Was I just part of his games with Barclay or was he genuinely interested in me? Had I imagined it or was there really a spark between us?

I'll never know.

And, speaking of things I'll never know, who was that

fucking gunman? Was he someone hired by Bartholomew to clean up after he left, ensure that no one escaped alive? Get us all together and take us out? Had that been his plan? Lure us with the promise of the money then pick us off, one by one? 'I don't like loose ends,' he'd said, and I guess that was all we were to him that night.

I don't know for certain. I never will. And, frankly, I don't care.

Already it seems so long ago, another lifetime almost. I will always have my limp to remind me of my time as low life, bad girl scum, but it seems a small price to pay.

One of the police said that Barclay would be looking at many years, maybe even decades behind bars or Perspex or whatever they build prison cells out of these days. But I doubt it. They won't make it stick, Tom's evidence will be shaky at best, and Barclay's family will lawyer him up big time.

Tonight I'm seeing Dawn back at home and we'll drink ourselves stupid yet again on Prosecco. Mum reckons I may have a bit of a drink problem developing but I can't shee it myshelf. (Did you see what I did there?) Besides, I can afford it even if most of my salary is still heading north to fund her recovery. I just tear up hearing her voice every time she calls. Her sentences can pause at times, her words lost as she reaches into the darker recesses for that *bon mot*. But I can wait – it's just lovely to hear her, not completely well but improving every day. A reminder of the better things in life.

I am grateful for that.

I had the Uno recovered but it was deader than Tom Thomas, my real fumble with the dark side. I bought another one but it's not the same.

I'm a one car kind of girl I guess, the girl in the Fiat Uno.

And if they finally manage to get Barclay to court I'll be there at his side if he needs me, of course, following his instructions and pleading innocence and shock-induced amnesia as long as my acting skills convince. Tears are good – everyone seems to well up in sympathy when I turn on the waterworks big time.

One thing's for certain though; my bad days are done.

Finished. Over. Kaput. That's enough veering off the straight and narrow from me. (For now, at least.) You won't find me playing with fast (ish) cars and guns again, that's for sure. (At least, not for a while.) I'd have to be an absolute bloody idiot to get involved in that kind of malarkey again, and there's one thing this girl isn't, it's an idiot.

Honest.

One year later…

It's gone midnight but my new iPhone is ringing impatiently.

'Hello?'

'Claire?'

'Yes.'

'2am. Pick me up. Number Two will be joining us.'

'Of course.'

And I'm grinning as I leap from my bed, the night barely begun, the dawn still hours away. I dress and grab my keys and dance out to my waiting rust-encrusted chariot, no rest for the wicked and all that.

You can't keep a good girl down. Or a bad one, come to that.

Acknowledgements

My thanks to
Barbara Henderson for her support and encouragement on the Random House Creative Writing course and beyond;
Kathleen Gray for her reassurances and guidance with the edit on the final draft;
Graeme Elkington for his friendship and parking the world's most beautiful Karmann Ghia outside my house so the other neighbours think it's mine;
Lesley, Mike, Colin, Neil and Jimmie for their understanding and support last year;
Dan, Mandy, Maggie, Tina, Lenny, Leah and all the other friends who have been so supportive and encouraging…
…but, most of all, my love and eternal gratitude to Jen, Els and the little man, who make me so bloody happy every single day.

Bad For Good

For Dill

Earlier…

It was gone midnight but my new iPhone was ringing impatiently.

'Hello?'

'Claire?'

'Yes.'

'2am. Pick me up. Number Two will be joining us.'

'Of course.'

And I was grinning as I leaped from my bed, the night barely begun, the dawn still hours away. I dressed, grabbed my keys and danced out to my waiting rust-encrusted chariot; no rest for the wicked and all that.

Of course, you just can't keep a good girl down. Or a bad one, come to that…

Chapter 1

'Left! LEFT!' Barclay yelled. I panicked and threw the ungainly Multipla to the right and went straight down a one-way street, the No Entry signs rocking in our wake. 'Bloody hell Claire! You're going the wrong way!'

'I know, I know,' my eyes widened and my hands gripped the wheel so tightly I feared it would snap. The speedo was screaming fifty as we shot down the sleepy suburban street, the parked cars all facing towards us. Little traffic and few people around at that absurd time of the morning, thank God. Only us.

And them? I checked the mirror and the police car was still there, about a hundred yards behind but being driven stupidly, recklessly fast. Just like our car. Closer, too close, the police lights violently flashing but the siren eerily silent.

Mustn't wake the neighbours whilst running down Barclay and MacDonald. How considerate.

It was gaining on us, headlights blazing, flashes of blue blinding me in the mirror. But there was no point in me looking back. Looking in that direction was pointless. The whole fucking night was proving pointless. I'd never liked New Cross.

'Sheeet,' said TNT from the back seat.

Yes, it was 'preetty sheeet' I had to agree. At the end of the street I yanked the car left and the tyres protested loudly, the rubber burning and screaming in pain. I felt TNT's enormous weight shift suddenly as he involuntarily rolled with the sharpness of my turn and our comical Fiat clown car almost rolled too, two wheels lifting from the road. I clenched my teeth, my jaw tight as I wrestled straight-armed with the wheel, turning left, right, left and then, with a bump and a thump, I had us back on all fours. Just.

I glanced over at Barclay. His eyes were squeezed tightly shut. From the back seat I could hear TNT quietly reciting something under his breath. It sounded like a prayer.

What was it that racing driver had said? 'If you're in control, you're not going fast enough'? I was not in control and I was still not going fast enough. The police were still gaining on us.

Sheeet.

'Left! NOW!' shouted Barclay, and this time I did as I was told, double de-clutching before executing a full handbrake turn with surprising ease, the car shuddering in response. But I had regained control and slammed hard on the accelerator again.

'Sweet mother of god,' muttered Barclay.

Too exciting for you, Mr Barclay?

The police seemed to have slowed to take that last corner and the dreaded lights had yet to reappear in my mirror. Up ahead was the main street. If I could make that then I could probably lose them at the next roundabout. For how long though? Not for the first time I cursed Barclay and his choice of the most conspicuous getaway car in town. A fucking Fiat fucking Multipla? As a getaway car?? Sure, we had an exceptionally wide load on the backseat in the shape of Barclay's Thug Number Two, AKA 'TNT', as wide as the average family all on his lonesome. But surely we could have used something else a bit less…stupid looking? Even a plain white van would have been better than the Multipla, the world's ugliest car.

Braking didn't even cross my mind as we shot onto the main street, jumping the far curb as I wrenched the wheel right too late before bouncing back onto the road. Barclay was gripping both sides of his seat, his rucksack bouncing on his lap as I forced the bulbous people carrier on, the dimmed lighting of the dozing shops blurring as we raced past.

Still no police car in the mirror. Had we lost them? Then the familiar flashing blue burst from the street we'd just leaped from and I floored the accelerator again and took the roundabout recklessly fast.

'Down there!' shouted Barclay suddenly, pointing to the third turning. Without questioning or even thinking, I followed his command and we circled the roundabout on two wheels then tore down another slumbering side street.

Only this one was a dead end, with an all-too-solid brick wall racing towards us.

I slammed on the brake and the Multipla went into shock, spinning in protest, its rear spiralling out of my control before we crashed into the wall side-on with a shattering, brutal crunch, the windows exploding with the impact.

And then suddenly, for a few confused, breathless seconds, the world froze.

I gasped for breath and shook my head. 'Fuck.'

'Quick. We can't stay here,' said Barclay, bursting into action and unbuckling his seat belt. 'We need to run. Number Two, you okay? No broken bones?' There was deep grunt from behind. I had no idea if it was a 'yay' or 'nay'.

I turned to my right and realised I was stuck. My door was pinned against the wall and was of no use in my 'making a speedy exit' planning. Barclay, though, was already out, thanks to the lack of brickwork on his side of the car. He brushed the glass from his suit, corrected his cuffs like he was James Bond and even ran his fingers through his hair before reaching in and dragging both me and his precious rucksack gracelessly through the passenger door.

'Ow! Careful!' I protested in vain.

The car was a right-off. There was shattered glass and twisted metal everywhere, tiny glass pebbles crunching under my Converses as I found my feet. Barclay seemed more concerned about his bloody bag than he was about me.

His precious Prada rucksack would be the death of me.

TNT had somehow extricated himself from the tight confines of the backseat and was nonchalantly brushing himself down. It was like a side-on collision with a solid brick wall was an everyday occurrence for these two.

'Number Two,' said Barclay, calm, composed and very much in charge, 'you stay here and detain the police. Give them the old *Désolé je ne parle pas anglais* and all that.'

'Oui, Monsieur Barclay.' Thug Number Two nodded obligingly, unquestioning once more in his loyalty to Barclay. What was it between that oddest of couples?

And how was he going to 'detain' the police when they caught up? Sod that, I wasn't hanging around to ask.

Nor was Barclay. He grabbed my hand and pulled me away from the misshapen wreckage of our misshapen car and the incredible bulk of the over-muscled man mountain that was our partner in crime, TNT.

'Quick, Claire. Down here.'

Barclay pulled me towards a poorly lit alleyway and I ran as best as I could. We'd just smashed into a solid wall doing at least thirty, but it didn't seem to have phased him at all. Me? I was struggling. My left leg suddenly throbbed, my wound from the Kent shooting last year waking and demanding I slow down. No chance of that happening.

'Run Claire, run!' he shouted as he let my hand slip and he raced down the alley. I didn't need telling twice and did my best to follow him, my arms gamely clawing at the air but my legs just not having any of it. Barclay was no Usain Bolt but he was leaving me for dust.

I stumbled, tripping over something on the pavement. Picking myself up I tried to get moving again. I was half expecting to hear a gunshot behind me and for it all to go tits up for plucky Claire MacDonald, but mercifully there was nothing and I forced myself on. It was like running in the shallow end of a swimming pool. The ache in my left leg reverberated through my body with every step as I tried to keep up. Fleeing the scene of a crime had never been so agonizing, so instantly exhausting. Even at three in the morning, the uncomfortably hot June temperatures had made the air thick, unmoving and difficult to swallow. My T-shirt so drenched with sweat that it turned instantly ice cold with the slightest breeze.

I just wanted to lie down and sleep. I'd had enough. I stopped and closed my eyes.

'Claire!' Barclay had returned and shook me from my moment of respite. He slapped my cheek and instinctively my fists clenched to return the blow. 'Claire! We can't stop. Number Two can only detain them for a few minutes. We've got to move away. We can't let them catch us. Claire!'

I nodded and somehow my legs finally got the message and broke into a desperate jog, left, right, left, right. Mechanical.

Unthinking.

The end of the alley was up ahead and some cruel, bright street lights brought the world back into some kind of focus.

'We'll stop in a minute,' he assured me.

There was a bus shelter and, miraculously, the night bus was approaching. 'Can we…' I was gasping, struggling for air. 'Can we get that instead of running?' I pleaded. It was all too much and my legs were calling it a night.

But Barclay hadn't heard me, or, worse, had just ignored me, and he disappeared into the darkness down another alley.

I couldn't follow. I threw myself on to the bus, fumbled for my Oyster and slumped onto a seat behind the driver, shattered, broken, finished.

'Tough night?' he asked jovially, desperate for company on his empty bus as it trundled away from New Cross. I guess that any company would do at 3.30 in the morning.

'I've got some 'difficult fella' issues,' I muttered before closing my eyes and surrendering to the contradictory cocktail of adrenaline and exhaustion that consumed me.

Chapter 2

'What the fuck was all that about?' My words were spat rather than spoken and the calm, peaceful afternoon air of Greenwich's Ashburnham Arms was shattered by my unladylike outburst.

'Fancy a glass?' asked Barclay, ignoring my obvious ire and pointing at the already open bottle of Sauvignon Blanc and expectant glasses on the table. The pub was in its usual empty 4pm library mode and the bar staff were nowhere to be seen. I wouldn't have been surprised if Barclay had forced the door and helped himself from the fridge – he was very capable at breaking and entering, and at making himself at home wherever he wanted.

'Sure. I need it after last night.' I picked up a glass and waved it in his direction. He dutifully obliged, the wine instantly misting the glass with its most-welcome chill. There were four glasses on the table but there were just the two of us. 'Are we expecting company?' I asked.

'Didn't you say Dawn was coming?'

I nodded. Barclay's sister, Dawn, had been recently picking up some bar work at The Ash and was due on shift later that evening. I say 'due' as whether or not she'd turn up was anyone's guess – she'd been somewhat unreliable of late, thanks to her efforts to shag every available man or woman in south east London. God only knew where my errant flatmate was most nights. And I used to think that I was the wild one?

'And the other glass?' I asked.

'Oh. That's for Hugues. He's joining us to go over what went wrong last night.'

Hugues? TNT? Joining us for a delicate glass of better-than-you'd-expect house white? I couldn't imagine the fragile wine goblet surviving more than a few seconds in his indelicate grasp.

'Ah – I think I hear him coming now.' Further down the road a car alarm had started up, probably an over-sensitive reaction to the mobile landmass of a man walking down the street. Sure enough, a few seconds later the light from the pub's open door was blocked out as TNT entered the lounge.

'Bonjour,' he rumbled, his face contorted in an ugly grimace that just maybe was an attempt at a friendly smile. It was difficult to tell. His expression, for all its size, rarely changed.

He pulled over two chairs and parked a buttock on each. Barclay offered him the bottle of wine and TNT held it close to his face, scouring the label. He took a sniff at the open neck, sneered and poured himself a third of a glass, doing an 'I guess that'll do' shrug. He sniffed it again, swilled it with surprising delicacy and took a sip. The face he pulled suggested it was not to his liking.

Bloody French and their wine snobbery.

'And,' I said, 'now that our happy little notorious Hole In The Wall gang is reunited once more, I ask again: what the fuck was last night all about? Where did the boys in blue appear from? Had they been waiting for us?'

I looked at Barclay. Barclay looked at Hugues. Hugues looked at me. I looked back at Barclay. Barclay was looking at his bloody phone.

'Barclay!'

'What? Sorry. Text.'

'I was talking to you!' Sometimes it was like trying to communicate with a bored school kid.

'What? Oh, I'm sorry. That was important. I'll put it away.' He slid it guiltily back into his breast pocket. 'There. You have my undivided.' Right on cue the phone chimed again. 'Don't ignore me,' it pleaded. Barclay glanced at his pocket but thought better of it when he heard my disapproving intake of breath. 'Undivided,' he reiterated.

Incorrigible. I sighed and for what I sincerely hoped would be the very last time: 'What happened last night? How did such a doddle of a job go so wrong that we end up hoofing it and wrecking the Barclaycar in the process?'

"Barclaycar? That's priceless!' laughed Barclay.

'No, that's Mastercard,' I said.

'Whatever. Lost your sense of humour, Claire?' scorned Barclay. 'Maybe we should go back to the Multipla and look for it.' His pocketed iPhone repeated its muffled chime in a childish, sulky manner. He took a sip of his wine. 'Anyway, I don't know exactly what happened. Like you say, it was the simplest of pick-ups so it probably was just a coincidence that they were there.'

'Didn't feel like a coincidence,' I said. 'It felt like they were waiting. Besides, I didn't think we believed in coincidences?'

Barclay looked uncomfortable. 'Even if it was one, we need a post mortem of sorts.' He reached down to his precious rucksack and extracted his bright red Moleskin notebook, flicking through the pages until he found what he was after.

'Right. Last night was the Rodgers pick-up?'

I nodded, tutting under my breath. It wasn't exactly hard to keep track of everything recently – we'd hardly had anything to do over the last few months and this had been in the planning stage for ages. In fact, for a while I'd started to think we'd never work again after Rochester and Barclay's arrest, but that didn't hold him up for too long – some puppet master somewhere pulled god-knows-what strings and he was back out on the streets and back in my life before I had barely been able to draw breath. But it wasn't quite the same and the Barclay who had emerged from his time in court appeared to be still bruised, emotionally at least, and quite fragile, delicate even. Definitely not the Barclay of old. He was a nervous shadow of the man I had grown to know, both physically and mentally traumatised by the beating and bullets that had shaken his body months earlier. Some may have thought that he deserved nothing less, that the final response to our games of blackmail and extortion were exactly what was coming to him. One might say that he… we…had been fully aware of the risks and had played knowingly such a dangerous, even deadly game and that we…he…had finally suffered the inevitable consequences of his walks on the wild side. What else did we expect? If anything, it was amazing it had taken so long for things, the authorities especially, to catch up with us and our little capers.

That was one view. But that was not my view. And seeing Barclay first humiliated and humbled, then tortured and finally pretty much destroyed by Bartholomew, that greedy big City fat cat had been simply too much, the punishment too violent, the price too high. It had just been plain fucking wrong. No wonder Barclay had taken months to recover, to regain that old swagger and infuriating arrogance of old. Shit, by the time he had that back I had almost missed it.

The only permanent external sign of his ordeals was that he had taken to wearing the finest, almost gossamer-thin black gloves all the time, whatever the weather. I didn't ask why, but I guessed he was concealing the brutally mutilated fingers of his left hand from curious eyes. He couldn't just wear the one glove, could he? That would just attract attention. No, far better to wear both gloves. Even in a bloody heatwave.

Anyway, Barclay, *my* Barclay, was back, more his old self, although he did get easily distracted.

'Barclay! Put your bloody phone down!'

He frowned at something on screen then sheepishly put it back in his pocket.

'Yes, where were we? Rodgers…Rodgers.' He read through whatever notes he had in the Moleskin, flipping through a few pages before shaking his head. 'Nope. Nothing I've got suggests there should have been a problem. Simple case of asking for two grand or revealing to his mother his online appetite for women old enough to be his granny, his mother's granny even. Meek little chap. Nothing here to suggest he wasn't going to play ball and simply hand over the cash, let alone involve the police.'

'Granny-philia or whatever it's called isn't illegal, is it?'

'It's not pretty, judging by the pictures I saw. That's why we were only asking for two grand. Shaming money. I'd be surprised if the police would have taken any interest even if he had reported us. Hardly worth it.'

'Someone told them it was something else then,' I mumbled to myself, my brow furrowed. I took another sip of my wine. Despite TNT's protestations it was rather special – certainly better than the flat Prosecco I had in the fridge at home.

TNT was looking confused and bored. I was never sure exactly how much of our conversations he actually understood – I'd never heard him speak more than a few words of English and, although Barclay insisted he was fluent in several languages including Chinese, I always imagined that when we were talking he just zoned out to some internal TNT lift music. I think I had finally managed to work my way through my stomach-churning fear of being in close proximity to him but I was still far from relaxed in his company.

'If you don't think it was Rodgers then, and we know that the police have closed the book on their own investigations into our…' I hesitated, trying to find a non-sensational euphemism, '…activities, how did the police know? Why did they bother to chase us?'

'Like I say, coincidence?' Barclay, clearly disinterested, wasn't taking me seriously.

'Nah. They saw something or had heard something. Even a couple of bored coppers at three in the morning wouldn't go on a breakneck speed chase through the streets of London on a whim, would they? A ridiculous race that resulted in me writing off our car and nearly us with it? Think of all the paperwork they'd have to fill in after…'

He shrugged. 'Then I have no idea why…'

'And how did TN…Number Two here manage to detain the police and walk free from that?'

'You'd have to ask him. He's a master at walking away without explaining himself.'

I glanced at our Gallic goliath and could understand that one hundred per cent. I decided to save that question for another day. He was still squinting at the wine. No pleasing some people.

We sat in silence. Not one sodding answer. And I could tell Barclay was just itching to get back to his phone.

'Surprise!'

Barclay's sister Dawn was at the open door, arms aloft, face beaming like we hadn't seen each other in years rather than just a few hours.

She strode boldly over and joined us at our table, nuzzling up to TNT like he was the world's largest, shaved grizzly bear.

Unlike me she had no fear whatsoever of our pet behemoth – if anything, he appeared a little unnerved by her each time they met.

'Wotcha Oooooog!' she laughed, tickling him under his right arm. He recoiled and flattened himself against the pub wall to escape her attentions. 'What's up with you guys? Oooh. Is that the new white here? That glass for me?' She helped herself and downed it in one, wiping her lips with the back of her hand in an overdramatic gesture. 'So, wazzzzzzzuuuppp, losers?'

Of all of us, Dawn had reacted in the most extreme manner to our fall in Rochester. But not in a negative, inverted, reflective way, oh no. Dawn had gone to the other extreme and had evolved into an even more explosive, louder teenager than before. It had either been the making or breaking of her – I still wasn't quite sure which. 'Life's just too short' had become her new motto and we were all caught in her tail wind as she breezed in and out of our lives. It wasn't fair: I was supposed to be the unpredictable one, the bad girl at Flat B, but for the last few months I was a poor second next to Dawn.

'We hit some local difficulties,' Barclay explained. 'The police were onto us this morning and it took a little work to extricate ourselves from their attentions.'

'A chase?' she asked. 'Please tell me there was a chase!'

'Yes,' I said wearily, 'there was a chase. And yes, we got away. Just. And yes, I totalled the car completely by slamming it into a brick wall doing thirty, maybe fifty. And I'm fine thanks. Thanks for asking.'

Wide-eyed, she didn't know where to look. 'You okay, Barks?' He cringed. Barclay really didn't like the new nickname she'd given him and, of course, that just made her use it more. 'Ay, Barks? You okay? Did you run away on those dainty little clown feet? And you, Oooooooogggggg, how did you escape on those fat little legs of yours?'

She poked TNT playfully in the ribs and he recoiled as if stabbed, no humour in his eyes.

'So are you guys now Britain's Most Wanted? Up on the Post Office wall yet?'

Barclay was not enjoying this but I was finding Dawn her

usual uplifting self. She may have turned into a complete tart of late, but she was by a Brazillion miles the most fun out of all of us and her wild laugh was so infectious, to me at least. I smiled and poured out the last of the bottle into her glass. 'Cheers!' I said, raising my glass. Hers didn't even touch the sides.

'That's it for me. I'm working in a few minutes. I'd better get things sorted back there.' She rose from her chair and went around the back of the bar, surprisingly keen to start her shift at the pumps.

Barclay's phone rang and he rose to take the call, turning his back on us.

'And another thing – where's the bloody money gone?' I asked no-one in particular. Barclay heard and held up his hand.

'Later,' he said, but I had no idea if he was talking to me or the person on his iPhone. He carried on talking into his phone while I sulked and finished my glass. I was already feeling sleepy – really shouldn't drink after lunch, not after a sleepless night at least.

Barclay continued his call and I saw he was smiling but in an uncomfortable, forced way. 'Of course I'm looking forward to it. Eight works for me. See you there.' And the phone slid back into his pocket. He picked up his rucksack from beneath the table.

'Got to go. Need a haircut before tonight.'

A haircut? It was almost 5pm – he'd be lucky.

'Why the hurry? I asked.

'Need to smarten it up a bit.'

But I wasn't really paying that much attention as something else had crossed my mind. 'Barclay,' I said, suddenly serious. 'You don't think it could have been that Bartholomew who called the police? If it wasn't Rodgers it could be that bastard coming after us again, like in Rochester?'

But Barclay was gone, racing out the door into the late afternoon's still shimmering heat.

'Bartholomew…' I said again to myself, the word tasting sour in my mouth and instantly unsettling my stomach. I'd hoped we'd seen the last of him but maybe not. 'Loose ends,' he'd dismissed us as, right before his hired gunman had peppered us and my beloved Uno with volley after volley of hot metal. We still were loose ends, I guessed, and Bartholomew didn't like loose ends.

I gulped down the rest of my wine. It didn't bear thinking about. Surely that game was over now?

Chapter 3

Barclay called me at the office the following morning.

'Claire? Okay to talk?'

My office email inbox was fit to burst but what the hell? 'Sure,' I said. The new office guidelines recently forced on us worker bees at Marshalls by our new HR fusspot said something about taking personal calls or using mobiles during the working day but I was buggered if I was going to pay any attention to any of that malarkey. 'What do you want? More importantly, how was your evening? Worth the emergency haircut?' He could probably hear my smile as I asked.

'It was fine. Thank you for asking. But that is not why I called, of course.'

'You've found out what happened on Saturday night?' I asked, whispering in code to avoid the radar ears of my co-worker Lizzie who was sitting opposite me in the open plan office. Lizzie had been at the company a thousand years and was our peerless office scandalmonger, the one-stop-shop for all the salacious gossip and suggestive nudge nudge wink wink hearsay she could get her grubbies on. She had long suspected that there was more to me than may have been suggested by my well-behaved professional demeanour in the offices of Marshalls Design.

'Saturday night? Ah, you mean Sunday morning of course. No, nothing further on that one. I guess we'll never know – like I said, coincidence.'

'Not our friend from Kent then?'

'Who, Bartholomew? No. I don't think so. We've heard the last of him I'm sure.'

'And the other guy? The guy with the motorbike?'

'The chap who was taking pot shots at us? We'll never see him again either, I'm certain. Hired hand who probably thinks he did his job and cashed the cheque. Besides, it's not like we've attempted to tangle with Bartholomew again, and with Tom's… demise…that book is closed. History. Ancient history.'

'Okay,' I mumbled, unconvinced.

'Forget them. Life moves on. And that's why I am calling. I've got another game in play. If I email the details can you have a look and see what you think?'

'Is it local?' I asked.

'Not far. Fulham. Is that a problem?'

'No, not at all. Is it big money?'

'Small-ish, but there's zero risk.'

Small-ish. Since that business with Tom it had all been small sums from people more likely to be embarrassed or humiliated than arrested for whatever dirt Barclay had uncovered on them. The new, super-cautious Barclay wasn't taking any unnecessary chances with big fish any more – he appeared content blackmailing the tiddlers.

'Okay. I'm interested. Send me some details and I'll have a look. I've got to go – work to do,' and with that I hung up. Barclay was teasing, dangling the bait and I was biting. Lizzie was desperate to hear every word and I looked up to meet her pleading stare.

'That sounded juicy,' she said, rubbing her hands together and leaning over the desk in anticipation. 'Job interview?' she whispered.

I laughed but didn't answer her. There's so much more to life than an office, dear Lizzie. She sat back, disappointed at my snub, and I turned my attention back to my fascinating screen of emails and spreadsheets.

Life at Marshalls Design had changed immeasurably over the last few months but what most of my co-workers didn't know that it was all about to change a hell of a lot more over the next one. All hush-hush, don't breathe a dickie bird but the company had been acquired by an American start-up run by some genius from Netflix whose bright idea to make him an even multier millionaire was to buy up struggling web companies like Marshalls, fire all of the local staff and set-up for pennies rather than pounds in India. Genius. Where do they find these morons? Probably a massive tax benefit in there, too, from what I could see.

And how did I know all about this if it was such a big secret?

Simples. Somehow, and I had absolutely no idea how exactly, I had been chosen to produce all the absolutely essential, 'mission critical' data and spreadsheets at Marshalls to detail the Netflix guy's masterplan. His name, by the way, was Anderson Andersonn III. Seriously. And don't ignore the 'third'; very important that, like some kind of royalty. He'd never been to our office and probably never ventured further than his own palatial office in California, but he was more than happy to wreck lives and companies from afar. 'Offshoring', they called it, 'offboarding', 'outsourcing', 'rightsourcing', 'subcontracting', 'distant working'. It had a thousand jargon-y names, all euphemisms for what it really was – firing everyone and fucking the service and customers up right royal and proper. But it was now his company and you can't stand it the path of 'progress'. Besides, who was I to suggest that I knew better than someone who had once been something or other at the mighty, all-conquering Netflix?

Anyway, it was now my job to turn everyone else's jobs into soulless rows of names and numbers, ripe for slicing and dicing. But even though the closest I had ever been to India was a lukewarm Tikka Masala after the pubs closed, I was quite enjoying the work. Besides, it would result in all my bored, whingeing workmates losing those awful jobs they were always complaining about behind the boss's back. Really, I was actually doing everybody a favour, wasn't I?

No, I wasn't even fooling myself, but I was only doing what I was ordered to do for my daily pittance, paying the bills when Barclay had nothing on.

I typed more names on my Made In China keyboard into another ominous, heartless spreadsheet. I paused for second when I added my own, but only a second. Yes, I was to be one of the casualties in the cost cutting war too, but I'd expect nothing less. At least there was a slightly bigger cheque at the end of it and even talk of a bonus. Whoopee.

'Hey,' said Lizzie, leaning too far over her desk and almost spilling out of her dress, 'guess who's supposed to be in the office at the end of the week?'

I shrugged, hopefully demonstrating both my lack of knowledge and interest.

'Sanderson!'

'Andersonn,' I corrected her, 'and don't forget the Third.'

'That's him. The Big Cheese himself. From Netflix!'

'He was only there a few months. We don't even know what job he had there – he could have just been a cleaner.'

'Whatever. He's flying in on his private plane to see us!'

'He's got a private jet?'

'Probably!'

'But you don't know that?'

'Don't all the billionaires have their own planes?'

'I really don't know,' I said, 'I don't mix in those circles.'

'Not yet!' she said. 'Maybe he'll fall for you and whisk you away to his private island!'

Lizzie lived in a fantasy world at times, fuelled by her obsession with her reality TV and Z-list 'celebrity' magazines and her copy of the Express every morning. The daily arguments we'd had about Brexit had led to us almost coming to blows and her xenophobic views on 'immigrants taking British jobs' beggared belief, but she was about to find that the truth and the real danger to her livelihood was far closer to home than some imaginary hoards flooding into the country from overseas.

The fact that big boss Andersonn was flying in explained the sudden urgency with the spreadsheets and shit. He must be coming to make the big announcement to the employees that they were losing their jobs. 'Oh, and on your way out please be so kind as to train these folks in India how to do your work. Thank you.'

'Can't wait,' I said, and I genuinely meant it – nothing better to brighten up a Friday afternoon in the office than a full head-on train crash of tears and tantrums.

As promised, Barclay's email was waiting for me on my MacBook when I got home from the delicately scented sweat fest that was my packed carriage from London Bridge. Damn the sudden, sweltering heat – why couldn't we enjoy a summer without the big fella turning the thermostat from its tepid spring setting straight up to the max? Only last week they'd been talking about snow, now it was a stifling, airless, sleep-depriving heatwave. It was like they'd got several pages stuck together when reading the weather forecast.

I showered, put on a pair of old boxers and fished the lightest tee I could find out of the dirty laundry pile. I gave it a cautionary sniff but it was still good for another few hours.

Refreshed, I fired up my laptop and delved into the super-secure email system Barclay had installed for me, precariously navigating my way through the required passwords, iPhone codes and thumbprint nonsense he insisted on.

His email was wittily entitled 'Job Opportunity' and it was brief, containing a couple of links and a picture of a middle-aged, middle-class woman that looked like it had been lifted from an old copy of *Country Life* you'd find in the dentist's waiting room. I clicked the first link. No great surprise: her name was Stella Partridge and she was a teacher, a head teacher no less, at some swanky award-winning private school. I read on but soon got bored. 'Outstanding Super Head,' blah blah blah; 'a rare example of an academic performance sustained over several years…' yawn, stretch; 'working in partnership with the community' etc, etc. All very impressive but massively dull and goody-two-shoes worthy.

The second link was more engaging. 'Stunning Chelsea Mature Milf Escort' screamed the flashing animated headline and there were dozens of lurid pictures of a barely-clad woman with a whip and furry handcuffs who must have been sixty if she was a day and…

Hang on a sec, surely not?

Bloody hell it was, it was the same woman. Her makeup looked like it had been plastered on with a trowel and the long, come-hither curls were undoubtedly a cheap, tarty wig. But it was the teacher. Oh my.

I needed to know what a 'Mature Milf Escort' was so I asked Google. Urgh. I didn't need to know that. Bad internet. Bad,

bad internet.

Clearly though, this respectable pillar of the community personally handled a few 'pillars' of a less respectable nature for cash after hours. Well, well. No wonder Barclay had seen her as ripe for one of his favourite blackmail games.

Barclay had also attached the Google map reference for a pick-up the next evening. He said he and TNT would be round at nine o'clock with some new wheels. I wasn't sure why we were taking the big fella if it was supposedly a risk-free pick up, but what did I care? The more the merrier.

My phone rang. It was Barclay. Sometimes I wondered if he was watching my every move. I wouldn't put it past him. Spooky.

'Claire – you've read the email.' It wasn't a question. 'Good to go tomorrow night?'

'Yes, of course, how did you…' I could hear someone talking in the background at the other end. 'Who's that?' I asked.

'What? Oh, no-one.'

'Were you on a date last night, Barclay? Is that a 'her'? Are you still with her? Was that the reason for the haircut? Did you pick up 'something for the weekend, sir?' too?'

He ignored my digging. 'You saw the stuff on Partridge. Good.'

'And I've learned some new things and seen images I can't now un-see. I know some new words that may prove useful in Scrabble, too. Are there 'Filfs' as well as Milfs?'

Barclay snorted. 'No idea. Anyway, Number Two's coming as I want you to do this Partridge job without me.'

That stopped me in my tracks. The last pick up I'd done solo had gone horribly wrong, resulting in me accidentally shooting a guy in the head. Yep, for real. Sure, accidents will happen, but that one was an absolute doozy – it still kept me awake at nights, replaying it second by second.

'On my own?' asked my littlest voice.

'Well, not exactly on your own. As I say, you will have Number Two with you for back up. I'm unavailable tomorrow night.'

I was not happy. 'Fuckin' hell, Barclay, you're outsourcing the dangerous shit to me and the big guy?'

'It'll be fine. You're good. He's good. She's easy. In every sense.' He chuckled at his own joke. Hilarious.

'It was supposed to be easy last time, remember?'

'This is different. It will be fine.'

I was not convinced. 'So we're doing it because you can't be bothered?'

'Claire. You wanted to be more involved and I'm giving you this.'

I guess I had asked for it. Okay, so I'd asked for it a long time ago, before Rochester, before Saturday's New Cross episode, but I had actually demanded more of the action. And, truthfully, I did want it.

'Okay,' I said, clambering down from my high horse, 'but we'll need wheels.'

'Of course. I will arrange for something appropriate.'

After the not-so-dearly departed Multipla I dreaded to think what auspicious chuckle wagon he would find for us this time. Oh joy.

Chapter 4

Actually, it wasn't so bad. A 53 reg Ford Transit van, dented and scratched enough to suggest a number of too-close encounters for its previous careless owners. It had probably been originally your archetypal 'white van' but now would have been better described as a 'once white' van, such was its unwashed, dilapidated state, the damaged paintwork skilfully concealed with some brush-applied emulsion. In other words, it was the classic cowboy builder's special, ten a penny on the streets of darkest 'sarf' London. Barclay promised it would be anonymous – he hadn't let me down on that front.

Barclay had parked it outside my building, TNT already safely on board in the back, lounging on an ancient, threadbare couch. 'I've borrowed it from a friend who's moving house at the weekend,' Barclay explained. 'The couch was already loaded on for the move and I said to leave it there. Not really fair to have him sitting on the floor and he doesn't fit in the front. Too tight.'

I could imagine. I waved to our oversized man in a van and he waved back, that scary grimace-come-smile again on his face.

'Claire, a word if you please?' Barclay closed the rear door on TNT and walked me over to the curb. 'I'm probably mistaken but I think our French friend appears to have taken a bit of a shine to you.'

I froze. 'A 'shine'? How so, a 'shine'?'

'It's nothing. Probably nothing. I'm sure it's nothing.' He turned to leave. 'I'm sorry I mentioned it.'

'Hold on, mister,' I pulled his arm and span him around. 'You're not just walking away from this one. A 'shine' as in a 'crush'?'

Barclay looked amused and seemed to be enjoying my wide-eyed glare. 'Possibly. A little one. It's after he came 'round in hospital and I told him that you'd escaped the police's attention by saying you were his girlfriend. I think he found that endearing.'

My legs felt weak and I found myself clinging to Barclay's

arm, no longer in anger, more for support.

'Me...and TNT?' I whispered, unable to believe what I was hearing.

'It's probably nothing. I've just misread some things. Sorry.' He pulled away from my grasp and I managed to stay on my feet. Just.

'You...you...' Was he joking? I sincerely hoped he was joking. Shaking my head I just didn't have the words. He smiled, turned and climbed into the front of the van

I opened the driver's door and brushed aside a pathetic little bunch of flowers sitting on the driver's seat. Flowers? That wasn't Barclay's style at all.

'Les belles roses rouges ne sont pas pour vous,' rumbled the familiar deep voice from the back of the van. That was a bit beyond my rudimentary schoolgirl French but I think he had just said the flowers were for me.

My blood ran cold as I turned the key in the ignition and the dirty diesel engine misfired into life.

Was I on a date with TNT? Sheeet.

Barclay and I sat in silence in the front of the van as we cruised the streets of Deptford, through in to New Cross and then, having successfully negotiated the tricky Goldsmiths University one-way free-for-all, onto the Old Kent Road again and out to Camberwell, Elephant and Castle and beyond; West London beckoned.

Barclay wanted dropping off around Earls Court tube but wasn't saying why. It was a minor diversion for us – the pick-up was near Wandsworth Bridge in a new but currently unoccupied business park. It would make a change from the old deserted car parks for sure, although I wasn't convinced I could make a speedy getaway if required as the A-to-Z had shown a succession of narrow, winding roads that I'd need to navigate to get us back to civilisation and the Fulham Palace Road.

Being summer it was still light – the combination of the long evenings of June and the head teacher's early start each morning meant that a pick-up after dark had proven impossible.

Mind you, her early school bell didn't seem to preclude her usual irregular evening activities, did it? Barclay had agreed that we'd pick the money up at eight and I wasn't in a position to argue? I was just the mug who was doing his dirty work in some dodgy van with an overdeveloped shaven silverback who had, allegedly, fallen for my girlish charms.

Not for the first time I wondered if it was all worth it.

'Here will do,' said Barclay, waving at a dangerous-if-not-impossible place for me to stop on the North End Road. I manoeuvred the unwieldy van to the curb and yanked on the handbrake. An irate BMW hairdresser honked his disapproval of my lack of signalling. Tosser. As if BMW drivers ever signalled...

I grabbed Barclay's arm as he made his move to leave us. I felt a sudden sense of foreboding tighten my stomach. 'Barclay. I'd...I'm...do you have to go?'

'Yes.' He brushed off my grip. 'Don't be silly, Claire. This is easy. It won't be like that time with the other teacher, it's completely different. Besides, Number Two will keep you safe. Nothing to worry about.'

It was Number Two I *was* worried about, so I wasn't reassured but Barclay's mind was elsewhere as he clambered out of the van and onto the still-heaving pavement.

'You'll be fine.' He smiled and disappeared into a crowd crossing the road to the tube station.

Bastard.

I checked my wing mirror, flipped the indicator and pulled out into the light traffic. The van was trickier to engineer around the smaller streets than I'd expected and the lack of visibility out of the rear was quite unnerving.

I turned south and headed for the new business park that was our destination. A turn off the main road and we were suddenly alone, no-one out at all and this little bit of residential Hammersmith felt quite sad and deserted despite the busy roads just being a few hundred feet away. The weather didn't mind the lack of audience though and the sky was a spectacular pink as the sun started its slow descent for the night. Great. It looked like Wednesday was going to be another hot one. I'd had enough of summer already and was already longing for a cold spell. Just can't do the heat, me.

I turned a corner and could see a lone woman standing around fifty yards ahead, looking around nervously, a small holdall at her feet. I pulled up and watched her. She was barely recognisable from the streetwalking 'Milf' on the website. Gone was the fantasy Ann Summers costume of her night work; instead she was dressed in her school ma'am splendour, all prim and proper in her Harvey Nichols finest. You wouldn't believe it was the same woman.

I put on my Raybans and a baseball cap and got out the van. I released TNT from his confinement, slamming the rear door of the Transit to announce our arrival. Partridge jumped, stared at us then tried to compose herself by lighting another cigarette. Man, she was nervous. I was nervous. TNT was making us both nervous but for very different reasons. As we walked towards Stella Partridge I thought for a second he was trying to hold my hand, but it was just an accidental brush. At least, I prayed it was.

Five yards away and we stopped. 'Stella Partridge?' I thought it best to check.

She nodded.

We walked a few more paces towards her. 'You have what we asked for?'

She threw her cigarette to the floor and stamped it out. She picked the holdall up and thrust it towards me. TNT lumbered forwards and she recoiled as he neared. I could so understand that. He was not a calming presence by any stretch. She should count herself lucky that this was purely business for her.

'Check the contents, Number Two.' I was growing more confident, her trembling fear placating mine.

TNT almost tore the bag open in his clumsy paws. He peered into its depths, poked a finger in and swirled its contents. Did he sniff it? I think he did. I wasn't going to ask questions. He lifted his head.

'C'est bon,' he grunted.

'Good. Thank you, Mrs Partridge. I can assure you that you will not be hearing from us again.'

'Is that it?' Her voice was quivering – she needed a drink. Several. And strong ones, too.

'Yes.'

She couldn't wait to leave and turned and half walked, half ran from us, her shoes' short heels clacking loudly on the unfinished paving as she fled, around a corner and out of sight.

TNT approached and handed me the bag. The cash was in loose crumpled tenners and twenties and I had no idea if it was all there. Later. Barclay had assured me that he had remotely disabled the business park's CCTV but I still wanted to get the hell away as quickly as possible. We'd have to trust her but I had a nagging feeling that it didn't look enough to me – maybe there were more twenties or fifties at the bottom. 'Let's go,' I said, keen to get the fuck out of there. I jogged back to the van, knowing full well that TNT wouldn't be able to keep up with me. I wanted some distance. I needed some distance.

The roads were quiet, that strange time of the evening when those going out were already out and those staying in were locked away for the night. A few couples were ambling along, holding hands and enjoying the early summer and the tranquil beauty of the fading sun on the Thames. I felt pretty tranquil myself: that was the easiest pick-up I'd done and it couldn't have gone better. What was more, TNT was safely shut away in the back of the van and I wasn't having to practice my schoolgirl French with him or resist his advances. Had Barclay been joking with me? Some joke. Was he winding me up and...

BANG!

The steering wheel lurched suddenly in my grip and our wheels bounced off the near curb as I wrestled with the van, desperately trying to regain control before we hit and mounted the riverside pavement. I had it. I had it. The van was pulling to the left but I had it. I braked hard and we stopped. What was all that about? I swung my door open and jumped down, walking slowly around to the passenger side. The left front tyre was a mess of shredded rubber. Was that a blow out? But I'd been keeping an eye out for the police speed cameras and had only been doing thirty, tops. Did tyres blow out at that speed? I had no idea.

I got TNT out of the back and pointed at the wheel. What was 'tyre' in French? What was 'flat'? What was 'can you please find the jack and change the wheel for me as I'm a helpless maiden in distress but not at all interested in you in any other way' in French?

I needn't have worried. My gallant hero knew exactly what to do and returned to the back of the van, lifting the couch and floor cover with no effort whatsoever to reveal a spare wheel and rotational spanner. Hurrah! But no jack. Shit! We were buggered.

'Fuck,' I sighed. TNT shrugged. He didn't look remotely phased. He picked up the wheel and spanner thing and trundled the spare around to the side of the car. He pointed at the wheel bolt crucifix and then at me. I was confused. How the huckens were we going to lift the car to change the wheel?

TNT crouched down and put both his hands under the side of the van. Seriously? He was going to lift the fucker? No way.

He nodded. I shook my head in disbelief and quickly set about loosening the wheel bolts. When they were all off, I nodded back to him, his arms tensed and with a grunt and grimace he braced himself and lifted the side of the Transit a few inches higher. I stood stunned, then hastily got to work, removing the old wheel and putting the spare in place as quickly as I could. Those wheels were so heavy – I couldn't imagine what the whole van felt like. With the first couple of bolts in place, Hugues let the van back down again. Bloody hell that was impressive. Superman. My Superman. I patted him on the arm and set about fastening the remaining bolts.

We were all done in five minutes. Pretty impressive if I say so myself. Well done, Team Claire.

He put the wheel with its burst tyre into the back of the van and clumsily clambered in after it and onto his couch. I got back in the driving seat and we set off the last five miles back home.

No such thing as an easy, straightforward night in this line of work.

I dropped TNT off at a bus stop to avoid any one-on-one farewells outside his home. He may have been my hero in my moment of need, but there's a limit to a girl's gratitude, y'know, and my limit definitely fell short of going up for nightcap with Monsieur.

By the time I got home it was finally dark. I sent a quick text to Barclay confirming the pick-up had gone okay and started for my front door, then paused. A blow out? Doing thirty? Surely not? I went back to the van; something was bothering me, something I thought I'd noticed earlier but hadn't double checked in my hurry for us to change the wheel.

I wrenched open the back door and shone my phone's screen on the burst tyre.

There. I was right. I tested it with my finger. No doubt. A few inches from the edge, almost hidden by the frayed rubber around it, was a hole. A very distinct, clean hole.

A bullet hole.

Chapter 5

'You're not bloody listening, Barclay!'

'I can't help but hear you, Claire. Everyone in Greenwich can hear you. I think it may be wise if you could keep it down a little rather than sharing your paranoia with the world.'

'Well you may be hearing but you're not bloody listening!'

Dawn tutted, already bored of the bickering. We, the three amigos, were walking down Greenwich High Street into the town centre. Barclay may have had a point though – the street was getting busier and maybe my volume control could do with a teensy weensy little tweak. I decided to say it lower and slower so he couldn't mistake what I was saying. 'I'm. Not. Being. Paranoid. Someone. Was. Trying. To. Kill. Us.'

'Nonsense. Who would want to kill Claire MacDonald?'

I threw my hands up in disbelief. 'Actually, Barclay, there's quite a list these days since I hooked up with you.' I started counting them off on my fingers: 'There's last night's target for a start and all the other people you've been blackmailing. Then there's the guy I shot in the head last year, and his girlfriend, another 'harmless' teacher who's probably been sticking pins into a little Claire effigy ever since that night. And Bartholomew, let's not forget the bastard who promised me he was going to take care of the 'loose ends' – and the three of us were the only loose ends around after that sorry affair. And there was also that bloody sniper who shot me and thee and killed Tom Thomas and…Barclay! WILL YOU, FOR FIVE FUCKING MINUTES, PUT DOWN THAT FUCKING PHONE!'

He looked up sheepishly from its glowing screen, narrowly avoiding a late commuter walking straight at us, eyes glued to his own phone. 'I'm sorry? It sounds like a conversation but all I hear is whining 'fake news', 'alternative facts' or whatever it is they call paranoia these days. Is all of this because Miss Partridge short-changed you last night?'

'What? No!' Actually, that wasn't strictly true – finding out that the head teacher-stroke-escort's holdall had indeed only held half the cash that we'd been expecting had put me in the shittiest and snappiest of moods all day. That...and being almost assassinated. 'Someone shot out the tyre on the van, Barclay. TNT and I could have been killed!'

He sighed and waved his gloved hand dismissively. 'You don't know that. Mick's old Transit's tyres probably just had a blowout. He bought it from Wardy last year and God knows where Wardy got it from. I don't suppose you checked the tyres before climbing in?'

'Did you?'

'I gave them a cursory glance. It looked roadworthy to me but you're the expert.'

'Expert? Since when? And no, of course I didn't.'

'So it could have been there all along, or plugged and the plug popped out at an inopportune time. I can assure you, Claire, that no-one is trying to kill you.'

'Aaaarrrrggghhhh!' He was infuriating. Why wouldn't he believe me? Dawn shook her head but knew better than to take sides when Barclay and I were at it in full flow. In her eyes we must have looked like an old married couple – constantly bickering and fault-finding but clinging together through whatever life could throw at us, a relationship with all of the noise but none of the danger.

'Do you know, Claire, how good a marksman you need to be to shoot out the tyre of a vehicle speeding along in low light conditions? Olympic gold standard at least. It's nigh on impossible. This is real life, Claire, not Jason Bourne.'

'That guy in Rochester was pretty handy. Hit you from a hundred feet in total darkness.'

'Hardly comparable. I was unconscious on the ground – it's not the same thing. Besides, he didn't manage to kill any of us and he fired enough bullets to rouse the dead.'

'He killed Tom, or did you forget that? He was an expert, Barclay, and you know it. I thought I was good with a gun but that guy was a sniper for hire and I bet he could take out a moving vehicle.'

He shrugged. He wasn't buying it.

'Not him. Not anyone.' He swung his rucksack from one shoulder to the other. 'Are we there yet?'

Like a big bloody kid at times. I gave up arguing and shrugged in defeat. 'Yeah, almost.' I turned to Dawn who had completely tuned out of the children's squabble. Time for Claire to change the record.

'You'll love this, Dawn,' I said, tying my hair back and putting on my sunglasses. 'You might even see another VW like that one Barclay and I hired for that trip to your parents that time.'

'I very much doubt that,' Barclay scoffed. 'They're not exactly common – I doubt there's another one around in south London these days.'

Always right, never wrong. Always impossible.

We almost fell over the three sparkling Volkswagen Karmann Ghias parked in the main entrance to the market square when we got there. Wrong yet again, eh Barclay?

This regular monthly meet-up for classic car enthusiasts, wittily named *Park It In The Market*, had rapidly become a summer 'happening' event for Greenwich locals and tourists alike. The enthusiastic and envious congregated from all over London to peek and poke at the masses of over-dressed middle-aged boys and their toys that lined the square. The early evening sunshine twinkled through the market's glass roof, bouncing off the finest gleaming chrome and over-loved paintwork that too much disposable income could buy. You didn't have to know anything about cars to fall in love here, it was a stunning homage to a distant, bygone era, the romance of Goodwood and Beaulieu and Monte Carlo all crammed into the thrumming market square. Every gleaming bumper and lovingly nourished leather interior was a stark reminder of how boring and anonymous modern cars had become. These days it's more about cup holders and convenience than chrome-detailed character.

I'd stumbled into the show the previous year when I'd been bored out of my mind convalescing from the shooting and had been boring Barclay and Dawn about it ever since. Now, with the first real blast of summer, they'd finally agreed to join me and we were there, back in time to a world when motoring was a joyful sunny Sunday out, rather than a lights-to-lights crawl on the M25.

Fanbloodytastic. I'd never been interested at all in cars when I was younger but since taking on employment as Barclay's getaway driver I had begun to appreciate them more, falling fully head-over-whatsits with that Karmann Ghia. Sadly, that had proven very much a one night stand and Barclay's motoring selection had quickly reverted back to type, buying the very ugliest and often most unreliable heaps of rusting shit known to man. That had done much to dampen my enthusiasm – the dangerous Ford Transit had followed the ugly bulges and bloat of a couple of Multiplas and (although it did hold a special place in my heart) an ancient rusty Fiat Uno that had just about held itself together for one last hurrah before finally giving up the ghost when I needed it most. My beloved hired Karmann Ghia had soured Barclay's opinion of classic cars at a stroke when it broke down on the way back from his family homestead that freezing winter's evening, leaving us fraught and frazzled waiting an eternity for the hire company to rescue us.

The Transit had gone back to its previous owner and so we needed some new wheels. Accommodating TNT was always going to be a challenge though, and even if he could be squeezed into the confines of a dinky dainty sixties VW camper van that Dawn, our own Little Miss Sunshine, was cooing over, they could hardly be relied upon for a fast and agile getaway. I didn't honestly expect Barclay to buy me a classic, but I hoped at the very least the cars here would inspire him to get something a little better. Besides, this was a fun evening out with the gang, even if I had – possibly an oversight but probably not – forgotten to invite TNT.

There's only so much stress a girl can take.

The market was heaving, packed solid. Engines revved with loud abandon and the deliciously masculine smells of oil and polish and leather were rife. The crowd swelled further and the noise intensified, a sixties classic disco belted out the irresistible Motown singles and there was even a hula hoop competition adding to the vibe of wild abandon and child-like innocence. The savage heat of the afternoon had barely died away and there was the giddy feeling of an illicit fairground that quickened my pulse and dried my mouth. I needed something to drink, and then, as if by magic, I saw Dawn weaving through the packed crowd with two bottles of Peroni in her hands. Sweet mercy.

'Got these. Couldn't wait another second. Where's Barks?' she shouted.

'I have no idea,' I hollered back. 'Loud, isn't it?'

'It's fan-fuckin'-tastic!' she laughed, her new blue bob bouncing in her excitement. 'This is just so wild Claire! You were right!'

I grinned and we dinked our beers in celebration. A jazz band over by a corner pub struck up in competition with the disco and the volume edged up to the level where neighbouring London boroughs would start to tut their disapproval. What did they know? We were alive, the cars were alive, the town was alive. There was summer magic in the air.

Suddenly, just when I thought it couldn't get any rowdier, there was a tremendous roar from the surrounding street and four thunderous Harley Davidsons made their grand entrance, the crowd doing a Moses to give them room. Loud, brash, completely impractical, they were so out of place amongst the grace and finery of the old-world Jaguars, Porsches and Mercedes.

Who let the bikes in for Christ's sake?

And then, wouldn't you just know it, Barclay appeared and instantly fell in love.

'What's...that?' he asked, pointing at a red motorbike that had followed the Harleys into the arena. Barclay's face was a picture. If this wasn't love at first sight I didn't know what was – he looked as if he was scared to blink in case the vision of loveliness would be snatched from him.

'It's a Triumph,' said Dawn. 'My mate Sarah's dad has one. It's got a funny name though – like that actor in Downton

Abbey. A Bonnington.'

'Bonneville?' I corrected her.

'That's it. Triumph Bonneville. You like, Barclay?'

He didn't answer but instead pushed his way forward through the crowd gathering around the bikes and attempted to immediately strike up a conversation with the bike's rider, not even giving the guy a chance to remove his helmet.

'Yes, he like,' I said.

'Typical,' said Dawn. 'Instantly forgets us when something more interesting turns up. Barks the Bastard.'

I smiled. I'd long since stopped being offended by Barclay's rudeness and I was slowly learning even to tolerate his miniscule attention span. But this seemed different – I hadn't seen him so excited by the prospect of a new toy since the last ridiculous not-so-shiny iToy was launched. Gimme shiny, gimme shiny – that was our Mr Barclay.

The conversation with the Triumph guy seemed to be getting a little animated – Barclay was after something, I was not sure exactly what, and the guy wasn't having any of it. I looked at Dawn and she nodded – time for some distance from her brother in case things got a little too heated. We started to edge away. Besides, Peroni replenishment was rather urgently required so we shoved and shouldered our way through the overheating crowd towards the Admiral Hardy on the corner. Suddenly Dawn went rigid and grabbed my arm.

'What? Oh.' I saw what she saw and froze too.

The bike was a classic, an ancient Norton, once the pride of British engineering and something of a mechanical marvel. But its rider was a jerk of the first order, a man I'd hoped I'd never see again. No such luck. Owen Ward, or 'Wardy' as he preferred, an old school friend of Barclay's and the creepiest, most deluded Lothario I'd ever had the misfortune to meet. He'd been meant to be teaching me how to fire a gun but had been more interested in molesting me with his over-attentive and suggestive instruction. Ward's attempted charm offensive had been low on the 'charm' but high on the 'offensive'.

'Shit,' said Dawn. 'Just when I was enjoying myself.'

Fortunately it looked like he hadn't seen us and we both planned to keep it that way. Dawn pulled me aggressively into the pub before he could turn in our direction.

Nice bike, ruined by a complete dickhead. Shame.

'Well that buggers up our evening then,' said Dawn. 'I'm not going back out there whilst he's leering around.' She, too, had previous with the odious Owen.

I nodded and ordered a couple of Peroni from the bored bar staff. 'Do you think Barclay invited him?' I asked.

'I'm not sure Barks and he are talking any more. Don't know what happened but I was under the impression he'd done a runner after some dodgy work he was doing backfired on him.' She looked me straight in the eye: 'I didn't like to ask though, in case it looked like me showing too much interest in him.'

'And that really would be too much to bear,' I agreed. 'Cheers.'

We chinked and chugged, the Italian lager gloriously cold on the back of my throat. Damn the heatwave. Damn the British weather. Damn Owen Wardy Ward ruining what had been a lovely evening.

Suddenly there was a familiar voice rising above the market square din – 'Ladies!' – and Barclay burst into the pub and made his way towards us, his face lit with quite possibly the broadest smile he'd ever attempted.

'Barks!' greeted Dawn, and his grin instantly lost its rigour.

'Don't call me that, Dawn, it's not funny, nor clever, and it actually belittles you rather than me.' She sniggered in defiance. He motioned at her beer. 'Where's mine?'

I rolled my eyes and signalled to the barman for another bottle. 'What are you so bloody happy about then, Barclay? And did you see who's out there?'

'I've just bought myself that Triumph Bonneville. Took a bit of negotiation but needs must. Picking it up on Saturday from Hank the Wank.'

'What?' I spluttered into my beer, 'Hank the Wank? Seriously?'

'That's how he introduces himself. Old Eton nickname

apparently. One shudders to think how he earned it. Something to do with Jacobs Crackers I believe.'

'How much?' Dawn asked.

'Huh?' He pulled his ear – the noise from outside had picked up again with more new bikes arriving. Dawn asked again.

He was beaming. 'Ten grand.'

'And that's good?'

'I have absolutely no idea. You can't put a price on love.'

I wasn't happy. 'So you won't spend more than a few hundred quid on the car we need to do our work, but are quite happy to spend ten grand on a shiny toy?'

'Oh, that's no toy, Claire. That's our new vehicle. I assume you can ride a bike?'

I straightened my back and pulled myself up to my full five foot six. 'Actually, Barclay, I can.'

'Really?' asked Dawn. 'Didn't have you down as a biker chick.'

'That's me, full of surprises. Got my licence when I was 17. Needed some cash so I was doing some pizza deliveries to make ends meet. Mum didn't like me buzzing around in London traffic so the licence was a compromise to keep her happy. Only had a cheapo Honda though, nothing like that Triumph. Not sure I can handle that beastie, Barclay.'

'You'll be fine. Nothing to it. He wasn't going to sell but when I met the asking price he was very happy. Just need to check the finances with Green and it's mine,' he said, then quickly corrected himself: 'I mean ours.'

Dawn laughed. 'You don't think he was asking for ten thousand sarcastically then, Barks?'

His smile faltered.

'What? No! Of course not!'

But we could both see the bleedin' obvious – poor Barclay had perhaps been taken, quite literally, for a ride.

'Who's Green? I asked, but Barclay ignored me, maybe didn't even hear me over the sudden din as a Harley parked right outside the pub fired up in a childish woman-repelling manner.

'Who's out there?' he asked, picking up a loose, dropped thread of the conversation. I furrowed my brow. 'You said, 'have you seen who's out there?'.'

'Oh. Owen Ward. Your mate,' I said. Dawn pulled a face – she looked as if she'd swallowed a wasp.

'Seriously? Nobody has seen him for ages – I thought he'd done a runner. There are loads of people looking for him.' He stretched his neck and lifted his head, staring frantically into the square. 'Can't see him. Where exactly? Bugger owes me money!'

'On the black Norton,' I said. 'By that poster shop.'

'Nope. No Norton there. You sure?'

I pushed passed him and leaned out the door. Barclay was right. The Norton, and its reprehensible owner Wardy, had gone.

'Thank fuck for that,' said Dawn.

'Bugger,' said Barclay.

'Beer?' I asked.

'Sure,' said Barclay. 'I feel in the mood to celebrate!'

And with that, he did something I had never seen him do before, not once in my entire year and a half of knowing that constantly baffling social misfit.

Barclay bought a round.

'What the fuck is that?' laughed Dawn.

'It's my latest ring tone,' I explained.

'It sounds familiar,' said Barclay.

'It's the Darth Vader music from Star Wars!' Dawn guessed triumphantly.

'It's the boss from the office calling. It can wait,' I said, killing the call and returning the phone to my bag.

Barclay had continued to bless us with his sudden and surprising generosity and the rounds had kept coming, continuing long after the last car had pulled out of the Market. Being the unscrupulous characters we were, his sister Dawn and I had taken full advantage and our table was starting to resemble a major recycling centre for Italian lager bottles and glasses.

Even Barclay was now showing signs of mild inebriation.

'Do you have one for me? What's my ring tone?'

'Oh, you wouldn't know it,' I giggled.

'He will,' said Dawn. 'And he won't like it.'

Barclay looked hurt. 'It's just a bit of fun,' I assured him, patting his gloved left hand then quickly pulled my own hand away in case even the gentlest of touches hurt his damaged fingers. Household pliers would never look innocent again.

I half expected him to immediately ring me to discover his ring tone but such clear thinking was apparently beyond him. Instead, my phone chimed with the arrival of a text, presumably Mr Insistent from Marshalls Design again. I took it out and checked.

'Bugger. They want me in at eight tomorrow morning. The big boss from America is flying in early and wants to meet me straight from something called 'The Red Eye'.' I had the feeling I'd have two of my very own tomorrow after all the evening's drinking.

Fun though the evening had been I really needed to make a move if I was going to get in on time for Anderson Andersonn the Turd the next day. 'I'd better go,' I said, tugging my bag over my shoulder. 'Have fun, guys – can't take a risk on my first meeting with my newest boss.'

'Laters,' said Dawn.

Maybe it was the heat or maybe it was the drink, but I was swaying unsteadily as I made my way to the door and left the pub for home alone.

The centre of Greenwich had quietened after all of the excessive noise and bustle of Park It In The Market. Sure, I'd had a few beers, more than a few to be truthful, but I still felt I could walk in a reasonably sober manner that wouldn't draw attention.

I was probably fooling no-one – I'd necked half a dozen Peronis at least, in all likelihood more, and my head was swimming. I had just stumbled past the Pizza Express and I decided to stop at the cashpoint and to get fifty quid out for the weekend. As I put my card in (three attempts before I got it 'round the right way) a couple came up and stood behind me.

Instant pressure. Why do I always feel bad for keeping people waiting at the cashpoint? I turned to apologise for my clumsy fingers mistyping my PIN and froze.

It was them. I'd seen their faces in my nightmares for months. My jaw went slack and I dropped my money on the floor. He looked older than before, almost haggard, but then kids grow up so fast. The twelve months hadn't been kind to her, either. The stress of the ordeal I had put them through had clearly taken its toll.

'She' was Samantha Fielding, a teacher and the wife (or was it now ex-wife?) of some multi-millionaire in the City. 'He' was a pupil, one of hers, and her lover. I had shot him in the head over ten grand and almost killed him. That was a year ago, and, as he kindly knelt down to pick up my dropped cash, I could see that he was still wearing some cushioned elasticated headwear to protect his ears and the side of his face.

'You dropped this,' he said. I couldn't blink. Could barely speak.

'Sorry,' I managed. 'Too much to...drink.'

He smiled and Fielding pulled him closer as if I was a threat. I couldn't breathe, either. Did they recognise me, was it fear that made her hug him or was it just affection? It had been so dark in that deserted garage and I'd kept my face hidden, but fortunately their eyes were blank as I nodded my thanks for the returned notes and edged to one side to let them get their own.

'You're okay?' I muttered, as much to myself as to them.

'I'm sorry?' Samantha asked. 'Do we know you?'

I hurriedly looked down and shook my head. 'No, no of course not. I was talking to myself. Sorry.' So many 'sorrys'. Too many 'sorrys'. Yet I could never say 'sorry' enough to them. I couldn't just stand there. I needed to leave, run away, but my legs felt suddenly ridiculously cumbersome and even walking was a challenge.

Christ, what must they think? 'Pissed little tart was probably as good as I could hope for – if they knew who I was and what I had done they wouldn't have been so understanding. Forget that he had shot at me first and I had been, as I'd told myself a zillion times since, firing solely in self-defence. Forget that. It was noise. Lies and self-deceit. I had ruined their lives and probably almost ruined mine too in the process. But I had continued working with Barclay regardless, recklessly. Any thought that my foray to the dark side had been temporary had since been smashed. I wasn't bad for just a little while. Turned out I was bad for good.

I managed to force one foot in front of the other and made my escape around to the corner to the bus stop. Mercifully, I was alone, as what followed was not pretty. I started shaking, a sudden cold sweat soaked me and a full-blown panic attack's dark clouds descended on me at speed, crushing me with their great weight. My stomach clenched and I could feel bile rising in my throat, its acidic taste filling my mouth and suddenly I convulsed and threw up, retching vomit all over my flip flops and the road.

I needed to get home. I needed to escape. I needed to sober up.

I needed another drink. Man, I needed another drink.

Chapter 6

It was the 'Morning After'. The worker bees at Marshalls were oblivious to my previous night's drinking and subsequent distress or the extreme effort it had taken me to get out of bed and into work earlier than my normal mid-morning appearance. I arrived promptly as required. 8am. Alright, 8am-ish – it was probably nearer 8.15. Maybe 8.30. Okay, it was around nine. Doesn't matter, don't judge me. I was still early, wasn't I?

Earlier than Anderson Andersonn, that was for sure. No sign of him when I arrived, nor for several hours afterwards. Maybe it had all been a ruse by my Marshalls' manager Pete to get us all to do a full day's work before Mr Netflix arrived. Even Lizzie was in early, around ten. Wonders never ceased.

'You know what I heard?' she asked me in a ridiculously loud whisper, her eyes flitting from side to side as if she was about to betray a great national secret.

'Go on, thrill me,' I said, stifling an early morning yawn with the back of my hand.

'I heard, from thin Sharon who heard it from always-hungry Sharon, that he didn't really work at Netflix.'

'Yes he did. It's on his LinkedIn thingy.'

'But not the famous Netflix apparently. She heard that he used to stuff DVDs in envelopes and was nothing to do with the telly Netflix. Just a post room boy.'

Big deal – he lied on his CV – who doesn't? I didn't know what to believe and didn't really care to hear any of it. It was not as if he was going to be that important to me anyway – a few more weeks and some poor sap in India would be doing my work and Barclay would be the only management (or maybe that should be 'mismanagement') I had to deal with. Besides, my Marshalls office job and all the tiresome office tittle-tattle that went with it was just a way of making some money for Mum's rehab, and that was hopefully soon to be history; the doctor had said he was pleased with her recovery from the stroke but that hadn't stopped some enormous medical bills hitting Dad right where it hurt most – his wallet. I helped where I could.

I really wasn't in the mood for Lizzie that morning. I was never in the mood for her, to be truthful.

'So?' I said.

'He just plays at being an internet tycoon. All the money comes from his dad.'

'And what does his dad do?'

'Nothing much these days apparently. Anderson Andersonn the Second is no more. Left Junior millions and...' She suddenly froze mid-sentence and kicked my foot under the table.

'Ow!'

'Shhh!' she hushed and started to look extremely (and unnaturally) busy. I looked around and saw the familiar five foot four of boss Pete and a squat, scruffy stranger emerge from the meeting room at the far end of our open plan office. Was that our new overlord? I'd never seen anyone who looked less like a successful businessman. He looked more down-and-out than up-and-coming, a late night doorway dweller who couldn't quite believe his luck that he'd been allowed in from the street. As they made their way through the tightly-packed desks I noticed that The Turd walked with quite a simian gait, an arrogant roll of the shoulders, his arms hanging loosely by his sides. He wore an unironed, stained black Def Leppard T-shirt that struggled (and failed) to contain his sizeable belly and some worn faded jeans that were baggy in all the wrong places. His greying hair was pulled tight into a ridiculous joke of a man-bun that made me want to reach for a pair of scissors to sever the monstrosity. To top it all, he had dark Raybans perched on his head like an Alice band, as if the effort to remove them completely when indoors was beyond him.

It was not impressive

Occasionally the Odd Couple would stop their management parade, Pete would wave his hands at some poor sod trying to do some work and Anderson Andersonn the Turd would laugh an absurdly Callow-like theatrical guffaw and the accompanying smug grin would threaten to break his face in two.

For me, it was hate at first sight.

This was like a nauseating Papal visit. We were blessed. I felt sick.

Eventually they reached our desks. Lizzie froze, paralyzed.

'And this is Elizabeth…Elizabeth…' Pete had clearly not done his homework and had forgotten (if he had ever known it) poor Lizzie's full name.

She stood and did an embarrassing little curtsy.

Andersonn's brow wrinkled. 'What are you doing?' he asked, shaking his head in confusion and almost dislodging his sunglasses.

She blushed and sat down again with a thump. Andersonn and Pete laughed cruelly. She visibly shrank.

He turned his gaze to me. 'And you are?' His eyes were dark, impenetrable, beady and cold like a dead bird's. There was no warmth or humour in his face, despite his widening grin. I shuddered involuntarily.

'This is the Claire MacDonald I was telling you about,' said Pete before I could speak.

'Ah. Cool. Hello Claire. How's it going?' Bizarre.

'Hello,' I said, genuinely unimpressed.

'You're the girl who's been doing that bunch of work for Pete with the big project.' He said it in a manner that suggested he didn't think I knew exactly what I was working on. 'Very important for us all, that thing. And highly confidential of course.'

He spoke to me slowly. Maybe he thought I was five years' old, or perhaps he had been told I had learning difficulties. Clearly he thought I was an idiot, and my first impression of him was not entirely dissimilar.

'We must talk, you and I, Claire. But not here. Pete?'

Ever ready to suck up when it mattered Pete jumped to attention. 'Claire. Can you please meet us in my office at eleven? Oh, and bring your laptop please, love.'

Did he call me 'love'? My teeth and fists clenched in unison.

I did a curt nod of the head and turned back to the work on my computer.

Tweedledee and Tweedledum continued their grand tour of

the office. No doubt Andersonn was marvelling at the battery hen-like conditions we were cramped into, our desks barely big enough for our keyboards let alone the mountains of paper we were expected to accommodate. 'Modern working', Pete called it, the 'hyper-efficient work space'. 'Modern not working', I preferred, 'a complete fucking waste of time' was another witty one of mine. One of us was right. I'm pretty sure it was me.

Lizzie was trying to catch my attention but my head was throbbing again and I really didn't need to hear about just how stupid she felt with her curtsy to Mr Netflix. Not my problem.

The morning was dragging even slower than usual and then, five minutes before the allotted hour, I unplugged my office laptop and rose from my desk.

'I'll be ten minutes I'd imagine,' I told Lizzie.

'Probably in there right now discussing how to get rid of me. What an idiot.'

'Probably.' Not one for sympathy, me. It was the kind of stupid, unthinking thing I used to do before Barclay.

She looked close to tears but I couldn't have cared less. She was rather stupid, and I was finding it all rather petty and tiring.

Pete's office had been tidied to within an inch of its life for the presence of Andersonn. Not that he struck me as a man who appreciated neatness or order; up close you could see evidence on the T-shirt of his airline breakfast, and his jowly cheeks were lightly covered with several days' tired stubble. Pete had nicked two leather chairs from some other floor in the building (certainly not standard Marshalls issue) and they were a little too big for the confines of his cell-like office, but Andersonn didn't seem to mind. I stood, uncertain whether one of the chairs was for me or if I was required to stand.

'You can go now, Pete,' said Andersonn, waving dismissively towards the door. 'Have a chair, Claire. Okay to call you Claire?' He winked. He fucking winked. Wanker.

Pete looked lost and shuffled towards the door, humiliated by the casual dismissal. Suddenly we were alone, me and the winking, slobbish supposed millionaire.

'Your man Pete doesn't know much about India,' said Andersonn. 'That's why the majority of stuff you've been sent has come from my office rather than through him.'

'I saw he was on that last list.'

'He doesn't know that particular detail of what's happening for a start. Best he doesn't – he's not professional enough to be able to work through that kind of thing – more worried about losing his own job than doing what's best for the company. I've seen his type before and I'm best shot of him. But you, you I don't have to worry about that with you, do I?' He was still smiling that forced Hollywood smile, not realising how unnerving the damn thing was. He made a motion as if to pat my knee but then withdrew, as if some internal HR disciplinary warning bell had sounded in his head.

Just as well, because if he'd have touched me I would have thumped him.

He sat back in his chair. 'Everything about India is strictly on a need-to-know basis.'

'I understand that. What I don't understand is why I 'needed to know'. Why me?'

'I wanted someone who…' he paused, as if struggling to find the right words that wouldn't confuse my dizzy little girly brain, 'someone who was a little…remote from the other staff.'

Was that me? Claire No Mates? Of course it was. It made perfect sense. 'Aha.'

'I was told that you are not one of the gang, that you don't disappear down to the bar with the rest of the crowd every Friday. That you show a marked disdain for not just the work, but also the workers and the company in general. I think Pete was saying that in the expectation that I'd kick you out, but, actually, that is exactly what I'm after.'

'Before you fire me.'

'Before I fire you.'

It was true. I shunned my co-workers like they had something contagious, were best avoided or, at least, kept at great distance.

'And that would mean that I, being a cold-hearted bitch who hates every one of them, would have no problems with you firing them all?'

His smile dimmed from full beam. 'Bitch?' he asked. He looked surprised.

I shrugged. 'Doesn't mean quite the same over here.'

'It doesn't? I didn't know that. Didn't pick that up at Oxford. So if I called you a 'cold-hearted bitch' you'd take it as a compliment?'

'I wouldn't sue,' I assured him. 'Okay, I understand. You picked me because I'm antisocial and too thick to ask too many questions.'

'I didn't say that.'

'But that's what you were thinking.'

'It may…' He was suddenly uncomfortable, wondering how he'd lost control of the conversation. His bravado was wilting. I, on the other hand, was beginning to enjoy myself.

'Whatever. It doesn't matter,' I said, 'because you're right. I don't care. Fire them all, I say. Every last one of them. And Pete. And me. Don't forget to fire me. And I'm more than happy to help you do it, but it'll come at a bigger price than that pathetic bonus I've been promised.'

He frowned. 'I'm not so sure about that. I think you're very reasonably…'

'Bollocks. I'm underpaid and you know it. We're all underpaid. But not paid as pathetically as those poor sods in India will be, I'm sure. I've seen the numbers.'

'They are extremely well paid by Indian standards I think you'll…'

'Doesn't make it right. Doesn't make it fair. No wonder you're forecasting such a high staff turnover every year – low salaries are low salaries and good people won't stay for them. Your projections for recruitment costs are woefully inadequate.'

He looked momentarily stunned. But it was barely a moment. 'How much do you want?' he asked quietly.

'I expect decent money for this. What you're having me do is ruthless, heartless work and I'm having to park my conscience to do this.' That was a little white lie if ever there was one, but needs must. 'And there could be consequences, personal consequences for me once the other staff find out I've been instrumental in getting them all the boot.'

'Seriously? If you're that worried about it I can just fire you now and put you out of your misery.'

'No you can't. You need me and you know it. I already know too much and you can hardly turn to that clown Pete.'

'You're very sure of yourself,' he said, and his eyes told me I'd hit the bullseye.

'A year's salary,' I said.

'Half,' he countered.

'A year.'

'Which is?'

He didn't even know how little he was arguing about and when I told him he just laughed. 'Done!' he said, and I knew I had been. Bastard. I should have asked for five years', ten even. 'Maybe we could discuss it over dinner this evening?' he suggested.

'Fuck off, Andersonn,' I laughed and I rose to leave. The smug smile returned to his face as I left the room. I guess you could call it a draw, not that I gave a flying monkey's.

Chapter 7

'I don't suppose there's any chance one of you bastards could move your seat forward?'

Dawn laughed and Barclay just tutted.

'I can't even get my legs down! I'm bent double here!'

'Boo hoo,' sobbed Barclay.

'I thought I was the driver?'

'It is only fair that the smallest sits in the back,' he said. 'Besides, I'm paying for the car, so obviously I am entitled to drive her.'

I crossed my arms in an unseen sulk on the back seat. There was barely enough room to even do that. 'Her'? What was it with the petrol heads that they felt the need to attribute our more intelligent gender to their testosterone-fuelled fantasy cars?

Barclay had hired a Porsche for the weekend, presumably to impress his new best friend, the curiously named Hank the Wank. It was a pretty old one – early seventies I reckoned – and the back seat, which was more of a padded shelf than somewhere to sit, couldn't even accommodate my size 10 frame without turning me into some kind of human origami. I may have done myself some serious, permanent damage squeezing in to the back and was beginning to doubt I would ever be able to straighten out fully again.

'Is it far?' I asked.

'Are we there yet?' they mocked in childish sibling unison.

'Seriously guys, I can't sit like this much longer. It would be more comfortable in the boot.'

'I doubt it,' said Barclay. 'That's where the engine is.'

I could have screamed.

'And why's Dawn with us? Couldn't just you and I have done this?'

Dawn turned to face me, but only confronted one of my knees, thanks to my excruciating contortion. 'I'm interested in bikes. It's childish, I know, but there's something about them.'

'Seriously?'

'More interested in bikers than bikes,' said Barclay. Dawn giggled.

It turned out that Hank had joined them for a drink or many after I'd left them in the Admiral Hardy and it had been lust at first sight. Dirty Gerty. I'm not saying she was 'easy', but...

Anyway, the meeting with Hank, despite his dubious nickname, had obviously been too much temptation for my bestest friend and there'd been no argument from me when she joined us – I just hadn't thought to ask how we'd all squeeze into the undersized sports car. More fool me.

'It's just up here I think,' said Barclay, pulling over to double check Google Maps on his phone. We'd been driving for almost an hour across Kent and were somewhere just outside Canterbury but I couldn't say with any certainty as I couldn't comfortably see ahead, only behind. We'd left the last town about fifteen minutes previously and it seemed rather unlikely we were going to stumble across another before we toppled over the White Cliffs into the Channel.

'Yep. It's over...there...' His voice trailed away and he was momentarily speechless. They both were. I had to see this for myself and painfully forced my head around to look through the windscreen and...

'Wow,' was all I could manage.

Hank's house wasn't any mere house. It was a mansion, a stately country mansion, so large it may have even been two, stuck together. Do you get semi-detached mansions? It was massive, regal, the kind of place featured in one of those BBC2 documentaries about how the other half lived, all Upstairs Downstairs and extensive grounds and, boo hoo hoo, bankrupting maintenance bills. My heart bleeds for the landed gentry at times.

It stood proudly at the end of a few hundred yards of winding sand-coloured gravel drive and had towers and spires and turretty bits, the full works, and was topped with flagpoles, their livery limp in the still air.

'Hello money,' I muttered under my breath.

As we approached the high portcullis gates, Barclay stopped and wound down his window to press an intercom button. But there was no need, and the gates magically, majestically opened without a word from him.

We were expected. I found myself curiously thrilled on entering a world previously denied to me, denied to any of us. I was going to see how the other half lived, or the other 0.05% to be more accurate. This palace was as much a fairy tale to me as anything Disney had ever dreamed up and I wouldn't have been surprised if we'd been asked to pay an entrance fee and buy a guide book to find our way around. I'd been disappointed when Barclay's family home had turned out to be a run-down, run of the mill suburban detached house rather than a minor National Trust property, but this was more like it. Barclay and Dawn could keep their childish motorbike fetishes; this was my bag – posh property porn. Mum would have been shocked but I couldn't wait to have a nose around.

It seemed to take an age to reach the actual front doors. We passed tennis courts, a maze (an actual MAZE!) and an outdoor swimming pool that looked like it had been airlifted from Miami and plonked down in the middle of the Kent countryside by mistake. The grass was so green it hurt my eyes and the pristine hedges had barely a leaf out of place.

As Barclay pulled up, the front doors of the mansion opened and a large and, I had to admit, rather handsome man emerged, overdressed in an oh-so-British stifling tweed jacket, check shirt and cravat. Did he not know it was almost thirty degrees? Did our Upper Classes not do 'weather'? I was burning up in just shorts and a vest.

'Barclay!' he bellowed in welcome, as if they had known each other for years. Barclay stepped boldly from the Porsche and they shook hands with a single, aggressive macho pump. 'You made it here okay?'

'No problems,' said Barclay as I started to unfold myself from the rear shelf of the car – I appeared to have lost all sensation in my left foot and my right had turned a worrying shade of grey.

'And there she is...' he beamed. Me? No, it was Dawn of course, who had adopted a dishonest, coquettish shyness as she edged out of her seat. Hank grinned, performed a gentle bow and delicately took her outstretched hand; a real gentleman if ever there was one.

'Oof!' I exclaimed as I finally fell from the car onto the driveway, an ungainly oversized knot of clumsy pins-and-needled limbs.

'And that's Claire,' said Barclay, turning from me in embarrassment.

'Hello Mr Wank,' I mumbled, brushing myself down as I attempted to straighten my aching back. But they were already ignoring me and were walking away, Dawn taking Hank's arm as he led them around the back of the mansion. I guessed my tour of the palace would have to wait for another day and I was starting to wonder why I'd bothered coming.

'Let's go see the Bonneville,' he said, his plummy voice a relic from a bygone era when Biggles and the RAF ruled the skies and Britannia the waves.

'Lead on sir,' said Barclay, clearly as captivated by Hank's air of privilege every bit as much as his sister was.

I followed up in the rear, very much the forgotten hired hand. I couldn't have looked more like a broken manservant if I'd been lugging their suitcases and hatboxes behind me. I knew my place.

Around the side of the mansion, just beyond the croquet lawn but before the helicopter landing pad, was a large barn. The driveway curved invitingly up to its doors, which suggested this was where he kept his car and bike. Cars and bikes, more likely. And possibly a small, private plane too; it was certainly big enough, hanger-sized even. And, as the doors slid open with a blip of a blippy thing in Hank's hand, we found out why it was so ginormous.

It was like a motor museum inside, a personal Park It In The Market. How many cars? I counted a dozen before I stopped – enough Aston Martins to make James Bond envious, vintage

Jaguars, Austin Healeys, Porsches, Mercedes and even a couple of Karmann Ghias.

No Fiat Uno or Multipla though. I guess he couldn't have everything.

All the cars were immaculate, the collection was a loving homage to outstanding twentieth century motoring engineering and classic design. All gleaming and buffed and sparkling in the sunlight as it flooded in through the open doors.

I was speechless. Even Barclay seemed lost for words. Dawn had tightened her grip on Hank's arm and was claiming him as her own.

'The bikes and the Bonneville are over down the back. It was the green one, wasn't it, Barclay?'

'Red,' said Barclay. It was an easy mistake for Hank to make, after all he did have four of the buggers. The red one we'd seen on Thursday in the market was there but so were two green bad boys and a marmalade orange one, too. They were all subtly different but all equally beautiful. I could see how Barclay had fallen so in love. In a word, they were magnificent.

'I don't really collect bikes but these are rather special, aren't they? The green one's actually the more modern version – see the disc brakes?' asked Hank. Barclay and I nodded, clueless. 'And the gear and brake levers are on the 'wrong' side. Modern bikes have the gear foot pedal on the left and the rear foot brake on the right.'

'Of course,' said Barclay.

'Older models were the other way around,' I guessed, a question more than a statement in a feeble attempt to sound knowledgeable. Barclay looked at me with raised eyebrows

'Exactly!' Hank smiled at me, hoping he'd found a fellow enthusiast. I smiled but decided that I'd say no more. Best not to push my luck on that front.

Like a child in a petting zoo, Barclay needed to touch and stroke. 'May I? he asked, removing the glove from his right hand as it hovered inches above the glistening red fuel tank.

Hank laughed. 'Irresistible, aren't they?'

'Why are you selling?' I asked.

'I wasn't intending to. I hardly need the cash, but your man here is quite persuasive with the old wheeling dealing and I could tell it was love at first sight. Most of these,' he waved his unadorned-with-Dawn free arm casually at the other motors, 'haven't moved in years. I've started to think it's all a bit of a waste, me just collecting tin for no other reason than it looks good. Hoarding would be probably a more accurate way of describing it. Why would anyone need more than half a dozen cars? It's not like these are particularly practical. I don't even enjoy driving that much.'

Barclay's affectionate strokes on the Bonneville were starting to look vaguely carnal and I figured it was time to move on before he made a complete fool of himself. 'Are they difficult to drive?' I asked.

Hank laughed his loudest aristocratic guffaw. 'Drive? You mean 'ride', my dear. You don't drive a bike!' The Barclays looked at me open-mouthed – surely she wasn't that dumb, was she?

'It's been a few years since I've been on a bike so I wondered if there was anything special we needed to know?' I said, regaining some of my composure.

'I'm not an expert myself, but why not take it for a ride around the estate before you hit the road. Have you ridden anything like the Triumph before?'

Barclay and I both shook our heads, embarrassed by our lack of experience.

'Ah. I see. Not too much to it, just a few pointers and I'm sure you'll be fine. You've got valid full licences?'

We nodded enthusiastically. Sorry, TNT, but I was really warming to the idea of a bike as our new getaway vehicle.

'Well I guess that's enough. Let's wheel her out and get moving.'

We stood back as he took the weight and kicked away the stand. It looked so heavy yet somehow fragile, too. Barclay could barely contain himself. Me? I was absolutely bricking it.

We moved to a small race circuit at the back of the barn, a

simple loop of tarmac, almost circular, no more than fifty yards across.

'The mechanic just uses it for testing,' apologised Hank. 'I don't like driving too fast and it's not really built for putting a bike through its paces, but it will do for us.'

'Don't we need helmets?' I asked, nervously.

'Private road,' said Barclay, matter-of-factly.

'I think I'd prefer a helmet,' I said.

'They're on a shelf just inside the door,' said Hank. 'The blue one should fit you nicely.'

I trotted back towards the barn, not quite sure what I was doing. There were about a dozen helmets all told, some modern and menacing, with visors like police riot gear, others older and with character, more like something you'd wear on an Italian moped as you buzzed down to the shops for some breadsticks and a bottle of Lambrusco. The blue one Hank had suggested was one of the latter and was very much my style. I removed my sunglasses and tried it on. Snug but not too tight, it would soon get hot 'n' sweaty in this heat and I realised that a bike was going to be a mixed blessing. The romance of a bike and the open road was beginning to fade for me.

I jogged back to the gang and our new wheels. The impatient, grinning Barclay was already on the bike and was pootling around the track. It looked easy, fun, and, even from a distance, I could see he was getting frustrated with the short, simple test circuit.

He stopped, standing astride the bike. 'Any chance we can take it out on the road now that Claire's got her helmet?'

'How about you take it just down the drive?' suggested Hank. 'But don't you need your own…'

Barclay revved the accelerator and drowned out the end of the sentence. With a jolt and a bump he rode the Bonneville over the manicured grass and onto the tarmac drive that meandered back towards the house. He accelerated and turned the corner, shooting off out of sight. We could hear him throttling it through the gears and racing away.

'He'd better not take it on the road without a helmet,'

muttered Hank.

'He's just a big child,' Dawn explained unnecessarily. 'He'll be back in a sec – even he ain't that stupid.'

Hank nodded and laughed nervously, but the smile froze on his lips as the roar of the bike diminished into the distance. It sounded like Barclay had lost his head and was already disappearing up the A2 back to town.

'He wouldn't, would he?' I asked, frowning.

As if he'd heard me the roar returned, increasing in volume and seconds later Barclay re-appeared, a grin so broad you could have seen it from the moon.

'Amazing!' he shouted. 'Claire, you just have to try this! Amazing! Amazing!'

Lost for words, eh Barclay?

He dropped the stand and dismounted. He waved for me to step forward. I wasn't so sure. It looked so…so heavy, and the beautiful polished metal looked dangerous. I stumbled forward, my knees struggling to carry my reluctant weight.

Barclay was enthusing to Hank and Dawn, his back to me. I was on my own. I touched the handlebars. It was quite daunting up close, a million miles from the Honda moped I'd had for my pizza job. That had been a kitten. This was a bloody great lion.

I put on my helmet, ready but my nerve suddenly gone. 'It's easy?' I called out, swinging my leg over the bike.

'It's heavy and the metal is very hot,' shouted Barclay over his shoulder. 'You should have worn longer trousers,' he said just as my right thigh touched the red petrol tank and I instinctively jumped away, releasing the bike and sending it crashing noisily to the ground.

'Claire!' shouted Barclay, turning and running towards the Triumph like a mother to a fallen toddler. He didn't give a bugger about me, the concern was all for the bike.

'I'm fine thanks, Barclay,' I said as he pushed me aside and lifted the bike.

'Ooh, nasty dent,' said Dawn, pointing at the exhaust.

Barclay swore but Hank just laughed. 'Graeme will sort that out, don't worry about it. Sorry Claire, but you can't ride a bike in this weather in shorts. I should have said. Didn't think. Can be a bloody fool at times. Never mind, let's go in for a cuppa and get out of the heat and I'll see if my man is around to fix it.'

Barclay looked crestfallen – he'd been planning to ride the bike back to London and I had been looking forward to getting behind the wheel of the Porsche, but now, thanks to my clumsiness, it looked like neither of us was going to be happy. Still, he had his new toy and we had our new getaway bike. Things were looking up for Barclay and MacDonald at last. It was about time.

Chapter 8

The Porsche had choked and spluttered its last on a quiet B road ten minutes from Hank's. It had failed dramatically and suddenly, something went bang and the engine shook and rattled and the car filled with thick, oily smoke in seconds. Impressively, Barclay kept control and managed to bring it safely to a stop. As we climbed out there was a distinct smell of burning and we all decided to put some distance between ourselves and the dying thoroughbred.

Last year the VW, now the Porsche. Maybe we were just cursed when it came to classic cars. Maybe that is actually why they just don't make 'em like they used to.

I checked my phone but I had no signal. Barclay shrugged, same problem. Same carrier in fact – we really should diversify. Dawn didn't even have her phone with her. Not enough room in her skimpy attire, I guess.

'How far back to Hank's?' I asked.

'Not too far. I reckon it's about a half hour walk, maybe a bit longer. Dark though.'

'I'll do it,' said Dawn, 'but can I take one of your phones to use as a torch?' Barclay surprised us both by giving her his. 'I'll probably get a signal nearer Hank's place – can't imagine him putting up with no coverage on his grounds.'

'Will you come back?' I asked, half joking.

'I'll see how tired I get. Don't wait up, children.'

And with that she was gone, leaving Barclay and me standing in the near darkness, just the moon and our dying Porsche's slowly dimming headlights keeping us company.

'This isn't much fun,' I said.

'No.'

'Maybe renting a classic car wasn't worth it,' I suggested, clearly on something of a roll.

'No.'

'She's been gone a while.'

'Yes.'

'You don't think she's forgotten about us?'

He didn't answer that one. He could be a man of few words in a crisis. It wasn't entirely beyond the realms of possibility that Dawn had abandoned us for her new man.

'Probably not,' I said, seeking to assure myself but failing miserably.

Minutes passed. They felt like hours but my watch confirmed they were only minutes. I couldn't read Barclay at all. Was he angry? With me? Himself? Dawn? The Porsche? He hadn't said any more than a few words since Dawn had left us, striding off into the darkness on her quest. The stony silence wasn't helping either of our moods – it was as if we were having a wordless row. I decided it was my duty to warm things up with some conversation.

'Barclay?'

'Hmmm?'

'If we're going to be doing our runs on two wheels rather than four in future, where does that leave TN...' I corrected myself, 'where does that leave Number Two, Hugues?'

'Hugues wants out.'

'He does?'

'He's not enjoying this life that's picked him. The hit and run in Docklands and all that time in hospital gave him lots of thinking time and he's asked if I will let him go.'

I felt a weight lifting from my shoulders. My first good news of the night. 'Seriously?' I was smiling and Barclay scowled in apparent disapproval.

'You don't like him?'

'I don't like him liking me. Not in that way.'

'Oh, that. I made that up. Thought it would be amusing.'

'What! Bloody hell, Barclay – I've had sleepless nights thinking he had the hots for me, you bastard.'

Barclay smiled. It wasn't funny. 'I don't see why you're so upset. He told you the flowers weren't for you. I heard him.'

'Is that what he said? You know I don't speak a bloody word of French. Barclay…that was not…you're pathetic! You're really pathetic at times, you know?' I was struggling to contain my anger, my jaw clenched and fists tightened.

'You really believed me?'

So bloody funny, eh Barclay? 'Of course I fucking did, you idiot! I suppose you bought those flowers, too?'

He laughed. 'I did, but they weren't for you, of course. I just forgot them and left them in the van.'

'Bastard.' And my clumsy punch hit him hard on the arm.

'Ow!'

'Serves you bloody right.'

He was still chuckling. 'I guess so,' he conceded.

Bastard.

I gave myself a few moments to take it down a notch or two.

'He wants out?'

'Truthfully, he never really wanted in.'

I was intrigued. 'What did you mean when you said 'the life that picked him' – shouldn't it be the other way around?'

Barclay nodded and gave a little shrug. 'He's not the man you think he is.'

'Seriously?'

'Let's sit over there.' He waved at a lopsided picnic table and bench, long neglected by the local Council. 'We've got probably an hour or two to kill. Never one to hurry things, my sister. Philanthropic acts don't come naturally to her.'

Runs in the family, I thought.

'She must have called a garage by now,' I said, more in hope than expectation.

'We'll see the sun rise before we see her again.'

For all their years apart I knew, deep down, that he understood her all too well. For me, Dawn was a great mate, a good laugh and huge fun, especially with a few drinks inside her, but was she reliable and dependable? I wouldn't put money on it and would have doubts about anyone who would. Much as it pained me to admit it, Barclay was almost certainly right.

The bench by the table was still covered in picnic debris, empty cartons of Capri Sun and crunched up Monster Munch bags thoughtlessly abandoned to the elements and local wildlife.

I scooped it up and dropped it in the nearby bin, only to find that it lacked a bottom. Oh well, at least the rubbish was now in a neat-ish pile on the floor. Barclay laughed when he saw my effort at Keeping Britain Tidy meet such a comical fate and I smiled too. I guess I couldn't be good if I tried.

'So who is Number Two, if he's not the man he first appears to be?' I asked.

'Who do you think he is?'

Games. Barclay liked his games.

'Well, it's pretty obvious, isn't it? He's your muscle man, 'Thug Number Two', a successor to he-who-must-not-be-mentioned Thug Number One. Your go-to-guy when the going needs to get tough.'

Barclay shook his head. 'Perfect. That is exactly what you should be thinking. Couldn't be further from the truth of course, but it's all about appearances, surface.'

'But he's huge, bloody enormous. He's not fast, I'll give you that – too heavy and big to even run from what I've seen – but he's as intimidating as anyone, any*thing* I've ever seen. He's the biggest, widest thing on two legs. And he barely says anything, just grunts and says 'sheeet' a lot. How can that appearance be even the remotest bit deceiving?'

Barclay gave me a glance than was bordering on pity. 'Well, you obviously know far more about Hugues than me then. I've never seen him fight, never seen him even throw a punch, let alone hit anyone.'

'You'd have to be an absolute bloody nutter to pick a fight with…' and I stopped abruptly, finally getting it. 'Ah.'

'Exactly,' a thin smile on his lips. 'It's all about appearances.'

'Like a nightclub bouncer then? All about the menace rather than actual fighting ability?'

He shook his head. 'I'm not so sure he'd welcome the comparison with a common thug earning a few quid while out on remand.'

'I didn't mean any offence,' my cheeks glowed in embarrassment. 'Sorry. You won't tell him I said that, will you?'

'It's the obvious mistake to make. Would you believe that

he's actually extremely cultured, a fine chef, widely read in several languages (although, sadly, not English) and a Master Sommelier?'

'I'd probably be more impressed if I knew what a 'sommelier' was – is it something to do with knives? Dawn found one once in my kitchen drawer. I didn't know I even had one.'

Barclay laughed. 'Of course she did. Typical. A sommelier's knife is for opening fine wine, wine with a cork of course, not a screw cap.'

'He knows wine then?'

'It's his passion.'

'You wouldn't know it to look at him.'

'And that, of course, is the whole problem. People judge and draw ill-informed conclusions from his appearance. He can't help being big boned.'

'He's a wee bit more than big boned.'

'Whatever. He's naturally huge. He can't do anything about that. And you can't be a professional sommelier if you can't glide gracefully between the tables in London or Paris. He's had trials in all of Europe's top establishments only to find that, no matter how knowledgeable he is and how sophisticated his palate, he scares the customers too much. It would be comical if it didn't break his heart when he clatters into a neighbouring table.'

Stop it, Barclay, you're breaking *my* heart.

'Couldn't he just talk or write about wine if he's such an authority?' I asked.

Barclay shook his head. 'Hardly. You know Number Two. He's a man of few words even at the best of times.'

That was very true. Aside from the odd dodgy expletive, he was probably the quietest man I'd ever met.

'Or grow wine? A vineyard perhaps?'

'Doesn't like heights, can't do ladders, up or down. And there's so much prejudice with potential employers and investors, they can't see beyond what's physically in front of them. They see a 'thug' rather than a man, and definitely not a…'

'…gentle man?' I was careful to separate the words.

'Indeed.'

'Not a violent man then?'

'What do you think? Of course not. But he's not stupid either, that's the other thing, and he needs to earn a living. If that luxury epicurean world was closed to him due to his appearance, he decided he may as well pander to society's petty prejudices and find something that could capitalise on his size and appearance.'

'And that's where you came in?'

'Not immediately, no. I didn't go looking for him – we met entirely by accident. It was about five years ago, in Monte Carlo of all places. I was in a bit of a dip and was emotionally all at sea. I'd run away from a bad situation rather than confronting it. I'd been pretty awful over something, childish and petulant with someone who, I see now, looking back, really didn't deserve it. But I was young and even brasher back then and thought relationships were an unnecessary encumbrance and beneath me. So I ran away.'

'You had a relationship? With another person?' I was surprised. I'd very much thought of Barclay as always having been single, a lone wolf separate from the rest of us.

He looked a little uncomfortable and glanced at his Breitling. 'It's a long story, but I guess we have the time for you to hear it.'

'I'm Gary Lineker. Fire away.'

"Gary Lineker'?'

'The crisps guy. Y'know. All ears. Doesn't matter. Tell me more.'

'As I said, it was about five years ago. Things were bad here so I ran to Europe and went a bit wild. I did things I wasn't proud of but I survived. Oh, don't look so surprised...you do *judge* people, don't you, Claire?'

I looked at my feet. I guess I did.

'Anyway, I was eating and drinking far too much for a lunchtime in the Café de Paris in Monaco, spending a fortune which *obviously* surprises you, and there was a commotion at the far end of the restaurant, voices raised, kids crying, a mother screaming, dogs yapping. They really shouldn't let children in the better places you know, it always gets quite unseemly and…'

'You're digressing,' I interrupted.

'I am. Sorry. Anyway, there was this almighty fuss kicking off and the wine waiter, who was of course poor old Hugues, was standing in the middle of it, his head bowed, massive shoulders shaking, tears dripping from his face, as the Maître d' tore into him at full volume, waving his arms around in a most indecorous manner whilst trying to apologise to the parents of the screaming brats.'

'Why were they screaming?'

'You said it yourself, his physical appearance can be quite intimidating.'

'And the kids just…'

'Did what rich kids do. Got their way. He was fired before I had even ordered my dessert.'

'Poor you. Poor Hugues.'

'Indeed. Anyway, that whole scene stuck with me for the rest of the day and later that night, when I was driving back to my hotel in Nice, I saw him again, sitting by the side of the road, his comical legs hanging over one of those sheer cliffs they have on the Riviera. I pulled over and walked back to him.'

'What was he doing?'

'Crying. Contemplating the rotten cards life had dealt him. Thinking of jumping. He was completely distraught. It took all my powers of persuasion to stop him leaping there and then. I wouldn't have been able to physically restrain him but my French is actually more expressive than my English at times and I was able to talk him around after a few hours.

'I gave him a lift back in my car – that proved a squeeze, I can tell you – and he stayed for a few days in the hotel while I sorted some stuff out for him. I even bought him a little dog as a companion, a tiny little black Toy Poodle which he still has and adores. That dog's love saved his life I think.'

'No, I think you saved his life, Barclay,' I said.

'Maybe,' he said with surprising modesty

'It was fate.'

'It was friendship. Two misfits shunned by the rest of polite society. He decided to come back to London with me and it was then that I realised that I could use his misfortune to purposes that would be mutually beneficial for the pair of us. That's when I came up with the job for him – he would be my Thug Number Two.'

'And what really did happen with Thug Number One?'

'I told you, we don't talk about that.'

'But…'

He sighed a pantomime sigh. 'You must never breathe a word of this to him or anyone.'

'Promise.'

'Okay. Truth is that there never was a Thug Number One. Hugues is an incredibly proud man, he wouldn't accept charity from anyone, and if he knew that I had created a job specifically for him it would massively humiliate and embarrass him, so I told him and everyone that he was an essential worker, replacing my irreplaceable heavy Thug Number One.'

'Who was fictional?'

'Exactly.'

'That's very thoughtful of you.' He smiled. 'Not Barclay-like at all.' He scowled.

'I wouldn't go that far. Besides, we both saw the opportunity even if I was a little loose with the truth with him over how it had arisen. He was literally at the end of his tether, unable to hold down any job. He's one of those odd types, desperate to serve, but as I say, you can't work in the service industry when you weigh thirty-five stone and terrify people, no matter how much you try not to. But what we do, you and I, we work in a field where such looks can be handy, a little soupçon of menace can go along way when you're doing what we do.'

I nodded. TNT had scared the living bejeezus out of me ever since Barclay had first introduced him but I'd never thought about the man, just saw the mighty behemoth. And Barclay hadn't done that, he had become his friend, his only friend, saving his life in the process. That explained the loyalty. It might have even been love. Barclay was perhaps, despite everything else, a better person than me.

'How's the dog these days? I asked.

'Fine. Hugues named him 'Barclay', you know.'

And with that I found myself choking back a little sob and had to wipe something from my eye.

'Ah, headlights,' said Barclay, and, sure enough, a large vehicle was approaching in the dim early dawn light, then slowed as it neared us. It was our own Dawn and her Hank in an ancient Land Rover, patched together with ill-fitting bolts, amateurish home welding and some serious countryside mud.

'Brought a proper car with us,' laughed Hank.

'Not a fan of vorsprung durch technik then?' asked Barclay.

'Can't beat British – German engineering's massively overrated in my book. Look at BMW and what they've done to the Mini…'

And the two of them were off again on another long discussion about the glories of a bygone era they could only have read about and never actually experienced. I wasn't interested, just knackered, and when we finally left the scene ten minutes later, I curled up on the backseat with Dawn and we both fell soundly asleep, the inane banter from the front droning us into the peaceful land of nod as Hank The Hero drove us home to the safety and security of good old London Town.

Chapter 9

Barclay wasn't happy. I wasn't happy either. I was back in Hammersmith on the Fulham Palace Road, minus the Ford Transit and TNT but now with Barclay perched behind me as I rode the Triumph Bonneville for the first time in London traffic.

I don't think I'd ever felt so nervous on the road before. Part of it was undoubtedly down to my inexperience on the bike, part of it was the fact that this was a quality piece of mechanical engineering thrumming between my thighs, but mostly it was the extreme vulnerability I was feeling with all of those Chelsea tractors thundering around me, like lions circling their prey. Do lions circle? Do they hunt like that? Mum's hero Attenborough would know but I had no idea. Must remember to ask her next time we spoke. One thing was certain though: I was bottom of this particular food chain and ripe for the taking.

I didn't have a clue why Barclay was so bloody miserable. My efforts on the bike hadn't been that lamentable. He'd muttered something about 'Green not being happy' with developments, but I had no idea what he meant by that nor who this 'Green' character was. Another of his well-dodgy business associates? His last business partner, Tom 'Thomas' Pedakowski, had turned out to be a nightmare and I really could do without being kidnapped, double-crossed and shot at by an unseen sniper again. A repeat prescription was certainly not what the doctor had ordered.

At least I wasn't having to listen to Barclay moaning about everything as he had been unable to get our intercom things to work so my helmet was a little oasis of muffled near-silence, isolated from the outside world. No more difficult small talk or macho bollocks from him. No more tiringly naïve questions from me. It was what we would both probably describe as a 'win-win'.

Of course, neither of us were going to be particularly happy chappies as we were having to clear up after my latest fuck up: that butter-wouldn't-melt head teacher Stella Partridge had short changed us by more than a thousand quid and that was bad. One of Barclay's 'flexible' business rules was that you never to go back to the same target twice, but Partridge had really riled him and we had, to his thinking at least, been conned out of what we had been promised. You may think that was a little unfair, given that we were playing an illegal game of blackmail ourselves, but you've got to have some ethics in life, haven't you? So we were back for more, hence him pressing her again for what we were 'owed', hence us returning to West London at midnight and the same, deserted riverside business park. Hence me saying 'hence' a lot – it was very much a 'hence' kind of thing.

She was waiting for us, standing under a king-size street lamp, puffing furiously on one of those electronic fag things, fluffy clouds of vapour rising from her like she was a steam train. She had dressed casually, leggings, trainers and a loose T-shirt. She looked like she may have just been out jogging. She didn't have a holdall this time, just one of those runners' light rucksack things you see sporty types with. I hoped all the money was in there. Barclay was determined that we did not make the same mistake twice and was going to be sure by doing this pick-up himself, not relying on me and TNT to learn from our mistakes. I kept the bike running as he swung his leg around and dismounted, his new bike leathers sticking for a second on the hot leather of the seat. He walked purposefully towards her. We both kept our helmets on as we were planning a quick getaway. The helmets were good for anonymity, but I still wasn't confident I could handle the bike if things got panicky.

Fuck, it was hot. Can't you wear lighter clothing on a bike? What's the point of the freedom of the road if you have to wrap yourself up in all the leather and stifling headgear? All seemed too health and safety to me but Barclay had insisted, said he wasn't taking any chances no matter how warm it was. I didn't have him pegged as a risk-adverse type, far from it, but, being something of a nervous Nelly myself on the bike, I didn't argue.

I had no visor but I still couldn't hear clearly what was being said. Barclay was doing his best seriously-pissed-off-man angry gesturing and I could see the conversation was not genial. Partridge looked terrified, Barclay's height, black helmet and dark leathers combo scaring seven shades of shit out of the cowering woman. I was actually starting to feel a little sorry for the short-changing bitch.

She timidly held out the bag and Barclay snatched it from her, fumbling it open with his gloved hands and poking at the contents. He lifted his head angrily and she shook hers rapidly, then nodded furiously. Barclay slung the bag over his shoulder and waved an angry finger at her before turning away and trotting back towards me and the bike.

'All there this time?' I said.

He nodded. 'Let's go.'

He climbed on the back of the seat and his arms encircled me. I kicked away the stand and nervously managed to execute a clumsy 180 degree turn before jerking through the gears and heading away at a less-than-impressive lick, slower than a learner rider taking their test. As rapid getaways go, it was modest in the extreme and once we'd turned the corner Barclay tapped me on the shoulder and motioned for me to pull over.

'What's wrong?' I asked, knowing full well what wasn't right.

'What are the hell are you playing at? You go any slower and we'll topple over! She could already be on her mobile calling the police – do you want to give them a sporting chance or something?'

'Sorry.'

'You need more practice on the bike,' he said, more than a little impatient. 'I'll ride. Swap.'

Damn, but he was right. For all my bravado I found the bike daunting and I was nowhere near as comfortable on two wheels as I was on four. We quickly dismounted and swapped positions. Another Claire fuck up averted. I was not having a good time.

He revved the accelerator and we roared away, Barclay shifting through the gears rapidly and with confidence, the Bonneville's throaty growl loudly announcing to the world that Barclay The Man was in charge. Bloody hell, Barclay – I thought we were supposed to be doing this discreetly, not turning the neighbourhood into your own personal Brands Hatch?

He slowed momentarily as we re-joined the Fulham Palace Road, then weaved in and out of the light night-time traffic like a reckless courier with a late delivery. It was exhilarating but I was bricking it at every turn, dropping to the left and right with Barclay's every movement, hanging on for dear life as he dipped and straightened, forty, fifty, sixty as we raced back through the sleepy streets before joining the Thames road.

This was more like it. This was a real getaway. Barclay slowed occasionally to appease the succession of speed cameras on the north side of the Thames, a token gesture to the law in our lawless escape. I hoped that he'd cross the river at the first opportunity to escape their imperious scrutiny and really let the Bonneville rip.

Mission accomplished. Success. I just had to get my bike riding skills up to scratch and I was sure that would come with a bit of practice. Assuming I could ever wrestle control of the bike back from Barclay – he was good, and boy did he know it. Regardless, things were picking up. Barclay and MacDonald were back on the road and in full control, nothing could stop us n…

It came from nowhere, darting out from a left turning onto the embankment and narrowly missing clipping us at the first attempt. 'It' was another bike, no idea what type but a big bugger, and it was fast. Fucking fast. I looked over my shoulder and it was gaining on us. Speed cameras be damned. 'Go, Barclay, GO!' I shouted.

He got the message and I felt the bike lurch into life beneath me, its thunderous power thrilling yet terrifying, the engine's roar reassuringly masculine and loud. Fuck the sleeping neighbourhood.

Barclay lent over the handlebars and we pulled away, accelerating from the bike and traffic behind us. He, whoever it was who thought he could take us, would eat our dust – no way was he going to catch us.

I glanced over my shoulder. Bloody hell – he was trying his damndest and was gaining again. Barclay was good but whoever was chasing knew his stuff too. Close. Closer. Too close. He was suddenly right behind us, his front wheel just yards from me, I could have almost reached out and touched it. I squeezed Barclay's waist and screamed as the other bike scraped our rear light and the number plate. Was he mad? Was he trying to kill us?

Barclay must have felt my panic and gave another sharp twist of the accelerator and threw the bike forward, pulling us a few feet further ahead but there was no way we could…

I leaned forward and squeezed Barclay tighter (as if that would make any bloody difference). Ahead were red lights and a small queue of law-abiding traffic. Barclay didn't slow but instead went even faster. 'Turn right, Barclay! Jump the lights and cut across right!' I screamed, unheard over the roar of the engine. But he knew, he knew exactly what to do and he accelerated towards the stationary traffic before executing a text book racing manoeuvre; he dropped the gears and we both dipped to the right perfectly, our knees stroking the tarmac as we leant into the curve and Barclay flew us passed the horn honking traffic and right, onto Albert Bridge. With no traffic ahead he expertly fired the bike up through the gears again. I glanced back. The other bike had made the turn too but was now several hundred feet behind us. So long, sucker.

We sped through Battersea Park as Barclay forced us eastwards. Another glance behind. The chasing bike was back and gaining again, its headlight swelling as it ate up the distance between us. I gasped and squeezed Barclay in alarm. He lent lower and somehow the Bonneville responded to his urgency. We'd just be a blur on a speed camera, we were beyond caring.

We shot around Vauxhall, narrowly missing a lumbering double decker, then Barclay surprised me by turning left and taking the river route through Lambeth rather than cutting up to Kennington. Across the river the Houses of Parliament loomed large. Why the fuck was he taking the scenic route? Another peek over my shoulder. The other rider was still there and accelerating, even under my helmet I could hear his engine, louder, coarser than our own. Fifty yards behind. Forty yards.

Thirty. Twenty.

Too close.

The Waterloo one-way system commanded that we went right but Barclay ignored it and took the direct route, straight ahead. A bemused Ford Fiesta honked and honked again in protest but we were gone. Vamoose.

Suddenly I could hear a police siren behind us, its loud wail piercing the cocoon of my helmet's padding. I turned and could see the blue light growing, the siren louder. It caught the bike behind us first, probably hadn't even seen us. Our pursuer slowed and Barclay, a glance backwards, made his move and turned left, breaking sharply and expertly, pulling us to a tidy stop right by the London Eye.

We quickly dismounted and walked from the Bonneville as if uninterested, removing our helmets before settling on a nearby bench. A police car paused at the top of the road and then carried on, ignoring us, a couple seemingly enjoying the views of the Thames and its tastefully-lit attractions.

Suckers.

'I thought he had us!' I was still short of breath and the adrenaline was pumping.

'Who?'

'The other bike!'

'What other bike?'

I punched his arm. 'Ow!' he exclaimed, then grinned. 'How was my riding?'

'Fanfuckingtastic! How did you learn to ride like that?'

'I didn't know I could. Instinct. Thank the video games I guess.'

I hadn't pegged him as a gamer, but what did I know?

'Amazing, just amazing,' I said.

'Yes, it was exciting, I'll give you that.'

'Who was he?'

'You're assuming it was a bloke.'

'Good point. Who was it?'

'No idea.'

'But they meant business – I thought we were finished when

they caught the back of the bike.'

'I felt something but it was a brush rather than a shove – wasn't sure he'd touched us.'

'He did. Broke the rear light I think. Just a few more inches and we'd have been finished.'

Barclay's eyes widened. 'I had no idea he was that close.'

'Or she?'

'Or she,' he agreed. 'You must have been terrified.'

I had been. I was starting to get the shakes. That was the third time someone had tried to get me in the past week or so. The same someone? No idea.

'Now do you believe me that someone's after us?' I asked.

'May just have been a thrill seeker,' he shrugged but I wasn't buying that. 'If it was someone specifically after us,' he reasoned, 'how did they know that we would be here? How do they know what we're doing, where we're going to be?'

'I don't know but I think it's something to do with that Bartholomew. I think he's looking to tidy away us loose ends.'

Barclay looked pensive and went silent.

'He's after us, Barclay. Somehow, he knows what we're doing and where we're doing it.'

'That wasn't him on the bike,' he said. 'No way could he ride like that.'

'No, of course not, but it's him pulling the strings, like he did with that gunman in Kent.' I shuddered at the memory.

'Possibly,' he said.

'Definitely,' I insisted.

'Maybe.'

Another pause. I could almost hear the cogs in his brain turning as he mulled it over.

'What are we going to do about it?'

'We can't do anything – we've nothing conclusive, nothing that ties it back to him or anyone else, come to that. Let me sleep on it. Besides, we can't stay here all night.' He rose from the bench and took my hand. 'Your ride awaits, Ms MacDonald.'

We returned to the bike and put on our helmets. Barclay took the front again and he got no argument from me. He was a natural and our roles had reversed. I decided I could live with that. For a while at least.

'Home, James,' I commanded and he kicked us off, this time at a sedate pace more appropriate for the time of night, my mind buzzing with all the questions but, sadly, none of the answers.

What the fuck were we going to do?

Chapter 10

Sleep and I were becoming strangers. I was all for the Barclay-generated excitement of the night before but all that 'danger' business with the other bike was not my idea of a fun night out, no sir, and my adrenaline levels were taking forever to return to normal, making a decent night's sleep almost impossible. My mind wouldn't shut up either – near-death experiences can do that to you, I guess. The flat was hot, my bed even hotter, but not in a naughty, Dawn-like way. This was in an uncomfortable, sweaty, anxiety-ridden Claire-like way. I tossed and turned, turned and tossed, just couldn't get comfortable. Hours passed. Hours of nothing. Wide-eyed, sleepless hours.

And then my phone sang into life and I was awake. When had I fallen asleep? I fumbled for the clock and saw it was almost midday. I had actually slept, and slept too long, too deeply after all. Shit. Another unplanned 'working from home' day from Marshalls – Andersonn had said that he was okay with me staying out of the office while I did his dirty work for him, safe from Lizzie and Pete's curious eyes. God knows when I'd find the time to get around to some of the spreadsheets though. Too much on my mind. All of it more important than his pathetic nonsense.

My phone rang. It was Barclay calling. He said he'd been doing some thinking and we needed to talk. He suggested lunch at the Cutty Sark. 'You paying?' I asked.

'If you insist,' he sighed.

It's not widely known outside the area but Greenwich is blessed with not just one but two Cutty Sarks of historical note.

The famous one of course is the legendary tea clipper, proud and majestically parked on a fancy fragile-looking glass cloud on the riverfront edge of the town's dilapidated tourist-trap centre. Once it had been the fastest ship on the seven seas, but it was a brief reign as faster, more economical steam ships were already being built before the clipper even got its bows wet.

I'd done the guided tour once and could bore for Britain on its history. A while back there had been a massive fire and the ship was burned to a crisp, gone for good. But then it was revealed that what burned wasn't the whole boat and that most of the original timbers had been taken away for a coat of Ronseal or whatever they use on these things and a few years later it re-emerged, Phoenix-like and fully restored, better than ever. Like magic. Very suspicious magic I'd imagine to the insurance company, but there you go.

Still they were quite adamant that it was the original boat, despite being all burned and whatnot. And the flocks of tourists don't seem to mind, so who am I to question it? It looks magnificent anyway, majestic even, and made me feel proud to be a local.

But the famous boat, ship, insurance swindle, whatever, is a pretty shit place to meet for a quiet word or three about the dangers that were encroaching on the night-time world of the Barclay and MacDonald gang, what with all the tourists hanging around it and all that post-fire CCTV threatening our privacy and freedom. That wasn't the Cutty Sark Barclay was referring to. No sir.

Fortunately for us, then, there's a *second* Cutty Sark. It's a fair-sized riverside Georgian inn just a brisk half a mile or so's walk east of the new-yet-old ship, boasting equally spectacular and panoramic views of the Thames, Millennium Dome (or whatever it's called these days) and the skyscrapers of Barclay's old Docklands haunt Canary Wharf, glinting in the dazzling summer sunshine.

The pub is one of the borough's finest, a throwback to simpler times and a refuge from the hurly and indeed burly of the 21st century. A marvellous, popular summer boozer and well worth the trip from Deptford. At weekends it overspills with visitors and locals escaping the arty farty namby pamby Greenwich craft market for a pie or roast. But during the week it was all ours, and as good a place as any for a quiet chat. Barclay and I needed to talk. Boy, did we need to talk.

I was sweating profusely outside the pub, sitting at one

of the outdoor tables perfectly placed for a little river front al fresco dining like they do in proper Europe. No shade though; Barclay didn't seem to be inconvenienced by the heat but I was melting quicker than the Wicked Witch of the West. The June temperatures were continuing to break records and I was starting to wonder if this was actually it, the tipping point when global warming, inspired by the climate change sceptics, was finally going to give it one final push and shift the British Isles from our modest north Atlantic climate into some brave new world of Mediterranean scorchio weather. God, I hoped not – never been a sun worshipper, me.

Bloody Brits moaning about the bloody weather. Typical. Anyway, on to other matters:

'Now do you believe me?' I asked.

'You honestly think someone's out to get us?

'Three times in a week, Barclay. First the police are waiting for us in New Cross...'

'I told you, that was coincidence. They got lucky.'

'We got lucky – we got away. How did they know? I wasn't exactly burning rubber when they turned on the blue meanie.'

'Like I say, coincidence.'

'Didn't you once say that coincidence was God's way of staying anonymous?' Barclay looked surprised I remembered his attempt at a bit of cod philosophy. 'Coincidence? Maybe, but unlikely. Two,' I was counting them off on my fingers, 'Hugues and I get shot at when doing the pick-up from the posh prozzie in Hammersmith.'

He exhaled like he was slowly deflating, bored already. 'There was a hole in a tyre.'

'A bullet-shaped hole. It scared seven shades of shite out of TNT.'

'I don't think you're thinking rationally – how would anyone know that it was you chaps fleeing the scene? It doesn't make sense. You're being paranoid.'

'It doesn't have to make sense. It's too fucking dangerous, Barclay! I didn't sign up for this shit.'

He quickly glanced left and right. Fortunately, we were still alone. I had got a little heated there. He motioned to me to quieten it a tad.

'Three,' I said, nearly a whisper, 'that bike last night. He was after us. He knew it was us. He tried to bump us into the Thames. Too close, far too close for comfort.'

He couldn't look me in the eye and squirmed on the wooden bench.

'Maybe.'

'No 'maybe' about it Barclay. Wake up! It might not even be a 'he', could just have likely been Stella Partridge, it could be Samantha Fielding…'

'Who?'

'The teacher whose boyfriend I shot last year!' Memory like a sieve that man.

'Could be the boyfriend,' said Barclay, helpfully.

'Yes, it could bloody well be him, too, thanks for reminding me. It could be the ghost of Tom Thomas for all I know, but I think it has to be that Bartholomew or his sniper or some other lowlife ne'er-do-well he's dredged up from some gutter and set on us.'

'But you don't know, Claire. You're putting two and two together and coming up with Bartholomew. You can't say that with any certainty. And what if it is? What do you suggest we do about it?'

'We go after him before he finally gets us.'

That stopped him dead in his denials.

'We…go…after…him?'

'Sure. You know where he lives?' He nodded unenthusiastically. 'You know how to break into places?' He nodded again.

'And we kill him in his bed?' he half-joked, mock alarm in his eyes. 'Claire, are you seriously suggesting..?'

'Of course not. But if we can find evidence that he's targeting us, we can plan our next move before he can make his. Doesn't have to be physical – you can do your clever hacking online magic on him again and crush him in cyberland.'

He said nothing, but gave a tiny nod of agreement. Good.

Things were looking up. We were taking the initiative, taking on our adversary at his own game. That was more like it. I was on a roll, Barclay was actually listening. 'Shall we order some food?' he asked, anything to shut me up.

Good. I was starvin' marvin. I could murder some decent fish and chips.

We ate inside – the midday heat had proven too much even for Barclay – and decided to try a couple of the guest real ales to whet our proverbial whistles. 'What's mine again?' I asked, sniffing my half of earthy smelling beer.

'It's called 'Goat's Scrote'. Not the most appetising of names, is it?'

I almost sprayed it across the table, laughing. 'Seriously?'

He chuckled. 'No. It's Ghost Ship from somewhere out Suffolk way. The barman recommended it. I quite like 'Goat's Scrote' though – a very real ale kind of name. Mine's a pale ale with a hint of elderflower. Surprisingly pleasant.' He smacked his lips like it was a fine wine. Hadn't figured him as a beer drinker.

'Tell me about this 'Green' then, Barclay.'

'Who?'

'This 'Green' you keep referring to. His name keeps coming up and...'

'Ah. Can we just leave it for now, please? It's private, delicate.'

'No we can't. This partnership in crime ain't going to work at all if we keep secrets from each other. Surely we've moved on from all the secrets now?'

'You kept your relationship with Tom secret from me,' he replied.

'But…'

I paused. He had a point. I had known that Tom was a business 'associate' of Barclay's, and I had then found out that he was actually the police consultant investigating Barclay, none of which I mentioned to my boss until it was all too late. I had also neglected to mention that Tom and I had been intimate in a very biblical sense on more than one occasion.

'Okay, my mistake and I agree that I should have told you earlier that I was seeing Tom, but let's just see if we can improve things going forward, shall we? Full disclosure, no more surprises, no shadowy puppet masters in the background pulling all the strings. That's not a lot to ask, is it? Partner?'

Barclay was looking distinctly uncomfortable and avoided my gaze.

'Barclay? I'm serious.'

He swirled his beer. He didn't say a word and picked at some lint on his trousers.

'Barclay? Everything on the table or I walk.'

He looked up and sighed. 'You're not serious, surely?'

I gave him my best Paddington hard stare. 'Try me.'

'This is…this is a little embarrassing.'

'Secrets always are.' I sound like a teacher scolding an errant eight-year-old. 'So who is this 'Green' chap? Another bent copper? A shady City wanker you're ripping off? Some 4x4 driving gangster Mister Big muscling in on your territory?'

'He's…he's a 'she',' he mumbled.

My eyes widened but I wasn't going to have it throw me completely. I kept my composure and sipped my ale. Arch misogynist Barclay was taking orders from a female of the species? I could scarcely believe it.

'You're working for a woman?'

'Not exactly, but I guess I am in a manner of speaking.'

Was it then…could it be?! Oh Barclay, you wag you.

'Is this Green your lady friend, Mr Barclay?' I smiled. I couldn't help it. Delicious.

'Kind of.'

Suddenly I wanted to know absolutely everything and more. 'A girlfriend! She's your girlfriend! Dark horse or what? What's she like? Older? Younger? Tall? Taller? Rich? Richer? Blonde or brunette…or ginger? I can see you going for a classy redhead and…'

'Not a girl. A woman. Her name is Green. And she's my…' he paused and took a big gulp of his pint, 'wife.'

The glass slipped from my fingers and shattered on the York

stone floor. Mum always said it was rude to stare but I couldn't help it, couldn't blink, could barely breathe.

There had not been any mention of a wife. Not one. Not from him, not from Dawn, not from Tom or Barclay's parents. My little world had been sent spinning. 'Your..?'

'Wife. Green.'

'It's…it's an odd name, 'Green'?'

'It's not her original first name – that was Philippa. But she's used just her surname since school. Goes with her eyes.'

Speechless. I was speechless. 'When you went so quiet for all those months I just thought you were tied up in the court stuff, but by the sound of things you were, what? Dating?'

He sighed. He didn't look remotely amused. 'Still managed to get myself a ball and chain after all.' It was a very un-Barclay thing to say and a wee bit sexist but I smiled regardless – he was uncomfortable confessing and deserved some slack for being so honest. Why hadn't he told me earlier? Surely he didn't think I'd be upset, did he? And where had been my invite to the wedding?

'And what's she like, this woman of yours called Green?'

'She's tall and elegant and quite the most beautiful woman I have ever met.' His cheeks reddened and his eyes were restless. 'She's complex, socially she's shy, a little awkward. She's cautious around new people. Takes a while to thaw. You might not take to her immediately. It all had to be done very quietly. Nothing public.'

I raised an eyebrow, a trick I'd only recently mastered. 'And that's why you haven't mentioned her before?'

'One of the reasons. When you meet her you'll understand. She needs ushering into my world slowly.'

I smiled. 'It's all very romantic, very Jane Austen.'

'Don't say that. I can't stand that woman's films.'

I didn't correct him on that one. 'And you're living together?'

'We do now. She's been away, overseas for a while but she's back now and we're very much…y'know. She is quite beautiful. I think I mentioned that.'

'You did. It's wow, Barclay, major wow. Have you met her

family? Parents? Are you planning a family and..?'

He shook his head. 'Slow down, Claire. No need to be so excited. Green and I are still getting to know each other. It's been a bit of a whirlwind.'

I grinned. 'Does Dawn know?'

He shook his head. 'Not really, no. Full disclosure, you demanded. Full disclosure you got.'

'But bloody hell, Barclay, I didn't expect this.'

'Would you like another drink? You were rather clumsy with the last one.'

'Sorry, yes I was, but you can't blame me. I think I need a proper one this time. G&T please. Double. Bombay Sapphire if they've got it.'

He left our table and headed to the bar, no doubt delighted to get out of my searing, inquisitive spotlight for a few minutes at least.

Bloody hell. Barclay and a Mrs Barclay. For real. I had no idea.

He returned with two glasses and a packet of salt and vinegar. 'Shall we order dessert?

'Sure. When will I get to meet Mrs Barclay?'

'Green. Just call her Green. We're going for dinner up in town at the end of the week. You could join us for a drink beforehand.' He visibly perked up at the prospect and smiled. 'Yes, that would be good. Let's do that.'

'She knows about me? Our work?'

'She knows elements. If you came along…'

'Let me guess; I'm a 'business associate' rather than a getaway driver?'

'Correct.'

'And you and me, we're completely legal, legitimate and not in the slightest bit involved in any hacking or blackmail activity whatsoever?'

'Exactly. 'Lifestyle Coaches' is what we are.'

'As in 'we know something about your lifestyle, how about giving us a coachload of cash to keep schtumm about it'?'

He smiled again. I think this little confession had helped

him, unburdening himself at last to someone, even if it was only Claire MacDonald, the social worker for social misfits.

A loud, over-excited family of Japanese tourists arrived, snapping everything in sight with their giant Canons and swarming over several tables right next to us. Barclay gave me a look to indicate that maybe we should drink up and move on. A shame to miss out on the Spotted Dick and custard, but we weren't going to be able to continue our conversation with all that 'did William Shakespeare live near here?' questioning. Besides, I needed some time to think this all through. And, of course, to prepare for meeting Green on Friday evening.

Chapter 11

'Have you ever been to Paris?' Barclay had asked on the Thursday. It was an exciting question to be asked.

I said I hadn't. 'I've never had anyone special to explore it with. That's what you're supposed to do, isn't it? That's what they say, it's a city for lovers, not loners. To go as a tourist on my tod wouldn't be right, it would feel a bit of a waste.'

'That's one way of looking at it,' he said. 'I didn't have you down as such a romantic.'

Don't you believe it mate, but I decided that it was best not to remind him of my thing with Tom. 'Why do you ask?'

'I'm not suggesting we go to Paris if that's what you're thinking. No, it's just the place I'm taking Green to tomorrow night is like a little piece of thirties Paris right in the heart of London.'

'Really?'

'You know, one of those little secret places that you keep to yourself.'

I never got to hear about those places for obvious reasons. 'Sounds interesting.'

'Why don't you meet us 'accidentally' outside Zédel at 7.30 and I'll introduce you to a little taste of Paris. And to Green, of course. I'll send you the address and we'll see you there.'

It was too enticing an invitation to turn down. I put my mobile back down on my desk and Lizzie gave me a conspiratorial look.

'You off somewhere nice then for the weekend?' she asked, grinning. 'I've got ears like a hawk, me.'

'Eyes. Eyes like a hawk. If you had ears like a hawk you wouldn't be able to wear your glasses.'

'Whatever. Is it Paris then?' It was like she was psychic at times but I was never going to tell her that. 'I'd love to go to Paris.'

'So would I,' I thought, but kept it to myself. 'Not this weekend,' I said. 'A little closer to home.'

'Or Venice? I always fancied Venice and...' but before she

could share another of her great, unfulfilled travel fantasies, Lizzie froze, wide-eyed, then suddenly started to sort through the pile of papers on her desk, a desperate attempt to look busy. Uh oh. That could mean only one thing, and I felt a shiver down my back as I felt his hand on my shoulder.

'Good afternoon girls,' said the now-familiar American voice. 'And how are my two most dazzling employees faring today?'

I turned and beamed my very best fake plastic smile. 'Oh, we're just fine and dandy, Mr Andersonn.'

'Anderson. How many times do I have to insist? Please call me Anderson.'

A huge difference. 'Sorry, I meant Anderson.'

He smiled. 'Can I have a few seconds of your time, Claire?'

'Sure,' I said.

'Somewhere private? Sensitive talk.'

'Oh. Okay.'

Avoiding Lizzie's glare I rose from my seat and followed him into Pete's office. He signalled for me to close the door behind me. I couldn't help but notice that Pete's desk seemed to be a little light on all things Pete that morning and the walls looked rather bare.

'Looks a bit different in here,' I said.

'Yes. Very observant. Peter has left the company by mutual consent.'

'Oh.' I doubted that there was anything remotely 'mutual' about it – he'd given no indication of looking elsewhere. It didn't really matter, of course, as I knew 'elsewhere' was very much on Andersonn's business plan for all of us.

'He was starting to ask just a few too many questions and went snooping around in the recycling bins. He reckoned he found some spreadsheets. I'm disappointed, Claire; I thought I'd given very clear instructions that you were not to print anything out?'

'I wasn't aware that I had.'

'Clumsy Claire. That doesn't sound at all like a Claire I can rely on.'

I shrugged.

He sighed dramatically. 'Well, I guess one can only keep a lid on things for so long. Probably best if you do this work out of the office or the others on the floor will suspect something's up.'

I nodded. Suited me just fine.

'And I need to move things much quicker. What are you doing at the end of the month?'

'I...ah, I don't actually plan that far ahead normally.' I couldn't – Barclay never knew what was happening from one day to the next, so what chance did I have?

'Good. Then you're coming to India with me. I checked and they've still got your passport here from when they sorted out that Visa for you a few months back and you were supposed to have all the jabs too, I think?'

I nodded, my right hand rose instinctively to rub my left shoulder where the doctor had painfully jabbed and probed a few months back. I had thought it all a meaningless charade at the time, but now I was beginning to realise it was actually quite real.

'We need to close the transition in the next few weeks and I need someone from here so I'm taking Claire MacDonald. You're done all the hard work so far, you deserve the chance to see it through. Besides,' he winked, he bloody winked, 'it will be the perfect opportunity for us to get to know each other better.'

I shuddered. Think, Claire, think quick.

'I'm not sure that's...I have to go and see my Mum!' I said too quickly; it was all I could think of.

'Your mother?'

'At the end of the month. It's her birthday. She's taken a turn for the worse. I need to go to her.' Lies, all lies, spilling out in such desperation even I wasn't convinced by them.

'Then we'll go at the end of next week. It'll only take a few days to double-check the facilities and close the deal. I will make sure that you're back in time for your Mom. India will change you – you'll come back a completely different woman.'

But I didn't want to be a different woman. He touched my hand in a ridiculous attempt to reassure me. 'The jabs will still be doing their thing, the visa's still got months on it. No need to do the malaria thing in Bangalore so there's no nasty stuff to worry about if we steer clear of the water and don't breathe in the shower.'

Had he just suggested that we would be showering together? I shivered.

'Nothing to worry about, nothing worse than those little pricks you've already had.'

As opposed to the big prick standing opposite me with a Cheshire Cat grin and no doubt a hard-on already tenting his chinos.

I grasped in my mind for an excuse, any excuse, but I couldn't think fast enough and found myself nodding involuntarily. 'Okay,' I mumbled. It certainly wasn't okay. I'd think of something. I may even be dead by then if we didn't stop Bartholomew.

'Excellent!' I'd obviously made his day. I realised then that it was all part of his cunning plan, there'd been no rogue spreadsheet that my former boss had found. This git had made all that up to get Pete out of the way and me onto that plane, into a hotel room, into the shower, into bed. Creepy little arrogant tubby shit. I'd have to throw a sickie as I had absolutely no intention of going to the airport whatsoever, let alone getting on a plane with him. Not to India. No way, Jose. Plenty can happen in a week. I decided that I would play along for now but I'd jilt him at the check-in on his big day and leave him to his own disappointment. It's not like I needed the job, the job was going to India without me anyway.

Besides, I was due in Paris at 7.30.

The restaurant was called Zédel, and it was on the pedestrianised end of Sherwood Street, just a few paces from Piccadilly Circus, the hub of the West End that never sleeps thanks to its weak attempt to be London's answer to Times Square, all neon billboards, begging statues and slow-walking crowds of visitors wondering what the hell all the fuss was about. Where was the circus? They'd been promised a circus but there were only pigeons and other bemused tourists. No clowns. They, the tourists, were the only clowns in town.

Never mind guys, Trafalgar Square's only a few hundred yards away and you'll feel far more at home there with those busloads of students with their selfie sticks. Sorry about the 'circus' thing. Move along now, nothing to see here.

Even from a distance Zédel was something else. Captivating. I'd arrived early and decided to have a nose around before I was due to try bumping in to Barclay's wife (I still couldn't get the idea of a Mrs Barclay straight in my head). Was she there already? I couldn't see any particularly breath-taking beauty elegantly passing the time waiting for her husband.

There was a small area at the front of the restaurant fenced off from the hoi polloi milling outside the theatre opposite and one of those celebrity chef chain restaurants, this one for the irritating cocky cockney on Channel 4. I bet he'd never been there. It looked insincere and plastic, fake Italian food for the masses.

It was the antithesis of Zédel – Zédel was pure class. A large, colourful canopy sheltered a few customers from the sun and there was a distinctly French air about the place, both inside and out.

Maybe Green was already inside? I made my way through the al fresco diners and a doorman, looking every bit the Parisian cliché, even down to the thinnest of moustaches on his top lip, opened the heavy door for me, a small bow to demonstrate his Gallic civility. 'Merci,' I said, proud of my masterful grasp of the language.

Inside… Wow. Just wow. Barclay had not lied. The place *was* Paris, or certainly the nostalgic Art Deco images of Paris we all imagine. The café area was small, fashionably compact and crowded with densely occupied tables, the clientele dripping with wealth in their sanctuary from the hustle and bustle of London and its chronic pollution. There was even Edith Piaf 'je ne regrette rien'-ing from the hidden speakers, a ghostly soundtrack from a long-lost era. I could imagine the room smelling of Gauloises. Maybe they had a special French fag air freshener?

It was ridiculously French! If you asked a class of school kids to draw a French café this was exactly what they would have come up with. Newspapers on poles? But of course. The smell of cheesy French Onion soup and strong, pitch-black coffee battling it out with the whiff of overripe brie baguettes and hoppy beer? Yes sir. A little old lady, extravagantly overdressed and with the obligatory handbag-sized Chihuahua that was showing far too much interest in her plate? Tick. Every inch of wall space crammed with framed black and white prints of long-dead celebrities? Inevitable. And aproned waiters skilfully ferrying trays of drinks, sandwiches and pastries between the tightly packed furniture (in a most un-TNT manner)? Oui! Oui! Oui!

So, so French. Extravagant. Expensive. A world apart. Pure class.

I felt so out of place.

I had no idea bars like this still existed, let alone in London. I instantly wanted to take Dawn there. Dawn would love this so much. But then I'd seen so little of her – nothing in fact – since she and Hank had dropped us off after rescuing us from that clapped-out Porsche. They'd ridden off into the early sunrise, mission accomplished, and she'd gone completely offline. No responses to my texts about the new man in her life. He wasn't my type but she appeared to be completely smitten.

Good for her.

'Mademoiselle – may I assist?'

'What? Oh, sorry, miles away. I'm waiting for someone and…'

'Maybe wait for heem outside? We are not very big in ze café and…' He signalled to the door and I nodded, embarrassed, before making my way back out onto the street…and bumping straight into Barclay.

'Claire!' He exclaimed. 'Fancy meeting you here!'

It sounded as false to my ears as that waiter's accent. I just had to smile, couldn't help myself.

'Why, if it isn't my old friend and occasional boss man big

boy Barclay himself! Well I never!' He didn't appreciate the sarcasm and shot me daggers before moving to one side and revealing his companion, standing a step behind him in his shadow.

'Claire, allow me to introduce you to Green. My wife.'

She smiled and the breath left my lungs, my world was ablaze. He had warned me, told me, insisted even, but nothing had prepared me for Green.

She was, I can honestly say, the most beautiful woman I had ever seen. Tall in her Jimmie Choo heels, unspeakably elegant in a tight, off-the-shoulder black number I would have killed a room full of puppies and kittens for, her shoulder length raven hair dancing in the light breeze. I wanted to be her. I wanted to be with her. She was a vision. My mouth dried and I swallowed hard. There were no words I could muster to greet her.

'So this is Claire?' She took my hand and delicately held it. A smile lifted the corners of her mouth but disappointingly fell short of her eyes. 'Barclay has told me so much about you.'

I still had no words.

'All good, I can assure you,' laughed Barclay, nervously.

'All…good…' I managed.

Suddenly I was all too aware of my mundane, off-the-shelf finest, I felt like a dirty, underdressed commoner compared to the immaculate, radiant couple before me, Barclay in his finest Paul Smith, Green in that figure-hugging number so fine and delicate that heads turned and jaws dropped. Men and women. Straight and gay. Chihuahua.

Green's porcelain beauty gave her a confidence that couldn't be faked, not so much an arrogance as a poised certainty that made me feel instantly clumsy and inadequate, inferior. Her eyes were really green, a soft, delicate, pale green, unlike any I'd ever seen before.

Oh Barclay, you lucky, lucky bastard. You've hit the jackpot.

As if he was reading my mind, he smiled. She smiled. I grinned.

'Nice to meecha!' I said, for some reason adopting an embarrassing East End accent I hadn't used in years. What was

I thinking?

'Were you just leaving?' Barclay asked. 'Maybe stop for a drink before you go?'

I nodded and we were guided to a reserved table for two by the door. As Barclay ordered the drinks, Green touched my hand and said 'So lovely to meet you at last. I've heard all about you and Dawn but I was starting to think I'd never get to meet either of you – Barclay can be such a secretive chap.'

'Can't he just,' I said.

'You probably didn't even know we were married!'

'Funny you should say that but…'

'This is nice,' said Barclay, turning back to us with impeccable timing having ordered three cocktails from the insouciant French waiter. Ever the gentleman, he opted to stand. 'I was hoping you would get to meet one of these days.'

'You should have arranged something, Barclay,' she said, 'but I guess you're always too busy.' She punched his arm playfully and he just took it without flinching.

'Indeed,' he sighed. Odd. It may have been me but it suddenly felt uncomfortable and forced, and as he leant down to kiss her cheek she edged away. It was slight and quick but I noticed it nevertheless. 'And how was your day, Claire?' he asked.

The cocktails arrived, potent-looking cream in gold (what else?) Martini glasses topped with a slice of passion fruit. 'What's this?' I asked, sniffing the surface with cautious enthusiasm.

'It's called a Porn Star Martini,' said Green. 'They're my favourite and rather special.'

You're rather special, I thought, but kept it to myself. I took a sip and it was glorious. I was in liquid heaven and these two were my accompanying angels. Don't fuck it up, Claire, please don't fuck it up.

'Your day?' asked Barclay, echoing his previous inquiry.

And so I proceeded to fuck it up, and for the next ten minutes I bored everyone, including me, senseless with my mind-numbing world of Marshalls, Andersonn and Bangalore. The Martini didn't last two gulps and once I'd found my voice

I couldn't silence it despite my mind screaming SHUT UP. My mouth just babbled and babbled, senseless office gossip that even Lizzie would have yawned at. Bless her, Green really tried to feign polite interest, smiling and nodding obligingly at my demented tattle. Barclay wasn't so subtle and quickly decided he was fascinated by the little French lady's tiny dog. Even I was mortified by what I was saying. Stop, Claire, just stop – you're making an absolute, Grade A arse of yourself. It was like having first date nerves and I seemed to have misplaced my Off switch.

'...and poor Lizzie she hasn't a clue what's just around the corner and as for Brian in Accounts he...'

Barclay decided he couldn't take it anymore. 'Fascinating,' he said, finishing his drink and rising to his feet as he checked his Breitling. 'Our reservation downstairs in the Brasserie awaits, Green. It gets très occupé downstairs and I want to show you the Crazy Coqs cabaret room before we eat.'

'Of course,' she said rising. 'You go ahead, I just need to visit the Ladies' room.'

'Sure,' said Barclay. 'I'll give you a call, Claire.' And he disappeared through the rear door, and down the stairs. Couldn't get away from me fast enough, the bastard.

I picked up my bag and smiled. 'So nice to have met you, Green, I just wish we had more time and...'

She grabbed my arm and pulled me close. Any warmth had suddenly left those green eyes and she leant over to my left ear, her perfect lips brushing my hair.

'You have one week to pack your bags, MacDonald, and exit Barclay's life. You will be history this time next week. For your own good, you must go.' It was a whisper but harsh and cold, brutal even.

I reeled away, stunned. She turned, almost a flounce, and followed her husband down into the restaurant. Not even a 'goodbye' or a wave.

Where had that come from? Was it me, or had the room temperature suddenly plummeted? I stumbled away, my feet feeling clumsy, my unsure steps carrying me out of the café and back into the evening throng of Sherwood Street and its surer-footed crowds. I bumped into strangers like a drunk after closing time, my world tilted, my balance lost.

'Careful love,' said a middle-aged lady trying to steady me before I did her and myself serious damage.

'I'm fine. I'm fine.' I said, convincing neither of us. I somehow made my way to the Eros steps and sat down, woozy, my head spinning.

That was a stunner. Had I misheard her? No, of course not. And what did it mean? Surely she didn't see me as a threat, a rival for Barclay's affection?

Who to ask? Who would understand? Not Barclay, and Dawn had vanished anyway. Mum? Where would I start explaining all this to my mum? TNT? Get real Claire, TNT??!!

I'd never felt so alone in my life.

Chapter 12

Barclay had promised a call but instead I got a text the next morning, brief and to the point:

Pick U up @7. Wear black. B

Black? Is there any other colour? There certainly isn't in my wardrobe.

I had slept fitfully and didn't rise until gone midday.

I just needed to talk, but there was no-one to hear me.

I had been emotionally exhausted the night before but my brain just couldn't process what had been said and it replayed the same inconclusive loop over and over and over again. The flat was airless, my window wide open but there was no relief from the heat in the bedroom and the distant rumble of the south London traffic, punctuated every now and then by a wailing siren or dog barking, wasn't helping. By 1am my old T-shirt was soaked through so I found another and considered changing the bed sheet. I flipped the pillow but even its dark side was too warm. I tried reading a book until gone two but my eyes were wider than ever. Lights out. Radio on. No good – even the banality of Magic FM didn't bore me to sleep.

At 3am I had decided that I would just ignore Green's demand.

At 3.30am I resolved to pack my bags and get a one-way ticket to Australia. It's nice there, isn't it? But a bloody long way. Maybe too far. And they have those big spiders that hide in the loos. Maybe not.

At 3.45am I was mentally booking a single ticket to Edinburgh, my plan being to hide at Mum and Dad's and move into the cupboard under the stairs. I figured if it was good enough for Harry Potter, it was good enough for a frightened Claire MacDonald. But Harry hadn't been happy…

At 3.55am I was considering boarding the plane with Anderson Andersonn for Bangalore.

At 3.56am I scolded myself for being so head-fuckingly stupid: things weren't quite *that* desperate. I told myself that the early hours were no time to be making such massive life-altering decisions and it would all be much more straightforward the following morning. I just needed to forget all about it and get some sleep.

It may well have been clear the following morning, but as I didn't wake until the afternoon any answers or solutions felt even further away than ever. Barclay was picking me up at seven – presumably we were going to Bartholomew's mansion or office or some such place in our somewhat desperate search for incriminating evidence proving that it was him who as behind the attempts on our lives. Whoever it was had been one step ahead of us and we at least needed to play catch up. Unless Barclay had come up with some other genius idea? Who knew what else he had up his sleeve, what other surprises he had lined up for in-the-dark Claire? As he was the supposed brains of our outfit I didn't think that he was exactly pulling his weight.

I'd soon find out. I wasted my Saturday, unable to think straight or make any plans. Desperate for company, I tried a long walk in Greenwich Park, joining the dog walkers, picnicking families and scantily clad tourists enjoying the large swathes of freshly mown grass that were already yellowing in the sun.

Everyone was making the most of the hot spell that was supposed to end in the mother of all thunderstorms at some point over the weekend. Christ, I hoped Barclay was going to pick me up in a car rather than on the bike – I really didn't fancy being on the back of the Triumph in the gleefully forecast monsoon.

I needn't have worried. Barclay arrived bang on seven outside my building in yet another nondescript car of questionable reliability and dubious quality. This time it was a Skoda, but not one of the more modern, reliable ones – this was an original from Eastern Europe, a vintage car only in terms of age.

'Nice,' I said, clambering in. 'You sure can pick them.'

He turned and smiled. 'We're undercover. No point in being conspicuous.'

'Evidently.' I sniffed. 'What's that smell?'

'Ah. You smell it too? I thought it was just me. I had fish for lunch.'

He wasn't making any sense. 'Why are you telling me about your lunch?'

'Don't you think it's a fishy smell?'

'I was getting more like wet dog pong.'

He shrugged. 'It's only for tonight.'

'And where are we heading?' I asked.

'Bartholomew's, down in Whitstable. I had trouble finding him – he appears to have gone completely offline, no trace of him in any of the usual places but I found that he's scheduled to be receiving some dubious back-slapping humanitarian award at a dinner in Oxford this weekend and there's a room booked in his name at the Macdonald Randolph – no relation, I take it?'

I didn't have a clue what the fool was on about so I just shook my head.

'So as he's out of town I thought we could pay his place a visit. He bought the house a while back but I was still able to get the floor layout from the estate agents' site. I've already hacked and disabled the alarm system. Should be a doddle.'

That was not reassuring – Barclay's 'doddles' were rarely anything of the kind.

The road to the dozy gentrified Kent seaside town of Whitstable was the same one that Dawn and I had taken with my Ex (in every sense of the word) Tom Thomas on our fateful encounter with Bartholomew the previous year. There was a nervous excitement mixed with trepidation in the car as we trundled east. A storm to end all storms was brewing and the sky looked biblically dark and angry.

Barclay was reluctant to talk and I really didn't want to push any Green buttons so early in the evening. I kept it light:

'Good meal last night?'

'Mine certainly was. They do a very passable *Truite aux Amandes* there and it never disappoints. One could be dining at Maxims or at Le Cinq in Paris rather than in central London.'

'And Green liked it?'

'It was a little…false for Green. We left early.'

A little 'false'? A bit like she had been with me then, I thought. Hypocrite.

'You have to tell Dawn about her, you know.'

'In good time.'

'And Green was okay with you being away 'on business' with me on a Saturday night?'

'She doesn't know. She's away this weekend herself doing something. I don't ask, she doesn't ask, it's important that there's some space for a little privacy in any marriage.'

That struck me as strange, the kind of thing couples say after they've been together for years and years, not just a few months, but I let it pass. We were on a mission, and the last thing I needed to do was rock the boat. Especially this particular Czech-built 'boat,' a painfully noisy reminder of just how low eastern engineering stooped before the fall of communism. Why, Barclay, why? What was wrong with getting an old Ford or Vauxhall, good old British cars?

'Have you got your gun with you?' he asked.

I nodded, sheepishly. 'You don't think it's necessary though, do you?'

'Shouldn't be. The place will be empty and we'll be undisturbed. As he seems to have abandoned all of his technology and resorted to an offline existence we just need to see if there's anything incriminating in his home. We can't really prove he isn't involved though, only if he is, assuming we are fortunate enough to stumble on something he's carelessly left lying around. It's not the best of plans. We're clutching at straws. It feels desperate.'

'It *is* desperate, but I think he is involved in some way and if we find something, anything, then we can confront him or at least try to come up with a way of stopping him.'

He sighed dramatically. 'If you insist.' His right hand instinctively rubbed the glove on his left, a nervous tic he'd developed when the stress got to him. I had no idea what condition Barclay's damaged fingers were in under that glove's soft leather. Do fingernails grow back if removed? I knew toe nails could but whole fingernails? And would they hurt when they were growing back? I shuddered at the very thought. He never mentioned them. Occasionally I'd noticed an involuntary wince when he clutched something in that hand. Sore point. Four sore points, to be more accurate.

The house wasn't actually in Whitstable but a few miles east of the seaside weekend retreat for affluent Londoners. It was really nearer to the less fashionable Herne Bay, something estate agents would describe as 'Whitstable borders' with no discernible sense of irony. It was on a minor side road, detached and isolated from any neighbouring properties, a mile or so inland from a stretch of beach where even a seaside shed can cost over twenty grand.

The house was what I once heard someone describe as a 'MacMansion'; an over-sized, tasteless, modern extravagance of red brick and an excess of unnecessary Doric columns, architecture-from-a-catalogue for the wealthy, presumably intended to imply status and sophistication but actually suggesting the exact opposite.

From the road it was partially shielded from curious eyes by a well-manicured hedge that must have been around eight feet high – too high for the nosey but low enough to give everyone an idea that someone wealthy and above them in the social hierarchy was living there.

Barclay had done some more research on Bartholomew. In the twelve months since our last direct encounter with him he'd been busy: lots of travelling, mainly to the US and Australia; he'd remarried (but it had barely lasted a month and divorce proceedings were already underway); he'd bought two businesses and sold three; and one of those new acquisitions had collapsed with the ink barely dry on the deal, leaving over a thousand workers suddenly ex-workers and their pensions mysteriously disappearing, apparently overnight, much to the bemusement of the financial authorities.

But little of this made the press – he obviously had

considerable influence with the billionaires who shape the nation's gossip and breakfast table agenda to their own needs. Funny that. Barclay had said he had to dig fairly deep for this stuff, which suggested there was a cover-up of sorts going on with Mr Bartholomew.

In an ideal world, the soon-to-be-former Mrs Bartholomew would go public when she took the bastard to the cleaners in the divorce, but somehow I doubted it. He'd get away with it again, shedding a few million of hush money to buy her silence.

But nothing that had happened to him even remotely justified him trying to nail Barclay and MacDonald. Although Barclay still had his doubts, it had to be him behind the attempts to get us, even if his own finger wasn't actually curling around any trigger.

We parked twenty yards from the entrance to the house. There was an impressive-looking gate protecting the property but it had been left ajar for some reason. Barclay pushed it open and shrugged.

'You're just pissed that you can't try that lock picking thing you bought on eBay,' I joked.

'You know me so well.'

The house certainly looked unoccupied. The storm clouds had hidden the sunset but it still wasn't completely dark. A security light sensed our approach and burst into life, dazzling me momentarily and making me freeze like an escaping convict caught in a guard's searchlight.

'Come on,' he said impatiently. 'We haven't got all night.'

My lack of sleep was starting to catch up with me and my limbs were feeling suddenly weary. I was nervous, too – housebreaking may have been second nature to Barclay but it did not come naturally to me. Although he assured me he'd hacked the CCTV and alarm system it wasn't unimaginable that he'd overlooked something, a guard dog for example. Barclay had a history with barking dogs and I wasn't overly keen on them either, but I had no intention of using the gun that was in the light shoe bag slung over my back.

We went around the back of the property and were surprised

to find a window open on the top floor, probably a bathroom's.

'Can you shin up that drainpipe?' he asked

'Fuck off. Get your street urchin, Fagin.'

Barclay tutted and disappeared down the side of a detached garage. After some muttered cursing and grunting he returned a minute later with a ladder.

'For a man with the state-of-the-art security system, he does make this remarkably easy,' he said.

He put the ladder against the wall – it was a few feet short of ideal but it would do. 'Ladies first,' he said with a sarcastic polite wave.

'Hmmm.'

I climbed hesitantly but there was no turning back, Barclay following me almost too closely up the rungs. The window opened easily and, although it was a bit of a stretch, I was able to pull myself up and into an extravagant, Roman-style bathroom that was bigger than my entire flat.

'Bugger me,' I said, turning on the over-bright lighting that bounced brilliantly off the mirrored walls and ceilings. Not a room for privacy then, but an ideal one for checking a bald patch or middle-age waistline.

'Classy,' said Barclay as he came through the window behind me.

We made our way out across the marble floor, past the enormous freestanding white enamel bath in the shape of a giant scallop shell, built for at least three occupants, maybe more. You don't see those down at Wickes.

No time to dally though – we were on a mission and we weren't going to find anything of interest in a bathroom. We exited into a dark hallway. The house was silent, just a distant whir of some unattended appliances elsewhere in the house. We were alone.

'According to Zoopla there are two offices: one down on the ground floor, the other…' Barclay turned a handle and barged the door with his shoulder, 'here.'

He turned on a light. It was an odd room to find in someone's house, more like a professional television production studio than a home office. A bank of massive flat panel TVs lined a wall, all blank except one which showed a mosaic of rooms around the property, changing every ten seconds. I stared at it, frozen to the spot.

'I thought you said you had hacked the CCTV?' I said angrily.

'Cleverer than that. I've rigged it so the monitoring company is actually seeing a loop from yesterday. Look – there's the bathroom but the window's not fully open. It's like we've never been here. I'll switch it back when we've gone. There'll be no evidence of our visit at all.'

I hated to admit it but he was a clever bugger at times. I would have just cut a wire or stuck chewing gum on a lens and been damned by the consequences no doubt.

'What's this stuff all for?' I wondered aloud.

'Not sure.' He turned on one of the TVs with a remote and it showed a dimly lit bedroom. He pressed a button on a complicated looking console and the room on the screen lit up. The bed was a huge circular number that looked like it could accommodate an entire rugby team and accompanying WAGs (if that's your kinda thing). For a second I pondered the impossibility of finding fitted sheets and bedding for a circular bed, but I doubted that was a concern of Bartholomew's. Barclay turned on another screen and we saw the same room but from a different angle, zoomed in on the centre of the bed.

'Ah,' said Barclay. 'So that's his game.'

'What's his game?'

'Home made porn. Fun for all the family.'

He turned on a third TV and again we had the same room, a different angle and the camera focused in even closer, this time the foot of the bed.

'It's all automated,' said Barclay, more to himself than me.

'Creepy. Please don't play me any recordings you find. I only ate five hours ago.'

Barclay laughed. 'Looks like it's transmitted, too – that's a broadcast console over there and there's a couple of those old Slingboxes things.' As always, his technical jargon meant nothing to me. The bible got it slightly wrong – it should have said 'Blessed are the *geeks*: for they shall inherit the earth'.

Barclay flicked a few more switches, twisted a couple of knobs and, proving that, like all men, he was still a big schoolboy, pushed a few faders up to the max to befuddle whoever used the room next.

'Nothing more here. Nothing that looks remotely like it's to do with us. Let's go check out that other office.'

We descended an ornate, curving staircase into a ridiculously massive marble floored hall.

'Office Two should be that room there,' said Barclay, pointing at a closed door halfway along the far wall. He strode over and tried turning the knob. Locked.

'Bugger,' I said.

'No worries,' he said, removing his rucksack. 'I got a little something for such inconveniences.'

I was anticipating some fancy clever hoojamaflip gadget for working out the combination, but instead he produced a small mallet.

Three loud whacks and the door swung open, the lock smashed to buggery.

'Some times the old ways are the best ways,' he smiled. He flashed his torch around the dark room. 'Good. No windows.' He turned on the room's lights.

Whereas the previous room had been an Aladdin's cave of modern technology, this was like a throwback to a bygone, pre-silicon time. It was a small, traditional office-cum-library, complete with teetering stacks of paperwork, bookcases and filing cabinets lining the walls, shelves bowing under the weight of encyclopaedias, maps, atlases, dictionaries in a multitude of languages, bound magazines, even a few dozen phone books from a variety of British cities.

In the centre of the room sat a large leather-topped teak desk, piled high with folders and documents, newspapers old and new, more magazines and, in the centre, pride of place, an ancient Remington manual typewriter, a half-typed letter still wrapped around its roller.

'That's pretty neat,' I said, brushing the keys. 'I've seen them in junk shops and movies, but I never thought anybody actually used them these days. This is like walking back in time…'

'Clever,' muttered Barclay.

My brow furrowed. 'How's a typewriter 'clever'?'

'He's off grid. Completely disconnected. No digital footprint, not even digital fingerprints. No profile. No logs. No data transfers. No traces or IP. No DNS server caches. Absolutely nothing online. No wonder he's been so difficult to track.'

Again with the techie mumbo jumbo, but at least this time I could make some sense of it. 'So whatever he's doing in here is…invisible to us?'

'To anyone, not just us. His research, his planning, everything's offline. Real privacy, the kind everyone has sacrificed to be part of the twenty-first century. Whatever he's doing, he wants it hidden from the outside world.'

'Except we're standing here.'

'Yes, indeed we are.' He smiled. 'I must have scared him with my hacking last year.'

'And we can see that,' I said, pointing at the far wall.

'And what's that?' asked Barclay, not even lifting his head from an old copy of the Daily Telegraph he was reading.

'That map with all the pins and string.'

'What?' That got his attention.

We walked over to have a closer look.

'Bloody hell,' Barclay said.

Bingo.

There were dozens of red pins and a similar number of green, a handful of blues and yellows, carefully dotted around the streets of London and the home counties. One immediately caught my eye: a cluster of pins, red, green, blue and even a purple one, all packed tightly together just outside Canterbury.

'That's…'

'That's Hank the Wank's mansion.'

'And that's…' I was pointing at a too-familiar street in Deptford, a pin cushion of green and blue, dotted with red.

'That's your place.'

'And so this is…' I took a few paces back to observe the map in all its glory.

'Everywhere we've been in the last few months. That's…'

'…not good.'

There were red, green and yellow pins in New Cross, where I'd crashed the Multipla. Green and yellow pins at the Hammersmith spot where that Partridge woman had short-changed me; red and green where Barclay and I had picked up the outstanding balance of payment due. And down by the Thames someone, presumably Bartholomew, had drawn a big cross. That was where the tyre had been shot out.

'Shit,' muttered Barclay. 'Looks like I'm red, you're green, Number Two is blue…'

'Dawn yellow?'

He nodded. Some pins were joined by a thread, presumably indicating a journey where the journey was maybe important.

'How does he know?' Barclay asked himself. 'It's pretty extensive. Not totally complete but pretty close.'

'It doesn't have enough pins to show everything, surely?'

'It's not tracking absolutely everywhere, just those that may present…' he paused, realising what he was saying, '…an opportunity.'

'Is he tracking our mobiles?'

Barclay looked pensive. 'Probably. It's easy enough to do, then just a matter of joining the dots. Look.' He pointed at two Hammersmith pins which were linked to two more on the Chelsea Embankment by a yellow thread. 'That's us on the Bonneville. Once he sees us there he knows we'll be heading back to Deptford after the pick-up, so he can map our route,' he traced the thread along the road until he reached another black cross, 'to here. That's where the bike started chasing us and tried to run us off the road.'

'So we *are* being tracked by him! I knew it!' I couldn't contain my triumph a second longer.

'Yes, but I doubt he's doing the dirty work himself, just acting as the puppet master. He's got other people doing the tech and the manual labour. He's taken measures to keep his own fingerprints off this. Fortunately for us, that someone's not particularly effective with the final act or we'd be dead already, but being one step ahead of us it's only a matter of time if he persists. He just needs a better hitman.'

He scratched his chin and went back to the desk. He started sorting through some of the cardboard folders stacked precariously by the typewriter. He paused and pulled one out, opening it.

'You,' he said.

'Me,' I whispered, spreading out dozens of grainy photos of me at work, me in Deptford, walking, shopping, driving, living my everyday life. There was me at the cashpoint in Greenwich with Fielding and her boyfriend. Me in the queue at Tesco. Us at Park It In The Market. Me ignoring the Big Issue guy down by the Post Office.

'They're from all over but mainly CCTV by the look of things.' He pointed at the timestamp on a picture. 'It may not just be phones he's using to follow us.'

'He's hacked in to the police systems?'

'I doubt it's him – like I said, he seems to have gone to considerable lengths to keep this stuff offline – but someone's doing this for him. Someone good. Someone technical.'

'Better than you?'

Barclay laughed and shook his head. It didn't matter. This wasn't a competition of technical competence. But it was a race. A race we had to win.

Barclay opened a few more files. There was one for Dawn, another for TNT, even one for my boyfriend of yester-year Henry, the Ex shared by me and Dawn. Stella Parkinson had one, too. And Hank the Wank. And…Mum and Dad?

Fuck. This was not funny. We should destroy them all.

'Is there one for you, Barclay?'

He pointed at a dozen folders on the other side of the Remington. 'I think those are me,' he said. The pile was over a foot high.

'Wow.'

'You were right,' he said and, despite the circumstances, I couldn't hide my grin. Go, team Claire! 'We need to get out of here, leave it exactly as we found it and plan. We've got to do something. We can't hide from this kind of surveillance or stop it. We need to turn this around, take the initiative in some way. Go after him, maybe.'

'And what?'

'I'm not sure.'

He looked uncertain as he straightened the paperwork he'd disturbed on the desk. I'd never seen Barclay look that worried before but the expression on his face was one of doubt and indecision.

He'd think of something. He always thought of something, didn't he?

Didn't he?

Chapter 13

'We're fucked.' I was gripping the wheel so tightly it was in danger of snapping in two.

'Nicely put,' said Barclay. 'Top marks for observation.'

'Don't tell me you're still not convinced …'

'Oh, I'm convinced – how could I not be? And I know we're in serious trouble if we do nothing. There's no point hanging around waiting for the axe to fall, either figuratively or literally. We need to do something all right, but I'm not exactly sure what.'

That was not reassuring. I'd been able to work out how bad things were for us all on my lonesome and it had been ridiculously frustrating waiting for him to finally cotton on to Bartholomew's plans for us. Coincidence? Never in a month of Mondays and it had been obvious someone was after us.

But now, at last, he was convinced. Now we were both convinced. Boy, were we convinced.

'Buggered,' he muttered, as I dipped the headlights to avoid blinding the driver of the car speeding towards us in the inky darkness that had enveloped the unlit M2 like black fog.

'Fucked,' I whispered to myself.

The car was not a Skoda full of joy, no sir.

I'd suggested that we cut up the SIM cards from our phones once we'd left Bartholomew's house but Barclay just turned off something called 'Location Services' and said he wanted to check the actual phones properly when we got back. I wasn't convinced it was just the phones – if he had that information, why hadn't he tried to stop us once we'd started to drive down to Whitstable at least? Then he could have had one of his henchmen lying in wait for us? It didn't quite add up. There had to be more to it than just tracking our phones, and there had been the CCTV in London too, of course. That had been chilling.

We'd taken photos of what we'd found; the map, the folders, the CCTV pictures, plus various other documents that had been gathered in the stomach-churning surveillance of our merry team – bank statements, embarrassing social media postings (are there any other kind?), that kind of thing. We even found a few cassettes of telephone conversations (including one between Barclay and TNT entirely in French) and DVDs copied from various CCTV cameras of us on the bike, our pursuer and the police interception. He didn't have anything that looked particularly incriminating – just us, faces partially obscured, picking up a bag or three, but then I'm no lawyer so I wouldn't be an expert judge of that. Besides, he wasn't trying to lock us away, he was 'tidying away the loose ends' himself.

He was out to kill us.

The Skoda was doing its best to assist with the speedy getaway but I was now wishing Barclay had brought his bike after all – the threat of the storm seemed to be subsiding and we'd have been home by now if we had been on the Bonneville. Even my beloved Fiat Uno would have been an improvement on Barclay's latest lamentable rusting false economy.

'Can't you hack him?' I asked.

He laughed. 'What, with a machete or something? That's a bit extreme even for you, Claire.'

I rolled my eyes. 'No, muppet. Online of course. Drain his accounts. Falsify his tax records. That kind of thing. You remember? THE STUFF YOU'RE SUPPOSED TO BE A BLOODY GENIUS WITH?'

He winced, like he had a mouthful of grapefruit.

'I'm serious, Barclay. We need to bring this guy down. You did it last time.'

'It's not the same now. He's gone offline, remember? He's been that way for months. He's smart, he knows how I got him before and he isn't going to fall for that again. He's tidied up his act and has taken measures to hide everything away securely. He's had the experts in and they've locked his stuff away so that even I can't get at it. There are limits to even my talents, you know.'

Seriously? We really were in the shit if even Barclay was admitting defeat.

'No. We're going to have to think along more traditional lines,' he said. 'He's abandoned his personal technology and resorted to traditional means to protect himself. We're going to have to do something similar.'

'Such as?'

Barclay paused for a second as if the tiny cogs in his noggin were finally, reluctantly whirring into some semblance of action. 'You're good with a gun.'

'Fuck no, Barclay. I'm not whacking him!'

'You're not up for that?'

'No!' I was shouting. I couldn't believe what I was hearing. 'I'm not a hit man...woman...whatever, Barclay – I'm not gunning anyone down in cold blood.'

'Even in self-defence? You took that teacher's boyfriend down in self-defence...'

'That was an accident and you know it was. I've barely slept since! No way, no way, I'm not doing that again. Forget that.' I shook my head so violently we almost careered off the road.

'Steady there,' said Barclay.

'You're joking, right?'

He didn't answer. I didn't really want him to.

I drove in silence for what felt like forever, waiting for him to have a more rational Eureka moment that wouldn't involve me doing twenty-years-to-life as a consequence. Eventually:

'You got anything better than me shooting him dead?' I asked, calmer.

'How about shooting him but not quite dead?'

'You mean wounding him? What would that achieve?'

'It would scare the shit out of him.'

'It would scare the shit out of me.'

'But you'd consider that?'

'There's nothing to consider: I'm not a good enough shot.'

'I think you are.'

'I know I'm not. Remember last time?'

'Which one?'

'You mean which fuck up – the one with the teacher's boyfriend or the one with Bartholomew's sniper? My track record isn't exactly great.'

'But you were amazing at Wardy's lock-up.'

'Hitting a stationary target from twenty feet isn't the same as hitting a moving person. You told me that – weren't you listening?'

It was a pointless argument. I wasn't going to do it and he'd have to think of something better.

A few minutes passed. 'Have you ever fired a rifle?' he asked, persevering.

'I hadn't even touched a gun before I met you.'

'How about you get some professional rifle training? Military grade, no more Wardy. And then you could just clip him so he gets the message that we're not for ...'

'Seriously? 'Just clip him'? From how far away? Fifty feet? A hundred? Two hundred? I don't think I could hit a paper target from fifty feet, let alone a person. And what if I miss and his skull explodes? I don't think any judge would buy my 'only trying to wound him, m'lord' defence.'

'He's a fairly big person.'

'Yes, but you're not listening to what I'm saying Barclay. I can't do it and I won't do it. I don't want to do it – I'm not up for this.'

'How about we go shooting and see how good you are?'

He was tenacious I had to give him that. Wrong, but persistent. Persistently wrong.

'And you have nothing else in the amazing Barclay's mind palace of incredible ideas? Just 'Boo. Bang. Scare him'?'

'You said yourself we need to go after him. How were you thinking of doing that? By text? Maybe a telegram? A Post-It on his fridge? Seriously Claire, we need to play him at his own game.'

'I'm not a hit man.'

'But you are a good shot. It would shake him up. Seriously shake him up. And then I can tell him simply, 'no more, or else...''

I wasn't buying it, but I was tired despite my anger and the adrenaline still surging from the tension of the break-in.

'Not Ward. I never want to see that fucker again.'

'No, of course not. Not sure he'd know one end of a rifle from the other anyway. Hank the Wank was boasting that someone on his staff won some shooting medal at the Olympics, bit of a local celebrity out that way. I'll call him first thing and see if he can set something up. Claire, all you need is a bit of training…you'll be brilliant.'

'I'm not…'

'How difficult can it be?' He was too excited and I was too tired to argue.

'So that is all we need to do? I shoot him and hope he backs off?'

'Unless I think of something better that's all I have. I'll sort out the phones so hopefully he won't be able to track us anymore.'

''Hopefully'? That's not exactly reassuring.'

'I'll call Hank and…' he checked his watch, 'I'll call him first thing in the morning.'

I didn't say anything. At least we had a plan of sorts, even if I couldn't imagine it actually working. It was better than having nothing. Or maybe it wasn't.

It was still a few hours until sunrise but the bright lights of the M25 and the city beyond were glowing warmly in the distance as the Skoda made its painful efforts to deliver us from evil.

'Why don't we just lay low for a little bit?' I suggested in one last desperate effort to avoid being trained as an assassin – it was all I had.

'And how do we do that? When could we safely emerge from our bunker? You don't think they'll notice you not going into work for a few years? And it's not just us – you saw the files he's got. There's potential collateral damage too. There was even one with your parents in there.'

That was true. The picture of my kid brother was about five years out of date – he was around twice that height already – but the file had enough details on Mum and Dad to make them achievable targets for any lowlife looking to earn a few grand, no questions asked. There had even been pictures of Lizzie and Anderson Andersonn. Bartholomew's web had spread terrifyingly wide. I shivered just thinking about it. What the fuck could we do? No-one was safe. I'd doubted I'd ever sleep again until this stopped.

We lapsed into another brooding silence, every mile feeling like it could be the Skoda's last.

Finally, Barclay spoke.

'Green likes you.'

Uh oh. 'You sure? I didn't think she did.'

'What makes you say that?'

'Y'know, just an impression I got.'

'She said she did. Wants to get to know you better.'

'Oh.'

A minute passed. I didn't know what to say.

'You're not so keen then?'

'Not hugely, no.'

'I said she can be a little awkward but...'

'I just got the impression she wanted me out the picture, that's all.'

'Did she say that?'

'Well not those exact words but...'

'Like I said, she can be a little shy but once she gets to know you and you her it'll be like you're best buddies. You're a very likeable person. I'm told.'

He laughed at his own little joke. A very tiny joke. I wasn't laughing. I just wanted to cry.

'You cold?' asked Barclay. 'You're shivering.'

I shook my head. Cold? No. Terrified? Yes, that was the word. I was fucking terrified.

Chapter 14

I was wrong. I slept like a hibernating dormouse once I got home. No drink, no pills, not even a shower, just sheer emotional and physical exhaustion. My head crashed down on the pillow and that was it for at least two hours. No nightmares. No mind-racing panic attacks. Queen Poopy was well and truly pooped.

I had probably been rattling the windows with my snoring but, frankly, sod the neighbours, I didn't give a shit. Boy, did oblivion feel good, even if it was just a few hours.

I was woken by a pounding on the door and a familiar voice, pointlessly trying to shout quietly, or maybe it was an attempt at an extremely loud whisper.

No need to shout, Barclay – it's not as if your fist hammering on the door hadn't already made me neighbourhood enemy number one.

'Claire? Claire!'

Well, he had said first thing.

I opened the flat's door a crack.

'What is it? Seven?'

'Six thirty. Get dressed, Claire. Hank said 'yes'.'

'You're fucking mad.'

'Dressed, Claire. I'll be downstairs. Ten minutes please. And someone left the front door open downstairs. You should have words with your neighbours.'

Absolutely off his trolley. But the fact that we were going on the bike cheered me and, besides, what else was I going to do on a strikingly beautiful, not-a-cloud-in-the-sky Sunday morning? May as well get myself a few more life skills under my belt and learn how to wing a fat bastard from a hundred feet. Gotta be some kind of fun, hadn't it? I decided to forego a shower and pulled on a T-shirt and jeans from the pile on the floor of the previous week's clothes.

What was I waiting for? A marksman to take me out?

The ride out of early morning lethargic London was spectacular.

Any Sunday traffic was still safely tucked up in bed and we had the roads to ourselves. Barclay had done some magic with a few pieces of black tape so that the bike's plates were suitably anonymous and our awesome Bonneville consumed the tarmac like it hadn't eaten in a month. It was exhilarating, electrifying, life-affirming. The absence of traffic and brilliant sunshine in an impossibly blue sky transformed the capital's humdrum roads into a glorious Californian Pacific highway despite the miles of cones for the eternal A2 roadworks that had been dormant for months. My eyes couldn't widen enough to take it all in and I was grinning like a giddy schoolgirl, the sheer thrill and excitement of the bike was all-consuming. This was living, this was life, and it was ours, just ours. For glorious mile after heart thumping mile everything else was gone from my head, I was finally empty of all that shit that was threatening to consume me. No Bartholomew. No Green. No sniper. No Andersonn. No India.

No Barclay? Not quite. I still had Barclay.

I gripped him tighter around the waist until my arms ached. Ride, Barclay, just ride. Never stop. Never turn back. Let's just ride forever, the roads are ours, let's leave that crazy dangerous world behind.

We were hurtling out towards Canterbury at a speed that was stealing the air from my lungs.

I felt reborn, reinvigorated, and, as Barclay slowly and skilfully negotiated the quiet country roads around the grounds of stately Wank Towers, life felt surprisingly good. No, better than good: bloody brilliant. Thank you, sunny Sunday morning in June. Thank you, Triumph Bonneville. Thank you, Barclay. You bugger, you.

And you know what? We're coming to get you, Bartholomew. No-one's safe…or hadn't you read that particular email? No-one fucks with Barclay and MacDonald.

My bike-crazed euphoria couldn't last for ever and, sadly, we were at Hank's in just over an hour. I wondered if Dawn would still be there? We hadn't seen or heard from her since she and

Hank had ridden off into the early morning sunrise the previous week and I needed to know that she was okay. New rules now – I made a mental note to ring Mum and check she was safe, too. But surely even someone as cruel and vicious as Bartholomew wouldn't stoop that low, would he? Threaten my innocent Mum and Dad? He was welcome to have some heavy-for-hire rough up my teenage brother Paul, heaven knows that little scrote had it coming but not Mum and Dad. Please god, not them.

Despite the day's early morning warmth I shivered, my reverie broken. The ride out had been a glorious distraction but there was serious business to be done, and I was still not happy with what was being expected of me.

We had reached Hank's gates and they gracefully opened for us again without us needing to stop. Barclay swept the bike up the drive and the large doors of the main house swung open and there was Hank. Too much Hank, in fact. All of him, every inch of plump, pink flesh, stark bollock naked as Mother Nature had originally intended.

'Bloody hell,' I muttered into my helmet.

'Hello, old bean,' he boomed, smiling, his arms thrown wide in welcome, his small meat and two veg sheltering from the strong sun under the pot of his stomach. His own 'old bean' looked mildly embarrassed.

We dismounted and removed our helmets, staring in disbelief at our grinning host.

'Barclay! Claire! Welcome back! It feels like just hours since we last met!'

'No hugs, no hugs,' I muttered furiously to myself as we approached the man and his manhood. 'Please don't expect me to hug you, Hank.'

Mercifully Barclay got there first and they shook hands with a strong, masculine pump.

'Nice out today, isn't it?' said Hank.

Barclay nodded.

'If it gets any nicer, Barclay may take his out, too,' I joked before I could stop myself. Barclay shot me daggers but Hank laughed heartily, his pink stomach jumping jollily and other parts presumably jiggling too – I just couldn't bear to look.

'Hi guys!' It was Dawn, running through the house and squeezing past him to greet us. 'Hank said you'd be up early.'

Fortunately she was fully dressed. Even unflappable Barclay would probably have flapped at the sight of his younger sister in the altogether – it was still a bit early on a Sunday morning for that kind of thing. She'd been shopping by the look things, still oblivious to the possible danger she was in.

Hank put his puffy pink arm around Barclay's shoulder and they strode off in a determined fashion through the main house's doors. Dawn and I followed, whispering conspiratorially.

'What's all this about then?' I asked.

'I was about to ask you the same thing.'

'I go first. Why's Hank starkers?'

'It's something he's always done apparently, on Sundays at least. He says it reminds him that, despite all the rich trappings good fortune and privileged genes have bestowed upon him, he's just flesh and bone like everyone else.'

I could see why the poor chap needed grounding; the interior of the house was even grander than the exterior and the hallway was lined with a parade of suits of shining armour, all standing to attention as we passed. It really was a bloody stately home.

'At least he's got the weather for it today and…'

'What's this about someone being out to get Barclay? I thought he'd poo-pooed you on that one?'

'It's not just Barclay – it's all of us. Thee, me, he…even Mr Natural there.' I pointed at the bare bouncing buttocks of Hank a few yards ahead of us. 'I was right. It was that Bartholomew from last year. It looks like he's after all of us.'

Dawn stopped, eyes wide and drew her hand to her mouth. 'Why?' she asked so quietly I could barely hear her.

'Not exactly sure but I think we're still considered to be 'loose ends', unfinished business. Maybe he thinks Barclay has more incriminating files on his business that could finish him. Dunno for certain.'

'And does Barclay really have stuff that could do that?'

'He has old bits but says it's not relevant or useful anymore and Bartholomew's now shrewder in what he has and where he puts it.'

'And he's trying to kill you?'

'Not with his own bare hands, no, but he has someone or even several someones out to get us. There've been a few attempts we know about so far, plus we think he was the guy who set the police on us a week or so back. We broke into his house and saw his files and plans and whatnot and he's after us, no doubt about it.'

'You broke into his house?'

I nodded. 'Had to be done.'

'And he had files on me?'

'He's been tracking you, too. Even Hank. Even my family.'

'Fuckin' hell.'

I nodded

We'd finally reached the end of the long hallway and were emerging into the back garden through an ornate pair of fancy glass doors. I say 'back garden' but I really mean 'grounds'; there must have been half of Kent out there, perfectly manicured grass going almost as far as the eye could see, a rose garden here, an orchard there, outbuildings (including the barn with all those cars and bikes), tennis courts and even another swimming pool, all perfectly maintained and impeccably tended by what I could only assume was a small army of attentive workmen and gardeners.

Barclay and Hank had stopped a dozen or so yards ahead of us. Barclay was waggling his arms about wildly, in that familiar, slightly uncoordinated pissed-off-pterodactyl style of his. It was all very good-natured, and, as if to prove my point, both he and Hank burst into laughter at some shared joke they'd stumbled upon.

'What's so funny?' asked Dawn as we caught up with them.

'Oh, it's nothing,' laughed Barclay.

'I was just telling Barclay about Willoughby,' chuckled Hank.

'Willoughby?' I asked.

'Yes, my dear, Loxham Willoughby, your instructor for the

day. Our very own Olympic champion. A bronze, I believe. It's just a shame the Games were so long ago though. Ah, here he comes now…'

From inside the house moseyed a grey-haired, short and comically rotund figure dressed entirely in heatwave-defying tweed jacket and a kilt that was dusting the ground. He must have been ninety if he was a day. He was ambling along as fast as his little legs could carry him, a rifle in each hand waving about furiously as he struggled to keep his balance.

'Hello there!' he called, waggling one of the guns at us in greeting.

This was my instructor? This was the London Olympic champion who was going to show me how to take the wings off a mosquito from a hundred feet away? Which London Olympic games exactly? The ones just after the war?

His movement, although enthusiastic, looked a little painful, almost arthritic, but there was a wide smile on his rosy cheeked face, which was framed by an impressive display of shockingly wild white hair that looked like it hadn't been tamed by a brush for many a decade.

'Hello lassie!' he said in a surprisingly loud and rich, warm Scottish brogue that made me instantly feel like I had found a long-lost beloved grandparent. Great grandparent even. 'You must be Claire. And this is Barley?'

'Barclay.'

'And you and Barley want to get some practise in with a rifle I understand?'

'We do,' I said. 'Just for recreational purposes of course, you understand.'

His brow creased. 'I was told you were going to take out that twat Farage? I sincerely hope I haven't been dragged out of my bed on a false promise?'

He looked serious but couldn't keep it up and his yellow teeth flashed again in another insanely wide grin.

'You've got me,' I said. 'I'm going to take out all of the Brexit nutters one by one. Bloody clowns.'

He chuckled. 'You need to get yourself a decent government

down here, like the one that beautiful Nicola has. She's my kind of woman. Gives me some serious wood, she does.'

Did he say 'wood'? Surely he wasn't referring to his..?

'So we'd better get down to business,' he said. 'Get those buggers whilst the sun shines before they fuck up the country completely, eh?' He suddenly noticed Hank in his birthday suit and did a comical double-take before joining us as we headed towards a nearby firing range nestled in a small copse of trees. 'Warm enough for you, laddie?' he asked. Dawn giggled and Barclay smiled. Hank had clearly heard it all before and wasn't going to let anything throw him from his Lord of the Manor stride.

This was going to be soooo much more fun than my lesson with Wardy.

'Hmm,' said Barclay. It was a very judgmental 'hmm'.

'Not my finest hour,' I admitted. 'I told you I couldn't do it.'

'But you started so well.'

That was true – my first shot had hit the centre of the target from fifty feet away but then…

'Not what I was expecting,' he continued. 'Very disappointing.'

'It was bloody difficult.' It was odd that I felt that I had to defend myself, even though I thought I'd been quite clear from the off that I wanted nothing to do with this madcap scheme, that I was not prepared to shoot someone in cold blood. Not my bag. It was dangerous and stupid and I shouldn't have even entertained the rifle lesson. Yet still I found myself on the defensive: 'Nowhere near as easy as it looks on the telly.'

'Obviously.'

'Look, Mister Barclay,' I pulled myself up to my full height, the blood starting to thud in my ears. 'If you think it's that fucking simple, you pick up the gun and try it for yourself!'

'Did his little talk put you off?'

I scowled but Willoughby's 'little talk', as Barclay so delicately put it, had scared the living crap out of me. I know he had just been trying to ensure that I understood the seriousness of hitting a living target and it was more in jest than anything, but I'd never realised what a bullet actually does when it enters the body. I didn't know that they're not meant to come out the other side but are deliberately flat-nosed to ricochet and ping pong around inside the body like some crazed bagatelle game, shredding organs and muscle and veins and bones and arteries and whatever else they can find in there before they lose their momentum. Eughh. My stomach had flipped at the very thought of the brutal savagery that a bullet can inflict. It made me feel sick, nauseous, and I didn't want any part of it. Never again, Barclay, never again. I never wanted to fire another gun as long as I lived. Which, of course, might not be that long anyway.

'You couldn't even hit the bloody target!'

'I told you this was a stupid fucking idea. I can't do it. I don't want to even try. We have to think of something else.' We were shouting and Dawn, Hank and Willoughby had gone back indoors to escape our drama but were watching from behind the glass, leaving us to our voluble domestic.

'You're giving up?'

'Look Barclay,' my forefinger was poking him hard on the chest bone, 'I'm not up for everything and I'm certainly not up for this. I gave it a go. It wasn't even close. I may have been okay in Ward's garage across a few feet but proper gun skills are clearly beyond me. How old's Willoughby? A hundred? Two hundred? He's a natural, still Olympic grade. But I'm not. It's not me. That was humiliating.'

'So you're giving up?' he repeated.

'You need to give this up! It would be me that's taking all the risk. I'm the one who could end up killing someone, shredding their insides! If I can't hit a target I certainly can't clip someone just to ruffle their feathers!'

'You could just send a few bullets past him, surely?'

'Are you fucking thick? I'm as likely to hit him as not! And we won't keep getting away with this shit, Barclay – we'll get caught if we shoot someone. I'll get caught! I'll get locked away! No sir, I want nothing to do with this.'

He reeled away from me.

'I'm very disappointed that you'll not even try…'

'I tried, Barclay, I fucking tried. But I was shit, okay? Completely shit at it. Couldn't hit the proverbial barn door. It's fucking difficult and I can't do it!'

'Then you're no bloody use to me whatsoever,' he stormed, and turned quickly, striding purposefully towards the house without looking back.

I stood motionless and threw my head back. 'FUCK!' I shouted as loud as I could, my fingernails cutting deep into my palms.

By the time I'd followed Barclay indoors he'd already gone, taking the bike and my lift home with him.

Bastard.

Chapter 15

'That sounded like it got a bit…emotional,' said Dawn. We were sitting in a bright red nineties' Volkswagen Golf convertible Hank had loaned us, heading back to London.

'He can be so…so fucking childish! His brilliant plan doesn't work and it's all my fault!'

'I didn't see him excelling out there, didn't even have a go himself.'

'Exactly! Why has it got to be me every time? What makes me so bloody special with a gun?'

'Er … didn't you say you were a natural?'

I snapped my head to the left and scowled at her. 'Don't you start!'

'But that time after you had your shooting lessons with Ward and…'

'Completely different! And what did I know? That was before I shot some wanker and almost killed him, remember?'

That shut her up. She didn't know what to say. There was nothing she could say. She was wrong, as wrong as her brother.

An uncomfortable silence filled the car as I ignored the signs demanding I kept it to fifty and forced the Golf up over seventy. Fuck them. Fuck everyone. Dawn was staring at her lap. We didn't do rows, her and me. This was pretty much our first. And it was all bloody Barclay's fault.

I had to calm down. Driving too fast was helping, the yellow speed cameras flashing us in acknowledgement that I'd just about lost control. Calm it, Claire, calm down.

'Can we go a little slower, please?' she whispered.

Maybe. My anger started to subside, I eased off the accelerator and dropped back down to the required fifty.

I wasn't just angry with Barclay and Dawn, I was angry with myself. Angry that I'd gone along with his stupid idea. Angry that I hadn't been very good at shooting after all. Angry that I hadn't been mature enough to realise the damage, the very real damage, a gun can do to a man. Or a woman. I'd been carried along by Barclay's belief in me, the confidence he gave me to be reckless and stupid. And I was disappointed too; everyone secretly longs to find that they have a secret talent, something they excel at but never knew about. My secret turned out to be that I was shit with a gun after all. Should have guessed.

Get used to it Claire, you're nothing special.

I looked at Dawn and attempted a smile. 'Sorry.'

'S'okay.' She looked tired. 'You're stressed. Barclay's stressed. It'll pass.'

'Yep.'

I felt bad for snapping at her. Still no regrets about letting loose with both barrels at Barclay, but Dawn hadn't deserved my ire. Another one for the list of Claire fuck ups in my special Month of Fuck Up sunshine shebang.

Dawn put on her aviator sunglasses and reclined the seat almost horizontal as if she was on a sun bed. She looked stunning in her new barely-there summer outfit of a hooped black and white tube top and the shortest denim skirt imaginable, making me feel even more average and dowdy and boring sitting next to her in my second-wear clothes of a few days' vintage – not a good look for such a hot day. Not a great smell, either. There was something about Dawn that made me feel that I was aging prematurely and ready for style tips from the stalwarts of the local Women's Institute. Maybe it was her blue hair where I seemed destined for an early blue rinse. Or all the piercings. Or the tattoos on her arms and thighs.

It was probably the tatts. Never fancied the pain of getting one myself but they did scream a deafening 'fuck you, I'm young and can do what I fucking like' statement. I was angry at the world. Maybe I should get one after all. Just a small one. Maybe on an ankle. Under my sock. Out of view.

'And how bad was it really at Bartholomew's place?' Dawn asked quietly, unsure whether Hurricane Claire had fully blown out.

I sighed, keeping my eyes fixed on the road and hands tight on the wheel. 'It was bad, Dawn, really, really bad.'

'Does he actually track your every move? Our every move?'

'Not all of mine and certainly not all of yours, but all of Barclays so whenever we're with him there was a record of it. There was video, too. He'd somehow hacked into that CCTV camera down our road – there were shots of you and me going in and out the building, walking down the road, even with the shopping. I felt quite violated.'

She nodded.

I shuddered. 'I know we aren't supposed to give a blue monkey's about privacy these days but there's a line, isn't there? How dare he? Bastard.'

Dawn nodded in agreement. 'Bastard. And Barclay's plan is that you scare him away by shooting him?'

'Shooting at him. 'Miss and Maim' is what Willoughby called it.'

'That's not a very sound plan.'

'Willoughby says it nigh on impossible, even for a sharpshooter like him. The movies lie. You don't just pick up a rifle and clip someone at the first attempt. But Barclay couldn't think of anything else and he really believed I could do it. I thought I could, too. For a moment I really thought I could. But now,' I bit my lip, 'now, I know better.'

She nodded but said nothing. Hurricane Claire had indeed subsided, probably now just Stiff Breeze Claire. It was time to lighten the mood or we'd be suicidal by the time we were home.

'What was that nude-y thing all about?' I asked.

Dawn's face lit up. 'Oh, wasn't that fun? He's just so wild and spontaneous, isn't he? You like him, Claire? You do like him, don't you? He's pretty cool, isn't he?'

'And rich. Don't forget stinking rich.'

'Psssh. Not important to me.'

'But it's that uncountable wealth and privilege that gives him the freedom to be so carefree and impetuous, surely?'

'Whatever.'

'And he's been in the nude-y nude all weekend?'

'Just today. He does it often on Sundays.'

'You weren't tempted to try it yourself?'

'I'm barely dressed as it is,' she said, waving at her scanty attire. 'Maybe I'll give it a try next week if the weather holds.'

I laughed. 'I know you won't do it if it turns a bit nippy.'

'True, but when the weather's like this,' she did a little ceremonial wave at the bright azure sky, 'you just can't believe it ain't gonna last forever.'

She had a point. I couldn't imagine it turning wintry again in my lifetime. Weather can be funny like that.

'Things are going well with Lord Moneybags then?'

'He's a lot of fun. Early days but it's nice to be with someone who doesn't worry about everything and just gets on with life.'

'Thanks a lot,' I said, frowning with amateur dramatics hurt. 'Leave the worrying to us disposable people.'

'You know what I mean.'

'This is a nice little car he's given us,' I said, our conversation swerving like a learner driver confronting pot holes for the first time.

'He said I could keep it. He's got a couple of old VWs he prefers to the flash boy toys. Guess I neglected to tell him I'm a nervous driver. Maybe you could give me a few lessons? I don't think I've driven since my test.'

'Deal. I am a professional, after all. I like this one – it makes a nice change from the shitty bangers Barclay keeps dragging back from the knackers' yard. I can't cope with that bike of his, either – too macho for me. Bit of a beast for my feeble girly arms.'

'Hank says he's a biker at heart. He likes the look of the classic cars but doesn't enjoy driving much. That's why they're all in the barn rather than out on the drive. He has this really obsessed bloke, Garage Graeme he calls him, who just looks after them all day, always has a rag in his hand, polishes them and polishes them. Sounds like he's some sad case who loves and cherishes them like they're his own rather than Hank's. Hank just buys and sells a few cars for pocket money. That's why he took Barclay's offer, even for one of those lovely bikes – it was more than twice the going rate.'

'That bike is a thing of beauty,' I said.

'Yes, but everything has its price, and Barclay paid double.

Besides, Hank's got three others, all in better nick than the one he flogged to Barks.'

She smiled. There wasn't any great sibling rivalry between the two of them but there was a wee bit of one-upmanship on show every now and again. I got the impression that Dawn had enjoyed seeing her brother diddled out of some of his dodgy earnings and it was something quite delicious in its own small way. Childish maybe, but then if siblings can't be childish, who can?

Even with the roof open it was hot. Dawn was struggling with the leather upholstery clinging to her bare legs and was fanning herself with a map but I had no such reprieve from the exhausting heat. I turned the air con up to the absolute max but any cold air was whipped away by the heavy warm gusts buffeting us. Hottest day yet, and my T-shirt felt like it was glued to me. Give me the chill of deepest, darkest winter any day.

'You need another plan,' she said as I swerved to avoid an overzealous Ocado van. We had been almost crushed by a giant lemon on wheels. That would really have been a bitter end. Ho ho.

'Obviously. Got any brilliant ideas?'

'Can't Barclay trace him online again? He really is good at that freaky geeky stuff.'

'He says that he can't. He says Bartholomew's gone completely dark and the only way he can find him online is third hand.'

'What's he mean by that?'

'When Bartholomew uses his credit card or something. Apparently he doesn't even use a proper mobile, just some Pay As You Go jobbie, doesn't seem to use a computer of his own now, given that dirty work to someone else. Barclay says Bartholomew has gone from the web, signed off from the online world.'

'And Barclay doesn't have a clue where he is from one moment to the next?'

'He may get the odd clue – a table or hotel room reservation, but they're few and far between. Otherwise, nothing.'

'And yet Bartholomew knows exactly where you are?' She paused, then added: 'Where *we* are?'

'Looks like it. Not exactly fair, is it?'

'He doesn't strike me as a man who is looking to play fair, just plans to finish the job he started.'

'Finish us, you mean. You're not exactly helping, you know, Dawn.'

Her sudden silence was deafening.

We were almost back home. The A2 slowed as we passed the Kidbrooke exit and I signalled to turn west. Dawn noticed a thin cloud of black smoke rising up into the late afternoon sky.

'That looks like there's been a fire in Greenwich,' she said, pointing at the thin, dark cloud that was rising steadily, unimpeded by any breeze.

'Could be the Cutty Sark again,' I half-joked.

'You could always try talking.'

She was switching the conversation faster than I was changing lanes. 'Sorry, what? Talk to who exactly?'

'Bartholomew.'

'Talk to him? Seriously? You think he'll actually listen? He doesn't strike me as a man who listens to anything except the sound of his own voice.'

'No harm in trying.'

'There could be plenty of harm in trying,' I exclaimed. 'He could grab me by the throat and throttle me.'

'Not if you picked somewhere very, very public where there will be plenty of decent, law-abiding people who will notice you being brutally strangled in their midst.'

'And what do I say to him, exactly? 'Please Mr Bartholomew, don't kill me. I promise to be good. I could be very goooood to you…'' I stroked Dawn's thigh and she laughed.

'Maybe not that, but you'll think of something. Play for sympathy, swear to eternal silence, tell him Barclay's fired you, you've grown up, you're emigrating, anything. It must be costing him money and time tracking everyone, surely?'

'Not sure that particularly bothers him. The thrill of the chase, the glory of the hunt and all that. What's if he's obsessed?

Obsession's not good. Not rational. No room for diplomacy if he's obsessed.'

'If he was that consumed by it he'd be trying to kill everyone with his own hands, not having some third-rate hit man buggering it up all the time. Must be pretty frustrating for him that you're still walking about.'

'Aren't I a bitch?' I joked. But Dawn may have been on to something. Besides, I wasn't exactly bubbling over with any great ideas of my own, was I? Diplomacy? As a desperate last resort? It might work, or at least buy me enough time to think of something better. Put some distance between me and Barclay, too. He'd want to talk to Barclay but that bad boy had made it very clear that I was of no use to him anymore – I was just looking after myself and Mum and Dad. And I guess Dawn, too. Barclay could whistle for all I cared.

'Maybe I could play the innocent card, pretend I was caught up in this by mistake?'

'You were, weren't you?'

'Not really, no, but Bartholomew wouldn't know that, would he?'

'You've not been exactly working under duress though.'

'I doubt he knows that. I could say Barclay has been threatening me or…'

'Careful with the lies,' cautioned Dawn The Wise. 'You'll only tie yourself in knots and they'll never work. Don't make too much stuff up – he'll see through them. He's a bad guy rather than a stupid one. Besides, you are a really, really shit liar.'

I tried to look hurt but we both knew it was true. 'Best then I say as little as possible,' I said. 'I like the idea of playing the innocent, trying my best doe eyes, make it a bit teary and lots of trembling lip. 'I was a bad girl but I'm trying to be good now', something like that. Bat the eyelashes, turn The Flirt up to eleven.'

'Careful now, you'll have me welling up…'

The lights changed and we continued our stop-start across Blackheath common.

'Where will you look to meet him?' Dawn asked.

Good question. Needed somewhere very public. Nothing sprang to mind, but then suddenly: 'When I first saw him he was at an Italian deli in Docklands. Barclay said Bartholomew went there every day without fail, like clockwork. Same place, same time, even the same lunch. Crazy busy place, lots of people around. Wall to wall CCTV too.'

'Sounds perfect.'

'I think you're right. Will you come with me?' The traffic stopped again, this time for a small crowd crossing from Greenwich park to Blackheath village.

'Of course. I'll keep my distance but I'm in this too so be sure to put in a good word for me when you're negotiating with him.'

'Done.'

'That smoke's further west than I thought,' I said. 'Can't be the Cutty Sark.'

We joined the crawling Sunday traffic queue down into Deptford. Where was everyone going on a Sunday? Didn't they know how much parking costs around here? Maybe they were all heading to see the famous tea clipper in flames again.

*

Dawn spotted the fire engines first, blocking the end of our road although their battle with the fire looked like it had been one they had lost big time hours earlier. Fuck. I parked the Golf on a double yellow and we both leaped out, cursing like troopers. A lone policeman was informing the curious public that 'there was nothing to see here' and that they should 'move along now'. He was clearly too young to have learned anything more than the tried and trusted constabulary clichés.

'You can't leave that there, Miss,' he said, pointing at our illegally-parked car.

'Sorry, but that's our bloody home that's on fire!' I shouted.

'Not any more it's not. Taken 'em most of the day to put that out. Not much of it left now.' He moved out of our way and let us through. We splashed through the puddles of water and foam that had battled with the flames on our behalf, all in vain. A few of our neighbours were wandering around looking bemused but by the look of things the main show had finished a while back. One last burning building a few doors along from ours was still sending up some smoke but the worst was over, the damage had been done.

'You live here?' asked a knackered-looking fireman, removing his helmet and mopping his dirty brow.

'Not any more, I guess,' I said. My voice sounded small and lost – I had no deep attachment to the place and I could only hope that the insurance would cover the costs. That feeling of being violated hit hard again. I was numb and realised it wouldn't really hit home exactly what I'd lost in the flames for several hours, days even. 'Hit home'. Oh, the irony.

'I don't suppose you left anything on whilst you were out, did you?' he asked. 'Heater, oven, iron, hair straighteners?'

Heater? In this heat? Did he think we were mad? 'No, nothing that I…' I shook my head, still trying to take it in.

Our building, my home for the last four years, was gone, completely gutted and burned to a charcoal crisp, flimsy wisps of roiling smoke still rose from the dampened, charred ruins. The roofs of our building and those either side had completely collapsed, a few remaining barbecued timbers pointing defiantly to the heavens at precarious angles. Must have been quite an inferno at its height. Other houses further down the street on both sides had been blackened by the flames but at least they'd be habitable again. One day.

Not ours though.

'You don't know how the fire started?' Dawn quietly asked the fireman.

'No idea love. Could have been almost anything. The neighbours say there was no explosion so we can rule out gas, but it could have been electrics.'

'Or maybe deliberate?' My stunned mind was drawing rapid and worrying conclusions.

'Got a lot of enemies after you then, love?' he laughed. I didn't.

I nodded then shook my head. No point in confessing on the spot to my crimes and misdemeanours. The fireman frowned at my confusion and wandered back to his mates, deciding it was probably safest to leave the two damsels alone in their distress.

'Fucking hell,' said Dawn under her breath.

'Too real. This is too real,' I muttered to myself. 'Not sure I can cope with this.' I turned to Dawn. 'It was him, wasn't it? Bartholomew? Sending a message to us, to Barclay. He probably thought we'd be in there.' My pointing finger was shaking as the shock finally hit. 'He meant to kill us.'

Dawn's face was ashen. My mouth was dry and I was having to blink away tears; I couldn't tell if they were from the acrid smoke still in the air or sheer emotion. We needed to end this, end this stupid fucking nonsense right now before someone gets seriously hurt. Like 'burned to a crisp' hurt.

'I will go and see Bartholomew tomorrow,' I said, trying to sound in control. 'You still coming?'

'Sure,' said Dawn, but I could tell she was having second and possibly even third thoughts.

'All our clothes have gone. All my photos and books and my laptop and...the sofa. The sofa's gone, Dawn, our sofa!' I was rambling, making no sense. Like with any loss, the emotional impact when it finally hit was so random and haphazard as to make me sound like a complete idiot, unable to determine what was important and what wasn't.

We staggered back down the street. There was little point in asking if we could look through the burned remains – there'd be nothing of ours worth salvaging in there. Anything that the fire had miraculously missed would only have been swamped by the deluge of water and foam the emergency services had needed to stop the whole area going all 1666 on us.

'Where are you going to stay tonight?' Dawn asked. 'Sorry, I meant where are *we* going to stay?'

I nodded at the Golf that some over-zealous twat with a Hitler complex had already ticketed. 'Fucking hell. Well, we can always sleep in there if we can't find a hotel room.'

Dawn shrugged and we shuffled back to the car. I dramatically tore the yellow plastic parking notice off the windscreen in my anger, letting it fall to the floor in an infantile gesture of defiance.

The car somehow looked much smaller now that there was the prospect of us having to spend the night in it.

'It's not exactly five star accommodation, is it?' said Dawn. 'I'll ring that Travelodge down the road and see if they've got any rooms for the night. Should be plenty available on a Sunday.'

No luck. They were fully booked. Typical. Shouldn't have expected anything different on the weekend when life decided to fuck us up right royal and proper.

We tried a few other hotels but no joy. In the end, exhausted, I drove us all the way back to Canterbury and we spent the night in a little cosseted luxury after all.

No point in slumming it when we still had Hank's country pile at our disposal.

Chapter 16

He didn't look particularly evil, but maybe that was the whole point. Real life villains don't dress in black and twirl their moustaches.

He didn't look like a man who would think nothing of hiring a crack sniper or demon motorcyclist just to tidy up some 'loose ends'.

He didn't look like an arsonist who would burn down my home, knowing that there was every chance at 7.30 on a Sunday morning that I would still be inside, innocently chasing sparkly unicorns in the land of nod.

He didn't look like anything out of the ordinary.

He just looked normal. Boringly normal. Anonymous.

I hadn't seen him for over a year and I had transformed the Bartholomew of my imagination from the short, overweight guy in the City pinstripe to a monstrous Bond villain, hiding in his tech-laden Kent coast lair stroking a white cat while carefully plotting the end of the world. Or the end of Claire and Barclay's world, at least.

Nope, he looked almost too normal, so much so that when I first saw him from our vantage point outside the Costa opposite the café, I actually wondered if it was the same guy. He was so…so...harmless-looking, blending in with the Docklands crowds of bankers and wankers shuffling out of their air-conditioned prisons for an hour of fresh air and sunshine. It was bloody baking that Monday, the mercury still soaring and the air motionless and still, no breeze to calm its almost tropically oppressive weight. My shirt was wet to my back and yesterday's, no, they were last week's clothes – what others did I now own? – already felt as if they were in dire need of the hottest of hot washes. I would have stayed in an office if I'd had the choice – it was not pleasant outside, no sir.

Bartholomew didn't seem to acknowledge the temperature. His navy pinstripe wool suit was a three piece, finely tailored to cover his lack of dietary discipline that manifest itself in a sizeable stomach the buttons did well to conceal…almost. His shirt was regulation white, and the tie was bright red silk. So far, so City, so clichéd.

I'd actually seen him twice before. The first time was here, as he queued for his lunch, Barclay showing me our quarry before we moved in for an ill-conceived sting. The second time was that fateful night on a deserted building site just outside Rochester. That encounter had been brief and lit only by moonlight, so I was confident he wouldn't recognise me. But then I remembered the file with all the pictures of me, the CCTV footage and screen grabs. He'd recognise me alright. He had been obsessing about all of us for months, like a celebrity stalker who had lost all grip on reality.

But at least we had the element of surprise; it would shock him to finally meet me again in the flesh, I was sure of it.

Dawn returned from her trip to the Ladies, two chilled bottles of sparkling Pellegrino in her hands.

'And work was okay with you taking the day off?' she asked, making herself comfortable.

'They're getting used to it. I told the American, Andersonn, that I needed some time to get myself set for Bangalore.' I smiled and opened my bottle of water, drinking deeply. 'The idiot still thinks I'm going to be joining him in the Departures lounge on Friday.'

'This Friday? Surely you're going to have to break it to him soon?'

'There's still plenty of time for me to fall ill. Just need to do a little internet research on what's going to strike me down. Besides,' and I couldn't help but broaden my smile, 'he can always take Lizzie.'

Dawn chuckled and pulled a face. She had met Lizzie once and once had been enough for them both as neither had impressed the other. Chalk and cheddar those two.

'Look at that,' she panted, nodding at a six foot plus piece of wealthy banking eye candy, all perfectly coiffured gelled black hair and artificially whitened teeth, his double-breasted suit defying modern convention simply because he was a rich, couldn't-give-a-damn-what-you-think bugger who knew he looked good in anything. He looked the classic villainous type.

'Focus, Dawn, Focus. Look, that's him over there.' I attempted a surreptitious nod in Bartholomew's general direction but it was probably just too subtle for Dawn. 'The one in the pinstripe, white shirt, red tie …' I stopped myself – I was describing at least half a dozen men in the general vicinity of our target. Christ, it was like someone was cloning them.

As if she'd been reading my mind, Dawn said 'They all look the same.' One thing you could never accuse Dawn of was that she 'looked the same' as anyone, but today she had attempted a feeble disguise so as not to alert Bartholomew to the fact that perhaps I had a familiar accomplice. A Baldrick-worthy cunning disguise at that – her aviator sunglasses. Brilliant. I'd have recognized her at a hundred yards, but fortunately Bartholomew wasn't looking in our direction and she was getting away with it, even if she was attracting quite a bit of attention from many of the men milling around. It was probably that ridiculous denim mini skirt that was barely the width of the average belt. Even I had to admit she had great legs and the attention they were grabbing was undoing any anonymity offered by her glasses. Ho well, I could never really expect someone like Dawn to cut it as a covert companion, could I?

'Remind me again what you know about him then,' she whispered.

I took a sip of my sparkling water. 'His full name is Anthony Aloysius St. John Bartholomew. He's sixty years' old and worth about seventy million, give or take a few quid.'

'Seventeen? Wow.'

'I said *seventy*. Seven-oh. Barclay said he's had a very good year. But it's not enough for him, and even with him having Midas-sized piles of wealth he still wants more, which is how Barclay and Tom found him, skimming off his financial consultancy clients who were too important to worry themselves with the smaller number after the first few commas on all the transactions they were signing off. What the NHS could use to fund a hospital or two he was pocketing for himself, always just out of sight of the financial authorities.'

'Said authorities not exactly renowned for honesty themselves.'

'Hexactly.'

'And which one is he?' she asked, pulling her shades down in an Audrey-like stylee.

'Back of the queue at that Antonio's deli.'

'You'd have thought with all that money he'd have somebody get his lunch for him, wouldn't you?'

'You would, but that's part of this 'humble, down-to-earth, butter-wouldn't-melt' appearance he puts on to keep any suspicions at bay.'

'Tubby little chap, isn't he?'

'If you ate a chicken escalope ciabatta every day for lunch you'd be carrying a few extra pounds too, I'm sure. Barclay says he's a man of habit, repetitive habit. He's here every day, come rain, snow, sleet or shine, buying the same roll for lunch.'

'Are you nervous?'

'Of course I'm fucking nervous!' I was smiling but my stomach was performing in the Olympics. 'Wish me luck!'

'I've got your back,' she said as I stood up, but I don't think either of us knew what exactly she was going to do to help me if the bugger turned nasty.

'The usual, Mistahh Bartolomew?' asked the smarmy Italian behind the counter. Bartholomew just nodded and looked out the window, waiting for his lunch to be assembled from a rather tasty looking selection of Italian ingredients. 'And for you, lovely Miss?'

I felt my face warm at the not-so-subtle compliment. 'The same as Anthony here,' I said.

He turned so quickly to see me he almost fell. Instinctively I put out a hand to steady him and our eyes met.

Bingo! His jaw dropped, nostrils flared and eyes widened.

'You..?' was all he could manage, barely audible above the lunchtime chatter and the clatter of the industrial cappuccino machine.

‘Hello Anthony,’ I said, sounding so much more confident than I felt. ‘I thought it was about time we had a chat, tried to iron things out and stop all the nonsense. Care to join me for lunch?’

He rocked on his heels and looked like he was going to have a heart attack, his breathing deep and audible, his eyes jittery and panic-stricken.

‘Sir, your escalope,’ called the guy behind the counter but Bartholomew wasn’t listening.

‘Please put it on the tray with mine,’ I said. ‘But he’s paying.’ Bartholomew was too shocked to argue – instinctively he tapped his wallet on the payment thingamajig and bought me lunch. I grabbed a handful of napkins and a couple of glasses. Like an errant child he shuffled after me as I took the tray with our lunches and found a table to the back of small deli.

Claire MacDonald, smooth operator under pressure or what?

‘How did..?’

‘How did I know you’d be here? You’re *always* here, Anthony, every bloody day, five days a week, maybe even seven for all I know. You don’t mind if I call you Anthony, do you? You strike me as more an Anthony than a Tony. Not that I care of course – I’ve got more than a few other choice alternatives I can call upon, especially as there are no young children around.’

‘No. I meant how did you escape the…’ and then he stopped short, just before he would have incriminated himself in a very recent case of murderous arson.

I winked. ‘Up too early for you, Anthony, I guess. But don’t ask where I was.’

I don’t think he’d blinked once since I’d confronted him. ‘Why..?’ He was struggling for words. I’d rocked his smug little cocoon of a world.

‘Why?’ I leant closer over the table, our noses were almost touching. ‘Why? Because I have nowhere else to be now you’ve burned down my fucking home, you fucking bastard. Because I can’t walk down the street without checking over my shoulder ever second step for some bullet from some hotshot assassin of yours. Because I can't step off a curb without half expecting to be thrown out of my Converses by a speeding motorbike or 4x4. Because this needs to stop and it needs to stop now, this very minute, before someone dies. It may be me, it could just as likely be you, it could…'

'Barclay,' he spat.

'Yes, it could be him. It could be any of us. It could be *all* of us. Enough. Too much. Too extreme. It needs to stop.'

I took an ambitious, forceful bite of my ciabatta to punctuate my words. I couldn't believe how forceful I sounded, how firm and convincing. I was queen bee, top of the world – this was turning out to be far easier than…

'No.'

He said it quietly but it was full of menace. My mouth dropped open and I froze.

'No, MacDonald, it doesn't end today, at least not at this table. I will talk but I will only talk to him, to Quentin Barclay, not his dizzy girl Friday. Unless you are being offered as a peace offering. In which case,' he sneered, 'he will have to find a lot better.'

I gagged and spluttered on the leaden mouthful of bread I just couldn't swallow.

He laughed. 'You don't think you're his 'first', do you?' He did little air bunnies with his fingers to show his contempt for me. 'That idiot has an eye for the young girls, the younger and prettier and more desperate the better, but he seems to have sunk to new depths with Claire MacDonald I have to say. You're not exactly his usual arm candy, are you?'

I couldn't breathe, my mind was scrambling for a response but was floundering. I'd plunged from soaring self-confidence to being horribly out of my depth, all of my advantage lost with a simple, personal slight. Too fragile, Claire, you're just too fucking fragile.

'We're not a…couple,' I mumbled.

'No, of course you're not. Nobody would make that mistake. I don't know exactly what you do for him or what he sees in you but then you're of little interest to me. You're an inconvenience.'

'A 'loose end'?'

'Exactly. I'm sure you have your uses but you're of no value to me.'

'If that's the case then forget about me and leave me and…'

He moved closer to me, his overpowering cologne cloying, killing my appetite immediately. 'MacDonald. I will do what I fucking well like. If I want you dead you are dead. If I want your family dead, they will follow you into the grave.' It was a chilling whisper.

I couldn't move, the half-chewed food inedible and solid in my mouth.

'But I will talk with Barclay. And I want you there. And I will see if we can come to some kind of arrangement. I have done my research. I know things about Mister Barclay that I am sure he would prefer didn't become public. It's a dangerous game, blackmail, and the tables can easily be turned.'

I swallowed hard, the food feeling sharp as it grazed my throat.

'Tell Barclay to meet me in the Island Gardens park at midnight. You come too – I'm sure he'd welcome your protection and counsel.' He smiled but his eyes were brutal and cut me to the core. I just wanted to punch him and punch him, shatter his nose and face until my fists bled, but I just sat there, paralysed.

'And you will be delighted to know that you have disturbed my lunch and I've lost my appetite. Feel free to treat yourself to my leftovers.' He spat something from his mouth onto his plate then pushed it towards me and rose from this seat. 'It may prove to be the last food you can afford for some time.'

Again he grinned, again my fists tightened, unseen. 'Tonight. Midnight. No more games, it is time, as you suggest, to talk.' And with that, he was gone, pushing his way in an arrogant, entitled manner through the bustling queue of people at the counter.

Shit. Fucking shitty shit.

I tried to compose myself but my hands were shaking. Had I made it worse? Should I have just stayed the fuck out of this rather than making a pathetic attempt to bring it to a close?

Dawn appeared in the doorway and made her way over to my table.

'He's gone? I couldn't see much from Costa.'

I nodded.

'Did it go well?'

'No,' I whispered, staring at the remains of my lunch.

'Oh. Not good then?'

'No.'

'Not even a little teensy weensy bit good?'

I took a deep breath and shook my head. 'No, not a little teensy weensy bit good. Just a fuckity-fuck load of massively massive bad.'

'He's not prepared to talk?'

'Oh, he's happy to talk alright. In fact, we're going to meet with him tonight, if I can convince Barclay that it's in his interest to do so.'

'Well, that's what you wanted. That's good, isn't it?'

'No, it isn't. He's says that he's going to turn the blackmail on Barclay, threaten to expose him…and me, I guess…unless we pay money we don't have into his bulging bank account.'

'Ah.' Dawn pulled Bartholomew's abandoned lunch closer to her. 'Still, talking may make a difference, don't you think? I don't suppose this is going spare is it?'

'It is. He didn't finish it but…'

Too late. She wedged the roll into her mouth. 'I'm shtarvin',' I think she said, but it was barely intelligible as she chomped down on Bartholomew's tainted food.

Dawn seemed to be taking it well, but then I couldn't blame her. She was probably still in shock from the fire and was coping as best she could. This wasn't her fight really. I'm sure she cared, for me, for Barclay, but probably believed that it was all a bit unreal. Besides, she was just an innocent, homeless bystander in all this shit, wasn't she?

And me? I was in it too deep to breathe. Fuck knows what would happen that evening, Barclay and Bartholomew in the garden at midnight. That was assuming I could convince Barclay to attend. And that Bartholomew wasn't planning to have some gunman there to pop us off, one by one like wooden ducks on a fairground stall.

What had I done?

Chapter 17

We were back outside Costa. I rang Barclay's mobile. It rang three times before it flipped to voicemail. 'Speak,' it commanded. Such charm.

'Barclay. It's me. Claire. I need to talk to you. Urgently. I spoke to Bartholomew. He wants to meet you tonight. At midnight. At that park in Island Gardens. And…' It all sounded so childish, so pathetic, little Claire MacDonald playing at being the diplomat, the negotiator, the oil calming troubled waters, the…

…stupid bitch fucking everything up. I hung up, my message incomplete.

'Shit.'

'Not there?' asked Dawn.

'No. Yes. Yes, he's not there. And my message sounded shit and…'

My iPhone suddenly burst into life. It was Barclay.

'You did WHAT??' He was so loud that I jerked the phone away from my ear.

'I…'

'You spoke to him? What, on the phone? Face to face? What the hell are you playing at?'

'It seemed like a good idea,' my voice sounded tiny, his was monstrously loud. 'It *was* a good idea, Barclay. And Dawn thought so too. We can't go on like this, Barclay, he burned down our flat for fuck's sake.' I swallowed hard, desperate to keep the guilt from my voice. 'I'm scared. We're scared.'

'He did what?'

'When we got back from Hank's our flat, the whole building, had been torched.'

He paused for a second. 'And you know for certain it was him?'

'Who else would it be?'

'I thought you had a long list of people who were out to get you?'

'It was him, Barclay, you and I both know it.'

He paused again, digesting the news. Then:

'And as a result you decided to confront him, face to face?'

'We didn't have any other plan.'

'I had a plan.'

'It was a shit plan, Barclay.'

'It would have worked.'

Not again. 'Forget that. It's never going to happen, Barclay. It is not a plan. It is impossible. Can you please park that one now, for good?'

Silence.

'And yes, I confronted him, face to face, mano a mano. I went to that Italian Deli he goes to every lunchtime and I sat him down and told him it had to end. Now. No more games. No more stupid, stupid games.'

'And he said 'yes'?'

I hesitated then said: 'Pretty much.'

'And he wants to talk to me in Island Gardens tonight at midnight?'

'Yes. He picked it but I had a look on Google and it might be a good meeting place as there are no tall buildings for a sniper and…'

He sighed as if he was talking to a child. 'He won't need a sniper, Claire. He can just shoot me at close range. And you too – presumably he wants you there as well?

'He won't shoot you. He wants something from you and…'

'He does? Intriguing. Okay. Let's talk this through properly. Can you come over in an hour?'

'You didn't give me your address when you moved. Are you still in Docklands?'

He wasn't. He gave me his address, somewhere around Plumstead Common by the look of it. There were some nice big houses out that way, but not really his style. More traditional I thought.

'An hour? I'll be over with Dawn and…'

But the line had gone dead. He was still angry with me. I couldn't blame him. I was still angry with me, too.

*

'Sorry but I'm not going.'

'But Dawn, you have to! I need the moral support! Don't desert me now!'

'I can't. I've got someone I'm supposed to meet this afternoon anyway, something I've been putting off for ages. You don't need me – you'll sort this out with Barclay. You need to kiss and make up with him. I'm not deserting anyone, but this really isn't to do with me. I'm just on the edges, this is about you guys, it's your bag.' Her eyes were wandering and I could see she was struggling with a guilty conscience and didn't really believe what she was saying, but I understood perfectly. She wasn't directly involved, hadn't asked for any of this. She wasn't one of the bad guys.

But I was.

'Can I call you?'

She pulled me close and gave me a massive hug, forcing the breath from my chest, probably snapping a rib or two in her attempt to comfort me. 'Of course, Claire, of course. Always.'

'Where are you going?' I asked.

'Like I say, got to meet up with someone for an afternoon cuppa then back to Hank's of course. There's nowhere in town now for me, is there?'

'Nowhere for me, either.'

'So, when this is all done, come and stay with us whilst we get us a new place sorted. It'll be safe – Hank will protect us. Hank's piles of cash will protect us. You could do with some luxury for once. It'll be fun.'

It would be safer, but I wasn't so sure that anywhere would be truly safe for me just yet. Besides, it would be running away and hiding. And I didn't want to spend the rest of my days living on tenterhooks, looking over my shoulder and peering fearfully into shadows every minute of every day.

'Maybe when this is done,' I promised, and kissed her brow.

She grinned and pulled away from me. 'Go sort it all out with my big brother. You'll think of something, I'm sure. I'll get Hank to plump up the pillows in one of the spare rooms for you.'

I attempted a smile but it was forced and fragile. I felt like crying. 'You're doing the right thing. Go see your friend. Go to Hank's. Take the Golf. I'll get the train to Barclay's. One of us is getting this right.'

'We both are, Claire, we both are.'

'I'll call you,' I said, and checked my phone. Battery down to 15%. Note to self: charge your phone, Claire.

I gave her the Golf's keys back. She smiled and dropped them in her bag. And with that she left me, alone in the Costa coffee shop, a little wave and she was gone. And for some reason I shivered, despite the weather. It felt like we were saying goodbye forever.

Barclay's new place, from the outside at least, was the complete opposite of his old one. That had been a tall steel and glass monstrosity of chaotic Boris-approved planning, so ugly in its uniformity. This was a small, semi-detached on a Barratt's estate cul-de-sac just off the Common. Totally non-descript. Totally un-Barclay.

Or maybe this was Green's place? Maybe she was someone who would have more traditional tastes than a high tech modern man cave in the sky.

I'd soon fine out. He'd said number 12 and I rang the bell. Ding Dong, mayhem calling.

No response. Nothing. Bugger. Barclay had said to meet him in an hour but either I was early or he was late. On past experience, I'd lay good money on it being the latter.

I tried having a nose through the front door's frosted glass. It looked very domestic and cosy in there. A little red – not very Barclay at all. I started to doubt that I had the right place, then suddenly there was movement, a blurry shape growing larger and she was there, slithering down the hall. Green. The Wicked Witch of the West. Run, Dorothy, run!

The door opened with a jangle of the security chain.

'Come to say goodbye?' she asked coldly.

'I've come to see Barclay.'

'To say goodbye.'

'To have a conversation.'

'He's not here and I don't know when he'll be back.'

'Oh.'

'He's not your number one fan right now, is he? He's started talking about you in the past tense, quite bitter about something by the sound of things. I had assumed you had done as I'd told you.' She was smiling but, again, there was no humour or warmth in her beautiful, pale green eyes. The Ice Maiden speaketh.

'No I haven't.'

'But you will.'

'You say you don't know when he'll be back?'

'No idea. It's not like I track his every movement, is it? We're husband and wife, not master and slave.'

Could have fooled me.

'He said he'd be here.'

'Then you know more than me, Claire,' she hissed. 'He most certainly isn't here. If I were you I wouldn't waste your time waiting for him. He was clear that it was over between the two of you and that you were very much history. Fly away, little bird, back to your nest. Get yourself a life of your own and leave ours.' She fluttered her hand like she was dismissing a junior member of staff.

I didn't fancy spending a second longer with the condescending bitch so I turned to leave. Nice dress though. Expensive.

'A pleasure knowing you, MacDonald,' she called after me as I strode away. Without turning I gave her the finger. 'How sweet. So lady-like.'

'Like you'd know,' I muttered bravely under my breath as I paced back to Plumstead station.

Barclay called me twenty minutes later.

'Where are you?'

'I'm on the train back to Deptford. Where were you?'

'I got delayed. I'm home now.'

'Didn't Green tell you I'd called by?'

'Didn't see her. She's just gone up to town for something.'

'Typical. Will she be gone long? I really don't want to see her again.'

'Didn't say, but if she has gone shoe shopping it will be hours. She likes her shoes. Has two special cupboards for them.'

I liked shoes, too. I used to have loads; a few pairs of Converses, some tatty New Balance trainers and an old pair of DMs for 'bests'. After the fire though, I was down to the pair I was wearing.

'I'll turn back at the next stop and come to you,' I said.

'You really don't like her, do you?'

'No. I didn't tell you but at Zédel she told me to get out of your life in a week or else.'

'Really? 'Or else' what, exactly?'

'I have absolutely no idea.' My train slowed into Greenwich, the doors opened and I jumped out and started making my way over to the other platform. 'I'll be about half an hour, Barclay.'

'Good. We need to talk. About Bartholomew…and Green. I'll fire the Gaggia up.'

Urghh. Another one of his 'special' espressos awaiting, coffee so thick and turgid you could stand a spoon up in it. 'See you in thirty,' I said as the down train for Dartford pulled in. For once my timing was spot on.

'Ciao,' said Signore Cappuccino.

At least we were speaking again, but for how long I wasn't sure.

Chapter 18

'This…is…nice?' I hadn't meant it to be a question – it just came out that way.

Barclay shrugged. 'Green's taste more than mine...'

I'd never have guessed. Barclay's apartment in Docklands had been very much a showroom for his macho small-mindedness, all chrome and glass, his boy toy gadgets displayed with pride. But it had lacked warmth, character, a feminine touch. This house was, to say the least, very different.

For a start there was all the pink. There was a lot of pink. And when I say 'a lot', I mean *everything* was pink. Not the subtlety of 'rose', or 'blush', just pink in its rawest form. Doughnut icing pink. Eye-watering pink. It felt like I was wearing rose-tinted glasses. There was a pink floral print sofa and chairs, pink teddy bears, fluffy candy floss coloured cushions, the walls were a light cherry colour ('Strawberry Breath', Farrow & Ball would no doubt call it, but to you and me they were really pink), the carpet a breathless magenta that would embarrass even Barbie.

For a woman named Green, she sure liked her pink.

Everything screamed 'not Barclay's choice'. The only technology on show was an ancient portable television, tucked away on a pine bookshelf amongst some well-worn Harry Potter paperbacks and Nigella cook books. The main wall had a giant mirror surrounded by several framed paintings of cigar-toking dogs dressed as gangsters playing cards in a bizarre animal speakeasy. The room was tasteless, almost sickeningly so. I felt quite dizzy and had to find myself a chair to take the weight off my eyeballs.

It was as if someone had deliberately decorated the whole house in as saccharine a manner as possible. Far too sweet for my tooth.

It was not Barclay. It was the very opposite of Barclay.

'Green's 'taste'?' The inverted commas must have been audible.

'I'll accept it is a little overpowering, a bit…'

'Much?'

'I suppose you could say that, yes. I've obviously become accustomed to it.'

'Barclay, it's horrendous!'

'If this is what she…'

'Don't give me that. This is most definitely not your style or even anywhere close. Nobody likes shit like this. How can you live here?'

His pained expression said it all really. He lived here under duress. There was clearly much more to this relationship than met the eye but it would be rude to pry into what was clearly a very private, loving and honest relationship and…

Sod that, it certainly wasn't an honest relationship and I was going to pry and get it all out there.

'What's she got over you, Barclay?' He squirmed, unable to meet my gaze. 'Where did she come from? And forget all that lovey dovey bollocks you fed me last week, what is it about you and Lady Green that condemns you to live somewhere like this??'

He stared at his tiny espresso cup. I'd never seen him so uncomfortable. No wonder he'd been looking to keep this place, this life so quiet. This house undermined everything Barclay was. Or, more truthfully, undermined everything Barclay wanted others to think he was.

'Some other time maybe and…'

I shook my head.

'Nope. Now.'

'When you're in love…' he began but I wasn't having that.

'The truth, Barclay,' I insisted.

He sighed, his shoulders slumped, his eyes on the floor as he toyed with the empty cup. 'It's complex.'

'I can do complex,' I said. 'Try me.'

'It's…I can't…' he pulled out a chair from under the dining table and sat next to me. He couldn't look up, the nauseating carpet appeared to have entranced him. He took a deep breath and lifted his head. 'Okay. It's like this.

'There was a deal. Yes, I'd guess you'd call it that, a deal.

After all that Kent business last year and my time in hospital things were looking bleak. The police didn't show any leniency for me nailing Tom Pedakowski and charged me with pretty much everything I've ever been involved with, even back to my Uni days with Wardy. Some stuff I'd long forgotten about. I could talk my way out of a few of the smaller things, but it just kept coming, charge after charge. I was in deep, deep shit. The only thing they didn't seem to have anything on was the Bartholomew blackmail fiasco – I guess your friend Tom had kept that particular indiscretion nicely locked away because of his own involvement. I was looking at many years, probably decades behind bars.'

'You say there was a deal? Who was the deal with?'

'My father.' His head dropped and shoulders slumped again. He suddenly looked smaller, like the confession was sapping all his strength. Barclay's father despised him and let everyone know it. According to Dawn, their relationship had long been broken and when I'd visited Barclay's parents' home the previous year I'd seen it myself first hand. I had needed to leave the room as the belittling insults flew. 'And he helped. Eventually. Reluctantly. And for a price.'

'And what's that got to do with Green?'

'Green...she was the deal. My father insisted I had to get my life back on track. No more what he called 'unconventional entrepreneurship'. He said I had to stop embarrassing him at every opportunity, that I needed to grow up and settle down. Start afresh. Do normal stuff. Get an office job. Join the rat race. Stop dreaming.'

'And marry Green?'

'Not exactly. More complex than that. It was more like 'not divorce her'.'

I shook my head, not understanding what I was hearing. It had suddenly stopped making sense. He was talking in riddles, as if I'd heard it all before and didn't need any details.

'You were already married?'

'Obviously.'

Obvious to who, exactly? 'And you were divorcing her?'

'Not really, no. But I should have been. It had been five years since we had separated. We lived as husband and wife for barely five weeks.'

'Five years? And you still weren't divorced?'

He shrugged. 'Never quite got around to it. You know what it's like, there's always something more interesting to do. All that paperwork and the solicitors and meetings – seemed to be more trouble that it was worth. It wasn't as though Green was in any rush to sign anything either – she just disappeared, I never knew where. No word of goodbye or anything, just vanished, and I wasn't exactly going to try to track her down. Of course, it had been an arranged marriage in the first place.'

'Arranged? Arranged how? What are you talking about, Barclay? I'm confused. Can we just rewind?' I could feel a headache coming on; the gaudy room wasn't helping.

'Sorry,' he mumbled. 'I was hoping you wouldn't be interested and we could skip the details.'

'You promised me full disclosure, remember?'

'I did.' He sighed and looked at me with a feeble attempt at puppy dog eyes. He wasn't getting any sympathy from me – I'd had enough of the lies.

'I got married to Green to appease my father. It was for one of his failing business deals, a last-ditch attempt to secure some backing for his tottering empire. He was in some serious trouble at the time as the global financial meltdown had almost bankrupted him. Never quite understood it but the marriage was part of this deal. I went along with it as I was looking for funding myself – I had this ransomware idea that just needed some seed capital so I could move quickly before the security improved on the Android phones and killed the opportunity.'

'Ransomware?'

'Google it. Anyway, my brilliant idea needed financing and my father and this investment partner of his said they'd fund it, if I got married to the partner's daughter.'

'And that was Green?'

'That was Green.'

'So you married for money?'

'Pretty much. A marriage of convenience. A means to an end. The usual story.'

'It was far hardly a fairy tale wedding then?'

'Is there any such thing? It was a business transaction. Most marriages are, aren't they?'

Cold, Barclay – have you never been in love?

'We weren't consulted at all. We were just chattels, easily traded.'

'It never worked of course – despite Green's obvious physical charms we didn't hit it off, didn't need to and we barely lasted five weeks as a couple as there was a problem with some money and the whole swaying house of cards came crashing down. It was quite unfortunate, ruined him and almost took Green's father down too.'

I didn't feel even the slightest bit sorry for Barclay; the great manipulator had been manipulated into a loveless marriage by his own father, all for financial gain. Boo hoo. 'What was he like, this investor, Green's father?'

Barclay shrugged. 'I never met him – very hands off, never directly involved. That was the way he did things, I was told. I did meet her mother though, she was at the Registry office. Green and I barely spoke. She may be beautiful but unfortunately, as you've also noticed, that beauty is only skin deep and she has a heart of ice to go with those eyes. We never even…the marriage was never consummated.'

'And this was when? Five years ago?'

'I'm not much good with dates, but it was around then, yes. Years before you and I met.'

'And you never got divorced?'

'No. I told you that.'

'And now you're trying to patch it back together or your father withdraws his calming influence with the authorities and inside you go?'

'My father is desperately trying to rebuild the business relationship again. I'm a little surprised her old man is up for it but maybe he's struggling too. Even more surprising was that Green was keen to try again. She's still beautiful...'

Typical male of the species; in lust rather than love, easily manipulated and manhandled.

'She hates me,' I said.

'So you say, although she honestly hasn't said anything to me on that front. If she does though, I don't think that makes you particularly special. Despite my best efforts I know she still hates me too. She's costing me a fortune, a bloody fortune. And this, all this…' he looked around the room, shaking his head, 'it's like a test to see how far she can push me. Living here is torture. Painful. Soul destroying.'

'And very deliberate on her part?'

'I would say so, wouldn't you? I mean, this can't be to anyone's taste, can it? Look at that ridiculous TV – my phone has a bigger screen than that. And I'll never finish paying for all this tat. And then there's the clothes and the shoes…especially the shoes.' Barclay was close to tears. 'So many shoes...'

I patted his right hand. 'Sorry, Barclay. I had no idea…'

He did a little shake of his head and sighed the most dramatic of self-pitying sighs. 'I don't want to talk about it anymore. My cross to bear, my life sentence. Besides, I may not have to bear it for much longer if Bartholomew gets his way.'

'True.'

'Sorry I snapped earlier.'

'S'okay.'

'Another coffee?' he asked. Wisely, he took my shudder as a 'no'. 'So what exactly did Bartholomew say when you confronted him? What's he after?'

I was still reeling from the rat-a-tat-tat of surprises that Barclay had unburdened himself of but managed to sound composed: 'He said he'd done some research and knew things about you that you wouldn't want public.'

'It's not unimaginable,' he conceded. 'He could have someone with access to those police's files and there's plenty in there he could use. Money talks and Bartholomew has far deeper pockets than my family. The palms crossed by my father may well have been treated to Bartholomew's cash, too.'

'He said he was going to turn the tables with the blackmail.'

He raised an eyebrow. 'Not without an element of risk to him, of course. I'm honestly surprised he didn't just leave us alone. We walked away, why couldn't he?'

'Or he just doesn't care. We're the loose ends, remember? He wants this finished and isn't the type to back away or just forget about it.'

'True,' said Barclay. 'And he said he wants to talk? More like make his own demands I suppose.'

'Yes. Island Gardens park, tonight at midnight.'

'Well, he can't take what we haven't got,' said Barclay. 'Even my overdrafts have overdrafts, Green's sucking me dry. What's the worst that can happen? I write him an IOU?'

'He shoots you? Us?'

'At the moment, that may not be the worst outcome in the world for me. I'll tell you what though, he's not getting his hands on my Bonneville.' He attempted a weak smile.

It was a feeble attempt to make light of the situation. He always gave the impression of being in control, in charge, but it was all looking like a fragile charade. Like his marriage.

'So you will go?'

'Sounds like I have to. You'll be there?'

'I'm in this shit with him every bit as much as you are. I lost my 'innocent bystander' defence when I went and confronted him, didn't I?'

He nodded but mercifully spared me any sarcasm. 'And Dawn?'

'She's run off to Hank's.'

'Sensible.'

'I'd join her but we need to sort this shit out first.'

He rose from his chair and left the room for a few minutes. I sat in silence, trying to understand everything he'd told me. Married for five years? It was crazy, and now he was trying to make it work with someone who he hated almost as much as she hated him, which was probably even more than she hated me.

He returned and put something frighteningly familiar on the table.

'And bring this with you.'

I froze. It was the gun that had first dragged me into Barclay's world. I pushed it away.

'I thought I'd made it clear that me and guns were history?'

'You did, but he'll likely be armed, Claire, so please, no arguments. Bring the gun. Empty it if that makes you feel more comfortable, but bring it as a deterrent. And I'll have Number Two come along too. A bit of intimidation sometimes is all it needs. I take it he didn't require that I come alone?'

'He actually insisted that I was there.'

'Then I'm sure he won't mind if Hugues comes too.'

'And what if he has a marksman again to take out all three of us?'

He shrugged.

'I should be going,' I said. 'Green may be back soon.'

Barclay didn't try to stop me as I rose. 'I shall be with Number Two at the northern entrance to the foot tunnel at 11.45,' he said.

'Okay.' It was all too incredible and yet too real. I had to get out of Barclay's pink prison and take a long walk, clear my head.

We said our goodbyes and I wandered, still somewhat stunned, back to Plumstead station. I had left the gun at Barclay's: no point weighing myself down with it if I had no intention of using it. He didn't seem too surprised.

It wasn't until my train pulled up to the platform at Deptford that I realised it was no longer home – I had no home. Bartholomew had seen to that.

When your world has turned to shit and there's nowhere left to run, no-one you can turn to, there is only one salvation.

A proper all-day breakfast, of course. From the station I trekked down to my favourite greasy spoon on Deptford High Street and the artery-hardening consolation of their 'Three Of Everything' special. I needed black pudding – every bad girl deserves black pudding.

The food was not going to win any TripAdvisor awards. It was lukewarm, the bacon burned to a crisp and the sausages suspiciously pink, all swimming in congealing grease. Blackened tomatoes, runny eggs, a trio of mushrooms the token veg, fried bread and over-buttered white sliced, too. Perfect. Indigestion was going to be the least of my problems before the night was out. Suddenly I was ravenous and devoured it in a matter of minutes, along with two pots of tea.

The café waitress looked at her watch, sighed, and came over again and asked if I wanted any more tea. I attempted a smile and shook my head. I couldn't eat or drink another thing. Last meal for the condemned woman before her date with fate and all that. Didn't want to spoil it. Mind you, there was one last slice of homemade bread pudding on the counter that I'd swear had my name on it. Tempting and…

My mobile burst into life. It was Hank. Odd – why was he calling?

'Hi Hank.'

'Hello Claire. Is she with you?'

My eyes narrowed. 'Dawn? No, of course not. She left me ages ago, just after lunch. Didn't she call you?'

'Yes, said she had someone to see but wouldn't be long. She should have been here hours ago. You haven't spoken at all?'

'No. Not a word. What time is it?'

'Almost ten.'

Bloody hell. No wonder the café was trying to close up around me. Dawn should have been there hours and hours ago. Why hadn't she made it back to Hank's yet? She couldn't have spent that long with that friend and it was only a few hours' drive even in the rush hour. Unless…

I felt the panic rising, my mouth dried and I struggled to keep my grip on my phone. 'I've no idea where she is Hank. She was seeing someone first but that was hours ago.'

'I've tried calling but her phone just keeps flipping to voicemail,' he was trying to sound calm but his voice sounded unnatural.

'I'm sure she's safe,' I lied, desperate to assure us both. 'Must be just the traffic. She drives like a granny, you know.'

'Sure. Must be traffic. But let me know if you hear from her,' he said, and with that my phone went dead and he was gone.

Like Dawn. Not the 'dead' bit – at least I hoped that wasn't true – no, the 'gone' bit. Dawn had gone. Disappeared.

As if stolen by the night.

Chapter 19

'Barclay. It's me. Claire. Have you seen Dawn?'

'Barclay. It's Claire again. Is Dawn with you? Let me know.'

'Barclay. Claire. Why don't you answer your fucking phone?!'

'Barclay! Call me! Dawn's gone missing! I don't think we should see Bartholomew tonight! Call me!'

Voicemail. Not exactly one of technology's finest achievements to be truthful. Conversations with Barclay often turned out to be one-way traffic, but this was ridiculous. I may as well have tried calling and texting a black hole. No replies. No response. What to do?

Barclay had said to meet at the north side entrance to the Greenwich foot tunnel at 11.45 so I started to make my way there. The café had thrown me out at ten on the dot and I'd quickly outstayed my welcome with the bar staff at the fancy new riverfront bar who had sneered at my order for a pint of tap water. I sat outside on a 'For Patrons Only' bench desperately trying to get hold of Barclay and Dawn. No luck. Then some moronic bouncer decided that I wasn't welcome even outside and he was revoking my charitable status, moving me on. 'Time you were gone,' he growled.

I took my phone out for one last attempt to get Barclay and saw that it was down to seven per cent. No charger. Nowhere to charge it, anyway. Wonderful.

Out on the street the sensible ones had looked at the skies and finally called it a night. There was a heaviness in the air as ominous thunder clouds had skulked in, almost undetectable against the inky blackness. Distant rumbles of thunder announced the incoming storm's intent; the weather was finally going to stop teasing and take itself seriously.

No more dallying. I could have joined the noisy queue for the DLR for a single stop but I checked my watch and I didn't have the time. Late. Shit. The Greenwich foot tunnel was my only option for crossing the river and meeting Barclay and TNT before the showdown with Bartholomew.

I fucking hate that tunnel. Sure, it's yet another masterful piece of engineering by those clever Victorian buggers, but it's a scary place at any time, especially at night. It can't be that long but when you go through it the tunnel feels endless, as are the iron steps that take you down under the Thames. There are unmanned lifts at both ends but I just don't trust them; the stairs are for me the preferred option, especially late at night.

Some locals say that the tunnel is haunted by a ghostly couple whose feet hover inches above the paved floor. I'd buy that – like I said, it's a bloody spooky place, eerie and unsettling. After a few hundred feet you lose sight of both ends as the tunnel dips to its lowest point under the river and the acoustics take on an unnatural, underwater quality. Not my favourite place and not ideal for the feint-hearted or a lone, late night over-fed-to-bursting idiot out of ideas and out of time.

I had lost track of time, had left things too late and I had no choice. I had to get to Barclay and TNT to warn them that Dawn had gone missing, that Bartholomew was, again, the likeliest suspect and that the stakes in this stupid game had been raised even higher. I strode into the tunnel's south entrance and spiralled down the steps, taking two at a time before spilling out at the bottom, dizzy, stumbling, and landing on my hands and knees.

Stupid Claire. Stay calm. It's not like anyone's going anywhere.

The tunnel was empty. Every sound, even my breathing, took on an unnerving, otherworldly quality.

A portentous crack of thunder sounded above and echoed menacingly down the stairwell. Shit. Could the tunnel flood in torrential rain? I doubted it – those Victorians thought of everything, didn't they? But where would the flood water go? I didn't plan on staying long enough to check on some long-dead engineer's handiwork and broke into a gentle jog. Instant stitch. Maybe the greasy food hadn't been such a great idea after all.

Scared? Me? Of course not. Big girl, me. I was more scared of what I was going to find at the other end and…

Another crack, a little more muffled as I made my way down

the tunnel but the accompanying long rumble reverberated around me.

Sod that. My jog became a gentle run and then suddenly I heard a loud clunk … click … thud … behind me. Something big and heavy was coming down the steps and I wasn't hanging around to find out what. I broke into my best take at a sprint. The pots of tea in my stomach were sloshing from side to side with each pace.

I passed halfway and the tunnel sloped upwards and there, thank fuck, I could see the lift doors invitingly already open. My stitch had gone and I picked up my pace, my heavy breathing echoing down the tunnel. Finally there, I threw myself into the cage and collapsed on all fours, gasping for breath.

The doors closed. Athleticism and Claire: not natural bedfellows, lest we forget. My thigh's old wound pulsed dully but it was a bearable, almost pleasurable distant pain. I pressed the big 'G' button and, after a heart-stopping few seconds, the jittery mechanics shook into life. Through the dirty glass I saw the monster that had been pursuing me – a smart but knackered-looking chap tugging along a large briefcase on loud plastic wheels. Probably a solicitor.

Terrifying.

Pathetic, Claire. Man up, buttercup, for Christ's sake.

The lift lurched and rose, shuddering as if exhausted by the sheer effort of its daily toil. I checked my watch again. 11.50. I'd had hours to kill and yet somehow had managed to be late. Typical Claire.

'You're late,' said Barclay, professor of the bleeding obvious.

'Late,' verified TNT, arms and brows crossed. No-one was happy to see me.

'Why the fuck,' I shouted, 'don't you fucking answer your fucking phone, Barclay?'

He muttered something unintelligible.

'Your phone!' I screamed. 'Didn't you get any of my bloody messages?'

Barclay pulled his phone from his pocket and checked the

screen, raising an eyebrow.

'Dawn's missing?'

'Yes!'

'Since when?'

'I last saw her at lunchtime. She was off to see someone then heading to Hank's. That's an hour and a half journey tops. He hasn't seen or heard from her.'

'Oh.'

'That the best you can do? 'Oh'?'

'It may be nothing.'

'Seriously?'

'It probably isn't nothing. Hello Claire, by the way.'

I scowled my best scowl.

'Besides,' said Barclay, 'we're here now. Too late to back out.'

We were where we were. Bartholomew would arrive in a few minutes.

I'd not been to the park at Island Gardens before. It looked a small but neat little affair, a small green with a café and kids' playground. It was well lit, which was reassuring for our clandestine rendezvous. I didn't fancy meeting anyone in the dark. No noticeable CCTV but presumably our tormentor had already checked that out for himself.

There was a flash of lightning and a loud crack of thunder directly overhead and the heavens suddenly, finally opened and the long-threatened rain started at last, the heavy drops thudding dramatically on the ground in their pent-up fury. The heatwave had finally broken.

At the far end of the park headlights appeared. We had company. The lights were bright and high; Bartholomew was in one of those ludicrous, gargantuan Chelsea Tractors.

The players were in place. The stage was set. The die were cast. The tension finally got the better of me and I broke wind and belched simultaneously. It was time to get this pantomime on the road.

You know that scene in *Reservoir Dogs* where Tarantino has Keitel and co walking in synchronized arrogance, all slow-motion strut with a 'let's go to work' swagger?

Well, that wasn't us. Barclay maybe a little, but definitely not me – I was already knackered and limping after being pursued through the tunnel by a petrifying solicitor; I had a stagger more than a swagger. And TNT? His sheer size may have been menacing when stationary but there was no bluster he could muster in his ungainly stride no matter how angry he tried to look.

Reservoir Pups more like. It was probably just my imagination but I thought I could hear someone laughing at us from the direction of the half-concealed car.

There was a rustle behind the hedge and a figure emerged from the dark – Bartholomew, in an expensive-looking long Dryzabone coat that almost reached the floor. The raindrops just bounced off him like he was impervious, a Superman.

Me? I was already soaked through, my flimsy top clinging to my curves and bumps like I was entering a wet T-shirt competition. At least my clothes were finally getting a long-overdue wash.

'Hello, Barclay,' said Bartholomew. 'I see you've brought the brains of the outfit with you.' He smirked and did a little nod towards me and TNT. Bastard. 'You can tell a lot about a man by the people he associates with.'

I think I'd just been insulted but I wasn't quite sure. At least we were the good guys. Well, I think we were now the good guys – it was a grey area at best. We were all just shades of bad.

'No cowardly snipers in the bushes then, Bartholomew?' taunted Barclay.

Bartholomew smiled. 'MacDonald reckons this game has gone far enough.'

I could barely hear him; the storm clouds had decided they weren't going to piss around anymore and had let loose the full force of their ire. 'Torrential' didn't do it justice – the rain was like a sudden tropical monsoon. We could barely hear or even see him, even though he was just a few yards away.

'Do you have my sister?' Barclay barked but I couldn't swear that Bartholomew heard him.

'I have taken out some…insurance,' Bartholomew shouted back, struggling to be heard over the storm that was crashing down around us. Did that mean he had Dawn? I wasn't sure, but Barclay assumed the worst.

'Then Claire is right: things have gone too far. Let her go and let's make that the end of this.'

'Let who go? And how can this end when I know so much about you?'

Barclay looked puzzled. 'What? I can't hear you!'

'The courts may have let you off but why should I? My people said that the police couldn't hand the files over to us fast enough.' I didn't hear what he said next – the deafening rain made his grandstanding pretty much redundant. Then I caught: "…are a lot of people out there who would like a taste of justice, Mister Barclay.'

I turned to Barclay, his hair now flattened by the rain. He looked broken, as if the deluge had washed away the last of his confidence and self respect.

'Cat got your tongue now, Barclay? I have everything I need to finish you once and for all, while you have...what exactly do you have now? Nothing. Fuck all. Even that…thing,' he waved a disparaging hand at TNT, 'is all bluff and bluster. My gran could put up more of a fight than that freak, and she's been dead twenty years. What to do, what to do…'

TNT's fists curled but he looked more confused than threatening. So Bartholomew had done his background checks on TNT too, and knew that our muscle man may have been the size of a vending machine but also was about as dangerous as one. We'd seen the files on us but hadn't read them – too much information, too little time. He had it all and we had zilch. Barclay had been outplayed, outsmarted, out thought and outfought.

'If you have all that, why did you take Dawn?'

'Your sister? I don't need your sister. Besides, I have you,' he poked Barclay in the chest. 'And them.' Again, the condescending sneer.

A brief feeling of relief raced through my body but it was

fleeting – he didn't have Dawn. But then, if he hadn't abducted her where was she?

'Why this meeting then?' asked Barclay, but before Bartholomew could answer a gunshot rang out from behind me. We all ducked instinctively except TNT. He just grunted and toppled to the ground, bouncing on impact like a felled giant redwood.

Barclay turned towards his fallen friend. 'Hugues!' he cried out – the big man had fallen face down and we couldn't see if or where he'd been hit. Bartholomew was cowering too and looked as shocked as us. This wasn't him. This wasn't us. I could just make out through the rain a figure running towards the foot tunnel's stairs.

'I'll get him!' I yelled, and sprinted towards the tunnel.

What was I thinking? Chasing an armed sniper? Bartholomew behind me, possibly aiming another gun in my direction?

I have no idea. Instinct? Panic?

Or just plain fucking stupidity?

I think it was the latter.

So I ran, following the gunman down into the foot tunnel.

Chapter 20

How I kept on my feet was beyond me. I stumbled and tumbled down the spiralling stairs. Two, three, four steps at a time, slippery from the rain. Round and round I descended, a clumsy out-of-control motion, half flying, half falling before I hit the bottom hard on all fours, picked myself up then started through the industrial steel rings at the opening of the tunnel's north end.

A bullet whizzed passed me, loud and deadly but wide of its mark.

Fifty feet ahead of me I could see a fallen figure scrambling on the floor. He'd tripped on the wet, uneven York stone floor and been sent him flying. And it looked like he'd hurt himself; he gingerly tested his ankle as he stood. That looked broken to me. Ouch.

Shame.

It didn't stop him firing off two more shots at me though as he struggled to balance himself. Both missed but I felt the movement in the air as the second flew passed, far too close to my arm for comfort. And loud. So loud in the tunnel. I needed to cover my ears but that would have slowed me down too much. Not that I was thinking logically at all. I started to run

I'd just have to live with the loud ringing in my ears.

I suddenly regretted not bringing Barclay's gun. But you don't do guns anymore, do you Claire? Bloody stupid time to develop a conscience.

The gunman was still moving slowly, dragging his left foot behind him. Broken ankle or just a twist? Didn't matter to me – I was going to catch him and he knew it.

He tried to fire again but there was nothing. He stared at the pistol for a second in disbelief and then threw it to the ground in disgust. Forty feet. I could easily catch him.

But then I slipped too, my foot stubbing an uneven paving slab and sending me sprawling. My knees and hands slammed hard into the floor sending shockwaves through my body. I'd live. Nothing broken. I picked myself up and found myself smiling at a 'No Running In The Foot Tunnel' sign. Yeah, right.

I was losing my advantage and he was nearing the far stairwell. I started after him again, picking up his discarded weapon on my way.

'Stop!' I yelled, but he just continued his hobbling, lop-sided scuttle. He was getting away and I was already tiring.

Even if there were bullets left in the gun I couldn't stop to shoot. I'd only fuck it up. Too out of breath. I thrust the gun into the back of my jeans. My lungs and legs were suddenly heavy but he had the upper hand now and luck was on his side – the south-side lift was waiting for him, its doors open, welcoming him in. He threw himself at the lift floor, reached up and pressed the button. The doors shook, faltered, teasing, then slammed shut just yards in front of me.

I smashed into them, banging on them with my clenched fists in frustration. 'Stop!' I screamed, but the mechanical cogs were turning and the cables were lifting him from me.

The stairs. I'd have to use the stairs.

Again.

Shit.

I went for the quick single steps rather than clumsy, tiring doubles. Ten, twenty, twenty-five…I counted them off. I was losing it though. I couldn't see him but could hear the lift shuddering to a halt at the top of its climb. Thirty – a third of the way up? Was that all? Just a third? Fuckin' hell. I'd never make it.

But I couldn't stop…couldn't let him get away...HE'D KILLED TNT!

Needed to change my step, tried two at a time…

Single steps too much…

The ringing in my ears had been replaced by the desperate rasps of my breathing. So short…so short of breath.

And the weight of that fucking breakfast, so heavy…

Fifty. Fifty-two. Fifty-three…forever…

'Stop!' I called out into the void above.

I could hear the lift gates sliding open above me.

Ignore that. Go, Claire, go!

It was all or nothing.

But my heavy legs only had nothing and were leaden and clumsy, failing to respond.

Just a little further. Twenty more steps...no more, surely... there couldn't be...more? I'd lost count...another turn of the spiral and I could see the lights from Cutty Sark Gardens just above me.

Almost there. Five. Four. Three...

I took the last steps in a single, desperate bound, a last burst of energy from god knows where and I emerged from behind the lift and into the open square, the great tea clipper looming overhead. My quarry had collapsed on to all fours in the hammering rain and was clutching his damaged ankle. He was going nowhere now. Catching my breath I finally caught up with him and he turned to face me.

'Hello...Claire,' he managed as he desperately gasped for air.

I couldn't believe it. Even in the lashing storm I recognised that pathetic face.

Wardy???

He was finished. Exhausted. Couldn't move.

Not me. From somewhere I'd got my second wind. I was on him without mercy.

I should have been thinking that he might have a second gun or a knife, of the bullets that had almost taken me out just minutes earlier. Should have weighed up the odds of his six foot plus against my knackered, out-of-condition, breakfast padded featherweight frame.

Should have thought it all through.

But I was beyond thinking. Thinking's not good sometimes. Gets in the way.

He'd been trying to kill us and now I had him at my feet.

Screaming, I unleashed my fury, I kicked and kicked, left foot, right foot, and punched and spat and scratched. It was not pretty. He folded up like one of those armadillo things, pulling himself into a tight ball to protect himself.

Fat chance.

My Converses were the only weapons I needed. I had his gun, too, but no idea if it would fire, using it like a hammer as my blows rained down on him.

Kick. Caught the side of his face and heard his cheekbone crack, his eyes wide in panic.

Kick. Hard on the elbow, forcing his left arm out wide as a reflex.

Stamp, on his left hand, the bones splintering under my weight.

He screamed. I was screaming.

'Why?' Kick. 'The fuck…' Stamp. 'Are you trying…' Kick. 'To kill us?!' A final kick in the small of his back unfurled his head from its safety and I put my Converse to his nose. Blood and bone sprayed out, splattering on the paving.

'Stop!'

No chance. He was lying prostrate now on the paving and I stamped the left foot hard on the side of his head and shifted my weight onto it.

'Please … stop.'

No chance. I bore down hard.

'Please…stop…Claire.'

I was pressing too hard and my foot slipped off in the wet.

I lifted it to stamp again then froze. What was I doing? The red mist started to pass. Suddenly my own exhaustion hit me and I felt the aching tightness in my lungs as I struggled for air.

I bent down and lifted him by his blood-soaked collar.

'Why?' I spat, my shoulders heaving with the effort.

'A second…give me a second…'

I shook my head.

'WHY?'

'I can explain, just give…give me a second.'

I threw him back to the floor and he closed his eyes, the onslaught had finally stopped and a faint smile curled his mouth.

'You're a … feisty one …' he said, grinning to reveal his bloody teeth.

'Why?'

'Unfinished business…he told me…I had to finish what I'd started…what he'd started.'

"He'? Who's 'he'?'

'Bartholomew.'

I knew it. Ward shifted his position, wincing as he propped himself up against the low riverside wall. He looked and sounded like he could pass out at any moment.

'What do you mean, 'unfinished business'?'

'Last year. Got a call.' He panted. 'Asking me to take out someone. Down in Kent. Good money. Silly money. Couldn't say no. Didn't care. No questions asked. Didn't know who.'

'Rochester – that was you?'

'What? Yes, down that way. I didn't know who!'

Didn't matter. Didn't fucking matter, and I kicked him as hard as I could in the side of his chest, driving the little air left from his lungs, probably snapping a rib or two. Bloody hoped so.

'I didn't know who I…was shooting…' His eyes were wide in his desperation. 'It was dark, remember? It wasn't easy with a hand gun. Misjudged it. Fucked it.'

'You fucking hit me! Put a few in Barclay!'

'I DIDN'T KNOW! Only found out later.'

I couldn't believe my ears. I didn't believe my ears – he was lying. He knew it was us. If he could see us to shoot he knew it was us.

'You knew. And no doubts? No remorse? Or was the money so irresistible you just had to come back and finish the job?'

'Not at first, no. I got paid. Job done. Then I found it had been Barclay…and some bent policeman I'd shot and the copper was dead but Barclay had survived...'

'And me!' I interjected angrily. 'And Dawn.'

Ward ignored me and was getting his breath back. 'It was all over, I thought. But then something went wrong and Barclay was out, back on the streets. And I got a call, that Bartholomew again, he came back and demanded I finish the job or he'd shop me to the police. And I'd killed a copper, so what could I say?

I had no choice...' For some reason he attempted a smile, his lips and teeth a bloody grimace. Bastard. I kicked him in the stomach. Hard. Fucking hard.

Enough. Show some control, Claire. Show some control.

I pulled his pistol out the back of my jeans. It was small, almost too small. It was a wonder it had felled TNT.

TNT. I'd almost forgotten. He'd killed TNT. Poor, sweet, misunderstood TNT.

'He wants you dead, you know? All of you. The big guy, too. Offered me even more money, so much I wouldn't know,' he shook his head, 'wouldn't know how I would ever spend it. I couldn't refuse, I'd never need to work again, I…'

I jerked the gun and thrust it into the side of his head, twisting it to make him cringe.

'I had to say 'yes', couldn't refuse. He said we were in this together. Said it was just insurance so I had to do it. If it wasn't me, he'd have someone else take me out and then get them to finish things, someone …'

'Competent?' I suggested.

That hurt him, really hurt him. But he nodded, knowing he was beaten, beaten by me, a bloody girl.

'So it was you who shot out our tyres, tried to crash us on the bike, set the police on us, that was all you?'

He nodded.

'I tried tampering with an engine on a hire car Barclay had but was seen by someone and had to leave it half done.'

The Porsche breaking down was him?

'You're a fucking lousy assassin, Ward,' I said, landing another kick on his ribs. 'I suppose I should be amazed you managed to hit TNT?' Not that he'd have been easy to miss.

'TNT? Who's that? The big guy? I was aiming at Barclay.'

Poor TNT. An innocent bystander again. I peered over the river at the park on the north bank. Couldn't see anything from that distance no matter how hard I squinted. No sign of Bartholomew's car. No sign of anything.

When I turned back Ward had somehow lifted himself up and was standing again, by the low river wall. I lifted the gun.

'Don't try anything, Ward!' I shouted.

'Or you'll what? You know that gun's empty.'

'Doesn't feel empty to me,' and I squeezed the trigger, the gun barking into life, shocking us both. The bullet caught him in the shoulder and carried him over the edge into the torrid Thames waters below. I ran to the wall but there was no sign of him, he'd disappeared below the surface, too battered and weak to swim.

Shit. Fuck. Shit.

Nice one, Claire.

I dropped the gun and crumpled to my knees on the wet paving, my shoulders shaking, overpowered by the huge dry sobs racking my chest.

It wasn't proving to be a great evening.

Chapter 21

Fuck. Bloody hell, Claire. That wasn't exactly your finest hour.

I tried to compose myself; big, slow, deep breaths. I needed to move quickly but my legs had other ideas. Standing they could just about manage but running? Forget it – they were ready to call it a night. I looked up and around me. Bloody CCTV cameras everywhere. Shit shit shit. I needed to move now, before someone at Big Brother central noticed that all was not well down in the centre of town.

I pulled out my mobile to call Barclay, only to find that some idiot had forgotten to recharge it in the café. Some idiot? That would be me. My shoulders dropped as the world conspired against me yet again. Like me – no stamina. I felt a sudden nostalgic pang for my ancient Nokia. What's the point of a mobile that needs charging every few hours? Not so smart those bloody smartphones, are they?

Whatever. That was the least of my problems. I shook my head, tucked the gun in my jeans, lied to my legs that the steps wouldn't hurt this time (honest) and started back to the tunnel entrance, one last trip back under the river.

Island Gardens was deserted. No Barclay. No Bartholomew. No Bartholomew's car.

No TNT.

And no sign they'd ever been there.

I couldn't see any blood, the rain would have washed that away anyway, but it looked like TNT had not just survived but had been mobile enough to get away under his own steam. There was no way that Barclay or Bartholomew could have moved him without the help of a passing fork lift truck, so he must have made it away on his own. Barclay had once abandoned him after a hit and run and wasn't known for hanging around the scene of a crime. No, the only person who could have moved Thug Number Two was the man himself, thank the lord.

Well done, sir, but with a friend like Barclay, he was used to looking after himself.

I parked my arse on a nearby bench and counted through my options. It didn't take long. I didn't have any. I was still fucked. Actually, it was worse than that – I was completely fucked. No home, no friends, no nothing. Completely, well and truly, no doubt about it, fuckity fuckity fucked. I lay back and closed my eyes, wishing the world and all my troubles away for five seconds. Just five. Needed to get away. Needed to…

A car horn woke me from my sleep. I'd hit a new personal low on a night of me reaching unprecedented depths of human behaviour: I had fallen asleep on a park bench. At one in the morning. In the rain.

Things could only get better.

A car flashed its lights at me.

It looked vaguely familiar. Couldn't distinguish the colour but was it? Surely not? It was!

Another honk. Bugger me, it was Dawn's car, the Golf she'd been given by Hank. A smile surprised my face and I grinned as I picked myself up, made a futile attempt to make myself presentable and brushed my wet clothes down and then ran towards it. She was okay! It was all going to be okay. Thank the lord for that. The passenger door was flung open and I threw myself into the seat, the sheer relief of finding her (or, more accurately, her finding me) was all-consuming and …

It wasn't Dawn driving.

It was Green.

Barclay's bitch of a wife.

I screamed and tried to get out, scrambling for the handle but she was quick, too quick, and she had locked it from some door control thingy. Before I could do anything else she stamped down hard on the accelerator and the car jumped and surged away. A hand from the backseat patted me on the shoulder. 'Hey, calm down Claire. S'all okay.'

Dawn?

'How? Who? What..?'

'Calm down, MacDonald,' Green said, jumping a set of

sleepy red lights and sending an insomniac dog walker leaping for safety with his yapping Schnauzer.

'How..? Why..? Dawn – what's going on?'

'Bloody hell Claire,' said Dawn. 'Chill out. I'm fine. She's fine. You're fine. Don't panic. I gave her the keys as I'd had one glass too many and didn't fancy getting stopped by the cops. We're your knights in shining whatnot.' I could sense her slightly squiffy smile behind me. I wanted to hug her but that was impossible within the tight confines of the hatchback.

'Green..?'

I wasn't finishing my thoughts let alone my sentences. Was I being kidnapped? By Green and Dawn? Since when? Barclay had said that Dawn didn't know Green but clearly that was wrong as they were acting like best buds. Barclay had been getting good at being wrong. It was not a quality in him I found particularly endearing. How had they found me? Why had they found me? What the fuck was going on?

'What the fuck is going on?' I asked.

Green smiled, her eyes fixed on the deserted roads ahead, her driving focussed, intent, intense.

'I don't understand,' I said.

'No, of course you don't,' Green said. 'You never do, do you? I don't get what he sees in you. Dim little Claire. All action Claire. Not thinking Claire. You know your problem MacDonald?' She turned to me, the aggression made me draw back in my seat. 'You don't listen. You don't think. I told you. How many times did I tell you? I warned you to get out. Put some distance between yourself and Barclay.'

'You threatened me…'

She threw back her head and laughed. 'Threatened? Threatened? You idiot, I was trying to save you from all this… this shit. And you thought I was *threatening* you? What a fucking idiot!'

Dawn was silent in the back. She could do that after a few drinks – just tune out. The way we were being driven, that was no bad thing. Green ignored more red lights and threw the car at a roundabout, the car coping admirably with her too-sharp steering. She took the third turning then braked hard to avoid rear-ending a slow lorry turning left. Impatient, she forced the accelerator back to the floor and the Golf picked up the pace again, the automatic gearbox making light of the sudden demand for speed. The professional in me hated to admit it but she drove well. Bet she couldn't have done that turn in a manual, mind, but she was good.

Green was still amused by what I'd said. 'Is that why you looked so worried when I last saw you? You thought I was jealous of you and Barclay?'

I looked at my knees. I didn't know what to say. 'There's nothing between me and Barclay,' I mumbled.

She laughed. 'Of course there isn't. Never has been, never will be. Anyone can see that. Even if there was, why would I care, anyway?'

'Because you're his wife.'

She stopped laughing and shook her head, giving me a look of disbelief. 'You really don't have a clue, do you?'

'I don't. I think I mentioned that.'

'Fine. Let me...' – she paused for a second as she slowed to manoeuvre the car through a pinch-point chicane, followed by a fast right-then-left – '...explain. In short sentences and simple words so you can keep up.'

I wasn't warming to her. Dawn seemed to have dozed off in the back seat and I checked my watch. It was so late it was almost early. There was traffic up ahead; a few lorries and cars heading south despite the hour, a rumbling procession heading from the choked-up capital to the sanity of the Dover road. Maybe Green would slow at the junction?

Fat chance. She accelerated at the crossing traffic and narrowly missed an Asda lorry, oblivious to its panic-stricken horn.

'Where to begin, where to begin,' she mused.

'At the very beginning?' I suggested. 'It's a very good place to start.'

She smiled and, for once, there was actually a little humour there, a little, a smidge maybe. 'Sound of Music?' she asked.

'Of course.'

'I do like you Claire. I meant that when I said that to Barclay that time. There's an innocence to your oddness I find quite endearing.'

Despite my misgivings, my cheeks warmed at the compliment.

'Let's start at the very beginning then…'

'It starts with my father. Everything bad starts with my father. Bad things often end with him, too.'

'When I said at the very beginning I wasn't meaning 'with your conception',' I joked, sensing a lightening in her mood.

She gave her head a little shake. 'It's probably best if you just shut up and let me talk. If you interrupt it'll take forever and you'll only feel bad if you joke once you realise the truth.'

Rebuked, I dropped my head as she stared at the brightly lit tarmac ahead.

Green said: 'I try to come across as someone confident, in control, hard even. But I'm not. Quite the opposite. And admitting to being…fragile…it fills me with a degree of shame and…this isn't comfortable. It really isn't.'

I nodded solemnly.

'As I was saying, it starts with my father, the man Barclay calls just Bartholomew.'

Suddenly there was no air. I couldn't breathe, couldn't think.

'Your…'

'…father. Yes. Anthony Bartholomew. Green was my mother's surname. Close your mouth, dear, that gaping makes you look a bit dim.

'Bit of a surprise I see. I'm surprised Barclay hadn't worked that out for himself but he's not as bright as he thinks he is, is he?'

She could say that again.

'As I was saying, it starts with him and his shitty fucking business deals. Shitty deals with shitty people. And, once I was old enough, I was just another commodity to be traded. Good job I grew up pretty. I'd hate to think what would have happened to me if I'd been plain like…' She stopped herself just short of firing the inevitable insult my way.

'Traded?'

There was a twitch of her lips but definitely no smile. 'He didn't put me out on the game, if that's what you're thinking. Mercifully that was beneath even him, although he no doubt considered it when I reached my teens. Nothing is truly beneath him and I'm sure he would have considered it if his business associates or clients had made enquiries.' She turned to me, eyes steely and cold again. 'He really is a…'

We both knew the word but she couldn't say it. I swallowed hard.

'And one of those business associates was Barclay's father,' I said, starting to piece the story together.

Green looked at me in surprise. 'Exactly. You're getting it. Our two fathers were very close for a while, worked hand in glove apparently. I didn't know what they did, such matters weren't for the ladies of the house of course. Mum and I were just decoration at his beck and call. There were lots of evening meetings, lots of whisky, cigars, phone calls. I locked myself in my room, headphones hiding me from the fake laughter of their false friendship rising from downstairs.

'They were cut from the same cloth: Barclay's father lacked any moral compass or decency too of course, that's why they got on so well, but I guess you already know that.'

I was learning but could barely picture the man I'd met the previous year. He had seemed rude, hard maybe but harmless to me – Barclay and Dawn hated him, Mrs Barclay obeyed his every command, but I must admit I just had him down as another weirdo from the Barclay clan.

'The two of them,' she continued, 'the two fathers I mean, had a genius plan that would make them both millionaires, but they got into arguments about the details, two alpha males rutting over who got what and they had a huge row, explosive, and Barclay's father stormed out of our house and we didn't see him for weeks – it looked like it was all over. Then suddenly he reappeared, a little meeker and with less bravado, with something different than just needed some start up cash and everything was back on track and they were best friends again. But the row had been a wake-up call, so they decided that they couldn't let that happen again and they came up with an old-fashioned business arrangement to ensure such a 'misunderstanding' wouldn't be repeated. I was half of that arrangement.'

'And Barclay was the other half.' She was filling in the blanks Barclay had left from his version of events. Did I believe her? The truth probably sat somewhere between the two stories.

'Exactly. Our two families tied by blood. I was seventeen when we were introduced by my mother – father didn't get involved in the details. Barclay of course was a few years' older than me. I thought I could give it a go. Okay, so Barclay's not exactly handsome like a fairy tale prince and he wouldn't be everyone's cup of tea but it could have been a hell of a lot worse for me. There's something about those eyes...

'But he was cold and aloof, distant from the moment we met. When you look like me, being ignored is so hard to take of course. Barely any eye contact. We were married within hours. There was no discussion, we'd barely said two words to each other. It was a business transaction, complete with filing cabinets full of pre-nups and various contractual obligations on all parties, stocks and shares swaps, all kinds of financial shit. The two of us were pretty incidental in the whole thing. No church, no wedding dress, no celebration, just a cold, dowdy registry office. May as well have been married in a corridor. The registrar muttered the vows to himself, like he was reciting a shopping list at the check-out. Must have broken some kind of speed record in getting to the 'do you...and you' bit. All the paperwork we had to sign took longer than making the vows. I don't even think Barclay's mother was there. I've never met her – I doubt she knows I exist.'

'I don't think she does.'

'You've met her? What's she like?'

'Obedient.' It was the only word that sprang immediately to mind but I couldn't have found a more appropriate one even if I'd had weeks to consider it.

'It started to break on the first night. We were supposed to honeymoon in some pathetic little cheap motorway motel they'd arranged for us just off the A4 but Barclay was on his mobile all evening and I was too upset. I never thought my father would actually do it, you see, marry me off without a care. And when Barclay finally spoke to me he had called me a dirty little…' She couldn't finish the sentence. Part of me didn't want her to.

'I'm sorry,' I said, and genuinely meant it. She shook her head, the tears spilling from her eyes.

'Cruel. So cruel,' she whispered, wiping her cheek with the back of her hand.

I felt a lump in my throat and moved to put a reassuring hand on her arm but she pulled away, not wanting any part of my attempt at an offer of comfort.

'And then my life just span out of control. Barclay wanted nothing to do with me. Nothing. It wasn't just the lack of affection; it was a total lack of attention. He couldn't even look me in the eye. I didn't know what to make of it. We went through the motions, moved into a pissy little apartment in Kennington. I hated it. That's where the true horror began. It was a tiny place but Barclay couldn't even stay in the same room as me; if I walked into the kitchen, he walked out. If I followed him into the lounge, he'd leave, slamming the front door behind him. We didn't share a bed – we barely shared the flat. He'd disappear for days, then return and ignore me for hours on end. I had no-one to talk to, I was so alone.

'And then something changed. Something had gone wrong, horribly wrong, something to do with Barclay's work, something he'd done for his father and that was when he started to abuse me.'

I felt my jaw drop. She glanced in my direction before fixing her eyes back on the road. 'No, not physical abuse. He never hit me. Nothing so obvious. Verbal violence. Emotional battering. Once he started, the bullying was relentless. He'd shout and scream, attack me with savage invective, cruel put-downs and cutting, caustic sarcasm. It wasn't just being mean, it was demeaning, remorseless, degrading. You hear about women being verbally abused on daytime telly but to actually live it…' the tears were flowing freely now, even in the dimly lit car I could see that her eyes were red at the memories.

'I kept telling myself it was just me being too fragile, too sensitive. I felt as though it was my fault, that I'd brought this upon myself. But I know now that it wasn't me. It was him. I felt worthless, considered suicide, I needed pills, so many pills, and there was no-one there for me, nobody cared. Barclay was so self-centred, self-absorbed, ignorant of the pain he was causing me, so brutal, heartless, callous, unthinking…' She paused. 'Don't look so surprised, Claire. He may seem different now but I reckon it's still there, tucked just below the surface. 'Reasonable Barclay' is just a veneer. I think you've changed him a smidgen, probably unwittingly but …' She attempted what may have actually been another smile but it looked painful, more like a grimace. 'Maybe he's easier now. Not quite mature but at least bearable.'

I couldn't think of anything to say. I thought back to how obnoxious Barclay had been when I had first met him, how he'd humiliated and embarrassed me in the pub with my bag, all of those long silences, how he'd abandoned me with a wounded TNT after the hit and run, how he had seemed to completely lack the basic social sensibilities. He seemed like a different person now. Maybe she wasn't exaggerating about how he used to be.

Maybe I really had changed Barclay. He'd certainly changed me.

'That's why he doesn't deserve what my father's planning to do. Everyone deserves a second chance. Even him.'

'What exactly is your father planning then?' I asked.

'He's going to kill him, of course,' she said.

Silly me. Of course he was.

Chapter 22

There was some nonsense coming from the back seat – Dawn was talking in her sleep. 'Claire!' she suddenly called out, 'Watch out for that marshmallow! Save the unicorn! You don't fillet salmon like that!'

A giggle, and then she was silent and sleeping again.

At least someone was happy.

It certainly wasn't Green or me.

Green's phone chimed with a text and she wrestled it from her pocket, the Golf swerving briefly towards the curb before she corrected it. One hand on the wheel but no eyes on the road.

'Shit,' she muttered.

'What's that?' I asked.

'Text from my father,' said Green. 'He says he needs help. He says he couldn't do it on his own. He says it can't wait until morning.'

'He can't do what on his own?'

'I'm trying not to think about it.'

'Think it's Barclay-related?'

'I'd imagine so.'

'Body disposal?'

Well, that was a conversation killer if ever there was one...

Several miles passed without a word being said, Dawn's sleepy breathing like a ticking clock counting down to fate o'clock.

I decided to try to fill in some of the gaps in what I'd heard and experienced. 'How did you find me? How did you know where to pick me up?'

Despite Dawn's earlier assurances I wasn't convinced I could trust Green, I still wasn't sure it all added up.

'We were already driving around trying to find you and Barclay. Barclay had an appointment on his phone for Island Gardens at 11.45 so we went there first but,' she shook her head, 'by the time we got there the show had left town. Must have been around 12.30. We drove around a bit but couldn't find you or Barclay or the big guy. We'd just about given up and doubled back for one last look on the off chance and Dawn spotted someone lying on a bench in the rain. Classy.'

'How did you know Barclay an appointment at Island Gardens?'

'Barclay had it in his phone's calendar.'

'And you have access to that?'

She gave me a withering look.

'Of course. I have a phone that's a clone of his. Everything he does on his phone, ever text, every message, tweet, whatever, I can see the moment he does it. My father gave it to me.'

'I didn't know you could do that.'

'My father got some real experts involved.'

'And that's legal?'

'I very much doubt it.'

'Oh.'

It explained so much about the surveillance we'd been under. Barclay was supposed to be an expert with all that technology stuff but this sounded like Bartholomew had someone who was in a different league.

We said nothing for five minutes. Dawn coughed, briefly threatened to stir but then the snoring resumed, still out for the count.

'My therapist says that I'm mentally scarred for life,' Green said suddenly, resuming the earlier conversation. 'She reckons Barclay should have been locked away for life, but the law is still lenient when it comes to verbal and emotional abuse. Harder to prove without the broken bones and bruises of physical abuse. All hearsay and after the event. I tried to tell my father but he was cruelly dismissive, thought it was a pathetic cry for attention. I even started to believe that myself. I'd suffered all that condescending verbal invective from him as a child and he'd only gone and ensured that it would happen to me in adulthood, too. And the really sickening thing was that he hadn't even realised he had. Didn't care. His daughter, his only child and he couldn't care less.'

She paused, staring at some on-coming traffic, lost in her pain. Then;

'I stuck it out for a few months – I wasn't really tracking the time passing, every day the same, the days became weeks and then months – and then several things happened abruptly at once.

'First, Barclay disappeared. I don't know where. One day he was there, storming around the house in a blind rage, god knows over what, the next morning he was gone. At first I was relieved. But as it continued into the next day I started to worry that when he came back he would be even angrier and maybe, this time, the abuse would turn violent, fuelled by drink or drugs or whatever he'd decided he'd needed. But he didn't come back, not that day nor the next and somehow, my mind flipped it around and I started to tell myself that it was all *my* fault, that I'd been in the wrong and that I would deserve a beating when he got back. I was so fucked up I really thought that it was all down to me. I wasn't the victim, I'd made *him* the victim.

'I was broken, desperate, and there was no-one I could turn to. I tried ringing my mother, only for it to ring and ring and ring. I'd never felt so alone. Then finally, after weeks, I rang and my father picked up the phone. I asked where Mum had gone and he told me that she'd gone away, 'past her Use By Date' was how he so tactfully put it. 'Oh, and by the way, your marriage is over.' He said it as brutally as that, another contract expired. That was all he saw it as. A shit deal gone bad. Not a life destroyed, just a fucking business thing.

'I was young and didn't know how to react. I felt relief that the farce of a 'marriage', which had only been a 'marriage' on paper, was finished, over, done. I asked why but he just mumbled something about things had turned to shit, Barclay had fucked up and everything had gone to hell.'

"Barclay had fucked up?"

'I thought he meant the younger Barclay, my Barclay, *our* Barclay, but he probably meant Barclay senior. May have been referring to both for all I knew. Anyway, it was over, the contracts shredded. I was free to leave. Legally I was still married but hardly anyone knew about that anyway except the lawyers. No-one seemed to care.

'I didn't need telling twice. There was no Barclay around to hold me back. I got out of that so-called-life as fast as I could. Packed a case with the essentials, withdrew what was left in the bank account – just a few thousand, Barclay had taken the rest of it by the look of things – and ran, flew as far away as I could.'

'Where did you go?' I asked.

'New York, of course. Doesn't everyone run to New York? Should have been far enough away from Kennington I figured. If I had thought about it for five seconds I would have gone somewhere cheaper, that way the money would have lasted longer, but I didn't, people who run don't think of consequences, they just run, the further the better. No planning or thinking, I wasn't used to having that kind of 'you can go anywhere, do anything' freedom. Stupid. No wonder it quickly turned to shit.

'I got to JFK and rang a friend of an old school friend who was living there, figured it would only be for a night or two whilst I found my feet. I knew he'd always fancied me. He couldn't believe his luck when I turned up on his doorstep, case in hand. He muttered something about we'd have to share a bed as he only had a single room but I didn't care. Needless to say, that ended horribly, too. Days turned into weeks and it got violent when I kept saying 'no'. Beat me senseless, actually punched and kicked me in the face, as if that would persuade me to sleep with him. Bastard – I seemed to attract bastards, I was like a complete-shits-magnet.' She sighed, her green eyes moist. 'Again, I blamed myself. It was my fault. All my fault. Green the victim. They say that's what emotional abuse does, turns you into a paranoid, self-pitying victim.

'I ran again, spiralling out of control, rapidly running out of money, nowhere to hide, nowhere to sleep. Yadda yadda yadda. The old runaway tale of woe. Within a week sleeping on benches in Central Park – can you imagine how low you have to fall to do that?'

As a matter of fact, I could…

'Within a week I had joined the great unwashed, begging

on the streets for loose change. It was winter, snowing, I needed somewhere to sleep and fell too easily in with the wrong crowd. They said that they could help me, save me, just a toke and everything would be better. Slippery slope, and I was sliding south and out of sight.

'I almost topped myself twice that year but I was so fucked up I couldn't even get that right. Told myself the drugs helped. Managed to do the full works – smack, crack, taking pills for thrills – you name it, I smoked it. I hadn't so much spun out of control as plummeted straight down, down, down Alice's rabbit hole. Truth is, I should have died. Probably did die a few times. Gone, completely gone.'

'And you blamed Barclay for it all? Him and your father?'

She shook my head. 'Yes, and me, of course, I thought I'd brought it all on myself. Victim number one, remember?'

I had nothing to say. I couldn't quite square it with the Barclay in my life and I couldn't imagine the stunning woman sitting next to me had ever slept anywhere but in feathered luxury.

'What changed then? How did you get to come back here? And, if things were that bad with him, why on earth did you return to Barclay?'

A sharp intake of breath: 'The months start to blur when you've hit rock bottom and every day you're out of your head. I'm not proud of those years and I was lucky to stay alive. Tried my luck on the West Coast, living on a beach, the hippy thing, flowers in my hair, nothing in my head. Ended up back in the cities. San Fran. LA. Even down to Mexico but couldn't speak the language. Found myself tempted to go on the game down there but couldn't do it. More drugs. More bastards. I was an easy pickup for the sugar daddies and just let myself get buffeted around by whoever was pushing. I appeared in some painful under-the-counter porn I never got paid for. That was the lowest of the low. And then, when I really was just about finished and was determined that the next suicide attempt would be the real thing…just one more bottle, one more fix…he, my father that is, he tracked me down. Sent a guy, some loathsome little rat of an underling, to dust me down, pick me up and drag me back to the UK. I was on automatic, just did as I was told. Didn't think. Couldn't think.

'First he took me to New York to straighten me out. I got checked into a suite at the Four Seasons and was told I could stay as long as I liked, but couldn't leave until I was straight. Even put an armed guard on the door to ensure I stayed put. It took weeks. I lived on room service and pay per view. Did the whole cold turkey bit – blanked that one out, which is no bad thing – but when I got sober I went stir crazy with the cabin fever and begged to be let out, even if meant going back home to Britain. Which was exactly what my father wanted.

'He flew back me First Class of course, said he was sorry, so sorry for the way he'd treated me. He said that it would never, ever happen again. Things would be different now. He just wanted his baby back home where he could care for her.

'I didn't ask questions, didn't have the strength or will to fight it. I'd been to hell and back, lucky to be alive but had finally been saved, I hadn't deserved that kind of luck. Forgiveness, even. My Daddy was saving me, at last he was there for me. I just had to do him one favour, that was all I needed to do.'

'Which was?'

'Move back in with Barclay.'

'For fuck's sake why?'

'I didn't know then. I do now of course, but at the time I was willing to try anything to get my life back on track. I didn't know what was going on between Barclay and his father but it must have been pretty major for him to need to come back so keenly to me.

'We were bought that house in Plumstead. I decorated it to show Barclay who was in charge this time around, not my style but I knew he'd hate it, absolutely hate it. I promised myself that this time it would be different. And when Barclay moved in he did seem to have gone through some kind of transformation himself. There was something there that had been missing before. He was almost human. Almost kind. Almost.'

My mind was racing at ten to the dozen as I tried to piece

the jigsaw together. No good – I had to ask and save myself the pain of working it out. 'What was in it for your father? It can't have been money. From what I know Barclay's dad is pretty much penniless these days.'

'Mine isn't, far from it, so that's why Barclay's father was interested. Barclay senior must have thought his ship had finally come in when my father contacted him again after all those years, talking about a new working relationship, new opportunities, whatever had happened in the past all forgotten. I didn't get it at first – just couldn't make any sense of it.

'But what my father was really after was information. My father wanted to watch and learn about Barclay. Everything. Where he was, who he was with, what he was doing. What he was eating, drinking. Every appointment, every conversation, every call. I thought it bizarre but was hardly in a position to argue. He gave me all this technology and gadgetry, the clone phone and laptop and clever shit like that. Barclay's stuff was all hacked. He had cameras and microphones installed in our home, everywhere, even in the bathroom. And when he realised how involved you and Dawn and the big bloke were, he did the same with you, too. It felt dirty and illegal but it was exciting, getting my own back on Barclay without him knowing it.'

'Why didn't he just kill us?'

'I think he was enjoying himself, the chase, the hunt. Childish but I could see where he was coming from. He kept changing his mind, too. One minute he wanted the police to get Barclay, the next he'd be briefing a gunman, then he'd think that wouldn't be as much fun as prolonging things by injuring the…others.'

'You mean me and TNT?'

'Who's TNT?'

'Hugues. The guy you call the 'big bloke'. He's more than that, y'know.'

'If you say so.'

It was almost a game to Bartholomew. It explained so much yet not quite enough. Was Barclay's blackmailing of Bartholomew entirely at Tom's bequest or was there more to it than that? Did Barclay know who Bartholomew really was? I had no idea.

But at least I now knew how Bartholomew had tracked us, known where we were, where we were going to be next. Fuck me, it was like being in a stalky revenge movie but on the wrong side. In normal circumstances I would have quietly enjoyed the fact that Barclay, who regarded himself as the best techie brain around, had been infiltrated himself, and that had led to Bartholomew turning the old blackmail game back on Barclay, too. But this was too serious for such flippancy. Serious face, Claire. Your life has been hacked too, remember?

And, to top all that, I still wasn't sure I could trust a single thing Green said.

We lapsed into silence. I needed time to absorb all of the details and she appeared to have reached an end to the explanations. Did I actually believe any of it? More to the point, why would she make all of this up if it wasn't true? Barclay being a bastard I knew all too well, and I could imagine that trying to live with him when he was at his worst and most savage would have been nigh on impossible. That might also explain the queen bitch personality she'd shown to me.

It was confusing, but I couldn't quite get it all straight in my head. Still so many questions. Ward – how did Owen Ward fit into all of this? She hadn't mentioned him at all.

And did she really have no idea how her father was using the information she was providing? Didn't she ask questions? Or was she just too scared after what happened before?

Because that's exactly how I was feeling. Too scared. Scared shitless.

We were nearly at the M25 turn off. 'I need to stop for some petrol,' said Green.

'I need to call Hank again,' said a sleepy voice from the back seat.

'Just stopping for a few minutes,' said Green. 'I think I know where Barclay is.'

'Good,' she said sleepily.

It wasn't good. There was nothing good about it at all.

I shouldn't have been drinking coffee at that time in the morning but I needed the caffeine to keep going – my adrenaline levels were slipping, although probably only temporarily.

Green had gone to the loo to sort out her makeup, which was a shame as the smudged mascara panda eyes had made her so much more human. Dawn had called Hank and he was coming to pick her up. She wasn't hanging around for more now that she knew I was okay. Hank had clearly thought enough of her that he was prepared to get onto one of his bikes despite the hour and rescue her from whatever lay ahead. Sounded quite a sweet thing to do. Sounded like things were getting more serious between them. Lucky girl.

She hadn't been surprised when I told her about Ward.

'Y'know,' she said. 'I did wonder if it was him when we were holed up in the Uno down in Rochester.'

'You never said.'

'I couldn't figure out the 'why'. The 'why' made no sense – he was Barclay's friend, oldest friend, possibly only friend. Even though he was a lecherous wanker and grade A tosspot there was nothing to suggest he'd kill a friend just for cash.'

'Turns out he would. Fortunately for us, it also turns out that he was a shit hitman but not man enough to admit it to his paymaster, although I think Bartholomew has now realised that and has taken things into his own hands. That's why he's grabbed Barclay.'

'And you reckon Ward's gone? He didn't come back up? Shit floats, doesn't it?'

'It was dark. I was emotional. All a bit of a blur. I don't think he surfaced but he might have. I could be wrong.'

'It sounds like you gave him one hell of a beating.'

'I'm not proud of it. I just lost it, big time. That bastard had been trying to kill us, burned down our home. The police probably have it all captured in high definition on CCTV – it was right by the Cutty Sark.'

'I doubt it – one of the guys I know once told me that those cameras in Greenwich don't work half the time. Budget cuts he said.'

Well if that's true that's the first bit of good news I've had this week.' Knowing my luck though, it probably wasn't.

'If it had been me,' said Dawn, 'I'd have probably kicked his head off and shat down his neck.'

'Charming.' I managed a little smile. 'Are you sure you're not coming with us?'

'I'm sorry. I really am. But I just had to ask myself if Barclay would do the same for me and, you know what? I don't think he would. Why are you doing it? Would he do it for you?'

'Call me delusional, but I think he would, yes.'

'I'm not so sure. Why don't you come with me?'

I finished the last drops of my triple espresso. 'No. In too deep I guess. Stupidly loyal, me. Like a dog. We'll see if Green can talk some sense into the pair of them. I may have misjudged her.'

'Or she's playing you, too?' Dawn looked doubtful. I shrugged. 'I'm not sure I trust my newly discovered sister-in-law,' she said.

'Me neither.'

'She called me when I was at Hank's, said Barclay had given her my number, telling me she was the sister-in-law I'd never even heard of. I tried calling my father about it but he's away somewhere and it sounded like such a stupid question to throw at Mum. 'Is Barclay married?' I agreed to meet her but wasn't sure I was up for it and kept delaying it.'

'Why didn't you mention it when I went to see Bartholomew?'

She shrugged. 'Didn't think to. Anyways, it turned out we actually got on well, too well, two bottles of Prosecco and more than a few sickly cocktails. Lost track of time.'

Right on cue Green returned. She looked stunning. She'd only been gone a matter of minutes. How do some women do that? It certainly was way beyond my capabilities.

'Are you coming with us, sis?' she asked.

'Just us two, Green; thee and me,' I said.

'Hank's on his way,' said Dawn.

'Don't blame you,' said Green. 'A shame that you got mixed

up in all this.'

A 'shame'? That was one way of putting it I guessed but then it was a shame any of us were caught up in this total Grade A shit storm, wasn't it?

Chapter 23

Hank was on one of his own Bonnevilles and looked quite the part. He was, literally, Dawn's hero to the rescue. He'd even brought some spare leathers along with a helmet for her and some clean, dry clothes for me. Thoughtful. He cared. 'Keeper!' my brain shouted.

We said our goodbyes and they were gone.

Green gave me the keys to the Golf. She said she was tired and probably still technically over the limit. As I climbed in Green's phone announced the arrival of a text. 'Fuck,' she said under her breath.

'What?'

'It's him again. Just says 'I need you here NOW'.'

'We'd better get moving then,' I said.

We got moving.

In the early hours of the morning the Kent traffic was mainly lorries, grumbling and rumbling their way down to the port. I reckoned we could do it in half an hour. I turned to ask Green what she thought and, bugger me, she'd fallen asleep. Asleep? How could she? Her husband, admittedly not her favourite person but her husband nevertheless, had been abducted by her father, her much-despised and reviled and possibly, probably, psychotic father. What a family. Made even the Barclays look normal.

Well, normal-ish.

Her head had slumped to one side and she was out for the count, snoring like a good 'un.

I still didn't trust her. I didn't trust any of them – Green, Ward, Barclay, Bartholomew, even Dawn – because they had so many secrets and lies I'm not sure even they knew what was real and what was convenient fabrication or half-truth. Would Barclay, who could be an arrogant, condescending bully as I knew all too well, really drive a woman to hard drinking, harder drugs, to suicide attempts and the depths of despair? Would a manipulative father really trade his own daughter for a business deal, then pimp her back to get revenge on a blackmailer who threatened his astronomical wealth?

And where was TNT now? And had Ward really been trying to take out Barclay and me or was that all a fiction, too? And was Ward now floating down the Thames facedown, heading out to sea through the Barrier? Or had I been too shocked, too tired and stunned to spot him as he resurfaced after me knocking and kicking seven shades of crap out of him?

Christ, what a mess.

And now I was driving east again, back to Bartholomew's and another date with destiny. The A2 widened from two to three to four, manning up to become a motorway and I floored the accelerator in celebration. Not long now. The car flew over the Medway and I could see the town of Rochester, slumbering peacefully on the estuary.

Green snorted in her sleep and a glob of drool escaped from her perfect lips, hanging like mozzarella on a pizza slice. Ha! Not so beautiful now, was she?

I still didn't know what to make of her. Was any of it even remotely true? Or was I being fooled again by the lies and deceits that tumbled from their lips with such ease. I felt like I was playing a game of draughts whilst everyone else was eighteen moves ahead of me in an elaborate game of chess.

Who are you really, Green?

And who are you, Barclay? Are you actually worth saving? Would I ever work that one out for myself or would I only find out when it was all, tragically, too late to matter?

She did another snort, this one even more unladylike and coarse, and she was awake. Kinda.

'Ah wee dare yit?' she asked.

'Are we…?'

'Are we there yet?'

'Not quite. A little further.'

She rubbed her eyes, smudging the mascara so that she looked like a panda awakening from hibernation again. I should have mentioned it as an act of womanly kindness. I didn't – she'd find out soon enough.

She checked her watch. 'What exactly happened at Island Gardens?'

'The usual. Your father was there. Things were said. We got shot at. TNT was hit. Y'know how it goes. Do you know Owen Ward?'

'Ward? I know that name.'

I turned to her. 'So it's true? He was contracted by Bartholomew?'

She shook her head. 'I don't know about that but the name rings a bell I know!' She snapped her fingers like a schoolgirl realising she knew a right answer after all. 'He was the Best Man at our wedding! Odd guy – always ogling me. Gave me the shivers. Barclay didn't have a lot of friends when we were together. Just that creep, actually. Until you.'

'Until me,' I mumbled under my breath. 'Lucky me.'

We drove on, the dark road easy meat for the speeding Golf. Green didn't seem sleepy anymore and I still had questions.

'Why?'

'Why what?'

'Why have you turned on your father? Why didn't you ask him why he needed that information on Barclay? And on me and the others?'

'Don't judge me. With hindsight, I guess I was stupid. I didn't know why he wanted it and didn't think to ask. Deep down I was thinking that maybe he was considering some kind of revenge on Barclay for the way he'd treated me when we were together, but of course he wasn't; that was years ago, and it's not like my father has ever cared about me. Maybe it was all a business thing? Was Barclay involved in the original bust up between the two companies? Don't know. I didn't care, to be honest. I needed some time to get myself straight. Didn't care about anybody else. What I hadn't figured on was finding a slightly more palatable version of Barclay, more amenable, less brutal. That must be your influence – you've done that to him.'

It was a compliment of sorts and I took it, although I wasn't convinced it was true. 'You haven't answered my question,' I said.

'Which was?'

'Why have you turned against your father?'

'Like I said, the Barclay I found was not the Barclay I'd left. I started to trawl through his computer and it was full of information about my father. As I said, he had never, to my knowledge at least, even met the man so I thought that was odd. I started to think that maybe things weren't quite as I'd been told and that I really should know what I was involved with. I went down to the house to talk to him but he wasn't there. No great surprise but someone had broken his office door and left it wide open,' Ah, that was probably us after Barclay had smashed the lock. 'And on the wall was a map of where Barclay had been, and loads of files about you all, including some stuff on a family up in Edinburgh and that ape Barclay is always hanging out with. I didn't know exactly what was going on but knew it wasn't good. I had already tried to get you out of Barclay's world but obviously that didn't work.'

I shrugged.

'So I contacted Dawn and arranged to meet. A sisterly chat, even though she didn't really know who I was. And as we talked yesterday afternoon the pennies finally all dropped and we both realised exactly what was going on. It was pretty sobering. That was when we knew we had to come and find you.'

'Sure,' I nodded, concentrating on my driving. 'We're nearly there.'

I signalled left and we peeled off the motorway and headed down to the coast.

'So you're one of us good guys now then?' I asked.

'You consider yourself good guys?' The panda looked surprised.

She had a point.

'Maybe we are the bad guys. But your father's even badder.'

'I wouldn't argue with that.'

Sleepy Whitstable twinkled ahead.

This was going to be yet another High Noon. At four in the morning. On little sleep.

What could possibly, possibly go wrong??

Chapter 24

Bartholomew's house looked different this time. I couldn't quite say how, but it felt menacing whereas previously it had felt docile, almost as if it had stumbled into this tangled web entirely by mistake, an innocent bystander of a house.

Now it looked dark and foreboding against the early dawn sky. The street lights blinked out as we approached, as if setting the stage for any drama to follow.

Maybe this hadn't been the best idea. Maybe I should have just left Green and fled to safety with Dawn. That would have been the sensible, rational thing to do. But I didn't do a great deal of 'sensible' now. Where was the excitement in being sensible?

The rain had finally stopped and the temperature had dropped a good ten degrees or so, the wind was whipping up like a good 'un – but it felt, to me at least, like the weather too had played a part in the grand deception that had ensnared me.

Us. That should have been 'us'. Me and Barclay. Barclay and me. Are you in that house, Barclay? Are you actually still with us? In one piece?

The drive gate was wide open again. I turned off the headlights and rolled the car onto the gravel as quietly as I could. As if that would make any difference. Bartholomew had been one step ahead of us at every stage and I had no reason to believe he was suddenly falling behind at this late stage. Besides, he'd told Green to get herself down here to help. Help? Help with what? Burying Barclay's body? Cutting him up into tiny, easy-to dispose-of body parts? My stomach lurched at the thought of cold metal severing still-warm flesh and bone. I could just about cope with it in a movie but the thought of someone doing it in real life was unimaginable.

With my phone still deader than a dead thing and Green no longer informing him of our every move I hoped that Bartholomew had no idea exactly when we were arriving. To some degree, that gave us a tiny element of surprise. That and

Ward's gun that I still had which may or may not fire if called upon. I had checked it at the service station and there were still two bullets in the chamber. I had no idea why it had failed for him earlier. It felt like a dead weight now.

I pulled the Golf up to the conservatory at the back of the house. The security light burst into life again, scaring the shaking shit out of me as we left the car. I shielded my eyes from the dazzling glare.

So much for us having any element of surprise.

'I take it you've been here before?' Green asked in an unnecessary whisper.

'Yes. With Barclay. We didn't exactly break-in though – he'd left a bathroom window open.'

'I think the law would still classify that as breaking and entering,' she said. I shrugged. I was getting good at shrugging when I had no answer. It was a very Barclay thing to do.

There were no lights on anywhere in the house. At least, there were none visible from outside. I looked up at the bathroom window Barclay and I had used previously – still ajar. I turned to Green as she had lifted a small plant pot by the conservatory door and picked up a key. She opened the door and we were in.

I'd found a small torch in the driver's door of the Golf that I'd brought with me in a stunning (and, for me, unique) act of forward planning. As we entered the kitchen area the only sound I could hear was the quiet hum of the enormous fridge freezer against the far wall and the ticking of a clock on the wall. It was beyond quiet, the silence hurting my ears as I strained for a sound, any sound, to give us a clue where Bartholomew and Barclay were.

If they were there.

No, nothing.

I opened the kitchen door and an overwhelming stench of bleach hit me, making me reel back a step. Urgh. What was that? Someone had been cleaning with a vengeance in the hallway. I pinched my nose but the damage was done and the odour caught the back of my throat. I swallowed hard.

Green pushed ahead of me and called out 'Daddy? Daddy?

Are you there?' I'd never have had Bartholomew down as someone who would be comfortably being called 'daddy' – maybe it was a deliberate goading on her part.

There was no reply. We were alone by the look of things. She turned on the hallway light and ran up the extravagant Hollywood staircase calling again. Nothing.

Somewhere along the line I'd instinctively removed Ward's gun from my jeans and was gripping it tightly for some kind of reassurance.

Empty houses. Even scarier than occupied ones.

I made my way along the hall. The door to the office we had been in previously was wide open. No more secrets, eh Bartholomew? I shone my torch in and my eyes widened.

I flicked on the light switch to see clearer.

Gone. All of it. Just a few oily Blu Tac marks on the wall from where the maps had been. Even the furniture had disappeared, the desk and table, the chairs, the typewriter, desk lamp, the teetering stacks of files and folders, papers, newspapers, all the directories and books. It had been completely emptied, every trace of its former contents gone, gone, gone.

Bartholomew had claimed he'd cleared away every trace of his indiscretions from the online world and now it looked like he'd removed them from the real world, too. That was why the place stank of bleach. Someone had been thorough, OCD thorough, and had wiped any evidence away.

Green was still calling out upstairs but that sounded like a lost cause. I poked my head into the other rooms on the ground floor but there was no-one there and it was all spotlessly, obsessively clean. It was like the Mary Celeste, but this was a ghost house rather than a ghost ship. I shivered as Green returned from upstairs.

'Anything?' Green asked.

'No. And he's cleaned out the room where he had all the plans and maps and stuff on us.'

She raised her eyebrows but I could tell that she'd been half expecting that. 'Covering his tracks,' she muttered under her breath.

'Nothing upstairs?' I asked.

'No. They're not here. Shall I call him?'

I shook my head – for some reason I still liked the idea of us having an element of surprise. 'Has he got anywhere else he may have taken Barclay?'

'Not that I know of. But then, of course, we aren't exactly close. I've only been here a few times myself.'

Should we wait in case they turned up, or was that wasting time when we could be looking elsewhere?

We made our way out through the conservatory and back to the car.

'He definitely said to meet him here?' I asked.

She nodded. 'If it had been anywhere else he'd have said.'

We were clueless. We needed a break, a sign. Anything would do.

I started the car and put the lights on full beam. No point in travelling incognito if there was no-one around. I executed the black cab special, a one-point turn in the drive and…

Wait. What was that?

The car's headlights had briefly lit up a barn, possibly a garage, at the end of the long garden. And parked outside it was the massive 4x4. I stopped the car and doused the lights.

'What?' asked Green.

'There,' I said, pointing at the barn, a hundred yards or more away barely visible in the dawn light.

She leaned forward, squinting. 'Is that his car?'

'Let's go,' I said, unbuckling and picking up Ward's gun again.

Time for action. Hang on in there, Barclay. We're on our way.

One hundred yards is actually a bloody long way when you're just about ready to drop. As we approached the barn I could see its large door was ajar, a pale light from inside leaking around its edges. We could hear movement from inside but no talking. Some music was playing. I may have been mistaken but I think it was an old Meatloaf song, something about being bad for good? That didn't bode well.

Green took the barn door handle. 'On three,' I whispered to her and I arched my back against the panelling on the wall, holding the gun to attention with both hands. 'One. Two. Three...'

And Green flung the door open as wide as she could. I stood in the classic shooting position Ward had taught me, feet shoulder-width apart, both hands supporting the pistol.

Finger on the trigger, not the trigger guard. Tut tut. I was ready.

I blinked furiously in the sudden burst of light as my eyes adjusted.

Bartholomew was slumped in a deckchair, a near-empty bottle of Jack Daniels in one hand, a large wooden rolling pin in the other. It looked like he'd been asleep but our overly dramatic entrance had put pay to that.

'Philippa?' He looked for a moment dazed, confused even. 'You're late,' he growled.

In front of him, bound with cable ties to an old wooden chair, lolled a familiar figure. Even though he was facing the wrong way I would have recognised that hair anywhere. It was Barclay, head hanging forward. He'd been stripped of his shirt and looked, from where we were standing, unconscious. At least I hoped he was unconscious – he could have been the other thing, of course.

Around his feet on the dirty floor were five or six large kitchen knives, splattered with blood.

This did not look good.

Bartholomew was staring at us, his eyes blinking furiously in an effort to wake up.

'What took you so long?' he said, slurring slightly as he rose from the deckchair, dropping the bottle on the ground.

'What the fuck..?' Green's eyes blazed and she lunged at him, fists curled and striking out blindly

'Whatthefuckwhatthefuck?' she screamed at him, as he swatted away her ineffective blows.

'Stop,' he commanded, and, much to my surprise, she did,

freezing like a statue. She still did what he told her. He poked her in the chest with the rolling pin and I half expected her to topple over like a felled tree.

The rolling pin had smears of blood on it. Keeping the gun aimed at him I sidled nervously into the barn so I could see Barclay better.

Green unfroze and threw herself at her father again, her fists raining violently down. He instinctively swung the pin at her, catching her with a sickening crack on her right forearm and sending her spinning to the floor. She landed hard, her knees smashing against the dirty concrete. Something went crack. Some bone broke.

'Stupid bitch,' said Bartholomew, dropping the pin on the floor where it landed with a clatter. Barclay jolted on the chair at the noise. He was alive. Just. I still couldn't see his face clearly but I reckoned it wouldn't be a pretty sight.

Green was down but not out and she lifted herself up on her good arm.

'Freeze, you fucking bastard,' I shouted, my arms straight, the gun pointing straight at his head. Ten feet. Maybe fifteen. I couldn't miss.

'MacDonald?' Bartholomew frowned at me – I don't think he'd noticed me before. 'Seriously? MacDonald? Wee Claire MacDonald with a gun again?' His mouth opened wide and his lips curled into a manic grin. He laughed cruelly. 'What are you going to do, Wee Claire, shoot an unarmed man?'

He took a step towards me, picking up one of the bloody knives from the floor.

'Now I'm armed. Is that better? You going to shoot me, Wee Claire?'

I panicked, suddenly gripped by fear. Couldn't move. I was paralysed by the thought of firing at his advancing bulk, at the feel of the pull of the trigger, the bark of the handgun, the deadly, organ-tearing ricochet of the bullets as they entered his bloated flesh. The gun felt so heavy. I was suddenly shaking, my vision blurring, doubling.

'It's not easy you know, MacDonald. I thought it would be

but even I am unable to do it. No matter how much I want to kill your beloved Barclay, this piece of fucking shit, I just can't do it, can't find the strength to hit him hard enough, stab him deep enough.' He turned to his daughter. 'That's why I need you, Philippa.'

Helpless. Impotent. Petrified on the spot. I couldn't even blink. My mouth dry, throat sore, every muscle tensed but useless. He didn't even need to look at me. I was nothing, no threat at all.

He laughed again.

'Shoot him, Claire, shoot him in the leg!' yelled Green from the floor.

But I couldn't move my arms, my legs, I barely managed a little shake of the head. 'Can't.'

Bartholomew stepped forward then span around and grabbed Barclay's naked shoulder, turning him and hurling him and the chair down in a single, terrifying display of his strength.

Barclay barely stirred as the chair clattered noisily onto the floor, his arms still tightly bound behind his back. His face was bloody, beaten, broken. Snot and blood dripped thick and rich from his nose, his nose looked broken and his eyes were bruised shut, already swollen from the beating. The work of the rolling pin, no doubt. Across his chest were dozens of small cuts, blood oozing from the wounds made by the knives.

Had Bartholomew been playing with him, torturing him or had he lost his nerve when he needed it most?

'It's not easy, you know,' repeated Bartholomew, waving the knife at me. 'Killing someone. It isn't easy. Not if they're not fighting back, if they're unconscious. It feels…sickening.'

He had been torturing Barclay, but he hadn't been able to kill him. First he'd tried with the Sabatiers, then his rage had exploded as he attempted cruder blows with the rolling pin. All failing, falling short of the ferocity needed to kill.

Unlike me with Ward. What did that say about me?

'That useless fucker Ward failed too, time after time he failed. Had to finish this myself but it ain't so easy with your own hands. Couldn't even strangle him in the end.'

'You sick fuck,' spat Green.

'What? This was for YOU!' He looked shocked. 'I got him! For you!'

'What?' She lifted herself painfully to her feet. 'What?' Screaming now.

'I was doing this for us. Close the book. New chapter. A new dawn.' He was mixing his metaphors. 'Your wretched husband nearly ruined me with those crazy get rich quick schemes he sold to his father, the stupid fuck. He almost cost us everything. Nearly got me locked up with his stupid computer nonsense. He hurt you, broke you, broke my little girl.' He held his arms out, imploring. In his mind, Barclay was to blame for everything. Bartholomew himself was blameless. As he moved closer, Green backed away, stumbling into me. She grabbed the gun from my trembling hands.

'No, you sick sack of shit! That was all you. YOU were the one. Barclay was a shit to me but it was all down to YOU! And this...' she pointed the gun at Barclay, unmoving on the floor, 'this has nothing to do with me. I asked for none of this. You used me, you used me twice! TWICE!' She was hysterical. 'This was all about fucking money, your money, protecting your fucking money! Nothing to do with me, don't you dare pretend this was anything to do with me!'

'He knows, you know,' Bartholomew looked stunned but still managed a cruel grin and he waved the knife at Barclay, still motionless on the floor. 'He knows now that you're my daughter, my blood, how you gave him up, gave me what I needed when I asked for it. I told him! He sobbed when I told him! Your fucking husband wept when I told him who you were, how you'd betrayed him! Doesn't that feel good? Admit it you little bitch, that feels really good!'

Green staggered, a look of complete disbelief on her face. 'Barclay?' she asked quietly, the tenderness apparent despite her shock.

'Shoot HIM, Philippa! Kill the man who made your life such a misery! He stole your life, your spirit! Drove your mother away! Sapped your strength! Your will! That's my gift to you!

Revenge at last! Kill him!' Bartholomew was shaking in his rage, his eyes wide and pleading, crazed.

Doubt in her eyes, Green had frozen again, the gun wavering, pointing at Barclay on the floor then at Bartholomew standing over him then back at Barclay, back and forth, back and forth, indecisive. Barclay. Bartholomew. Husband. Father.

For fuck's sake keep the gun still Green…

And then she pulled the trigger and killed him.

Chapter 25

It was loud, brutally loud, the gunshot echoing around the solid brick walls of the barn, deafening us all.

Barclay lay motionless.

Bartholomew stood over him, stock still. The top of his head had disappeared, a bright red splatter of flesh, bone and brains covering the wall behind him. I just had time to register the shock on his face before he tumbled backwards and bounced on the floor.

'Sheeet,' I muttered.

Nurse Claire found some scissors, towels and a bowl in the house. I filled the bowl with warm water before taking it out the barn but it had cooled by the time I got there. As I said, a hundred yards can be a bloody long way.

Barclay had come around surprisingly quickly but still looked dazed. I cut the cable ties and got a better look at him. There was blood and it wasn't pretty but he hadn't been beaten quite as brutally as I had at first feared. He squirmed, trying to evade me, shaking his head as I attempted to clean his wounds and wipe the worst of the mess away. He was looking more human already, less like an extra from The Walking Dead. Sure, the nose was broken and his teeth would be expensive to fix, the eyes probably wouldn't open fully for a day or two and the cuts on his chest would scar impressively, but all told he was going to come out of it pretty well for a bad guy.

Unlike Bartholomew, who had quite literally lost his head in our little exchange.

Green was still frozen, paralysed by shock and hadn't moved a muscle, the gun still grasped firmly in her hands. 'Green? Give me that,' I said and took it from her rigid fingers.

'Thanks,' she mumbled, unblinking.

'We should go,' I suggested.

'And just leave him here?' asked Green.

Barclay coughed and spat more blood on the floor. He

pushed me away and stood, straightening his back with a grimace. He stepped towards me, unsteady and wobbling, leaning a chair to get his balance.

He fixed me with his eyes then removed the glove from his right hand. 'I'll have that,' he said, taking the gun from me. 'Cover your ears.'

Instinctively both Green and I did as we were told. Before we knew what was happening Barclay fired the last bullet into Bartholomew's chest. Even Barclay couldn't miss from that distance.

I was stunned. 'Why did..?'

'Self defence. I killed him in self defence.'

'But...'

'It was just me and him – you weren't here. Neither of you. All me. All down to me. See?' He held up his right hand. 'Even have the residue on my hand to prove it.'

'But Barclay...'

'But nothing, Claire. It's been a long time coming. Time for me to grow up and take what's due for this...this fuck-up.'

He was going to hand himself in?

He looked at Green and attempted a smile. For once, it was probably genuine. 'My way of saying sorry for the way things were between us. Shouldn't have done that. No excuses.'

Green was stunned. 'I'll...I'll never forgive you...' she stammered.

'Promise?'

'I promise.' A little smile, but her beautiful eyes were swimming in tears.

Barclay nodded at me and pulled his phone out of his pocket. He pressed something on the screen and held it to his ear. 'Police,' he said. As he waited he scowled at us.

'Go. Best you two go now. Leave this with me. I'll make sure there's no trace of you before they come. Trust me.'

Green tugged at my sleeve. 'He's right. We need to get out of here,' she said, pulling me towards the door.

'Goodbye Claire,' he said and turned his back to us.

Surely this wasn't the end? It couldn't end like this. I hesitated but he waved me away, talking on his phone. Green grabbed my arm and forced me out of the barn. I turned to wave to Barclay but he didn't see, too busy staring at the body on the floor, his phone pressed to his ear.

'Barclay?'

Without looking up he walked towards the barn door but only to close it and shut us out.

'Barclay?' I whispered.

'Move, MacDonald,' said Green, impatiently, and we made our way back towards the house and our waiting getaway car.

Later

'You really need to turn that off now please, Miss,' says the stewardess, all smiles and cloying cologne. It's the third time she's asked and I suspect there won't be such a polite fourth. I'd better look like I'm behaving myself for once – no point in buggering up this final getaway by getting thrown off the bloody plane.

I return the smile and put my phone face down. I'm not turning it off no matter how much she smiles. Besides, it's been of little use – Barclay still isn't answering. Nothing back from my texts or emails either. Radio silence since our goodbye at the barn. It really is over.

The captain finishes his cheery assurances and advises us to 'just enjoy the flight'. How, exactly? How does one enjoy ten hours squeezed into an Economy seat sitting next to a nerdy web developer who has already hit on me twice, asking if I have a boyfriend and what my plans are when we arrive in Bangalore. 'The name's Giles,' he leers. I just put my headphones on.

Joy.

Yes, big brave Claire is running away. It seems the best option, the best immediate option at least. Probably my only option. I guess the police have Barclay locked away again – there was a report of somebody being questioned after the body of Anthony Bartholomew had been discovered and that had to be Barclay, finally handing himself in. There will be no escape this time I'm sure – he's fucked, big style, and it wasn't actually him in the wrong this time. C'est la vie. What people do for love. Or maybe that should be 'love' in inverted commas – I still can't figure out what he really feels about Green. There's something there, but it isn't anything like a regular relationship, that's for sure.

Green and I went our separate ways once we got back to town. Despite her finally turning out to be on our side – and killing her father wasn't something even she would have done lightly – I still don't trust her. Will Barclay crumble and give her up to the police? Will my part in this shitfest be exposed? Will they be able to tie it back to last year and all the other crime scenes I've so willingly been at? And Ward? Was my assault on him caught on CCTV? Had anyone been watching? Is he dead? Am I a killer?

I don't think I am. I don't feel any different. But I can't risk finding out. So many things I don't know. Possibly never will, so this is the easiest way for me to buy myself some time to get my head straight. Buggering off out of the country ASAP is the obvious, logical thing to do.

But deserting TNT…that doesn't feel good. What if he needs help? Who else can he turn to if I fuck off to India? Barclay's no use to him now and there's no-one else. Maybe Dawn, Dawn and Hank? How do they get hold of him without Barclay?

I can't think about that now. I've got plenty of my own shit to consider. Anderson Andersonn is travelling up front, First Class of course. He's offered me the seat next to him but I declined – my willingness to oblige his 'friendly' requests is limited to say the least.

Our plane reaches the front of the queue and the engines are revving up. There is a final 'bong' on the cabin's PA and we start to surge forwards. I should be excited. I've never flown so far before. Never been outside Europe in all truth. But I feel empty, lost, hollow, and as the plane thunders down the runway the tears start rolling down my cheeks and I'm choking back the sobs.

Suddenly my phone chimes. I turn it over and, as the acceleration pushes me back in my seat and the front wheels lift from the ground, I read...

Call me. B

Acknowledgements

Hugs and kisses to…

Karen Myers, for her skilful editing work, tidying away the author's mistakes, correcting his grammar and reigning in his (and Claire's) occasional excesses

Tina Pugh, for her enthusiastic review of my first attempt at *Bad For Good* and for helping me shape something much better for the subsequent versions

Alan 'Not Wardy' Ward, my knowledgeable gun expert and possibly the scariest mate a man could have

Barbara Henderson and her amazing, inspiring Random Penguins

All those readers who so kindly gave the first book their attention, especially those who found the time to write such encouraging reviews

And Jenny of course, who designed another great cover, listened to all my moaning and groaning as I struggled with the tricky bits, then read it from cover to cover, helping *Bad For Good* over the finish line

Barclay and MacDonald will return…turn the page for an exclusive preview of book three:

The Frenchman

An exclusive preview from Barclay MacDonald 3

He had never known pain quite like it.

The Frenchman tried to lift his body from the saturated grass but the bullet had ripped brutally into his back and he lacked the strength to move, and was fading in and out of consciousness. Any attempt at movement was excruciating, even the slightest effort sending a wave of nausea rushing through him that pinned him to the ground. He closed his eyes. The two voices were arguing, arguing about him, arguing about Number Two. He felt someone briefly tug at his arm but still he couldn't move, not a muscle, couldn't even re-open his eyes to show he was alive, the inky blackness washing over him, tempting him, soothing him with its promise. He heard Monsieur Barclay call his name, pleading, as the two men wrestled. A car door was opened, something was shouted in English, there was a loud thud then someone straining as if attempting to move a heavy object. The door slammed shut and the car sprayed stones as it raced away.

Silence. He was alone, and the darkness returned and he welcomed its comfort.

'Is this him?'

'Oui.' A familiar voice.

'We can't move him. He's fuckin' huge! He must way a fuckin' ton!'

'Oui.'

'Is he dead?'

'Non.'

'Sod this. I never signed up to this and…'

There was a loud whack and Hugues heard the sound of the Englishman staggering backwards, stumbling for balance.

'Ow. No need for that. I thought we were bloody partners?'

'Oui.' Familiar, but Hugues couldn't place it. He tried to lift his head but again the muscles failed to respond and oblivion threatened to take him again.

'You think you can move him? You're about his size, aren't you?'

The other man laughed and Hugues tried to resist as he felt two enormous hands roughly forcing their way under his chest and then, with surprisingly little effort, he felt himself being lifted vertically and draped over a shoulder.

'Oui,' laughed that voice, and Hugues felt his paralysed, useless body, all 500lb of it, being carried a few yards, raised then dropped into the back of a vehicle.

'C'est bon,' said the almost-recognisable voice. 'Bonne nuit mon frère.'

And with that Hugues suddenly remembered who the voice belonged to and he felt the panic rise in his chest. He silently prayed and cursed his terrible luck, and wished with all his soul, with every ounce of his being, that the gunman's bullet had hit true and had killed him first time.

For this was going to be much, much worse.

Sheeet.

Bad For Good Author Q & A

Tina Pugh: Was writing a sequel easier or harder than your first book?

Neil: It was difficult at first and I wrote plenty of different opening chapters before I got Claire's voice right in my head again. Once I had that though the writing flowed relatively easily. I had received plenty of reader feedback on what they had enjoyed in *When She Was Bad* and that was a great motivation for the second book.

The tricky thing was to find a story that would work with the characters but would not feel like just a predictable retread of the first book. I also needed to resolve a few of the unanswered questions from the original story. I hope that the two together make a satisfying whole in the omnibus paperback, *Barclay & MacDonald.*

Tina: We certainly learn more about some characters in this book, Barclay and TNT in particular. Did you always know their back story or did you have to create this whilst writing book two?

There was a lot of Claire in book one so it was time to look at the others. I had most of Barclay's back story mapped out when I was writing *When She Was Bad*. For example, I'd worked out the whole 'ransomware' scam he attempts and knew that its failure would almost bankrupt the family and be the reason for the breakdown of his relationship with his father. He's not the same thoughtless man that we met at the start of book one – Claire has changed him – and his past (as told by Green) is a flashback to the pre-Claire, self-obsessed Barclay and it's quite shocking.

I had no back story for TNT whatsoever – he was just a throwaway, a one-dimensional character I didn't really think about. But he was fun to write and subsequently proved to be one of the most popular characters in the book. I wrote three or four different versions of his back story before I was happy with it. The puppy was the clincher.

Tina: Did publishing your first book change your process of writing?

With the second book I was writing for an audience, which is more challenging that writing just for yourself. I had to be more professional; if people are good enough to give me several hours of their time I mustn't let them down with an ill-conceived story or lazy writing. Rule number one: never let the readers down - they trust you, don't disappoint them or waste their time.

Tina: What was your hardest scene to write?

Without a doubt, TNT's back story. It needed it to be amusing rather than comedic, sad but not tragic, and I really wanted the readers to feel a little like Claire, a bit guilty about how they've judged him on his appearance alone. It was rewritten dozens of times before I was happy with it.

Tina: You seem to have a lot of knowledge of what happens when a bullet enters a person. Did you go on your own Willoughby firearms training course?

Originally this book was going to be about Barclay quitting the blackmail game and exploiting Claire's shooting skills by hiring her out as a 'hitman'. I'm not into guns in the slightest but wanted to get things right and spent hours on a gun range in Bisley with my friend Alan Ward, who is an incredible marksman and top bloke to boot (albeit a little scary at times). Some of things he told me made my blood run cold and changed the story I had for this book completely. I realised that Claire would never willingly fire a gun if she knew the real damage a bullet did and that Barclay's plan to have her 'aim to maim' was a fantasy. She'd never agree to be a hitman, but her reluctance to fire a gun could ultimately prove to be her downfall. It creates a nice tension between the two of them, too.

Tina: You broke your ankle last year and were on crutches for months. Did this impede your research and progress on the book?

It didn't help! Most of the research was completed before my accident, but I did plan to spend some time on a Bonneville. Sadly, that never happened. Maybe next time.

Tina: What's the most difficult thing about writing characters from the opposite sex?

I find it easy, to be truthful. Readers were complimentary about the female characters in book one so I hope they're still convincing. My three 'early readers' are all women so that acts as a safety net before it goes into print.
Writing young characters is actually more of a challenge as I often make references a 26-year-old wouldn't know, let alone the teenager Dawn. Fortunately, the editors on both books spotted these and they don't make the final draft.

Tina: Are some of the characters based on people you know?

Not really, but I do lift certain characteristics or speech patterns. TNT's physical appearance is an exaggeration of someone I know in New York and Anderson Andersonn is a combination of several people I used to work with. My mum says 'whatnot' a lot, and Claire says that a fair bit. I do know a 'Wardy' but he's absolutely nothing like the Owen Ward here. Oh, and I've a friend who's a jogger with a schnauzer and his wife buys far too many shoes!

Tina: How do you feel now you have published two books? And does writing energise or exhaust you?

There's a sense of achievement but I know I can write better. I think the second is better than the first and the third will top

them both. The best feeling is when I write something, have no idea where it has come from and it makes me smile. That's energising.
The re-drafting and editing processes are necessary but tiring.

Tina: A few general questions now so we can find out about you. What authors give you inspiration to write?

Believe it or not, bad ones. Great writers intimidate me with their skill and imagination but a badly-written best seller is massively inspiring.

Tina: What's your favourite under-appreciated novel?

Larry McMurtry's *Lonesome Dove* is my absolute favourite novel of all time and has characters who will live in my heart until the day I die. It won the Pulitzer Prize so it's hardly under-appreciated but it is almost unknown in Britain.

Tina: What authors did you dislike at first but grew into?

When I was at school I wasn't clever enough to appreciate John le Carre and found his novels confusingly obtuse – I wanted my spy novels to all be James Bond - but now I'm in total awe of his writing. I'm re-reading them and they're wonderful.
J K Rowling's Harry Potter books left me stone cold but her Cormoran Strike novels are thrilling and beautifully written.

Tina: Do you read your book reviews? How do you deal with bad ones?

I do read them, and the good ones help me through the dark times when I have serious doubts that I can write. With a poor one I'll take it really, really badly and sulk for weeks. To date though, they've all been very positive so it's not something that I've really had to deal with yet.

Tina: Do you suffer from writer's block?

Writing can be hugely frustrating but if you accept that some days the words come far easier than others then stumbling into a 'block' isn't that bad. Once you have the characters you can usually work stuff out.

Tina: Finally, will you go for the trilogy? You left a lot of cliffhangers and I'm sure readers would like to know what happened to Wardy, TNT and Barclay himself.

It's Claire I'm most worried about...